SCIENCE FICTION STORIES VOLUME 1

SCIENCE FICTION STORIES VOLUME 1

KEVIN J. ANDERSON

WFP

WordFire Press

EBook ISBN: 978-1-68057-720-4
Trade Paperback ISBN: 978-1-68057-721-1
Dust Jacket Hardcover ISBN: 978-1-68057-722-8
Library of Congress Control Number: 2024937268
Cover design by Janet McDonald
Cover artwork by Tithi Luadthong "grandfailure"
Kevin J. Anderson, Art Director
Vellum layout by CJ Anaya
Published by
WordFire Press, LLC
PO Box 1840
Monument CO 80132
Kevin J. Anderson & Rebecca Moesta, Publishers
WordFire Press eBook Edition 2024
WordFire Press Trade Paperback Edition 2024
WordFire Press Dust Jacket Hardcover Edition 2024

Printed in the USA
Join our WordFire Press Readers Group for
sneak previews, updates, new projects, and giveaways.
Sign up at wordfirepress.com

CONTENTS

Why not start at the beginning? I'll open this collection with my very first published story, a short that I wrote on a manual typewriter when I was a sophomore in high school. It was 1977, and I had already wanted to be a writer for years.

When digging through old boxes and files a few months ago, I came upon my high school scrapbooks and found the magazine that printed the story, a Wisconsin High School Writings publication called Excerpts. *I was 14 years old.*

Maybe Steven Spielberg will see it now and decide to make it into an epic $200M film! Or maybe not. Nevertheless, I was off and running.

MEMORIAL

The roar of the ocean echoed through the empty sky, but no one was left alive to hear it. Waves, glinting from filtered light, lapped up against a long beach, leaving a deposit of deadly radiation which had made even the life-spawning sea sterile.

The sun burned down through a radioactive haze, warming nothing but the dead sands. No bird flew in the sky, no fish swam in the sea, no man walked the earth. Apart from the roar of the poisonous sea and the gentle sound of the just-as-deadly wind, the world was silent—the earth was dead.

The waves washed the shore again, taking with them a few grains of sand, exposing something to the sun's glare. More sand washed away, and the days passed.

The object became uncovered, something made of glass, clear, uncolored, but clouded slightly. Its shape was not what it had been, but was now warped slightly from exposure to the furious, raging heat of countless atomic blasts.

It had been a bottle once; and now it comprised the entire remnants of mankind. The bottle was the only representative of the human race, a memorial, a monument to the way of life which had been so suddenly destroyed.

Visitors coming and finding the earth dead would find this bottle, and from it try to reconstruct the civilization which had spawned it.

Paint on the bottle formed letters, now meaningless. The paint was blistered and burned, but the message, for all who could read it, was plain.

The words read: COKE ADDS LIFE.

Everyone tends to edit their memories of lost loved ones or lost relationships. We emphasize the admirable qualities and good times, while downplaying the unpleasant aspects.

Early in our relationship, Rebecca and I had some friction when we realized that we each remembered some experiences or discussions very differently. We were either having some sort of selective amnesia, or we each looked at things through quite different filters.

I was married once before, back when I was only 21, and it lasted only three years. It wasn't much of a marriage, and we had little in common, but after several years of being alone following the divorce, I began to view those memories through rose-colored glasses, forgetting the unhappy times, clinging to and even emphasizing some of the good parts. Maybe those miserable times hadn't been so bad after all.... When Neil Peart and I had a long talk about that "halo effect" during a hike together, it partially inspired the song "Halo Effect" on the last Rush album, Clockwork Angels.

Do we willfully edit our memories, or is it just a defense mechanism? And if we could remake our past the way we wanted to remember it, would we do it?

FONDEST OF MEMORIES

The stars in the bowshock are blueshifted as the ship soars onward. With each passing moment, the difference between my age and Erica's becomes smaller. Her newborn/reborn body, still on Earth, continues its second life as I grow farther away in distance, but closer in time.

I lean back in the comfortable Captain's lounge. The ship runs by itself, and I am its lone crewmember. Time passes much swifter for me, thanks to relativistic effects. But it still seems like an eternity until I can return home, until I can have Erica back the way she was.

This is my favorite memory of her, the one I recorded first:

Erica and I had met hiking in the back country. Both of us enjoyed the isolation, to get away from the gleaming cities. We introduced ourselves during the long walk, and two weeks later we arranged to meet again, to go rafting down the river.

The current was languid and warm at the heart of summer. Erica brought her own inflatable raft, and we laughed, so caught up with seeing each other again that we forgot to bring along the auto-inflator pump. Embarrassed at our mistake, we took turns using our own lungs to inflate the large raft as we knelt in the rocks and sand of the bank. Red-faced and puffing, we thought the situation seemed ludicrous at the time, but it forged a golden thread in our relationship.

"I'm glad you're not upset about it," Erica said.

I shrugged and said exactly the right thing. "The point, my dear, is to spend time with you. It doesn't particularly matter what we're doing."

Our embarrassment was strained further when we saw that we hadn't brought the oars either. We got into the raft and pushed ourselves into the current, kicking with our feet, paddling with our hands, using our rubber thongs to move us toward the center of the river.

We spent hours that day, floating under the sun, talking to each other. We ate bread and cheese from the cool-pack nestled between us; we drank cans of cheap beer. When we got too hot, we would roll over the flexible side of the raft into the river, splash around until we were cooled, and then crawl back in again.

Once I swam up to Erica and, on impulse, slid my hand against the bumps of her spine and pulled her close for a stolen kiss. She let it last a full second longer than I had expected, and time seemed to stop as we hung there in the warm current, buoyant, as if in a place without gravity.

Neither of us worried about how sunburned we were getting. I paid altogether too much attention to how beautiful the diamonds of drying water were as they shone on her skin....

Of all the scenes I relived for the recorders, that is my favorite memory of her.

I had already seen the explosion of the lunar passenger shuttle on the news before the authorities tracked me down. I watched the rough picture on screen as the craft took off from the crater floor and headed back on its two-day journey to Earth orbit. At the extreme range of the lunar base cameras, the liquid fuel tanks erupted, turning the shuttle into a cloud of dissipating wreckage and scintillating chunks of ice and frozen air. The image was streaked with pops of video static because the news crews had enlarged it so much.

Erica had been on that shuttle. The irony was, she had gone to the moonbase for its bimonthly safety check. Erica had gone to inspect the underground tunnels, the above-surface domes, making sure the wall-plates and life-support systems would keep the base inhabitants safe for another couple of months.

No doubt Erica had been perfectly relaxed, thinking her job done, as she departed the gravity sphere of the Moon. Someone else had seen to the safety of the transport shuttle....

I got rid of the Transport officials and their preprogrammed sympathy as quickly as their protocol would allow. I stared at the wall, at the home Erica and I had made for ourselves over the years. The lights turned into garish flares through the distorted lens of my tears.

I went into our bathroom and picked up a hairbrush Erica had forgotten to pack. I held it in my hand and stared at it, at the few strands of golden hair trapped by the bristles. She was gone. They would never bring back any sort of remains. A few strands of hair, like golden threads, were all I had left of her.

The first time I went to her apartment, Erica didn't think I was watching as she primped in front of the mirror, using her brush with a snap of her wrist, and came back out to meet me. I had dressed in my finest clothes.

Erica had the music turned low, candles lit. She normally didn't cook, but had studied food-preparation tapes to get everything just right. That she would do that for me impressed me more than the food ever would.

She made me sit down and accept her attentions as she served salad in a transparent bowl, as she ladled steamed broccoli (which I don't even like) onto the plate, and then bronze-colored chicken breasts. She poured us each a glass of frigid burgundy in a chilled goblet, and we proposed a silent toast, smiling.

"Everything perfect?" Erica asked.

I made an "umming" satisfied sound and said, without thinking, "Well, burgundy isn't really supposed to be chilled. You serve it at room temperature."

Her reaction shocked me. She seemed devastated. My one

thoughtless comment had destroyed all of her preparations. I hadn't realized how fragile she was.

"But it doesn't matter—" I tried to say, but Erica stood up so quickly from the table that her chair wobbled, and she—

NO. I rewound and edited that from the memory recorder. A trivial detail, not worth condemning to permanent archive. A simple thing. Fingering the controls, I deleted my tactless comment, ran back to a few moments earlier.

I closed my eyes, focusing on my imagination. This would be better for Erica.

YES. She had kept the burgundy at room temperature after all; we ate artichokes instead (which I do like). The meal went perfectly. We ended up smiling and holding hands across from the candle flame.

The man from the clone-bank sealed Erica's golden hairs in a sterile, transparent envelope. "No need to worry, sir. This is quite sufficient. I expect no problems at all." He tucked the envelope away. "I am indeed sorry about what happened to your wife, but we can fix that now."

I sat back in their self-adjusting chair and tried to feign a relaxed appearance. I felt so empty, so desperate. Part of this seemed completely wrong, but it also seemed the only thing to do.

The man from the clone-bank—I can't recall his name now— sensed my hesitation. He was a professional, accustomed to nervous people like me. He had a thin, clipped accent, not identifiable as any particular foreign language, but the inflections sounded too *processed,* as if he had learned to speak through language implants.

"You have been through our counseling sessions, have you not?" he said. His eyes did not waver as they looked at mine; they appeared too small for his face. "You understand that we will use information from these hairs to fertilize a donor egg. The resulting child will be the genetic equivalent of your wife."

He held up one finger; the nails were neatly manicured. "However, she will be a newborn baby. The body will be the same, but the age difference, some thirty years now—"

"I'm taking the star-freighter option," I interrupted.

This caused the man's eyebrows to raise. "Most people do not. While they can bring themselves to do the actual cloning, they are not willing to abandon their friends, their lives."

"Erica counts more than any of that," I said.

The man from the clone-bank smiled again. "We can help you choose an appropriate star-route with the relativistic difference you desire. When you return, your wife will look exactly as you remember her, the same appearance and the same age. But the memories, ah, the memories ..."

I looked the other way. I didn't want to hear about this part. I had been avoiding it. Those memories were lost, and I would never truly have the same Erica with the same past.

But the man from the clone-bank waited and then said, as if sharing a secret, "For that, we have a way."

Reliving these memories, focusing my mind to resurrect every last detail and bring it into the recorders, is the kindest form of pain imaginable.

Of course, I deleted all memory of my affair entirely. It's gone. It never happened, as far as the new Erica is concerned. I saw no need to put her through that kind of pain twice.

I realized, even while I was doing it, that I didn't want her to be unaware of my dissatisfaction, the reasons that drove me to seek companionship and understanding other than her own. Though the affair tore apart many of those precious threads that bound us together, if Erica had been able to *learn* from it, she could have understood more of the things that I needed, the things I found missing between the two of us.

And so, when I rewrote my memories I retained some of the minor quarrels and resentments we had toward each other. But instead, I rationalized a way for her to recognize her inadequacies before it became too late. Erica saw what she was doing, how her work shut me out, how she paid too little attention to me—and now, in my imagination, I rebuilt some of the events.

This time, she fixed things between us in the ways I wish she had done before. This time, as I recall it for permanent record, instead of her red-faced and tear-stained expression, instead of her anguished screaming at me for what I had done to *her* ... this time, still with tears in her eyes, she bowed her head a little, apologized, and said she did indeed love me.

The man from the clone-bank made sure I understood the apparatus before he left me alone in the room with my thoughts and memories. The mesh-net of contact electrodes, the soothing subliminal music in the background, the warm lights and gentle air currents were all designed to lull me into a semi-hypnotic trance so I could recall everything for Erica.

"The memories we record are extraordinarily vivid," the man said. "We take everything. Our lives are more than just grand events, but a sum of little details as well.

"We have a frame-of-reference processor that can shift the viewpoint of everything it records. When you recall something that happened between you and your wife, you naturally remember it through your own eyes, through your own filters of perception. With the frame-of-reference parallax, we can change that, adapt it, so that when we implant those memories into the clone, she will recall them as if she had experienced them herself. In such a way, you can indeed share everything you remember together. She will be your wife once more."

The man's voice tightened as he looked at me. His mouth curled into a button of fleshy lips. "Please attempt to remember as many details as possible, even the most trivial things. Summon them up and record them. The more input we have, the more exact will be the recreation of your wife."

They scheduled me for eleven sessions, and I began the task with relish, because I wanted to relive every single one of my precious moments with Erica.

Our largest fight, the one I regret the most, came when—after months of subtle hints that I carefully ignored—Erica finally approached me and asked me if I wanted to have children. The tone of her voice and the way she acted made it obvious how badly she wanted them herself.

I had heard about the "biological clock," how many of my acquaintances had suddenly and irrationally decided to toss away their careers and have families instead. Erica and I had just moved into a large home of our own. We were moving up in the world. We had everything we wanted. Erica's sudden request took me by surprise.

She routinely accepted more inspection jobs than she could handle; her job already took us apart more than I wanted. She was always off on the lunar shuttle, or checking the trans-Channel tunnel, or the Bering Straits bridge. Adding a child to the equation (or more than one, from the way she presented the question) would swallow up the little private time that remained to us.

I didn't feel either of us had the time or the energy to be good parents, and I knew how children could be ruined by parents who had come to resent their existence. I told Erica that we were not in a position to be good parents and therefore, for the sake of our potential child, we should not become parents at all.

This devastated her. She refused to make love to me for weeks. She moped around, saying little to me. The whole thing soured our relationship. It seemed almost a relief when job duties called her to the moon for a routine inspection tour, her last.

Now the most important thing was just to have Erica back.

So, as I recalled our discussions and my persuasive arguments, instead of Erica acting childishly and refusing to see reason, I altered the memories again, making her think for a long while about what I had said. Then finally, with dejection but genuine understanding, she nodded and agreed.

"You're right," she told me. "It was just a nice thought. I don't want to have children after all."

I was happy with the new memory. It would make things stronger between us.

I sit at the helm of my ship and think of Erica as the stars rush by. The chronometer continues to reel off two sets of numbers: my subjective time inside the Captain's cabin, and Earth-normal time, which flies by as the ship streams toward its destination. Before long, I can turn the ship around and begin my swift journey back to Earth.

Three decades will have passed by the time I return. I have put all our income into trust, and the star-freight company has deferred my salary into interest-bearing accounts with a regular stipend paid to the clone-bank to prepare Erica's clone.

When I arrive home, she will be the same age, the same appearance … the same *person* who was lost to me. I lean back and smile again. I picture Erica coming to greet me at the starport. I can't wait to see her again.

She will be just the way I remember her.

I was particularly touched by the news of mountaineer Rob Hall who died on Everest in 2005, slowly freezing in his tent and knowing he wouldn't make it through the night. He talked with his wife on the sat phone as he died, having the technology to say goodbye.

My friend Dr. Harry Kloor has been involved with the XPRIZE since its inception, and he was particularly enthusiastic about the new "Avatar" XPRIZE. Avatar technology is filled with exciting possibilities, in which a human can link with a separate robotic body via telepresence and use that separate body for myriad purposes. It might be a remote surgeon using a medical avatar to perform an operation on the other side of the world, or a tourist visiting hazardous and exotic places in a surrogate body, or an invalid doing daily activities but inhabiting a technological avatar. Harry was so enthusiastic about the possibilities of avatars that he asked me and Mike Resnick to edit an anthology of science fiction stories that would showcase the things avatars can do. This story shows how amazing avatars can be, and how they can help us become more human at the same time.

THE NEXT BEST THING TO BEING THERE

The immersive view of the rugged mountainside vanished as a white wave of snow and ice swept over them, experienced real-time by thousands of spectator-participants worldwide—armchair mountaineers, tourists, schoolchildren.

And Francesca.

The avatar tumbled, rolled, slid with sickening disorientation through the kinesthetic sensors. The optics became a whirlwind of pummeling snow; sensor touches conveyed the pounding pressure before the governing software dampened the input; haptics added a vertigo of falling.

"What happened?" Francesca cried. "What the hell happened?"

Her two young daughters were screaming next to her in the soft chairs of the control lounge. The media representatives connected to the SHERPA avatar flailed their hands against the unexpected avalanche that had struck the climbers on Mount Rainier.

In a separate room, some of the reporters tore off their interface sets, but Francesca maintained her telepresence connection as the rolling roar slowly ground to a halt. The SHERPA synthetic used its reactive software to stop its fall and anchor its polymer body in the sliding ice and snow.

Once stabilized, SHERPA scrubbed powdered snow away to clear its field of view, then used autonomous systems to dig itself free. Francesca experienced every moment through her passive interface, as well as the biting cold on her skin, the pressing weight of the snow.

Under a brilliant blue sky, she could see the breathtaking expanse of the glaciated volcano, the dazzling ice field, the gray rock jutting out of the white sea. Tens of thousands of virtual spectators experienced the same thing. The bright sun, uncommon for the Pacific Northwest, had made for spectacular visuals and a perfect ascent of the mountain, but several days of warmth might have melted just enough snow to make the ice field near Disappointment Cleaver unstable for the crossing.

Dr. Carlos Kingman, the program director, was shouting, and Francesca experienced a disorienting duality—hearing his panic next to her in the control lounge, while her real focus remained high above 13,000 feet. In a subwindow in the upper left corner of her field of view, she saw Kingman run to the summary screens.

"Full assessment—now." He whirled, his deep brown eyes wild, his coffee-colored skin darkening with urgency. He yelled to his techs, "Use the disconnects, interrupt the educational feed. We don't want the schoolchildren to see this."

The participating reporters in the secondary lounge were already uploading commentary filled with questions and speculations, even though they knew nothing. Kingman knew nothing. Francesca knew nothing.

Dizzy and stunned from experiencing the avalanche, she gathered up the two young girls, wrapping her arms around Tanya and Tammy. A separate part of her experienced the avatar climbing out of the fallen snow, recalibrating itself and getting its bearings.

She was too confused in the first minute to understand the implications, but then the realization plunged down like a different kind of avalanche. She peeled off the optic interface and stared at Kingman. She had seen no sign of her husband or the mountain guide accompanying the robotic avatar. "What about Stephen? And James?"

She glanced at James Tobler's slender wife, Nouri, who sat in another lounge chair, her knees drawn up to her chest, huddled in shock. Nouri still hadn't figured it out.

Francesca raised her voice. *"What about Stephen?"*

Mount Rainier in Washington State, 14,411 feet high, had always been a bucket list item for her husband Stephen. He was outdoorsy and fit, though he had put on a little weight since the birth of their daughters.

Francesca and Stephen had met through a common love of hiking. Living in Colorado, they had set out to complete all five hundred miles of the Colorado Trail, which they did. Together, they climbed all 58 of the 14,000-foot peaks in Colorado, the Fourteeners. As a young couple, fully in love, they supported each other, learned skills together, and ticked the peaks off their list, one by one. Stephen had even dropped to his knee and proposed to her on the summit of Mount Sneffels.

They were both schoolteachers, a career choice with the added advantage of summers off—hiking season, mountain climbing season. After Tanya was born, though, Francesca retired from her teaching duties, while Stephen was promoted to vice principal; the resulting raise allowed her to watch their daughter, and then, a year later, Tammy as well.

They had done so much before they started a family, but Stephen occasionally dreamed of climbing either Everest or Kilimanjaro—admittedly unrealistic goals—as well as Mount Rainier, also difficult but much more accessible. He and Francesca both knew it wasn't likely to happen.

Then last year, during a backyard barbecue with a few neighbors, Stephen had waxed poetic about mountain climbing in general and Mount Rainier in particular. Their neighbor, Carlos Kingman, had been intrigued with the conversation.

While Francesca rounded up the girls and let them play an inept but entertaining game of croquet in the backyard, Kingman lounged back in a lawn chair and looked at Stephen. "I bet there are countless people who would love to make the climb, but simply can't arrange the trip, or who aren't physically capable. What if you could do it?" Kingman raised his eyebrows. "What if you had the chance to climb Rainier, and tens of thousands of others could join you for the experience?"

"Sounds like an awfully crowded trail," Stephen joked.

"I meant figuratively. What would it take for you to do the climb?"

"Other than getting in better shape?" Stephen cocked an

eyebrow. "There'd be a lot of logistics planning, and I'd need the time off from school. It's typically a three-day expedition, led by a professional guide. Even from the highest trailhead, the ascent is still nine thousand feet—a lot harder than any Fourteener in Colorado." He sipped his beer with a wry expression. "Believe me, I've looked at all the details. I've dreamed. I've tried to make it happen. But … family obligations, you know."

Kingman wore a secretive smile. "I think there's a way we could make it happen, with the full support of your school. It would be an educational opportunity you could share with the world, and I'll have the funding. It would be a pilot project, a great demonstration of the ANA Avatar work—a surrogate experience for students all around the world, and an opportunity for many frustrated mountaineers who would like to subscribe." He began talking faster. "We have a brand-new telepresence unit that would be perfect for this use."

As she gathered up the croquet balls and made sure the girls didn't accidentally hit each other with the mallets, Francesca could tell that Stephen was excited by the idea. He tried to cover it up with skepticism. "Using an avatar? You mean, people would sit at home and experience a real, gritty mountain climb without having to lift a muscle?"

"That would be for the subscriber base of spectator-participants," Kingman said. "But somebody actually has to do it. You and a guide would accompany the avatar. Schoolchildren and paid participants would be connected via the SHERPA synthetic and experience everything you do." He grinned.

"SHERPA? Is that an acronym for something?"

"Of course it is," Kingman said with a chuckle, "but don't ask me what the letters stand for. Somebody was being cute." He set his own beer aside and stood from the lawn chair. "This would be a wonderful opportunity to show off the remote educational capabilities as well as the virtual tourism aspects the technology offers."

In the dozen years since the awarding of the ANA Avatar XPRIZE—a bold initiative that encouraged the development of remote operation and experience via sensory technology—various "avatars" had blossomed throughout the industrial, creative, medical, and service worlds. The rapid development and widespread uses were far beyond what had been envisioned by Dr. Harry Kloor, the instigator and lead of the XPRIZE. Now, in 2036, avatars in all their forms were penetrating everyday life. Francesca had been aware of Dr. Kingman's engineering work, but had not thought much about it. Neither had Stephen, but he was obviously intrigued with this new idea.

SHERPA was a sophisticated unit that would do more than just carry their packs and supplies; the robot was also a climbing partner that allowed Francesca and their daughters to virtually ride along. The plans came together smoothly, generating a great deal of media excitement.

Their experienced guide up Rainier, James Tobler, had summited the mountain more than fifty times. After a year of planning, Stephen and the robot set off from the Paradise trailhead on the first day, starting at an elevation of 5,000 feet in the thick forest. Guided by James, they headed across the Muir snowfield to the Muir Camp hut at 10,000 feet.

Classes tapped in, with thousands of students virtually participating in the climb; Stephen paused to give lectures, turning to face the avatar robot so he could explain geology, climate, or weather patterns on the mountain. Nearly 40,000 paid spectators worldwide also subscribed, paying a fee to vicariously experience the climb of Mount Rainier.

After a brief sleep in the cold Muir hut, they headed out at midnight under a full moon, ascending the glaciers. Thanks to the specialized permits Kingman had obtained for this project, their group had the normally crowded trail to themselves. James, Stephen, and SHERPA had reached the high point of Columbia Crest just in time for a breathtaking sunrise—all alone on the mountaintop, but silently accompanied by countless spectators and virtual companions, as well as Francesca and the two girls.

It had been glorious. Francesca had reached out, briefly allowed to use SHERPA's interactive interface. With the avatar's haptic sensors, she could take Stephen's hand and share in his victory from the summit.

Kingman had been delighted at the demonstration of SHERPA's abilities. A complete success, showcasing beneficial aspects of innovative avatar technologies inspired by the XPRIZE competition. The control lounge was filled with shouting celebrations.

But on the descent, while the three traversed the ice field near Disappointment Cleaver, disaster struck ... while the whole world watched, and participated.

As SHERPA oriented itself in the broken snow, recovering its bearings on dangerous ground, Francesca remained connected, desperate to help, but she experienced only as an observer. The two girls were terrified. Tanya was trying to comfort her little sister.

As Kingman barked orders, his staff jacked into the active interfaces. "How much damage did the avatar suffer? Did we lose any physical integrity? Is the first aid suite intact?" He ran to the external readout deck, calling up screens, staring at diagnostics. "I need remote emergency physicians, now! Bring in our team of active medical responders."

"We have to find the two men first, sir."

"Then find them!"

Still listening to the diminishing rumble and slide of displaced ice chunks, Francesca asked, "What can I do to help? How can I pitch in?"

Kingman was hyperfocused. "We're still assessing. We don't know what's happening yet."

Francesca was desperate to do something, but she was too far away. She was just a former teacher, former hiker, now a mother. Unwilling to interfere with the avatar team in the crisis, she withdrew to the background. She watched through the optical sensors as SHERPA searched for the two men in the avalanche field.

"Cycle through wavelengths," Kingman said. "We've got to find them. If they're buried under the snow, we have only a few minutes. We know exactly where they were—run a back projection."

James Tobler's wife Nouri shook herself and stood from her own seat. "Where's James? They're buried!"

Francesca spoke aloud to the room, even though her eyes saw the silent, bright ice field and the gray comb of rock. "Is search and rescue on the way?"

"Full teams from Paradise base camp are heading up on foot."

She knew how many miles that was. "They'll take most of a day!"

"The weather's good. We are also trying to launch helicopters. Rescue teams should be able to drop down on ropes—if we can find Stephen and James on the snowfield."

Francesca watched through artificial eyes as SHERPA cycled through the spectrum, using various EM windows to search for the two men who had been tossed about on a wave of ice and snow. They would leave a significant thermal trace with their body heat, unless they were buried too deep.

SHERPA scrambled through the loose, cold rubble, scanning along the obvious avalanche path, looking up the slope to where the climbers had been. The avatar projected their drop path based on their precise last-known positions. The technicians jabbered, going over rough calculations.

Francesca felt adrift in the middle of the activity, but she kept looking, then spotted a bright smear in the garish infrared imaging. "Look, over there!" In her mind and ears, she heard countless other participants also identifying the heat signature—a human-shaped lump buried only a few feet beneath the fresh blanket of snow.

SHERPA bounded over on artificial hands and legs, extruding traction crampons. The robot was designed for agility on rough terrain, and during the climb from Paradise and across the glaciers to the summit, it had learned and adapted to the terrain. Now the avatar raced toward the thermal image. Digging furiously, it used polymer hands to scoop and shove the snow, exposing the head and shoulders of one of the men.

Nouri let out a sudden cry from her chair, and through the optical sensors, Francesca saw that it was James Tobler. The man wasn't moving, and his head was bloody. Moving gingerly, SHERPA cleared away more debris to free the fallen guide and stabilize him on the uncertain slope.

"Get the emergency surgeons jacked in!" Kingman said. "Use the medical sensor suite to check him out. Is he still breathing?"

"He's still breathing," one of the techs said. "Getting vitals now."

Francesca felt the control shift in the avatar body as medical teams took over the manipulation. She watched its robotic arms move, detected sensors activating, first aid apparatus locking into place from embedded channels in the robotic arms.

SHERPA rapidly pushed through layers of clothing to assess cardiac activity. Simultaneously, the avatar detected breathing, with no atypical sounds or gurgling. Airway, check. Breathing, check. The full electrocardiogram revealed no arrhythmias. With one polymer articulated hand, it pulled open James's eyelids to assess the pupillary response.

In the background audio track, one of the physicians announced, "Both pupils are equal and responsive. If there were stroke or bleed, they'd be different, or they wouldn't constrict. Brisk—they look good. Good chance there's just a concussion. What's the blood pressure?"

The remote doctors used the avatar's embedded equipment to inflate securing pillows that stabilized his neck, packing quik-clot on the superficial scalp bleed. SHERPA held its hand just above James's elbow and remained completely still for an eternity of 30 seconds, detecting the sound of the blood flowing as the robot gradually released its hold on the elbow and assessed blood pressure.

"Blood pressure is low, but in the normal range," the remote physician announced. "Doesn't seem like he's lost much blood."

Francesca was glad to see the guide cared for, but she longed to take control of the avatar and keep searching for Stephen along the avalanche path. He was buried out there somewhere.

Though she remained immersed in the connection, Francesca felt the warmth of a body, two bodies next to her. Her daughters were curled up beside her in the wide, comfortable experiential chair.

"Where's Daddy?" Tammy asked. "Is he going to be all right?"

Despite the other connections through SHERPA, Francesca used real nerves and skin, a true sense of touch with her daughters, not through any haptic interface. She pulled the girls close and hugged them. "I hope so."

Kingman touched his ear, listened. "Helicopters are ready to launch soon. We'll have them on scene as quickly as possible."

"Will it be fast enough?" Nouri Tobler asked in a rough voice. "Will James survive?"

The physicians took full control, worked to stop the bleeding from the head injury, ran a final check. "He has the best possible chance," Kingman said.

"But where's Stephen?" Francesca still attempted to look through the corner of her eyes, SHERPA's eyes. The optical sensors scanned, and at the periphery she saw another thermal image. "Off to the left. Up on the slope near those three exposed rocks."

SHERPA's head swiveled, and all spectators could see the smear of body warmth, and more than that—movement. It was Stephen, clawing free of the snow that had buried him. "He's alive!" she cried, then squeezed the two girls curled up against her. "Daddy's alive."

Stephen got his head and shoulders free. "Over here," he gasped, his voice weak.

"We have to get to him." Francesca struggled to move inside the avatar body, but hers was only a passive interface. The physicians had taken full control, tending to James.

"If your husband is moving, that's a good sign," Kingman said.

Francesca longed to scramble across the ice field and pull Stephen out of the cold, smothering embrace. She would use the robot's body, the artificial limbs, the haptic sensors, to wrap her arms around Stephen and hold him, use the robot's waste heat to keep him alive.

Stephen pulled himself farther out of the snow, propping himself up. He brushed ice chips away and coughed. Francesca recoiled to see blood splashing out of his side, a bright red stain on the freshly exposed white snow.

SHERPA's optical sensors swiveled back to the still-unconscious form of James. Inside the link, the coordinating surgeon said, "That's good for now. Let's go check the other patient."

After ensuring James was stretched out and in a place where he wouldn't slip down a slope even if he moved or rolled, SHERPA covered him with a thin thermal film to keep him warm. Then the avatar dug polymer hands and feet into the loose snow to make a cautious ascending traverse across the field to where Stephen struggled to extricate himself.

Suddenly, large chunks of frozen debris slid out from under Stephen's hips, and he began to slide down the slope. He yelled, and Francesca yelled with him. He reached out his gloved hands, flailing, trying to slow his fall. He left more blood on the snow.

The avatar shifted its approach to intercept Stephen, working itself downward and across as snow slid under its textured feet. Stephen spread himself out, increasing his surface area, halting his fall. Finally, the unstable snow chunks caught on a rock ledge, and he came to a stop. He groaned in pain.

SHERPA picked and climbed its way over to him. From where he sat slumped on the ledge, Stephen looked gray, and his face was slack. He panted hard. He managed to sit, then pulled on the rock, trying to drag himself upright, but the effort was too much for him.

Through the eyes of the avatar, Francesca saw a wide maroon patch on his clothing, wet, soaked with blood from an injury in his left mid-torso. A large wicked shard of ice had pierced him like a crystalline spearpoint.

Breathing fast and ragged, Stephen reached out to grip the avatar's body. "I'm here. I'm okay."

"Help him!" Francesca shouted into the passive link.

The medical team took over, assuming full fine control of the medical suite in the artificial body. They scanned Stephen's vitals, assessed his injuries. "We can't remove the ice shard. Pack gauze around it so we can apply pressure."

"Traumatic injury, upper quadrant."

The doctors had been reporting through the speakers in SHERPA's plastic face, but Francesca said, "Let me talk to him."

Kingman nodded, gestured to one of his techs. Her audio link became active. "Stephen—it's Francesca! I'm here."

"You're very far away." He sounded disoriented.

"Not as far as you might think. It's the next best thing to being there." She reached out, used SHERPA's polymer hand to clasp her husband's arm. "Hold on. Helicopters are on their way, a full rescue crew. It won't be long."

"I'm fine," he said. "I hate to have the whole world watching this. Don't want to go down in history … as a klutz."

"Sorry, but we have to do our work," one of the physicians cut in over her private audio interface. "We need control back."

She said quickly, "I'm here, Stephen. The doctors have to take over now, but I'm watching. I'm with you."

"Yeah, a doctor would be a good idea." He forced a wheezing laugh. The spreading bloodstain in his side was growing ominously larger around the gauze and the ice shard.

Francesca retreated into the avatar's background as the surgeons took over. She had always been an active person, wanting to participate. She had climbed so many mountains with Stephen, summiting one Fourteener after another. Once, alone on the top of Mount Lindsey after a grueling hike, with the Sangre de Cristo range all around them, they had decided to make love in the rocky windbreak shelter. What could be more romantic? But they had been so sweaty and so exhausted, the experience had left much to be desired. They spent more time gasping for breath than gasping with pleasure.

Once the girls were born, Francesca had become a mother instead of a mountain climber, caretaker and teacher of her own daughters instead of classrooms of students. She had been happy with her life and with herself. She had been proud of Stephen.

But they both jumped at this chance Kingman's avatar program offered. Stephen could at last climb Mount Rainier, and she could be with him—and Tanya and Tammy had climbed the mountain, too. Connected through SHERPA, they had all stood on top that morning, surrounded by rocks and the sweeping plunge of the crater, the vast fields of the mountain's multiple glaciers.

As the sun rose on the top of the world, Stephen and James had thrown their arms up, howling into the thin air with excitement, and all those many thousands of spectators and participants linked in through the avatar connection did the same as SHERPA raised its synthetic arms.

The Rainier summit was the highest high … swept away only hours later in a roar and sweep of falling snow.

"Is … James all right?" Stephen gasped to the avatar as the remote physicians poked and prodded at his wound, muttering amongst themselves as to how best to treat the injury. He slumped back to a sitting position against the rough volcanic rock. "I'm dizzy … but I can help. With SHERPA I can work my way over to him." He pressed a hand against his stomach.

The emergency physicians were using the avatar's full capabilities. They had a backchatter on their own channel, but Kingman allowed Francesca and Nouri to listen in. One of the doctors spoke through SHERPA. "You need to stay put. Mr. Tobler has a concussion, but he is stabilized. We're more concerned about you now."

"I'm better off than he is," Stephen insisted. "Francesca, are you still there?"

"I'm here. And so are the girls. The helicopters are on their way. They'll be there soon."

Kingman signaled to her in the external real-world window in a corner of her field of view. "Two hours," he mouthed.

"They'll be there in an hour, Stephen. Just hold on."

He made a weak sound. "I'll hold on." The remote physicians tried to hold him down and keep him still. Their backchatter became ominously quiet.

Francesca continued, "Just relax. Let them tend you." She could feel Tanya and Tammy snuggling next to her, as if they could get closer to their distant father that way.

Kingman touched her shoulder and signaled for her to drop out of the immersive link. As she came out, disoriented to find herself in the mundane control lounge, his grave expression made her feel sick. "What's the matter? Everything's all right now. We've got them."

"I won't lie to you," Kingman said. "It's far worse than it looks. I … I want you to know."

"But Stephen's conscious. He's talking. He wants to go help James."

The lead scientist swallowed hard. He looked at her, looked away, then with a visible effort turned back to her. "The ice shard, that wound in his side—he has traumatic internal injuries. The physicians think it's a splenic laceration, but it may have hit the aorta, and there's no way to block it off. He's got so much adrenaline he may not feel pain, but he's bleeding a lot." Kingman swallowed again. "In fact, his systolic blood pressure has dropped twenty since the first reading, in only a few minutes. That's a strong indicator he may be bleeding out. SHERPA's sensors and diagnostics are quite sophisticated, but the medical suite can't stop internal hemorrhaging on that scale."

Francesca felt cold, couldn't formulate a question. Finally, she said, "But you have the very best telepresence doctors. Bring in any specialist to link up to the avatar. They can be right there."

"We have access to the world's best expertise, but he's out on a snowfield. In order to have a hope of saving him, the surgical environment is … is just not there. Best case, the helicopters couldn't get him to a real hospital in under two hours." The man shook his head. "Maybe the doctors are misinterpreting the signs, but if the internal injury is what we suspect, it … may be fast."

Her world collapsed and broke apart. "How long?"

Kingman just looked at her. "Our experts might be wrong, but prepare yourself. SHERPA has administered epinephrine, but the blood pressure isn't responding. The remote medics have done everything they possibly can."

"No, I don't accept that!" she said. "He's right there!" That's when the girls started crying, but she wasn't sure whether either of them understood what was going on. Her voice hitched, and she struggled to be strong. "Can I talk to him?"

Kingman drew a breath. "I can do more than that. I can let you be with him, through the avatar. SHERPA will project your face, your voice. With haptic sensors you can hold him."

Francesca felt cold, a layer of ice around her growing panic. "What about our daughters?"

Kingman didn't hesitate. "They can be there, too. We've deactivated the public connection, and no one else is watching him right now except for the doctors and you. The media is clamoring."

"I don't want reporters with my husband as he dies," she snapped.

"No, it'll just be you. You, and Tammy and Tanya."

Tears streamed from her eyes. "Let's hook up the girls again. We don't have much time."

Tanya and Tammy crowded next to her on the padded seat while a technician hurriedly reapplied the contact web to the girls. Kingman said, "I'm going to drop you into avatar mode again. The physicians will back off."

Francesca braced herself, thought about the summits she and Stephen had achieved, the high points of their lives—and not just on mountains. She thought of the open air, the expansive views, the exhilaration of endorphins, the fresh sense of accomplishment. Now she was so far away ... but through the haptic sensors she could feel him so close. SHERPA's hands were her hands, and she was with Stephen again.

"Something isn't ... right," Stephen said. He seemed very dizzy and disoriented, lightheaded. "I'm hurt bad, aren't I?"

She wouldn't lie. "I'm sorry."

"I thought so. Helicopters coming?"

"They're on the way, right now."

When Stephen looked up at her, his expression fell. Through the projected overlay image on the avatar's face, he could read her real thoughts. "Won't get here in time."

"There's always a chance, Stephen! Always a chance."

"I see your face. After all these years … I can read you."

He would not have wanted her to sugar-coat the situation. With so little time left, he deserved to know, to face his fate, to be with them. "They think you have severe internal bleeding."

"I feel … loopy."

She squeezed, and SHERPA's hand clasped his arm. "I wish you were here," he said.

"Actually, I wish you were *here*. Just one of the armchair mountaineers letting someone else take the risk." Her voice cracked.

"I like to do things for myself." He spoke slowly, as if each word were a heavy weight to be lifted out of his mouth. "Is everyone else watching, too?"

"No, just us … and the girls. Tanya and Tammy are holding you along with me. Can you feel this?" She squeezed again. "They have the touch sensors, too. We're all here."

"Good, I'll take that. Better than dying alone on a mountainside."

"You're not alone. We're here." Francesca leaned forward in the control lounge chair, and SHERPA's arms extended on the ice slope, embracing Stephen, wrapping around him and holding him. She could feel his solidity, feel his touch. Through the avatar's haptic sensors, they were right beside him. The girls felt the same thing.

Francesca was shuddering and trembling as she stifled her sobs so Stephen wouldn't notice. "I love you." He grew quieter, but he was smiling, comforted to have them next to him.

Francesca held him. His daughters held him. With a simple adjustment, the whole world could hold him in his last moments, but for now she had him to herself. They were there for him, and Stephen went quietly under the cold, bright sky after summiting a mountaintop he had always wanted to do—with his family.

In the control lounge, the three remained connected to SHERPA long after he was gone. It wasn't until the audio pickups brought her the sound of approaching helicopters in the high, thin air that she relinquished control so the telepresence physicians and the search-and-rescue teams could save James.

They would also bring Stephen's body back to her, but through the avatar she already had an experience that was far more meaningful, far more precious to her, and she held onto that, even as she let go of her husband.

There were rats in the soufflé again.

The biggest cliché question for authors is "Where do you get your ideas?" In this case, it started as a gag.

Author and artist Jon Gustafson came up with that opening line and challenged his writer friends to write the story that followed. He got so many responses that he published all the stories in an anthology, but they kept coming. He asked me to contribute to the second "Rats in the soufflé" anthology, and I took the challenge.

Where do you go from that opening line? I decided to write a full-throttle action-adventure science fiction story.

CONTROLLED EXPERIMENTS

There were rats in the soufflé again.

Tricia screamed and dropped the plate as she withdrew it from the station's food-prep unit. Behind the metal walls of the circuitry, she heard clunks and sounds of the other rats stirring, scrambling, *coming at them.*

"Look out!" Captain Kennedy Brandt shouted, knocking her aside as he pointed his blaster at the unit, firing in one long, continuous stream of energy that sputtered and popped through the air. Metal shards spat out of the chamber along with globules of molten plastic. Sparks flew as slagged circuitry, plexiglass, and steel dripped down the cracks.

Rats screamed one last time as they regrouped, tried to fall back into formation, then died in smoking masses of fur and cooked flesh. Others deep behind the panel squealed from their injuries and fled. But they would find another way to get in. It was only a matter of time.

Outside the airlock of the one safe module on station SS-1, Tricia could hear the scrabbling of claws against the door, the scrape of metal. God, they were using *tools* again!

Tricia regained her composure and looked at the ruined food-prep unit and wide-eyed Captain Brandt staring down at the depleted blaster in his hand. "Great, Captain. That was your last blaster charge. Now what are we going to do when they finally do break in?"

"They're not going to break in!" he shouted, his voice husky with panic.

Behind them, low to the floor, Tricia heard a slow chuckle from the only other survivor aboard the orbital research station. Dr. Sonnya Lyov, with her amazon build and long gray-blond hair, looked out of place curled up like a terrified baby, drawing her knees up to her chin. "They'll get smarter and smarter," she said. "It'll never end. They'll find a way to get us."

The captain whirled toward Tricia defensively, misdirecting his helplessness. "You said you purged the life-support systems!"

"I did, and the food channels, too. I dumped hard vacuum into all the ducts." She shook her head. "But you know how smart the rats are. They must have rerouted everything to protect themselves." Tricia sat back down again, gasping, trying to stop from hyperventilating. "Now we don't even have a food-prep unit. Thanks, Captain."

Kennedy Brandt whirled at her, wild-eyed. "The rescue shuttle will be here in a few hours! We won't need any more food."

Sonnya Lyov moaned and covered her eyes. "The rats will get us before then. There'll be no rescue shuttle."

Tricia lunged to her feet, screaming at the doctor. "Lihue's message did get through! It was acknowledged! Just shut up."

The first officer on SS-1, Kai Lihue—now dead—had run bellowing out into the corridor as Captain Brandt covered him. When the airlock door to their module had opened, rats screamed and scattered, white fur flying as Lihue charged. His muscular Hawaiian frame looked enormous compared to the scurrying super-intelligent rats.

"Good luck," Tricia had whispered after him.

The last she saw of Lihue was him ducking around a corner as the rats regrouped to mount a defense. Scattered along the corridor she had noticed tiny pieces of metal, electronics, pointed objects— *weapons.* The rats had been building bizarre, rodent-sized weapons.

She saw sparks flying, minuscule projectiles. The rats were shooting at Lihue! He stumbled, but kept running, firing his own weapon and making blackened holes on the walls as bolts of energy *spanged* off the metal plates.

Captain Brandt had sealed the door immediately behind his first officer.

Through the station intercom, they heard Lihue reach one of the other separable modules. He had locked himself in, panting, then blasted the few rats he found tinkering there. He had managed to reconfigure the transmission antennas that the rats had sabotaged, then began broadcasting to unsuspecting Earth below, telling their story and begging for an emergency rescue before they were forced to set off the station's automatic self-destruct.

Just as Lihue began to repeat his message, the rats outside had somehow figured out how to blow the explosive bolts. They jettisoned Lihue's module from the main core of the station, sending it adrift in orbit. It would likely have crashed flaming through Earth's atmosphere—but the rats couldn't wait for that. They managed to reconfigure SS-1's solar-power mirrors, focusing the concentrated energy onto the side of Lihue's drifting module, breaching its containment.

Over the radio, they could hear the first officer's screams fade into a hissing rush of vacuum.

The rats had done it out of revenge and their own scientific curiosity. That was all they seemed to want.

Now, Sonnya Lyov struggled with her long legs and muscular arms, trying to stand up, but it seemed too difficult a task for her. She slumped back into her corner. "Everything we do, everything we try and fail, teaches them more and more. They keep learning." She grinned. "That was what they were designed to do."

"Then we'd better not fail anymore. Right, Captain?" Tricia said.

Brandt swung around with his dead blaster ready to fire, as if that would help anything. Tricia finally snatched the weapon out of his hand and tossed it clattering to the deck.

Station SS-1 had been designed as an orbital isolation lab for genetics research, but after a decade it had been adapted for nanotechnology research. Well-known investigator and Nobel Prize winner Dr. Sonnya Lyov was trying to increase human mental abilities by developing cellular machines to fit inside the brain, acting as vast warehouses that could organize information, store countless encyclopedias of facts where they could never be forgotten.

After a year of final prototyping, Dr. Lyov and her assistant Billy Donatelli had tested it out on their dozens of captive lab rats to see if they could master mazes better, run through them faster. And did they ever!

After only two days, the results were remarkable. Somehow, the rats could communicate with each other the correct routes. Those watching above in the cages would help direct the test rat through the maze, offering a bird's-eye view.

Excitement ran high. Several live newsnet interviews from orbit astonished the scientific world.

Until, one sleep period, the rats escaped from their cages. Every one of them. When Lyov and Donatelli came into the lab the following morning, they found the cages sprung open with tiny ladders dangling down from the high shelves. Melted spots on the metal sides glimmered beside tiny contraptions that could only be miniature welding tools put together out of lab junk, hooked into the station's primary power supply.

And the rats had all vanished. Lyov had kept it secret for half a day, searching the modules while Lihue, Tricia, and Captain Brandt smiled patronizingly at the oddball scientists.

That night, during their year-anniversary celebration meal in the mess, Tricia had called up soufflé from the food-prep database. All of the crew had gathered for the meal. When she pulled it out of the chamber, the dish was infested. The rats had been trying to rig an explosive into the food package.

Another check showed that the rats had broken into the food stores and stockpiled everything for their own uses. Billy Donatelli found that the rats had also removed the access panels to several of the station's computer terminals. The rats had tapped into SS-1's entire database, downloading every scrap of knowledge stored in the master computer.

And they kept learning....

That night, while Billy Donatelli worked alone in the lab, the rats caught him.

They vivisected him.

The following morning, Sonnya Lyov found her assistant's body and various organs strewn throughout the module. Body parts had been locked in empty cages. Tiny clawed footprints, smeared in the plentiful blood, skittered along the stools, the tables. Small paw prints marked the keys on the computer terminal. A brief message had been typed onto the screen.

"WE KNOW WHAT YOU HAVE DONE TO RATS FOR CENTURIES IN THE NAME OF SCIENCE. NOW WE HAVE DISCOVERED HOW ENJOYABLE SCIENTIFIC RESEARCH CAN BE. WE WILL CONTINUE OUR OWN SERIES OF EX-PERIMENTS."

Now, only the three survivors remained, trapped in a single module with the doors barricaded and no way out. They continued to hear scratching at the door and tiny hissing noises. The rats were experimenting with more gadgets.

Suddenly a large hollow *thump* reverberated through the station. Dr. Lyov whimpered. Captain Brandt dove for his empty blaster on the floor. "What is it?" he cried. "What is it!"

Tricia gripped the metal stem of a mounted chair as the station rocked. "I think they've blown another one of the detachable modules. Just like Lihue's."

Captain Brandt scratched his square jaw. "I don't know why they haven't just jettisoned us, if they're so anxious."

"That wouldn't be any fun for them!" Dr. Lyov said, then started giggling again. "They're observing our reactions under stress."

Station SS-1 had begun to spin crazily, knocked into an off-center axis that made their module wobble with each rotation. Out of the tiny porthole, Tricia couldn't see Earth. The stars of the Galaxy spun overhead.

Outside the metal door, the murderous rats kept trying to get inside....

The 'incoming message' indicator chimed, startling Tricia, Dr. Lyov, and Captain Brandt. The light blinked again. Tricia rushed to the message pad and pushed RECEIVE. Capital letters spilled across the screen.

"RESCUE SHUTTLE *ACHILLES* APPROACHING STATION SS-1. UNABLE TO REACH YOU ON VOICE BAND. ESTIMATED

ARRIVAL, 25 MINUTES. WILL DOCK AT YOUR MODULE'S AIRLOCK. PLEASE ALLOW ACCESS."

"We're saved!" Captain Brandt shouted.

"ACKNOWLEDGED," Tricia typed. "All right, now we just wait." She pushed aside sweaty strands of hair.

The metal plate below the main bulkhead door felt warm. The rats must be trying to burn through. She heard skittering noises, as if the rats were redoubling their efforts. Tricia clenched her hands together.

Before fifteen minutes had passed, they heard the *clunk* of something heavy striking the walls of SS-1 on the outside. The message terminal chimed again.

"RESCUE SHUTTLE *ACHILLES* RENDEZVOUS SUCCESSFUL. ASTRONAUT TROY IN YOUR AIRLOCK IN 5 MINUTES."

"We're going to make it!" Captain Brandt shouted. Even Sonnya Lyov crawled to her feet.

Tricia heard the rats on the other side of the door renew their scrabbling. They had only a few minutes left.

The lights on the outer airlock blinked on, indicating that someone had opened the external hatch. The colors turned from red to amber.

Captain Brandt pounded on the door, as if to communicate his desperation. The rescuer knocked back once, signaling. Dr. Lyov stood up to wait by the airlock door, taller than either Brandt or Tricia.

Tricia felt ready to break down now and allow herself to feel the panic. She looked out the porthole again to take one last look at the wheeling stars overhead—and she saw shards of metal, wreckage of structural supports, white ceramic heat tiles. "What?"

Captain Brandt opened the inner airlock door, allowing the astronaut to enter. The rescuer took two slow steps forward. Captain Brandt ran to grasp the hand of his savior.

But something wasn't right. Tricia turned to look at the newcomer. "That's one of *our* suits!" She saw the markings of SS-1 and the station logo plain as day on the helmet, on the breast. "That suit's from one of our EVA lockers!"

Out of the corner of her eye she saw more wreckage drift past the porthole. It was the twisted remains of a destroyed shuttle. The real rescue shuttle. Then a human body drifted across her field of view.

The shuttle had never rendezvoused. The rats had destroyed it somehow, perhaps by knocking one of the detachable modules right into its path as it approached. They had been faking the transmissions.

At the airlock, Dr. Lyov started laughing hysterically one last time as the faceplate of the rescuer's suit burst open, revealing five rat-pilots sitting in tiny command chairs hauling joysticks rigged to pulleys and gears mounted inside the suit, making it walk, making it raise its arms, making it move toward them.

Other compartments of the suit split open, and more rats boiled out holding tiny guns, projectile launchers, possibly poison-laced needles.

Tricia shrank back against the wall and thought about the shuttle *Achilles*, the astronaut *Troy*. "We fell for that old trick again," she thought. "Maybe we're no smarter than rats after all."

Captain Brandt fell down trying to *clonk* the rats with his dead blaster. Dr. Lyov offered no resistance whatsoever.

As the rats swarmed toward her, firing paralyzing needles into her arms and legs, Tricia wondered exactly what type of experiments the rats intended to perform on them.

Before the release of Dune: House Atreides, *our first novel set in Frank Herbert's classic universe, Brian Herbert and I wrote this short story, published in* Amazing Stories *magazine before the book came out. (We also had a* House Atreides *excerpt published in* Playboy, *which allowed me to proudly display copies of the magazine on our coffee table "for the fiction.")*

Rather than being connected to the prequel events in House Atreides, *"A Whisper of Caladan Seas" is set during the events of* Dune, *a side story about brave Atreides soldiers trapped in the Shield Wall during the battle of Arrakeen, after the Harkonnens swept in to crush Duke Leto.*

I love how this story turned out, although one reviewer responded with a baffling complaint (as reviewers so often do) that we had included mystical aspects of this story, since he couldn't recall any mysticism in any of Frank Herbert's books! I still haven't stopped scratching my head over that one.

This story was also inspired by the 1967 Bee Gees song "New York Mining Disaster 1941." If you listen to the song after reading the story, you'll know what I mean.

Since that first short story, Brian and I have written and published over three million words together—with more to come.

A WHISPER OF CALADAN SEAS

(with Brian Herbert)

**Arrakis, in the year 10,191 of the Imperial calendar.
Arrakis … forever known as Dune….**

The cave in the massive Shield Wall was dark and dry, sealed by an avalanche. The air tasted like rock dust. The surviving Atreides soldiers huddled in blackness to conserve energy, letting their glowglobe powerpacks recycle.

Outside, the Harkonnen shelling hammered against the bolt-hole where they had fled for safety. Artillery? What a surprise to be attacked by such seemingly obsolete technology … and yet, it was effective. *Damned effective.*

In pockets of silence that lasted only seconds, the young recruit Elto Vitt lay in pain listening to the wheezing of wounded, terrified men. The stale, oppressive air pressed heavy on him, increasing the broken-glass agony in his lungs. He tasted blood in his mouth, an unwelcome moisture in the absolute dryness.

His uncle, Sergeant Hoh Vitt, had not honestly told him how severe his injuries were, emphasizing Elto's "youthful resilience and stamina." Elto suspected he must be dying, and he wasn't alone in that predicament. These last soldiers were all dying, if not from their injuries, then from hunger or thirst.

Thirst.

A man's voice cut the darkness, a gunner named Deegan. "I wonder if Duke Leto got away. I hope he's safe."

A reassuring grunt. "Thufir Hawat would slit his own throat before he'd let the Baron touch our Duke, or young Paul." It was the signalman Scovich, fiddling with the flexible hip cages that held two captive distrans bats, creatures whose nervous systems could carry message imprints.

"Bloody Harkonnens!" Then Deegan's sigh became a sob. "I wish we were back home on Caladan."

Supply sergeant Vitt was no more than a disembodied voice in the darkness, comfortingly close to his injured young nephew. "Do *you* hear a whisper of Caladan seas, Elto? Do you hear the waves, the tides?"

The boy concentrated hard. Indeed, the relentless artillery shelling sounded like the booming of breakers against the glistening black rocks below the cliff-perch of Castle Caladan.

"Maybe," he said. But he didn't, not really. The similarity was only slight, and his uncle, a Master Jongleur … a storyteller extraordinaire … wasn't up to his capabilities, though here he couldn't have asked for a more attentive audience. Instead the sergeant seemed stunned by events, and uncharacteristically quiet, not his usual gregarious self.

Elto remembered running barefoot along the beaches on Caladan, the Atreides home planet far, far from this barren repository of dunes, sandworms, and precious spice. As a child, he had tiptoed in the foamy residue of waves, avoiding the tiny pincers of crabfish so numerous that he could net enough for a fine meal in only a few minutes.

Those memories were much more vivid than what had actually happened….

The alarms had rung in the middle of the night, ironically during the first deep sleep Elto Vitt had managed in the Atreides barracks at Arrakeen. Only a month earlier, he and other recruits had been assigned to this desolate planet, saying their farewells to lush Caladan. Duke Leto Atreides had received the governorship of

Arrakis, the only known source of the precious spice melange, as a boon from the Padishah Emperor Shaddam IV.

To many of the loyal Atreides soldiers, it had seemed a great financial coup—they had known nothing of politics ... or of danger. Apparently Duke Leto had not been aware of the peril here either, because he'd brought along his concubine Lady Jessica and their fifteen-year-old son, Paul.

When the warning bells shrieked, Elto snapped awake and rolled from his bunk bed. His uncle Hoh Vitt, already in full sergeant's regalia, shouted for everyone to hurry, *hurry*! The Atreides house guard grabbed their uniforms, kits, and weapons. Elto recalled allowing himself a groan, annoyed at another apparent drill ... and yet hoping it was only that.

The burly, disfigured weapons-master Gurney Halleck burst into the barracks, his voice booming commands. Flushed with anger, the beet-colored inkvine scar stood out like a lightning bolt on his face. "House shields are down! We're vulnerable!" Security teams had supposedly rooted out all the booby traps, spy-eyes, and assassination devices left behind by the hated Harkonnen predecessors. Now the lumpish Halleck became a frenzy of barked orders.

Explosions sounded outside, shaking the barracks and rattling armor-plaz windows. Enemy assault 'thopters swooped in over the Shield Wall, probably coming from a Harkonnen base in the city of Carthag.

"Prepare your weapons!" Halleck bellowed. The buzzing of lasguns played across the stone walls of Arrakeen, incinerating buildings. Orange eruptions shattered plaz windows, decapitated observation towers. "We must defend House Atreides."

"For the Duke!" Uncle Hoh cried.

Elto yanked on the sleeve of his black uniform, tugging the trim into place, adjusting the red Atreides hawk crest and red cap of the corps. Everyone else had already jammed feet into boots, slapped charge packs into lasgun rifles. Elto scrambled to catch up, his mind awhirl. His uncle had pulled strings to get him assigned here as part of the elite corps. The other men were lean and whipcord strong, the finest handpicked Atreides troops. He didn't *belong* with them.

Young Elto had been excited to leave Caladan for Arrakis, so far away. He had never ridden on a Guild Heighliner before, had never been close to a mutated Navigator who could fold space with his mind. Before leaving his ocean home, Elto had spent only a few months watching the men train, eating with them, sleeping in the barracks, listening to their colorful, bawdy tales of great battles-past and duties performed in the service of the Atreides dukes.

Elto had never felt in danger on Caladan, but after only a short time on Arrakis, all the men had grown grim and uneasy. There had been unsettling rumors and suspicious events. Earlier that night, as the troops had bunked down, they'd been agitated, but unwilling to speak of it, either because of their commander's sharp orders or because the soldiers didn't know enough details. Or maybe they were just giving Elto, the untried and unproven new comrade, a cold shoulder....

Because of the circumstances of his recruitment, a few men of the elite corps hadn't taken to Elto. Instead, they'd openly grumbled about his amateur skills, wondering why Duke Leto had permitted such a novice to join them. A signalman and communications specialist named Forrie Scovich, pretending to be friendly, had filled the boy with false information as an ill-conceived joke. Uncle Hoh had put a stop to that, for with his Jongleur's talent for the quick, whispered story—always told without witnesses because of the ancient prohibition—he could have given any of the men terrible nightmares for weeks … and they all knew it.

The men in the Atreides elite corps feared and respected their supply sergeant, but even the most accommodating of them gave his nephew no preferential treatment. Anyone could see that Elto Vitt was not one of them, not one of their rough-and-tumble, hard fighting breed....

By the time the Atreides house guard rushed out of the barracks, they were naked to aerial attack from the lack of house shields. The men knew the vulnerability couldn't possibly be from a mere equipment failure, not after what they'd been hearing, what they had been feeling. How could Duke Leto Atreides, with all of his proven abilities, have permitted this to happen?

Enraged, Gurney Halleck grumbled loudly, "Aye, we have a traitor in our midst."

Illuminated in floodlights, Harkonnen troops in blue uniforms swarmed over the compound. More enemy transports disgorged assault teams.

Elto held his lasgun rifle, trying to remember the drills and training sessions. Someday, if he survived, his uncle would compose a vivid story about this battle, conjuring up images of smoke, sounds, and fires, as well as Atreides valor and loyalty to the Duke.

Atreides soldiers raced through the streets, dodging explosions, fighting hard to defend. Lasguns sliced vivid blue arcs across the night. The elite corps joined the fray, howling—but Elto could already see they were vastly outnumbered by this massive surprise assault. Without shields, Arrakeen had already been struck a mortal blow.

Elto blinked his eyes in the cave, saw light. A flicker of hope dissipated as he realized it was only a recharged glowglobe floating in the air over his head. Not daylight.

Still trapped in their tomb of rock, the Atreides soldiers listened to the continued thuds of artillery. Dust and debris trickled from the shuddering ceiling. Elto tried to keep his spirits high, but knew House Atreides must have fallen by now.

His uncle sat nearby, staring into space. A long red scratch jagged across one cheek.

During brief inspection drills while settling in, Elto had met the other important men in Duke Leto's security staff besides Gurney Halleck, especially the renowned Swordmaster Duncan Idaho and the old Mentat assassin Thufir Hawat. The black-haired Duke inspired such loyalty in his men, exuded such supreme confidence, that Elto had never imagined this mighty man could fall.

One of the security experts had been trapped here with the rest of the detachment. Now Scovich confronted him, his voice gruff and challenging. "How did the house shields get shut off? It must have been a traitor, someone you overlooked." The distrans bats seemed agitated in their cages at Scovich's waist.

"We spared no effort checking the palace," the man said, more tired than defensive. "There were dozens of traps, mechanical and human. When the hunter-seeker almost killed Master Paul, Thufir Hawat offered his resignation, but the Duke refused to accept it."

"Well, you didn't find all the traps," Scovich groused, probing for an excuse to fight. "You were supposed to keep the Harkonnens out."

Sergeant Hoh Vitt stepped between the two men before they could come to blows. "We can't afford to be at each other's throats. We need to work together to get out of this."

But Elto saw on the faces of the men that they all knew otherwise: they would never get out of the death trap.

The unit's muscular battlefield engineer, Avram Fultz, paced about in the faint light, using a jury-rigged instrument to measure the thickness of rock and dirt around them. "Three meters of solid stone." He turned toward the fallen boulders that had covered the cave entrance. "Down to two and a half here, but it's dangerously unstable."

"If we went out the front, we'd run headlong into Harkonnen shelling anyway," the gunner Deegan said. His voice trembled with tension, like a too-tight baliset string about to break.

Uncle Hoh activated a second glowglobe, which floated in the air behind him as he went to a bend in the tunnel. "If I remember the arrangement of the tunnels, on the other side of this wall there's a supply cache. Food, medical supplies … water."

Fultz ran his scanner over the thick stone. Elto, unable to move on his makeshift bed and fuzzed with painkillers, stared at the process, realizing how much it reminded him of Caladan fishermen using depth sounders in the reef fishing grounds.

"You picked a good, secure spot for those supplies, Sergeant," Fultz said. "Four meters of solid rock. The cave-ins have cut us off."

Deegan, his voice edged with hysteria, groaned. "That food and water might as well be in the Imperial Palace on Kaitain. This place … Arrakis … isn't right for us Atreides!"

The gunner was right, Elto thought. Atreides soldiers were tough, but like fish out of water in this hostile environment.

"I was never comfortable here," Deegan wailed.

"So who asked you to be *comfortable*?" Fultz snapped, setting aside his apparatus. "You're a soldier, not a pampered prince."

Deegan's raw emotions turned his words into a rant. "I wish the Duke had never accepted Shaddam's offer to come here. He must have known it was a trap! We can never live in a place like this!" He stood up, making exaggerated, scarecrowish gestures.

"We need water, the ocean," Elto said, overcoming pain to lift his voice. "Does anybody else remember *rain*?"

"I do," Deegan said, his voice a pitiful whine.

Elto thought of his first view of the sweeping wastelands of open desert beyond the Shield Wall. His initial impression had been nostalgic, already homesick. The undulating panorama of sand dunes had been so similar to the even patterns of waves on the sea ... but without any drop of water.

Issuing a strange cry, Deegan rushed to the nearest wall and clawed at the stone, kicking and trying to dig his way out with bare hands. He tore his nails and pounded with his fists, leaving bloody patterns on the unforgiving rock, until two of the other soldiers dragged him away and wrestled him to the ground. One man, a hand-to-hand combat specialist who had trained at the famous Swordmaster school on Ginaz, ripped open one of their remaining medpaks and dosed Deegan with a strong sedative.

The pounding artillery continued. *Won't they ever stop?* He felt an odd, pain-wracked sensation that he might be sealed in this hellhole for eternity, trapped in a blip of time from which there was no escape. Then he heard his uncle's voice....

Kneeling beside the claustrophobic gunner, Uncle Hoh leaned close, whispering, "Listen. Let me tell you a story." It was a private tale intended only for Deegan's ears, though the intensity in the Jongleur's voice seemed to shimmer in the thick air. Elto caught a few words about a sleeping princess, a hidden and magical city, a lost hero from the Butlerian Jihad who would slumber in oblivion until he rose again to save the Imperium. By the time Hoh Vitt completed his tale, Deegan had fallen into a stupor.

Elto suspected what his uncle had done, that he had disregarded the ancient prohibition against using the forbidden powers of planet Jongleur, ancestral home of the Vitt family. In the low light their gazes met, and Uncle Hoh's eyes were bright and fearful. As he'd been conditioned to do since childhood, Elto tried not to think about it, for he too was a Vitt.

Instead, he visualized the events that had occurred only hours before....

On the streets of Arrakeen, some of the Harkonnen soldiers had been fighting in an odd manner. The Atreides elite corps had shouldered lasguns to lay down suppressing fire. The buzzing weapons had filled the air with crackling power, contrasted with much more primal noises of screams and the percussive explosions of old-fashioned artillery fire.

The battle-scarred weapons master ran at the vanguard, bellowing in a strong voice that was rich and accustomed to command. "Watch yourselves—and don't underestimate *them*." Halleck lowered his voice, growling; Elto wouldn't have heard the words if he hadn't been running close to the commander. "They're in formations like Sardaukar."

Elto shuddered at the thought of the Emperor's crack terror troops, said to be invincible. *Have the Harkonnens learned Sardaukar methods?* It was confusing.

Sergeant Hoh Vitt grabbed his nephew's shoulder and turned him to join another running detachment. Everyone seemed more astonished by the unexpected and primitive mortar bombardment than by the strafing attacks of the assault 'thopters.

"Why would they use artillery, Uncle?" Elto shouted. He still hadn't fired a single shot from his lasgun. "Those weapons haven't been used effectively for centuries." Though the young recruit might not be well-practiced in battle maneuvers, he had at least read his military history.

"Harkonnen devils," Hoh Vitt said. "Always scheming, always coming up with some trick. Damn them!"

One entire wing of the Arrakeen palace glowed orange, consumed by inner flames. Elto hoped the Atreides family had gotten away ... Duke Leto, Lady Jessica, young Paul. He could still see their faces, their proud but not unkind manners; he could still hear their voices.

As the street battle continued, blue-uniformed Harkonnen invaders ran across an intersection, and Halleck's men roared in challenge. Impulsively, Elto fired his own weapon at the massed enemies, and the air shimmered with a crisscross web of blue-white lines. He fumbled, firing the lasgun again.

Scovich snapped at him. "Point that damn thing away from me! You're supposed to hit *Harkonnens!*" Without a word, Uncle Hoh grasped Elto's rifle, placed the young man's hands in proper positions, reset the calibration, then slapped him on the back. Elto fired again, and hit a blue-uniformed invader.

Agonized cries of injured men throbbed around him, mingled with frantic calls of medics and squad leaders. Above it all, the weapons master yelled orders and curses through twisted lips. Gurney Halleck already looked defeated, as if he had personally betrayed his Duke. He had escaped from a Harkonnen slave pit years before, had lived with smugglers on Salusa Secundus, and had sworn revenge on his enemies. Now, though, the troubadour warrior could not salvage the situation.

Under attack, Halleck waved his hands to command the entire detachment. "Sergeant Vitt, take men into the Shield Wall tunnels and guard our supply storehouses. Secure defensive positions and lay down a suppressing fire to take out those artillery weapons."

Never doubting that his orders would be obeyed, Halleck turned to the remainder of his elite corps, reassessing the strategic situation. Elto saw that the weapons master had picked his best fighters to remain with him. In his heart, Elto had known at that moment, as he did now thinking back on it, that if this were ever to be told as one of his uncle's vivid stories, the tale would be cast as a tragedy.

In the heat of battle Sergeant Hoh Vitt had shouted for them to trot double-time up the cliffside road. His detachment had taken their weapons and left the walls of Arrakeen. Glowlamps and portable illuminators showed firefly chains of other civilian evacuees trying to find safety in the mountainous barrier.

Panting, refusing to slacken their pace, they had gained altitude, and Elto looked down on the burning garrison city. The Harkonnens wanted the desert planet back, and they wanted to eradicate House Atreides. The blood-feud between the two noble families dated all the way back to the Butlerian Jihad.

Sergeant Vitt reached a camouflaged opening and entered his code to allow them access. Down below, the gunfire continued. An assault 'thopter swooped along the side of the mountain, sketching black streaks of slagged rock; Scovich, Fultz, and Deegan opened fire, but the 'thopter retreated—after marking their position.

As the rest of the detachment raced inside the caves, Elto took a moment at the threshold to note the nearest artillery weapons. He saw five of the huge, old-style guns pounding indiscriminately at Arrakeen—the Harkonnens didn't care how much damage they caused. Then two of the mighty barrels rotated to face the Shield Wall. Flames belched out, followed by far-off thunder, and explosive shells rained down upon the cave openings.

"Get inside!" Sergeant Vitt shouted. The others moved to obey, but Elto remained fixated. In a single stroke, a long line of fleeing civilians vanished from the cliffside paths, as if a cosmic artist with a giant paintbrush had decided to erase his work. The artillery guns continued to fire and fire, and soon centered on the position of the soldiers.

The range of Elto's full-power lasgun was at least as far as the conventional shells. He aimed and fired, pulsing out an unbroken stream but expecting little in the way of results. But the dissipating heat struck the old-fashioned explosives in the loaded artillery shells, and the ragged detonation ripped out the breech of the mammoth cannon.

He turned around, grinning, trying to shout his triumph to his uncle—then a shell from the second massive gun struck squarely above the entrance to the cave. The explosion knocked Elto farther into the tunnel as tons of rock showered down, striking him. The avalanche sent shockwaves through an entire section of the Shield Wall. The entire contingent was sealed inside....

After days in the tomblike cave, one of the glowglobes gave out and could not be recharged; the remaining two managed only a flickering light in the main room. Elto lay wounded, tended by the junior medic and his dwindling supplies of medicinals. Elto's pain had dulled from the broken glass to a cold, cold blackness that seemed easier to endure ... but how he longed for a sip of water!

Uncle Hoh shared his concern, but was unable to do anything else.

Squatting on the stone floor off to his left, two sullen soldiers had used their fingertips to trace a grid in the dust; with light and dark stones they played a makeshift game of Go, a carryover from ancient Terra.

Everyone waited and waited—not for rescue, but for the serenity of death, for escape.

The shelling outside had finally stopped. Elto knew with a sick certainty that the Atreides had lost. Gurney Halleck and his elite corps would be dead by now, the duke and his family either killed or captured; none of the loyal Atreides soldiers dared to hope that Leto or Paul or Jessica had escaped.

The signalman Scovich paced the perimeter, peering into darkened cracks and crumbling walls. Finally, after carefully imprinting a distress message into the voice patterns of his captive distrans bats, he released them. The small creatures circled the dusty enclosure, seeking a way out. Their high-pitched cries echoed from the porous stone as they searched for any tiny niche. After frantic flapping and swooping, at last the pair disappeared through a fissure in the ceiling.

"We'll see if this works," Scovich said. His voice held little optimism.

In a weak but valiant voice, Elto called his uncle nearer. Using most of his remaining strength, he propped himself on an elbow. "Tell me a story, about the good times we had on our fishing trips."

Hoh Vitt's eyes brightened, but for only a second before fear set in. He spoke slowly. "On Caladan … Yes, the old days."

"Not so long ago, Uncle."

"Oh, but it seems like it."

"You're right," Elto said. He and Hoh Vitt had taken a coracle along the shore, past the lush pundi rice paddies and out into open water, beyond the seaweed colonies. They had spent days anchored in the foamy breakwaters of dark coral reefs, where they dove for shells, using small knives to pry free the flammable nodules called coral gems. In those magical waters they caught fan-fish—one of the great delicacies of the Imperium—and ate them raw.

"Caladan …" the gunner Deegan said groggily, as he emerged from his stupor. "Remember how *vast* the ocean was? It seemed to cover the whole world."

Hoh Vitt had always been so good at telling stories, supernaturally good. He could make the most outrageous things real for his listeners. Friends or family made a game of throwing an idea at Hoh, and he would make up a story using it. Blood mixed with melange … a great Heighliner race across uncharted foldspace … the wrist wrestling championship of the universe, between two dwarf sisters who were the finalists … a talking slig.

"No, no stories now, Elto," the sergeant said in a fearful voice. "Rest now."

"You're a Master Jongleur, aren't you? You always said so."

"I don't talk about that much." Hoh Vitt turned away.

His ancestral family had once been proud members of an ancient school of storytelling on the planet Jongleur. Men and women from that world used to be the primary troubadours of the Imperium; they traveled between royal houses, telling stories and singing songs to entertain the great families. But House Jongleur fell into disgrace when a number of the itinerant storytellers were proven to be double agents in inter-House feuds, and no one trusted them any longer. When the nobles dropped their services, House Jongleur forfeited its status in the Landsraad, losing its fortunes. Guild Heighliners stopped going to their planet; the buildings and infrastructure, once highly advanced, fell into disrepair. Largely due to the Jongleurs' demise, many entertainment innovations were developed, including holo projections, filmbooks, and shigawire recorders.

"*Now* is the time, Uncle. Take me back to Caladan. I don't want to be here."

"I can't do that, boy," he responded in a sad voice. "We're all stuck here."

"Make me *think* I'm there, like only you can do. I don't want to die in this hellish place."

With a piercing squeak, the two distrans bats returned. Confused and frustrated, they fluttered around the chamber while Scovich tried to recapture them. Even they had been unable to escape....

Though the trapped men had held out little hope, the failure of the bats still made them groan in dismay. Uncle Hoh looked at them, then down at Elto as his expression hardened into grim determination.

"Quiet! All of you." He knelt beside his injured nephew. Hoh's eyes became glazed with tears ... or something more. "The boy needs to hear what I have to say."

Elto lay back, letting his eyes fall half-closed as he readied himself for the words that would paint memory pictures on the insides of his eyelids. Sergeant Vitt sat rigid, taking deep breaths to compose himself, to center his uncanny skill and stoke the fires of imagination. To tell the type of story these men needed, a Master Jongleur must calm himself; he moved his hands and fingers in the ancient way, going through the motions he'd been taught by generations of storytellers, ritualistic preparations to make the story good and pure.

Fultz and Scovich shifted uneasily, and then moved closer, anxious to listen as well. Hoh Vitt looked at them with glazed eyes, barely seeing them, but his voice carried a gruff warning. "There is danger."

"Danger?" Fultz laughed and raised his grimy hands to the dim ceiling and surrounding rock walls. "Tell us something we don't know."

"Very well." Hoh was deeply saddened, wishing he hadn't pulled strings to get Elto assigned to the prestigious corps. The young man still thought of himself as an outsider, but ironically—by staying in the line of fire and destroying one of the artillery weapons —he had shown more courage than any of the proven soldiers.

Now Hoh Vitt felt a tremendous sense of impending loss. This wonderful young man, filled not only with his own hopes and dreams but also with those of his parents and uncle, was going to die without ever achieving his bright promise. He looked around, at the faces of the other soldiers, and seeing how they looked at him with such anticipation and admiration, he felt a moment of pride.

In the hinterlands of Jongleur, a hilly rural region where Hoh Vitt had grown up, dwelled a special type of storyteller. Even the natives suspected these "Master Jongleurs" of sorcery and dangerous ways. They could spin stories like deadly spiderwebs, and in order to protect their secrets, they allowed themselves to be shunned, hiding behind a cloak of mystique.

"Hurry, Uncle," Elto said, his voice quiet and thready.

With intensity in his words, Sergeant Vitt leaned closer. "You remember how my stories always start, don't you?" He touched the young man's pulse.

"You warn us not to believe too deeply, to always remember that it's only a story … or it could be dangerous. We could lose our minds."

"I'm saying that again to you, boy." He scanned the close-pressed faces around him. "And to everyone listening."

Scovich made a scoffing noise, but the others remained silent and intent. Perhaps they thought his warning was only part of the storytelling process, part of an illusion a Master Jongleur needed to create.

After a moment's hush, Hoh employed the enhanced memorization techniques of the Jongleurs, a method of transferring large amounts of information and retaining it for future generations. In this manner he brought to mind the planet Caladan, summoning it in every intricate detail.

"I used to have a wingboat," he said with a gentle smile, and then he began to describe sailing on the seas of Caladan. He used his voice like a paintbrush, selecting words carefully, like pigments precisely mixed by an artist. He spoke to Elto, but his story spread hypnotically, wrapping around the circle of listeners like the wispy smoke of a fire.

"You and your father went with me on week-long fishing trips. Oh, those days! Up at sunrise and casting nets until sunset, with the golden tone of the sun framing each day. I must say we enjoyed our time alone on the water even more than the fish we caught. The companionship, the adventures and hilarious mishaps."

And hidden in his words were subliminal signals: *Smell the salt water, the iodine of drying seaweed … Hear the whisper of waves, the splash of a distant fish too large to bring aboard whole.*

"At night, when we sat at anchor alone in the middle of the seaweed islands, we'd stay up late, the three of us, playing a fast game of tri-chess on a board made of flatpearls and abalone shells. The pieces themselves were carved from the translucent ivory tusks of South Caladan walruses. Do you remember?"

"Yes, Uncle. I remember."

All the men murmured their agreement; the Jongleur's haunting words were as real to them as to the young man who had actually experienced the memories.

Listen to the hypnotic, throbbing songs of unseen murmons hiding in a fog bank that ripples across the calm waters.

The shroud of pain grew fuzzy around Elto, and he could feel himself going to that other place and time, being carried away from this hellish place. The parched, dusty air at first smelled dank, then cool and moist. As he closed his eyes, he could sense the loving touch of Caladan breezes on his cheek. He smelled the mists of his native world, spring rain on his face, sea waves lapping at his feet as he stood on the rocky beach below the Atreides castle.

"When you were young, you would splash in the water, laughing and swimming naked with your friends. Do you remember?"

"I ..." And Elto felt his voice merge with the others, becoming one with them. "We remember," the men mumbled reverently. All around them the air had grown close and stifling, most of the oxygen used up. Another one of the glowglobes died. But the men didn't know this. They were anesthetized from their pain.

See the wingboat cruising like a razorfin under dazzling sunlight, then through a warm squall under cloudy skies.

"I used to body surf in the waves," Elto said with a faint smile of wonder.

Fultz coughed, then added his own reminiscences. "I spent a summer on a small farm overlooking the sea, where we harvested paradan melons. Have you ever had one fresh out of the water? Sweetest fruit in the universe."

Even Deegan, still somewhat dazed, leaned forward. "I saw an elecran once, late at night and far away—oh, they're rare, but they do exist. It's more than just a sailor's story. Looked like an electrical storm on the water, but alive. Luckily, the monster never came close." Though the gunner had been hysterical not long before, his words held such an awed solemnity that no one thought to disbelieve him.

Swim through the water, feel its caress on your body. Imagine being totally wet, immersed in the sea. The waves surround you, holding and protecting you like a mother's arms....

The two distrans bats, still loose from the signalman's cages, had clung to the ceiling for hours, but now they swayed and dropped to the floor. All the air was disappearing in their tomb.

Elto remembered the old days in Cala City, the stories his uncle used to tell to an entranced audience of his family. At several points in each of those tales, Uncle Hoh would force himself to break away.

He had always taken great care to remind his listeners that it was *only a story*.

This time, however, Hoh Vitt took no breaks.

Realizing this, Elto felt a moment of fear, like a dreamer unable to awaken from a nightmare. But then he allowed himself to succumb. Though he could barely breathe, he forced himself to say, "I'm going into the water ... I'm diving ... I'm going deeper ..."

Then all the trapped soldiers could hear the waves, smell the water, and remember the whisper of Caladan seas....

The whisper became a roar.

In the velvet shadows of a crisp night on Dune, Fremen scavengers dropped over the ridge of the Shield Wall, into the rubble. Stillsuits softened their silhouettes, allowing them to vanish like beetles into crevices.

Below, most of the fires in Arrakeen had been put out, but the damage remained untended. The new Harkonnen rulers had returned to their traditional seat of government in Carthag; they would leave the scarred Atreides city as a blackened wound for a few months ... as a reminder to the people.

The feud between House Atreides and House Harkonnen meant nothing to the Fremen—the noble families were all unwelcome interlopers on their sacred desert planet, which the Fremen had claimed as their own thousands of years earlier, after the Wandering. For millennia these people had carried the wisdom of their ancestors, including an ancient Terran saying about each cloud having a silver lining. The Fremen would use the bloodshed of these royal houses to their own advantage: the deathstills back at the sietch would drink deeply from the casualties of war.

Harkonnen patrols swept the area, but the soldiers cared little for the bands of furtive Fremen, pursuing and killing them only out of sport rather than in a focused program of genocide. The Harkonnens paid no heed to the Atreides trapped in the Shield Wall either, thinking none of them could have survived; so they left the bodies trapped in the rubble.

From the Fremen perspective, the Harkonnens did not value their resources.

Working together, using bare callused hands and metal digging tools, the scavengers began their excavation, opening a narrow tunnel between the rocks. Only a few dim glowglobes hovered close to the diggers, providing faint light.

Through soundings and careful observations on the night of the attack, the Fremen knew where the victims would be. They had uncovered a dozen already, as well as a precious cache of supplies, but now they were after something much more valuable, the tomb of an entire detachment of Atreides soldiers. The desert men toiled for hours, sweating into the absorbent layers of their stillsuits, taking only a few sipped drops of recovered moisture. Many water rings would be earned for the moisture recovered from these corpses, making these Fremen scavengers wealthy.

When they broke into the cave enclosure, though, they stepped into a clammy stone coffin filled with the redolence of death. Some of the Fremen cried out or muttered superstitious prayers to Shai-Hulud, but others probed forward, increasing the light from the glowglobes now that they were out of sight of the nighttime patrols.

The Atreides soldiers all lay dead together, as if struck down in a strange suicide ceremony. One man sat in the center of their group, and when the Fremen leader moved him, his body fell to one side and a gush of water spewed out of his mouth. The Fremen tasted it. Salt water.

The scavengers backed away, even more frightened now.

Carefully, two young men inspected the bodies, finding that the uniforms of the Atreides were warm and wet, stinking of mildew and damp rot. Their dead eyes were open wide and staring, but with contentment instead of the expected horror, as if they had shared a religious experience. All of the dead Atreides soldiers had clammy skin ... and something even more peculiar, revealed when the Fremen cut them open.

The lungs of these dead men were entirely filled with water.

The Fremen fled, leaving their spoils behind, and resealed the cave. Thereafter, it became a forbidden place of legend, drawing wonder from anyone hearing the story as it was passed on by Fremen from generation to generation.

Somehow, sealed inside a lightless cave in the driest desert, all of the Atreides soldiers had *drowned*....

This is my first story featuring "Alternitech," a futuristic company where explorers hunt parallel timelines for subtle differences that might be profitable in this world.

The tiniest of circumstances, the most trivial of decisions, can have ripple-effect consequences for our lives—but then, we'd never know it, would we?

If you had just stomped on the brakes half a second sooner, you would have avoided the fender-bender that gave you whiplash. If you hadn't chosen that particular moment to run to the grocery store, you would have gotten the phone call that you'd won the radio station's grand prize contest. If you had chosen to stay home and read instead of going off to the coffee shop, you might not have bumped into the person who would turn out to be the love of your life....

Who can say?

Back in high school, I read Ray Bradbury's classic short story, "A Sound of Thunder," in which he portrays time and destiny as an easily unraveled web, where the untimely death of a mere butterfly back in the age of dinosaurs is enough to alter all of human history.

Think of all the possible variations on our world there could be, the multiple parallel universes with only the smallest of differences. It would be worth exploring.

You'll find several other Alternitech stories in these collections.

The original title for this story was "Time in a Bottle," but the Jim Croce estate wouldn't allow me to use it. Apparently, Croce's widow doesn't like science fiction. Oh well, I like my new title better.

MUSIC PLAYED ON THE STRINGS OF TIME

He arrived, hoping to find a new Lennon, or a Jimi Hendrix. Or an alternate universe where the Beatles had never broken up.

As the air ceased shimmering around him, Jeremy staggered; with his head pounding, he sucked in a deep breath. His employers at Alternitech always made him empty his lungs before stepping through the portal. The company had strict rules limiting the amount of nonreturnable mass shuttled across timelines, even down to the air molecules. Take nothing tangible; leave behind as little as possible.

The air here smelled good, though; it tasted the same as in his own universe.

He snatched a glance around himself, making sure that no one had seen him appear. It had rained recently, and the ground was still wet. Everything about this new reality appeared the same, but each timeline had its subtle differences.

Jeremy Cardiff simply needed to find the useful ones.

The Pacific Bell logo on the phone booth had the familiar design, but with a forest-green background color instead of bright blue. He had always found a phone booth in the same spot, no matter which alternate reality he visited. Some things must be immutable in the Grand Scheme.

Jeremy reached into the pocket of his jacket and withdrew the ring of keys. One of them usually worked on the phone's coin compartment, but he also had a screwdriver and a small pry bar. His girlfriend Holly had never approved of stealing, but Jeremy had no choice—in order to spend money in this universe, he had to get it from somewhere here, since he could leave none of his own behind.

The third key worked, and the coin compartment popped open, spilling handfuls of quarters, nickels, and dimes—Mercury dimes, he noticed; apparently they had never gotten around to using the Roosevelt version. He scooped the coins out of the phone booth and sealed them in a pouch he took from his pack. Never get anything mixed up, the cardinal rule.

Time to go searching. Jeremy picked up the phone book dangling from a cable in the booth and flipped through the yellow pages, hunting for the nearest record store.

Before he had left his own timeline that morning, everything had happened with maddening familiarity.

"Your briefing, Mr. Cardiff," the woman in her white lab coat had said. The opalescent Alternitech: Entertainment Division logo shone garishly on her lapel, but she seemed proud of it. Her eyebrows were shaved; her hair close-cropped and perfectly in place; her face never showed any expression. This time Jeremy saw she was attractive; he had not noticed before. Every other time he had been too preoccupied with Holly to notice.

"You tell me the same thing every trip," Jeremy said to the Alternitech woman, shuffling his feet. He felt the butterflies gnawing at his stomach. He just wanted to get on with it.

"A reminder never hurts," she said, handing him the high-speed tape dubber. It had eight different settings to accommodate the types of music cassettes most often found in near-adjacent timelines.

At least the woman had stopped giving him the "time is like a rope with many possible strands" part of the speech. Jeremy was allowed only into universes where he himself did not exist at that moment; it had something to do with exclusions and quantum principles. He chose never to stray far from his own portion of the timestream, stepping over to adjacent threads, places where reality had changed in subtle ways that might lead to big payoffs in his own reality.

Other divisions of Alternitech sent people hunting for elusive cures to cancer or AIDS, but they had been by and large unsuccessful. A cure for cancer would change history too much, spin a timeline farther and further away from their own, and thus make it harder to reach.

"Ghost music," on the other hand, was easy to find. Jeremy wanted to find new work by Hendrix or Morrison or Joplin, a timeline where these stars had somehow escaped freak accidents or avoided suicide.

"Do you have everything now?" the woman asked him.

"All set." Jeremy stuffed the tape dubber into his shoulder pack. "I've got my money bag, a snack, some blank tapes, and even a bottle to piss in if I can't hold it." Sometimes the precautions seemed ridiculous, but he wasn't here to question the rules. Alternitech would deduct from his own commission the transport cost for every gram of mass differential.

"You have five hours until you return here," she said. The portal opened, shimmering inside its chrome framework. "I trust that will be enough time for you to search."

"I've never needed more than two hours, even if I have to walk to the mall."

She ignored that. He was disrupting her memorized speech. "You are entitled to your commission on whatever new music you locate, but according to our contract we retain all rights and royalties." She smiled. Her lips looked as if they had leaped off the screen from the *Rocky Horror Picture Show*.

"Of course," he said. He had already learned that once, with his first big payoff, finding three new albums by Buddy Holly—he had actually been looking because of Holly's name, and he had been so surprised he had almost forgotten what to do. Almost. He had coasted on the triumph for a year, but he had found nothing new in a long time. He felt the anticipation building each time, wondering what he might find.

Exhaling the air in his lungs, Jeremy went sailing into the timestream.

Shopping malls had to be the most ubiquitous structures in creation. Jeremy had never encountered a timeline where the mall did not exist.

Inside the record store, Jeremy scouted down the aisles. The new releases displayed the appropriate Big Hits; a familiar Top 40 single played on the store's stereo system. The important changes would be subtler, difficult to find.

He checked under the Beatles first. At other times he had found strange but useless anomalies—a version of *Abbey Road* that did not include "Maxwell's Silver Hammer," a copy of the White Album that actually listed the songs on the back, a release of *Yesterday and Today* that had retained the disgusting butcher shop cover censored in the US. But since he could not take anything physical back with him, cover variations were worthless. In this store, however, everything looked the way it should have.

Disappointed, he next tried Elvis, the Doors, Led Zeppelin, John Lennon—those would net him the most commission if he brought an undiscovered treasure back.

He might as well have stayed home.

With a sigh, he finally searched for Harry Chapin and Jim Croce, Holly's favorites. New songs by these two wouldn't sell well back in his own timeline, but he always checked, for her. He stopped himself—it didn't matter anymore. Who gave a damn for Holly? But he looked anyway.

He thought of Chapin, killed in a car accident … his Volkswagen smashed under a truck, wasn't it? And Jim Croce, dead in a plane crash at age 30, two weeks after his song "Time in a Bottle" had been a theme in a TV movie: *She Lives*, one of those oh-so-typical "my lover is dying of a terminal disease" films of the early seventies. Jeremy considered the song sappy and sentimental; Holly insisted it wasn't.

"You know, if it were me saving time in a bottle," he had said to her, "I could think of a lot better things to do with it. Like find more time for my own music."

He knew just how to push Holly's buttons. After one fight, he had left a box on her doorstep for her to keep "all those wishes and dreams that would never come true." He had intended it to be ironic; she had called it cruel.

He and Holly had such different needs that they clashed often over the two years they had been together, coming close and drawing apart. He decided it was probably over now for good. Jeremy had his music, his need to write songs and work toward breaking into the business. Holly, though, just wanted to hang out with him, wasting hours in conversation that had no topic and no purpose. She said it brought them together; he resented her for draining away time that he could have used for composing.

In the house he kept his own mixer, a MIDI sequencer, synthesizers, music editing programs, a set of panel speakers mounted on marble blocks and an amp that could lift the house two inches off its foundations if he decided to crank the volume. He had all the gadgetry, he studied the hits, tried to come up with a sure-fire blockbuster. Listening to the crap on the radio, he couldn't see that his own stuff was any worse.

He just needed a break. You had to know a name, get under the right label, and somebody would make your songs hits, crowbar you to the top of the charts. Otherwise, music people tossed unsolicited demo tapes out the window. Reject. Sorry, kid.

But Jeremy planned to get in through the side door, to make a name for himself by bringing "ghost music" back to his own timeline and taking credit for it. Then the studio execs would be ready to listen to his stuff....

But it wouldn't happen here, not in this timeline, not in this record store. Jeremy sighed. No Beatles, not even any new Chapin. He flicked his gaze down to Croce.

Holly disagreed with Jeremy's approach to songwriting. She worked as a nurse and sometimes treated him like a patient with psychological problems. Therapy. Pop psychology. "You can't just find a formula and imitate it. You need the depth, the emotion. And you can only get that by drawing it from yourself, by being brave enough to look deep. But you're afraid to. You need to have something inside yourself before you can share it with anyone else."

But he knew Holly must be wrong. What did a nurse know about music? He played in bars on weekends, drawing a few crowds. Holly herself came to watch, sitting at a table near the stage and mouthing the words to his own lyrics that no one else recognized. Somebody would notice him. One of his songs would catch on. He needed a foot in the door and some more practice.

Startled, he found five different cassettes with Jim Croce's name on the side. In his own timeline, Croce had made only two albums, and most of those cuts had been compiled into varied "Greatest Hits" collections. After a moment of excitement—Jeremy always felt his skin crawl at finding an obvious change—he picked up the cassettes, glancing at the titles, reading the package copy.

In this reality, Croce's plane had never crashed. In the late '70s he had changed his style dramatically, but the cassettes didn't seem to be big successes. Croce had gone for dance music, funky R&B, with more and more desperate attempts at reaching the Top 40 again. Songs like "The Return of Leroy Brown" were sure danger signs of waning creativity. On his last album Croce had not even written his own material, instead doing covers of old hits. When Jeremy found "Time in a Bottle: Disco Remix" he couldn't stop from chuckling.

Personal zingers aside, the alternate Jim Croce would have little commercial value for Alternitech back in his own timeline. And Holly would hate him for bringing this stuff back, for spoiling the memories. That would be too petty. He couldn't do that to her.

Not knowing quite why he didn't want to rub her face in it, he decided against the cassettes. Alternitech wouldn't be impressed anyway, and it would be a poor shadow to those new Buddy Holly tapes he had found. Better to leave old Jim dead in his plane crash. Jeremy shook his head, feeling pleased about completing his good deed for the day.

Then he noticed another tape shelved under "Misc. C." It bore his own name: JEREMY CARDIFF—*This One's for Holly.*

He paid for the cassette by stacking up the quarters from the phone booth, one dollar at a time. The clerk looked at him strangely for paying in coins, but Jeremy was already tearing the cellophane wrapping from the tape case. The blurb sticker said "Contains the SMASH hit 'For Holly'!" Promo material tended to exaggerate the magnitude of any song's success, but he felt enthralled that something of his had actually been called a hit.

By the time he emerged into the scattered crowds wandering the mall walkways, Jeremy had popped the cassette into his player. He sat down in one of the mall lounge areas, closed his eyes next to a trickling fountain, and listened.

Jeremy recognized the first two cuts as variations—sophistications, actually—on songs he had already written. The third cut was one he had just begun in his own timeline. He felt a sense of unreality drifting over him, euphoria at having achieved his dream. In at least one timeline he had succeeded. He wondered what his alternate self was doing now, how he was planning to follow up a successful first album—

Then the other part of it struck him with a force great enough that he sat bolt upright on the padded bench. He shut off the player. He could not enter another timeline where he himself still existed. Exclusion principles. The Jeremy Cardiff in this reality—the one who had been a hit musician—must be dead!

He checked the copyright date on the cassette liner. Last year. His counterpart must have died not long ago.

Jeremy had never dared to check before, had never been interested to find out what altered circumstances had erased his own existence in these other timelines. But here he had achieved his best goals, his dreams—what had happened to him? Another pointless plane crash like Jim Croce's?

Jeremy checked the timer that would send him back through the portal to Alternitech. He had three hours to find out.

"But can you tell me how he died?" Jeremy tried to keep his voice calm on the telephone. The record company receptionist had kept him on hold long enough that he had already needed to plunk four more quarters into the pay slot.

"Self-inflicted," she said. Record company receptionists must go to school to learn that perfect "go screw yourself" attitude, he thought. "You know, the old couldn't-handle-success story."

Jeremy's heart caught in his throat. Self-inflicted? "Don't you have any other information? Please, this is important."

"Look," she answered, clearly impatient now, "he took sleeping pills, or shot himself in the head. I can't remember. Jeremy Cardiff had one hit, he made a little money, now he's dead. So what? The price of gas hasn't changed."

Jeremy swallowed as he hung up on her. "No, I don't suppose it has."

While waiting for a bus, Jeremy used the high-speed tape dubber to copy *This One's for Holly* onto a blank cassette from his own timeline, one he could take back with him. He would have to discard the original before he returned through the portal. The sky overhead was gray, as if preparing to rain again.

He listened to the rest of the tape after he had found a seat on the bus and sat back. He munched on a granola bar from his pack, careful to stow the empty wrapper back in the zipper compartment.

As the songs played, the initial astonishment wore off, and he began to hear his music with a fresh ear, like a listener would. Sadly enough, he was forced to admit that the songs seemed rather empty, the "oooh, baby, baby, yeah!" kind he had always scorned. Had he been too close to them? How could he have missed it? None of them had any punch.

Until the last song, "For Holly," which stood head and shoulders above the rest of the cuts. This had been the reason for the album. This had been the demo somebody had noticed.

He couldn't put his finger on the difference here—the music, the quality of his singing voice, the words? The pain sounded real. Somehow, it combined into a punch of emotion the others had lacked. He rewound the tape and listened to the song again.

When the bus stopped, he got out. The library was three blocks away.

He flipped through eighteen back issues of Rolling Stone until he found his own obituary. It occupied a quarter of a page, showing the cover of his album and his photograph. Jeremy felt an eerie chill seeing his own face stare at him from a photo he did not remember ever having taken.

The uncredited obituary stated the facts and little else. It carried the distinct flavor of an "also ran" notice. Jeremy Cardiff had had one hit, reaching #23 on the charts. He had been unhappy with his modest success, ended up washing down a bottle of sleeping pills with a pint of Jack Daniels. He would be sorely missed, but by whom it did not say.

"That's it?" He blinked up from the pages of the magazine, looking at the other people around in the library. No one noticed him, no one knew who he was. "That's all?"

He left his original cassette on the table in the library, hoping that someone would pick it up and listen to it.

During their last fight, Holly had said, "I hope you do become famous. I really do. Because I love you." Her voice was low with an undertone of exhausted anger, as it always was after the shouting stopped and they had both gone to their separate corners. "But you won't make room in your life for anything else. It doesn't have to be that way."

She tugged her blond hair behind her ears, keeping it out of the way. Faint mascara tracks marked her tears. Few people even recognized that Holly wore makeup, but Jeremy knew she spent half an hour each morning carefully constructing that impression.

"You'll never understand it," Jeremy said. He had tried to explain it over and over to her, but still she refused to give him the space, to let him have the time and energy he needed to devote to creating music. Instead, she was like a sponge, demanding his devotion, wrestling his attention to her own personal needs instead of to his composing.

"This isn't just a job like being an auto mechanic—" or a nurse, he did not add, "I really have the power to move people. I can send out a message that could make everyone think. But I have to take time to get it just right. I can't just drop what I'm working on whenever you're feeling insecure." The anger crept into his voice once more.

But Holly was having none of it. Quietly, she picked up her purse and went to the door. "Take all the time you need. Follow your yellow brick road. I don't want to be the one responsible for you not achieving your dream."

He couldn't think of anything to say in response before she closed the door behind herself. He stood alone in his studio with the tall speakers, the amp, the MIDI equipment, and all his unfinished music. The house was very quiet.

He listened to his copy of the tape as he made his way back to where the return portal would open for him. He treasured the song "For Holly." *Would I want to go through time with you? Are you the one?*

What if he had given up everything with Holly for a chance that was ultimately a flop? What if practice and brute strength and determination were not enough? That was the way to manufacture songs, like the empty derivative stuff on the rest of his album. Listeners could see right through that façade. He could never send a message to the world if he had nothing to say.

As he walked along the road, Jeremy removed the last quarters from his money pouch. Since he couldn't take them with him, he tossed them in one big handful into a puddle in the gutter. Like a wishing well—but he no longer had any idea what to wish for.

He needed the substance inside himself before he could put it into the songs, but he had tried to bypass that part, to skip an important step. Sorry, no shortcuts allowed. With a sinking feeling he knew it would be a hell of a lot more difficult.

As he stood in position and waited, Jeremy listened to the last song on the tape one more time. He had managed the true inspiration once, and he could do it again. He could use "For Holly" as a model—and it would be a great gift for her. He must swallow his pride, tell her he had been stubborn.

His chronometer showed only a minute or so before he would return to Alternitech. The executives would be upset when he returned empty-handed again. But Jeremy felt anxious now, ready to start a new timeline of his own. He could get some studio to listen to "For Holly"; he could scrap the empty songs he was working on and spend the time he needed. Maybe Holly would even want to help him; he had never let her actually help him before.

Jeremy froze with his hand on the cassette player. He was not, after all, returning empty-handed. He had his own music—and the contract stated that any songs he found in alternate realities belonged to Alternitech/Entertainment. Everything. The whole copyright, hook, line, and sinker. He had signed it, knowing full well what it contained. If he tried to cross them, they would press the legal buttons and swallow him up.

He could not let that happen to a song like this. He had only one choice, but there was no use crying about it—Alternitech would deduct for the mass differential of a fallen teardrop left behind. He felt his throat trembling as he pushed the button.

The cassette made a thin whimper as it zipped through the high-speed dubber, sending his music back into nothingness, erasing it forever.

Even if he could remember the tune, the words, he could not copy the emotion that had made the song so powerful. Such things could not be imitated; they had to be felt. He didn't want to end up with a minor hit he could not repeat. He had to learn how to do it, not how to copy it.

The air shimmered in front of him, opening into a brief doorway back home. His chest felt like lead, but he exhaled, pushing the foreign air out of his lungs. Shifting his pack on his shoulder, he stepped into the portal.

Reality changed subtly around him. It was all right, though. He had new inspiration, new work to do. He opened his eyes in his own timeline.

It might not be the same cut he had heard on his own tape, but it would be different from his other attempts. His focus would be different. He had a song to write, for Holly.

I have always read a lot of adventure science fiction, and I wrote "Comrades in Arms" when I was young and inexperienced. The early version was never published, but it had a great core idea—two enemy soldiers in a future war, a human and an alien, flee the battlefield together and go on the run when they discover they've been betrayed by their respective commands.

Then my friend Loren Coleman, a writer and game designer, suggested a military SF anthology, Five by Five, to consist of five military SF novellas by five military SF writers. I vividly remembered "Comrades in Arms" and knew it would be perfect for the project. But it needed a lot of work. I knew where to find the original manuscript in my old files, and I thought I'd just give it a quick polish, and that would be that.

Well, until I reread it. I was glad to see that my writing had improved dramatically since those college days, but the original story would need a complete overhaul and rewrite. The idea was solid, though, and I remembered the characters and scenes very clearly.

So I had to start from scratch, rebuilding the core idea and the plot structure, and then I wrote a brand new "Comrades in Arms" from the first word to the last. Here's a very old story that's also completely fresh.

COMRADES IN ARMS

—I—

Palming the power stud on his laser rifle, Rader leaped into the alien trench and sighted on his enemy. Targeting vectors appeared on the inner surface of his helmet face shield, and the tactile sensors on his gloves linked to his artificial hands.

Ten Jaxxans skittered along the angled trenches they had dug as they made progress across the planetoid's contested landscape. Moving in ranks, they all reacted in unison to his arrival. The enemy did not like, did not *understand,* unpredictability.

As a Deathguard, Rader was unpredictable. He had been designed that way.

He found his balance on the loose pea-gravel, used his momentum to keep charging forward. In their open bug-tunnels, the Jaxxans had no room to scatter, nor did they have time.

The brain fire pounded through him, the Werewolf Trigger that insisted he kill, *KILL!* He was a well-armored bull-in-a-china-shop, brain still alive along with a patchwork of his original body, hooked up to spare parts that allowed him to be sent back onto the battlefield. The chaos he provoked was part of a tactical plan issued by officers far from the battlefield; Deathguards weren't expected to survive long, though.

Rader had been briefed about this as a new recruit, though he hadn't ever considered it a real possibility while he and his squad mates laughed about squashing roaches. But the officials had made him the offer, showing him the contract as he lay there hooked up to complex life-support mechanisms in the med-center bed. Rader had barely been able to read the type with his one remaining eye.

"You want this, soldier? Or would you rather just be disconnected?"

The answer had seemed obvious. At the time.

Now the first alien died before he even saw the Deathguard: a pinpoint of red laser light burned through his chitinous face. Cyborg components kicked in, and Rader swiveled, sweeping the area with the nose of his weapon. Energy gels and synthetic adrenaline kept him moving, kept him shooting.

There were ten Jaxxans, then seven, then four in the invisible wake of his beam.

Much of the surface of the planetoid Fixion was a no-man's land, slashed with enemy trenches and tunnels interspersed with watchtowers. The aliens liked geometric order, but used unsettling angles, tilted planes, rarely straight lines. They had already occupied twenty asteroids in the Fixion Belt, just as the human army had; now both sides fought over the rest of the territory, particularly this central planetoid.

No longer part of the Earth League forward lines, Rader had already served his term as a soldier, given it his all, and now had this "opportunity" to give some more, for as long as he might last. He was there as an independent berserker, armed and juiced, sent into the no-man's land without any obvious military objective—it drove the Jaxxans nuts.

Deathguards were expensive and effective, categorized as Vital Equipment rather than Personnel—and so far the PR victories had been worth every penny of the military's investment. Or so Rader had heard; he was not on the list for explanations.

In short order, he killed eight of the Jaxxans in the trench, but he found himself wound in the luminous green threads of an energy-web cast by the last two aliens. The mentally projected web closed around him in a glowing net that would short out his armor and destroy his components—both the artificial ones and his biological ones.

But the Werewolf Trigger screamed at him like a drill sergeant inside his head. *KILL! KILL!* And he obeyed. The last of the Jaxxans fell to the trench floor, angular limbs twitching, and the coalescing energy-web faded.

The mindless Werewolf Trigger died to a whisper as the threat diminished and he calmed himself. Now that Rader could see more than a red haze, he gazed upon the carnage. The filters in his helmet blocked out the stench of burned meat and boiled ichor.

Alone, Rader recorded high-res images of the dead enemy in the trenches, transmitted his kills to HQ, and received acknowledgment but no praise.

He didn't need to remind himself that these Jaxxans weren't *human*. He stared at their scattered bodies, trying to compare them to something from Earth; they evoked locusts, lizards, and skeletons all at once. The aliens were unnaturally thin, with tough skin that resembled chitin. Their eyes were striking, large black globes that reflected the goldenrod light of Fixion's sun.

The Jaxxans carried no weapons, nor did they encase themselves in armor. All their power, their energy-webs, and everything else about them (he wasn't sure how much was rumor and how much was truth) originated in the minds behind those eerie polished eyes. Many Jaxxans supposedly studied human culture and language, but he hadn't had a chance for conversation to confirm it.

The walls of the shallow trench rolled inward, sliding down to cover the bodies. The sandy, gravelly soil of Fixion was lousy for digging trenches in—not to mention lousy for growing things in, lousy for building things in, lousy for living in. As a matter of honor, the Earth League would never let the Jaxxans have it, and the alien command apparently felt the same way.

Time to move on, keep finding targets, keep causing trouble—Commissioner Sobel had told him he might have four weeks of operational capability before the brain/cyborg interface deteriorated. He followed the Jaxxan trench, taking the path of least resistance, but he encountered no other Jaxxans. The trench bent in one direction, then another, but ultimately went nowhere.

Off in the distance, near the asteroid's foreshortened horizon, human artillery brought down a tall Jaxxan watchtower, and soldiers clashed in a forward offensive as part of the official military plan. His comrades. *Former* comrades.

Rader didn't belong there, would not be going back to the main base on the far side of Fixion, would not be going home.

He climbed out of the trench and set off across the open landscape.

—II—

On the very last day that Rader (Rader, Robert: 0166218: Earth-Boston) lived as a grunt, he rode inside a spearhead-shaped assault fighter, enthusiastic about the impending engagement. He crowded next to his buddies on the hard metal benches, hunched over, counting down the seconds until they reached the Jaxxan nesting asteroid.

They were a team, comrades in arms. No time for second thoughts now.

The cold metal air had been recycled too many times but still carried the unmistakable odors of sweat and farts, obvious indicators of human tension. Rader was pumped up on metabolic supplements and foul-tasting power goo. At the Base, he had wolfed down a chewy high-protein breakfast cake, which was supposed to taste like bacon and eggs, before rushing to the assault ship, grabbing his weapon, securing his body armor, and getting mentally prepared.

His squad mates were ready to go squash some roaches. They had been cooped up far too long at the Earth League's Fixion Base #1, participating in simulation after simulation, blowing up fearsome holographic Jaxxans during practice sessions.

So far, Rader had been on only one real assault mission, a raid on a Jaxxan supply ship. Hundreds of Earth League forces had captured the small alien craft, and they had slaughtered every enemy aboard without any difficulty; Rader barely got off a shot. In battle simulations, the holographic alien warriors had always fought much more fiercely. He suspected that the Jaxxans on the supply ship were just civilians hauling crates of packaged food.

Today's assault was bound to be much more challenging.

The night before, while prepping for the mission, Squad Sergeant Blunt had given them the full briefing—and "blunt" he was indeed, although the word "gruff" seemed equally appropriate; some of Rader's squad mates preferred the term "psycho-bastard."

Rader had sat joking with his buddies, nudging ribs with elbows. Since being thrown together into the same pressure cooker with the same goal and the same enemy, their squad had become very close—Renfrew, Chaney, Coleman, Rajid, Gonzalez, Huff.

In the briefing room, Sergeant Blunt projected a map of the asteroid belt, a smattering of space gravel strewn along an orbit that just happened to be in the star's habitable zone, though no one would really want to live there. Nevertheless, the Earth League deemed the Fixion Belt worth fighting for, and Rader had signed up in a fit of patriotism that had lasted significantly less time than his term of service.

The Sarge pointed to illuminated asteroids on the diagram, indicating the ones held by humans and an equivalent number held by Jaxxans. (The score received boos and hisses from the squad members.) The largest planetoid, Fixion itself, was the most hotly fought-over piece of real estate in the Galaxy.

Blunt pointed to another flyspeck amid the dots in the asteroid belt. "Intel has discovered a roach hatching base, or a nest, or whatever the hell they call it. We're going to wipe it out. Squash the bugs before they can hatch a thousand more disgusting soldiers."

The Sarge paused for a moment, looking at every member of the squad. "Payback. The Roaches did the same thing to us on Cephei Outpost. They saw that little colony and assumed it was our breeding station, killed all those poor colonists, those children. I don't think they understand how humans breed." Sergeant Blunt's voice became grim and angry. "We've got embassies set up on the Détente Asteroid, and the Jaxxan higher-ups speak better English than you do, but neither side talks."

The mood in the briefing room grew resentful; many of the grunts sneered at the very idea of peace talks. Huff let out a rude snort. "How can you talk with the *things* that slagged Cephei?"

Sergeant Blunt got them to concentrate on the priority. "It's not your job to think about the big picture. We don't pay you enough to consider the complicated things. Commissioner Sobel decides when it's time to talk to them. For you guys, we keep it simple: Enter the roach hatching station, destroy everything, and go home."

Rader raised his hand. "Any intel on Jaxxan defenses there, Sergeant?"

"Doesn't matter." The Sarge gave the closest thing to a smile that

Rader had ever seen. "We'll have a Deathguard with us. A fresh one, all systems still fully functional."

A quick hesitation of surprise, then a round of cheers …

Later, as the assault fighter closed in on the targeted Jaxxan hatching base, Rader checked his weapon, his suit, his med kit, his backup power pack. He pretended to relax. Waiting … gearing up … waiting … joking … waiting. Typical Earth League operation: hurry up and wait.

Voices grew louder in the spacecraft as the conversation became edgier, more rushed. He and his buddies talked about what they would do on their next R&R, reminisced about their homes, their families, their sweethearts. Although his squad mates were not a particularly handsome lot, each man claimed to have a gorgeous girlfriend who put porn holostars to shame and yet was entirely loyal and head-over-heels in love.

After the massacre on Cephei Outpost, he'd been too young by a month when the first call went out. But his best friend, Cody, was two months older and just barely squeaked into the Earth League military, ready to go after the Jaxxans. Before he left for basic training, Cody said goodbye to Rader with a quick embrace and then a studiously practiced League handshake. "There'll be plenty of roaches for both of us to kill, don't worry! Get your ass in the League as soon as you can sign up, and I'll meet you out there." He gestured vaguely toward the sky. Rader promised, waving … but wishing his friend had waited, just a couple of months.

His parents and his sister worried about Rader going off to war, but it was the patriotic thing to do. All healthy young men were pressured to join up, and he was anxious to follow in Cody's footsteps. A month later, on his birthday, he filled out the forms.

One week into basic training at the lunar military base, Rader received word that Cody and his entire squad had been wiped out by an equipment malfunction. An airlock hatch blew open when the troop transport was approaching a space station. Explosive decompression killed all personnel, sucked them out into space. Simple mechanical failure, bad luck—nothing that could be blamed on the enemy.

Rader had joined wanting to fight alongside Cody. They had always been a team, and he had hoped they could support each other, stand together against the Jaxxans. But the Earth League had him now, and he couldn't change his mind. His squad mates were his comrades now, his new best friends....

As soon as the assault shuttle landed on the Jaxxan nesting asteroid, explosive bolts would blast the hatch open so that the soldiers could storm out in a howling rush. His companions whooped, winding themselves up during the final approach, and Rader joined in. But as he looked warily at the hatch, suited up and holding his laser rifle, he thought of Cody's last moments ... willing to die in a blaze of glory out on the battlefield, not from a stupid malfunction.

Sitting wordless on an empty bench, the Deathguard in their team was an ominous, armored form, like a knight in shining armor. Rader respected the powerful cyborgs—resuscitated, revamped, and restructured to become perfect fighting machines— though he wondered what thoughts kept them going. Did they focus on the mission, even knowing what had happened to them, and what *would* happen to them? He supposed it was better than being declared dead. All Deathguards got an honorable funeral, and their families received full pensions; no one knew the former identity of any individual Deathguard. Rader hadn't thought twice about it when he enlisted in the League. He'd signed up body and soul.

Huff leaned over and whispered to him, "I can't wait to see that Deathguard go bonkers on the roach nest."

"So long as he doesn't go all Werewolf on us before it's time," Rajid said.

Rader found himself staring at the silent cyborg. "Not going to happen. They're too sophisticated for that." The Deathguard made no comment, one way or another.

Through the small window port on his side of the craft, Rader could see the potato-shaped asteroid as they closed in. The large craters were covered over with domes like large blisters, as if the space rock had reacted with an outbreak of boils to the alien presence.

Sergeant Blunt walked in heavy boots from the front bulkhead and stood before them in full uniform armor. "Listen up. Based on the small number of roach military ships stationed at the asteroid, looks like the enemy has no major defenses here. We have no intel on the interior of the base, so you'll have to find your way. Get to the main hatching chamber and destroy it. Clear enough? Your job is simple—point and shoot."

On the way in, the assault ship's pulsed lasers disabled the four Jaxxan ships stationed at the nest asteroid. Even though the nest asteroid sent emergency calls for Jaxxan reinforcements, Sergeant Blunt had expected it. The plan was to strike fast and finish the operation before alien backup vessels could fly in.

"All right, children," the Sarge said. "Saddle up, take your toys, and let's go scramble some eggs. Just don't let them scramble you. We're coming in hot, going to blow through one of their entrance domes. Do I need to remind you that this is *not* a prisoner capturing mission?"

"No, Sarge!" they all chimed in.

"Good, I was hoping you weren't all as dense as you looked. Now let's move it." The Sergeant fitted a breathing mask over his face; Rader and his companions did the same. The Deathguard sat waiting, like a missile prepped for launch.

Once the assault shuttle careened up against the largest blister dome and a shaped-charge explosion blasted open the hatch to let them loose, Rader's squad mates boiled out, swinging their laser rifles and yelling; they exercised just enough restraint to keep from shooting one another.

The alarms inside the hatching base sounded like staccato clacking beetles. Rader bolted forward and used his laser rifle to cut down any aliens he encountered. It wasn't his place to decide whether the roaches were civilians, politicians, medical personnel, or soldiers.

In the back of his mind, he wondered if the Jaxxan assault squad on Cephei Outpost had operated under similar orders.

As they rounded a corner into the main base, a Jaxxan in front of them raised his thin forearms and wove a deadly psychic energy-web. Gonzalez let out a cry more of surprise than pain, then the incandescent green lines disintegrated him.

Astonished, Rader used the sudden jolt of shock and fired. He blasted the Jaxxan before he could move his angular arms again.

Behind the main squad, the Deathguard lurched into the fray, mowing down targets, yet never coming close to hitting one of his human comrades. The cyborg blew open door hatches, thrust his armored body into well-lit research chambers, annihilated any aliens he found working in their labs. Then the Deathguard pushed forward, leading the way along skewed corridors and through angled intersections, deeper into the hatching base.

Still off-balance and angry from the loss of Gonzalez, Rader ran headlong with four of his comrades into a chamber of horrors—a nursery. Five Jaxxan attendants had lined up to protect more than a dozen fat, squirming grubs, white segmented things like maggots the size of alligators.

Coleman said, "That's just *wrong!*" He opened fire, and the grubs spilled open like fleshy sacs filled with entrails and ichor.

Frantic, one of the Jaxxan caretakers cried out in English, "No! Not the offspring." The alien's comprehensible words were so startling that Rader hesitated. But it was just a ruse: other aliens nearby worked together to weave a sparkling energy-web, filling the air with a mesh of green that they cast toward the human soldiers.

Rader focused and shot one of the roaches, then the next, working his way down the line, just like in the simulation. Huff knocked out the other two, and their incomplete energy-web dispersed. The rest of the Earth League soldiers made swift work of the remaining grubs in the nursery, chopping them into chunks of meat.

The Deathguard, who wasn't part of the formal operation, had already moved ahead on his own, continuing his rampage. Apparently, the cyborg soldier wanted to make the most of his second chance.

Over the implanted radio, Rader heard Sergeant Blunt yelling from a different sector of the asteroid, "Just woke up a hundred roach warriors in the deep tunnels! And they look angry. Called Base for reinforcements. Another ship should be here in an hour or two, so hold the roaches off 'til then."

"Roger that, Sarge," came a chorus of responses.

The Sarge added, "We know they sent off a distress signal too. It'll be a race to see who gets here first."

Rader said with genuine bravado, "Won't leave anything for them to rescue, Sarge."

As the squad pushed into the asteroid's most secure chambers, desperate Jaxxans fought harder and harder. Energy-webs rippled down the angled corridors, ricocheting off stone walls and frying several more human soldiers. Rader kept a rough score in the back of his mind, tried not to name his friends who lay dead. *Concentrate on the operation, on the objective.*

So far, he thought the humans were taking a greater toll.

Explosions rippled through the nesting base, and overpressure waves made his ears pop. Sergeant Blunt shouted over the implanted radio, "Heavy resistance—fresh warriors from below." He paused, as if to listen to a report. "Ah, crap—there's a roach ship coming in! Don't know if we can hold 'em off long enough." Rader heard another explosion, a sizzling sound, then a cry of pain from the Sarge—a high-pitched yelp that did not at all sound like the gruff, hardboiled man—then only static on the comline.

Rader shoved aside his alarm and dismay, not sure how the survivors of his squad were going to get out of here, but they would keep pushing toward the objective.

He, Coleman, and Huff fought their way into a large guarded chamber where the roaches made their last stand. The entrance hatch was sealed, so the three soldiers used their laser rifles to melt an entrance through the putty-like polymer metal wall.

"This must be the place," Coleman said.

Inside the protected chamber, Rader and his comrades discovered row after row of polished black casings the size of coffins.

"Giant eggs," Huff said. "Look at all of them!"

The soldiers opened fire on the casings, cracking them open and spilling out white and slippery humanoid forms with backward-jointed arms and legs, ovoid heads, and giant black eyes that were covered with a milky caul.

So they were chrysalises, not eggs.

With a high-pitched chitter, three Jaxxans lunged out from between the rows of black casings. When they hurled half-formed energy-webs, Rader dove out of the way, but Coleman was too busy shooting the chrysalises. The energy-web snared him, killed him.

Huff began firing wildly at the Jaxxans. From their cover, the aliens formed another energy-web that shimmered in the air and came toward them. Rader dropped to the floor and took cover, rolling up against one of the tall black casings. He yelled a warning, but Huff kept firing even as the web encircled and disintegrated him.

From his position of dubious shelter, Rader shot the two Jaxxans, then waited, listening.

Moving in a scramble of excessively jointed arms and legs, another alien skittered forward to a split chrysalis and caught the albino, mostly formed creature as it slumped out of the cracked shell. Like a soldier holding a wounded comrade, the roach cradled the dying, half-formed creature in segmented arms.

Rader rose to his feet, and the Jaxxan swiveled its head toward him, showing those large, black eyes like pools of sorrow. "Look what you have done!" Though the creature's chitinous faceplates showed no emotions, Rader felt that the Jaxxan was giving him an accusatory glare.

A red spot appeared on the Jaxxan's forehead, and a laser blast cooked his encased head, exploding his entire skull.

The Deathguard strode into the chrysalis chamber. From behind the helmet, which was no more readable than the alien's face, the Deathguard looked at Rader, then turned back to the black cases. He began shooting them one by one.

Rader's implanted radio burst to life again. "This is Lieutenant Nolan with the reinforcement ship, closing in on the nesting asteroid. Two roach defenders got here before us. The asteroid's overrun, but we'll take 'em on! We don't leave men behind."

Rader didn't cheer the speech. He and the Deathguard were trapped in the chrysalis chamber. In the corridors outside, he could hear the ominous sound of hundreds of skittering legs—warriors that had been hiding deep inside the asteroid, and were now closing in on the chrysalis chamber. Rader joined the Deathguard, standing together as they shot the rest of the casings, knowing they didn't have much time … knowing they weren't likely to get out alive.

At least he had a chance for some payback for his lost comrades. It was the only thread of hope he had to cling to. He wished he and Cody could have been here together doing this.

The armored and silent Deathguard turned around and opened fire on the Jaxxan warriors that surged into the chamber. Sergeant Blunt had counted more than a hundred of them; to Rader, it seemed like a thousand. Sergeant Nolan's reinforcements would never get here in time. The radio channel remained silent, no transmissions from the rest of his squad mates.

Backing deeper into the chrysalis chamber, the Deathguard

worked his way in among the black casings. Rader thought their position by the door was more defensible, but then he realized that the Deathguard was making a calculated move to lure the roaches inside.

The Deathguard turned his unreadable helmet toward Rader again, expecting him to understand. From his armored casing, he removed a thermal-impulse grenade.

Rader's heart froze. The cyborg had nothing to lose. Rader could have made the same calculation as the Deathguard, but he was unwilling to come to the obvious conclusion. Nevertheless, the Deathguard was going to do it.

When all of the roach warriors charged into the chrysalis chamber and tried to corner the two remaining humans, the Deathguard lifted his grenade and depressed the activation button.

Rader dove among the cocoon casings in an instinctive, but futile gesture. The flash of dazzling white light was the last thing he ever expected to see.

But it wasn't.

The quality of light that came into focus had a harsh, sterile quality, and the surrounding brightness resolved itself into clean ceramic-plate walls—the Base's medical center. He could hear diagnostic scanners, medical machinery, a respirator breathing for him like a gasping schoolgirl. He felt no pain … he felt nothing at all.

Rader couldn't move his head, only his eyes—one eye, actually —which limited his field of view. He tried to move, but could barely twitch his head … in fact, he could feel nothing but his head. The rest of his body remained numb. Maybe he'd been paralyzed. Maybe he'd lost limbs. Maybe he'd lost everything.

A worried-looking orderly appeared in his field of view, staring down with brown, clinical eyes. Even in his condition, he didn't consider her pretty. "You're awake, aren't you?" she said. "Don't try to move. You're not ready for that yet. We haven't connected all the necessary pieces, still waiting for one part to be modified." She fiddled with one of the tubes hanging at his side. "There. Give it a few seconds."

Tranquilizers flooded into him, and he dropped back out of consciousness.

When Rader awoke again, a smiling man stood over him, a face that looked oddly familiar—not from personal experience, but from images on the news broadcasts. "Congratulations, soldier!"

Rader placed him as Commissioner Sobel, the man in charge of the Earth League forces in the Fixion Belt.

"The rest of your squad mates gave their lives to destroy the Jaxxan nesting asteroid. You fought bravely and kept yourself alive ... just barely, but it was enough. Your mission isn't over—not yet."

Rader tried to talk, but only croaking noises came out. He still had tubes in his throat.

Commissioner Sobel continued, "I'm congratulating you, soldier, because you have a second chance. A chance to join an elite group. Every one of your comrades gave their lives in service to the war, but you have an opportunity to keep fighting. Don't you want to hurt the enemy that did this to you?" He smiled. "We're offering you a position as our newest Deathguard."

Propped in the med-center bed, paralyzed in place, Rader couldn't see how much damage he had suffered from the explosion ... how much of *him* actually remained. Once they hooked him up to the cyborg components and encased him in his permanent armor, he doubted he would ever know.

Did it really matter?

A little extra time to carry on the fight. At the moment, he didn't quite see why that should be his priority; he would rather go home, say his farewells to his family, see Earth one more time. That second chance seemed more important.

"You're a hero and will be remembered as such, soldier. We're declaring the mission a success, now that we've looked at the cost-benefit ratio in detail. We did lose your Sergeant and your entire squad, but we successfully wiped out the Jaxxan nesting base. And you can honor them by replacing the Deathguard who died in the operation."

Rader was trying to speak, but no words came out. Sobel patted him on the shoulder—so, at least he *had* a shoulder. "We'll hook up your vocal cords in time for the official announcement, and then we'll turn you loose as a one-man army on the main Fixion battlefield. That's where you'll be most useful. Singlehandedly, you can create a hell of a lot of trouble. You'll have weeks, maybe even months before the interface breaks down. Cherish every moment of it—I know you'll accomplish as much as you can. We're all proud of you."

Sobel smiled again and then left. Rader hadn't been able to say a word.

—III—

Commissioner Sobel scowled at the insignia on his collar, still shiny from his recent transfer here. He was a dark-haired man, thirty pounds past good-looking: the kind whose face turned red very easily, and lately his face was turning red more than usual. He brushed off a few specks of dust and leaned back in the seat of his shuttle taking him from the Base to the Détente Asteroid. After six months, the useless embassy there was just beginning to feel familiar, though he doubted he would ever get used to Fixion.

As Commissioner, he was not foolish enough to believe the optimistic projections he sent back to Earth through the Information Bureau, but he had to make others believe them. Each report submitted for public dissemination had to show the human soldiers as faultless heroes and paint the Jaxxans as monstrous and alien. Fortunately, the Jaxxans looked hideous, and people had been programmed for centuries to fear bug-eyed monsters. How else could the Earth League maintain support for this abysmal war in this godforsaken place?

Humanity had a long history of shedding blood over worthless scraps of land, and this broken asteroid belt was one such place. Humans had visited there, established a tiny astronomical observatory, set up small outposts, planted their flags. So had the Jaxxans. When both governments dug in their heels, possessing Fixion and its entourage of habitable worldlets became a matter of honor.

Sobel was savvy enough to know that this war was not as senseless as it seemed. Rather, the Earth League—and no doubt the Jaxxans as well—used it as a practice field to test the mettle of the rival species and determine whether they wanted to prosecute a larger war across numerous star systems.

Three years ago, the aliens had shown their aggression (or maybe it had been a retaliation for something) by wiping out Cephei Outpost. So humans responded by blowing up any Jaxxan outpost they could find, and the two militaries began their nose-to-nose warfare on the main planetoid.

The people back home rallied, and recruiting offices had lines out the door. As the battles went on, the Deathguard cyborg killing machines were portrayed as warriors so tough that even death on the battlefield could not stop them from continuing the fight against the Jaxxans. Poignant, tragic, glorious.

Sobel's two predecessors had put in their time, and now he was stuck administering the Earth League forces. He ran the show out here, organized the military, sent back the PR dispatches.

For appearance's sake, he was also the designated spokesman, an ambassador for humanity, charged (on paper at least) with finding a peaceful solution to the conflict. His superiors had never indicated that they genuinely desired a resolution; nevertheless, he needed to maintain appearances—he was good at that.

One of the small drifting rocks with a tenuous but stable atmosphere was named the Détente Asteroid, complete with a human embassy building and an adjacent Jaxxan embassy. By mutual agreement, each side was required to have a representative available at the embassy a certain percentage of the time, but due to a loophole in the agreement—intentional, Sobel thought—the human ambassador and the Jaxxan ambassador were not required to be on the Détente Asteroid *at the same time*, which made substantive peace talks difficult.

After a two-hour flight, Commissioner Sobel's shuttle landed on the Détente Asteroid. He was preoccupied enough with his thoughts that he forgot the oxygen mask until the last moment and fumbled it into place just as the hatch slid open.

He gathered his briefcase full of files and followed a small honor guard across the landing zone to the embassy building; a vanguard entourage had already restored the power, heat, and air-generators. No one had occupied the building for weeks.

Not surprisingly, the corresponding Jaxxan embassy building was shut down: windows shuttered, doors locked, no one inside.

Sobel made quick work of settling in. Though it seemed a pointless obligation to be here, he did look forward to a few quiet and uninterrupted days. He had paperwork to review, forms to finish, consolation letters to write.

No matter what the Earth public saw in the glorious video footage sent by the Information Bureau—how human forces had pushed forward to gain a few more acres of the no-man's land, how the Deathguards continued to attack the enemy like heroic vigilantes—Sobel knew the war was not going well.

Something had to change soon. An unqualified victory would bring a surge in support on Earth, but even a devastating defeat would inflame their passions, and he could take advantage of that as well. The worst case was that the battle for the Fixion Belt was a stalemate that would continue for a long, expensive time. Since he and his Jaxxan counterpart, Warlord Kiltik, had no particular reason to hold meetings, no resolution was in sight.

Seated at his temporary desk, Sobel opened his briefcase. Before delving into the files he needed to review, he glanced through the tinted window at the closed Jaxxan embassy. As soon as the Commissioner left, Kiltik would arrive to serve his own time as mandated by the interim treaties, and he would go through the same motions.

—IV—

Fixion's amber sky was barren of clouds, always. Even during the day, the tiny lights of other asteroids in the Belt were strung like a necklace overhead.

Dark spots speckled Rader's sandy brown armor, some camouflage, some just stains. Leaving the Jaxxan squad he had just killed, the Deathguard dodged across the landscape. Cover was easy to find on the torn-up terrain of canyons, craters, and angled trenches.

He noticed fighting in the distance and chose to head toward a collapsed Jaxxan watchtower. The Earth League operation had moved on, but if the roaches returned to begin repairs, maybe he could charge in among them. The Werewolf Trigger remained quiescent, but he didn't need it.

So far, all of his components functioned well. His brain moved the replacement parts in tandem with what remained of his body, but the breakdown could come at any time: a failed neural interface, a mechanical fault in the cyborg parts, or a collapse of life-support maintenance. The Earth League had drilled the duty into him: his commanding officers and comrades expected him to do everything in his power to defeat the Jaxxans.

He had accepted the terms in the med center: the extent of his injuries already categorized him as terminal, and he could either become a cyborg or be disconnected. In exchange for his new superhuman abilities he pledged to take on a solo mission that would not end until his final breath. His friend Cody had had no such opportunity.

Rader pushed on, alone, for as long as he might have left.

He dodged from one huge boulder to another, closing the distance to the damaged watchtower. He climbed an outcropping of rock above a steep gully, a crack in the shattered landscape from an ancient meteor impact. He stopped short, staring at the single Jaxxan that had taken cover in the gully below.

The alien was bent over a burnt human form—an Earth League soldier who had been charred by the backwash of an energy-web. Moving sharp-angled hands, the Jaxxan busily touched, inspected, prodded the soldier, who let out a groan of pain. The alien plucked a vial from a small open kit on the ground.

During basic training, Rader had heard of the awful things the roaches did to human bodies. He brought up his laser rifle and prepared to fire.

The alien looked at him with polished black eyes. He held a vial in long fingers, tilted it, and turned back to his work on the burned soldier.

With a jolt, Rader realized the open package on the ground was a standard-issue Earth League med kit. The Jaxxan was *tending* the wounded man. The alien fumbled with the kit, swiveled his head back to Rader. "Assistance. Help me understand."

Roaches moved in groups, fought together, crowded in their trenches and hives; they were rarely encountered singly. This one would be easy prey. He kept the laser rifle pointed toward the alien, but did not fire.

The Jaxxan put a gauze pack down, inspected a different bottle. "How do I revive him?" He spoke in short, clipped syllables.

Confused, Rader slid down the side of the gully, still keeping his rifle ready. The injured man stirred, and Rader saw how horribly burned he was. He croaked with a voice he had rarely used since being turned loose as a Deathguard. "What are you doing?"

"No time." The alien chose a stim pack from the kit. "This one, I believe." He pressed it against the dying soldier.

Rader jabbed the laser rifle forward. "Stop!"

The alien continued his quick and efficient movements, either not intimidated by the Deathguard, or driven by other priorities. "I need to wake him before he dies." Although the Jaxxan's hard lips did not allow him to pronounce certain sounds correctly, Rader couldn't believe how well the Jaxxan spoke English.

His response should have been clear; he wasn't supposed to wonder. Why hadn't he killed the Jaxxan on first sight? Why hadn't the enemy tried to kill him?

And why was the alien trying so hard to revive a dying soldier?

The soldier's uniform identified him as a recon scout, a member of a small team sent to assess the aftermath of the earlier military operation. A moan escaped the man's blackened lips, and his eyes flickered open in terror and pain for an instant before he finally died.

The Jaxxan sat back on the ground, folding his long legs. He made a satisfied sound, then raised his face to the Deathguard. "Now you will kill me?"

Rader's eyes narrowed behind his darkened visor. "Why did you do that? Explain." He kept the laser rifle trained on the roach's chest.

The Jaxxan bowed his head, in what seemed to Rader an alien expression of guilt. *Anthropomorphizing.* Nothing more to it.

"My energy-web hit him from behind. I was afraid. He did not see me. He had no chance to know he was going to die." He paused as if waiting for Rader to understand. "His soul did not have time to prepare for the departure of death. Had he died without awakening, his soul would have remained trapped within the body, forever. I would not wish such a fate upon even my enemy."

Rader felt the hard rock against his armor as thoughts flashed through his mind. He also recalled the Jaxxan in the chrysalis chamber of the hatching asteroid, who had clung to the half-formed but dying alien as it slid out of the broken cocoon case. *Look what you have done.*

"How do you know our language?" He couldn't imagine any of his squad mates trying to learn to speak Jaxxan.

"I studied."

"Why?"

"Because you are interesting." Rader didn't know what to say to that. "Many Jaxxans study humans. We review your broadcasts, your culture. I am a scholar, teacher, imaginer."

"Then what are you doing on the battlefield?"

"I was assigned to the System Holystal project. My interpretation of facets contradicted my superior's, and so I was transferred here."

Rader assessed the skeletal, bug-like Jaxxan. He seemed scrawnier than most. "You don't look trained to be a soldier."

"Not trained. I was meant to die, in service." The alien studied him with eyes like molten pools of ink. "Why did you not kill me, Deathguard?"

Both remained silent for a long moment in a strange standoff. A shooting star sliced across the sky, bright enough to be seen against Fixion's amber daytime sky. "I don't know."

"You are confused, your emotions in turmoil. We are each supposed to kill the other, yet neither wants to."

Rader stiffened. He had not moved the laser rifle. "I may kill you yet."

"No. You will not."

"How can you be so sure?"

"I can read it in you." The Jaxxan cocked his head. "Did you not know we are empathic?"

"No." Command had neglected to include that detail in their briefings.

The Jaxxan shook his head in disappointment. "What is your name, Deathguard?"

The question itself opened old wounds. A name signified he was somebody, an individual. A hero killed in action during the raid on the nesting asteroid. That name, that person was dead; his family had the certificate to prove it, even though Rader continued fighting for a brief period, like a mayfly in its final days.

"My name was Rader, before I was ... Now, I'm just a Deathguard." He sounded more gruff than he wanted to. He paused, wasn't sure why he even asked the question. "And your name?"

The Jaxxan proceeded to make a series of unpronounceable clicks from his alien gullet. Rader knew he could never repeat the name and said with a hint of humor. "I'd better just call you Click."

The alien seemed satisfied with that. "Rader, I must contemplate this turn of events. I was not prepared for such an occurrence. Please let me meditate." Still holding his laser rifle like a toy soldier positioned in place, the Deathguard regarded his enemy. Click answered the unspoken question. "I am not afraid of you. You will not harm me."

Rader was confused at such unwarranted trust, until he realized an empath could *feel* that Rader wasn't going to harm him. But how could he be so sure about Click? Maybe this was just a ruse to get him to drop his guard.

"You will want to bury your comrade." Click stood and moved away from the burned soldier. "That is the tradition."

Rader had just left the group of Jaxxans in the trench after killing them.

He could put the recon scout in a shallow grave, although Fixion had no known scavengers or predators that would disturb the body. He'd send a locator signal for an Earth League pickup crew to retrieve the fallen soldier. But, depending on where the fighting lines were, there was no telling when or if they would come. Due to interstellar shipping costs, bodies were never returned to Earth.

Yes, the recon scout deserved to be buried.

But Rader didn't know where he would go afterward. He had never let the question trouble him before. Days of running, fighting, killing tried to catch up with him, but internal mechanisms pumped stimulants into his body. He could rest here, but he could never sleep again—not after what they had done to him.

—V—

Since he already knew what Deathguards were, Rader figured out the implications even before the counselor came and rather impatiently explained his new situation. He'd had enough time in the med-center bed to draw his own conclusions.

"Your family has been notified of your heroic death, and the Earth League gave you a funeral with full military honors." He realized afterward that she did not use his name. "We sent home a clean packaged uniform, along with a posthumous medal of honor. The heirs designated on your enlistment form will receive a generous military combat pension."

His throat made noises, and he had to try several times before he could form the words. "Thank you."

She brushed the comment aside. She was rattling off a memorized speech and didn't want to be interrupted. "I regret to inform you that you are a terminal case. What remains of you belongs entirely to the Earth League. We will provide and maintain the machinery that keeps you alive." The counselor leaned closer to Rader. "We supply all of the equipment and components to make you whole again, temporarily. If you choose not to accept reconfiguration as a Deathguard, we will reclaim that equipment."

"Expiration … ?" He wanted to say much more, articulate a full sentence, but the counselor understood.

"How long will you last? Is that what you're asking? It varies. Each Deathguard is different, depending on the scope of injuries that put you here and the quality of the interface between your remains and our equipment." She looked down at a screen, touched a tab that activated his chart. "Not much left of you. I'm surprised you made it to the life-support bed on the rescue shuttle … in fact, I'm amazed they bothered to carry the scraps there in the first place." Frowning, the counselor read further. "Ah. No other survivors from your squad. The Information Bureau must have needed to salvage something from the mission."

Rader didn't want to think about it, didn't want to recall his family either, or his friend Cody, or Earth. He wasn't supposed to have anything to look forward to. He was just an afterimage of his life.

"Look on the bright side, soldier. If you accept, you'll have years, or months, or weeks to keep up the fight—extra time that you wouldn't have had. When the Jaxxans try to understand our strategy and tactics, Deathguards are our ace in the hole, an element of random destruction they simply cannot predict." He had seen more convincing smiles on plastic mannequins. "You could well be the key to winning this war."

Rader had heard the pitch before, had even believed it when he went through basic training. He didn't argue. Judging by the counselor's flippant attitude, he imagined that she had little difficulty convincing other new Deathguards. He allowed them to put him back together again, Humpty-Dumpty in combat gear.

With the potential for malfunctions building day by day, the Base was anxious to get him tested and functional and back out onto the front lines. When they brought Rader up to speed on his defenses and prosthetics, he seemed to have one of everything he needed. The components functioned to design specs. He had his armor, his weapons, and his training.

Occasionally, during test exercises, he would catch glimpses of his skin, small patches that showed in between the armor plate. His flesh was so burned and scarred it looked like wadded, dried leather. He had no desire to see what he really looked like anymore.

He was trained to shoot automatically, accurately, and without remorse. A Werewolf Trigger had been implanted in his brain, activated by stress and perceived danger in a battlefield situation. And his self-preservation drive was dampened.

Without mentioning Rader's name, Commissioner Sobel introduced him with great fanfare in a cheery patriotic broadcast sent out by the Information Bureau. "I give you the newest member of the Deathguard!" He raised Rader's gauntleted arm. Cheers resounded from the soldiers who had gathered at the Base for the formal announcement.

Despite the celebrations, Rader knew he could never be around people again. The Werewolf Trigger was like a firing pin in his brain, a siren that sounded off at oddball times. A Deathguard couldn't live back at the Base, nor bunk with other soldiers, not even fraternize with them. If something triggered his rampage, Rader could rack up countless casualties before he was terminated. From now on, he would be on his own.

The Commissioner's voice grew more somber. "Unfortunately, peace negotiations have broken down. Neither side is talking, and I don't expect the situation to improve. We'll need our Deathguards now more than ever."

More than a hundred of the deadliest, most powerful soldiers had been turned loose on the battlefield. Rader would join them, without comrades, in a last independent mission to create as much havoc as possible until his systems failed.

—VI—

When he finished digging the grave and covering up the fallen recon scout, Rader looked across at Click. His cyborg senses and sensors had remained alert during the burial, but the Jaxxan hadn't moved.

The alien meditated peacefully, obsidian eyes staring off into nothingness. The air shimmered in front of his face to reveal a scintillating crystal that opened like a rosebud, a projected object half a meter across, glowing with prickly facets and spires—not a weapon like the energy-web, but a crystalline snowflake that hung by unseen threads. Click remained motionless, peering into the facets as if hypnotized.

Rader came closer, intrigued. This seemed delicate, wondrous.

Click spoke without looking up from his scrutiny. "This is my *holystal*: a holographic crystal that I create in my thoughts. A three-dimensional map of my life, what has happened and what may yet occur. Every possibility has its own facet, constantly shifting and re-emerging as circumstances change. This ..." He reached out to touch a portion that was not symmetrical with the others. "This is where you fit in, Rader. Your presence has distorted all probable futures, giving me chances I should never have had, adding dangers that were not present before."

Rader was fascinated. "Can all Jaxxans do that? Or is it only you?"

Click made a rattling sound, and he realized the alien was laughing. "I am an imaginer, a scholar. My caste specializes in interpreting holystals, advising our leaders. Warlord Kiltik has his own expert on the System Holystal we are constructing in the Fixion Belt."

"And you disagreed with the expert, so you were punished."

"Yes. I was transferred to the battlefield." As Click spoke, the projected holystal shifted slightly, a gentle flickering of one facet into another. He pointed to the most prominent pinnacle. "This spire symbolizes that which is most important to me. It has stopped growing now. My work was my life, back in our home system ... before I was assigned here. To this war."

Rader thought of Cody, their own boyhood dreams, their plans for the future, but nothing so concrete as this crystalline blueprint of the Jaxxan's life.

Click continued with a distinct undertone of awe. "A team of engineers, scholars, imaginers, and dreamers was working on our race's History Holystal out in the free, empty space beyond the influence of Jaxx's sun ... a holystal so vast that it took our ships days to circle around it. Every facet, polished down to the finest detail, chronicled the events in the history of our planet, Jaxx's wars and triumphs, peoples, leaders, arts ..."

Click sighed, and Rader could almost feel the icy pain in his voice. "Then I was dispatched to the Fixion Belt, assigned to construct and interpret the System Holystal here. Now I shall never see my great project finished, or even look at it again...."

Rader thought of his own brief military career, the capture of the alien supply ship, the assault on the nesting asteroid, and the Jaxxans he had killed, all leading up to a brief encore as a Deathguard. Since being turned loose in the no-man's land, he had spent much of his solitary time considering the paths that had led him here. He relived all the living he had done.

Now that he objectively reflected on his past, Rader realized he hadn't accomplished much in his years. His friendships were what he cherished most, how he and Cody wanted to do everything together, and then the close bond he had formed with his squad mates. But Cody, and his squad mates, were all dead now.

"At least you built something," Rader said. The only things his parents had received were a letter of condolence, a posthumous medal of honor, and a pension.

He realized he was consoling the alien, and the thought appalled him. He had enlisted in the League to kill roaches, Cody had died in the service, every one of his squad mates had given his life to wipe out the enemy. Rader had already killed ten Jaxxans today.

But not this one, who had used a human soldier's own med kit to try to save his soul, even though the recon scout would surely have killed Click, given the chance....

The alien was staring at him with unreadable eyes, agitated to feel the waves of emotion emanating from the Deathguard. Rader tried to calm himself, fighting the tension so that it wouldn't activate the Werewolf Trigger. In frustration, he picked up a handful of dead soil and flung it at the rocks around them.

With a scrabbling of pebbles above, a human soldier came over the lip of the gully, sighted on the enemy, and fired without hesitation. The holystal shattered, dissolving into fragments and then nothing.

Click let out a high-pitched chittering sound as he scrambled for cover. The laser rifle followed him, and the rock wall next to his head ran molten.

The Werewolf Trigger yammered to life in Rader's head and he sprang into action before he could think, driven by the pounding command KILL, KILL! Unseen in his camouflaged Deathguard armor, he burned a neat hole through the human soldier's chest.

Click wheezed a terrified gasp and pulled himself to his feet. "Thank you."

Shock like cold water doused Rader's berserker rage, and the Werewolf Trigger fell silent inside his head.

Another soldier, the third member of the recon scout team, appeared at the top of the gully, saw his companion drop to the ground, noticed the Deathguard's laser rifle—and the huddled Jaxxan. "What the hell?"

Rader whirled, raised his laser rifle, but the scout dashed back to the safety of the rocks before the Deathguard could fire. In control now, Rader amplified his voice through the helmet, "Halt!"

He climbed up out of the loose gravel in the gulley, worked his way to higher ground in pursuit of the third soldier. But in the broken terrain with craters and a labyrinth of Jaxxan trenches, the seasoned scout had infinite places to hide. Rader looked half-heartedly, knowing the scout would head back to Base with his shocking report.

Rader returned to where Click waited, looking up at him, and the Deathguard stared at the human soldier he had just killed.

"Oh, damn! What have I done now?"

—VII—

Tapping his fingers on the desktop (pressed fiberboard, of course —not real wood, not out here in this godforsaken asteroid belt), Commissioner Sobel pondered the news.

Very serious. An embarrassment. Incomprehensible.

One of his Deathguard had turned sour, abandoning his duty,

killing two recon scouts—in the presence of an alien. Had the Deathguard been brainwashed somehow? The Jaxxans did have strange mental powers.

Or had the Deathguard suffered some kind of psychological breakdown? Sometimes, the cyborgs were so damaged mentally and physically that they were unstable, hence the impetus for turning them loose on the battlefield. Over the course of the war, four other Deathguards had failed spectacularly, and three had gone catatonic out on the front lines, where they were quickly killed.

But not a single one had ever cooperated with the enemy before! Sobel was infuriated. They had saved the life of this—he shuffled his papers, searching for a name—this Robert Rader. Earth League cyborg engineers had taken the burned, blasted remnants of a man, patched him up enough to keep going for a final stint on the battlefield. Wasn't that what soldiers wanted?

He reviewed the records. Rader had suffered extensive damage, but he had agreed to the cyborg conversion; nothing exceptional had showed up on his psychological tests. Given a Deathguard's typically short service life, it wasn't cost-effective to waste months on extensive evaluations. The Deathguards were activated, pointed in the right direction, and turned loose on the battlefield.

As soon as the high command learned about a traitor among the lone-wolf cyborgs, however, they would crucify Sobel. The Commissioner didn't understand it. What would make the man turn against his own kind and consort with the enemy?

Sobel punched a rarely used sequence on his communications console. The viewscreen shimmered before him, as if reluctant to reveal the image of his Jaxxan counterpart.

The desiccated-looking alien's black eyes stared impatiently at him, trying to fathom the human's expression. All the roaches looked the same to Sobel but, judging by the ornamentation on the rigid hide, he ventured a guess. "Warlord Kiltik?"

When the alien tried to answer, he broke into a coughing fit before he could speak. "Commissioner Sobel? Yes, it is you."

At least the alien recognized him. "Warlord, you know I wouldn't call you if the matter wasn't urgent."

Sobel looked past the alien, gleaning details from the background of the enemy headquarters. The walls were odd planes, tilted at random in the spirit of insane Jaxxan architecture, but his eyes were drawn to a spiny mass of crystals that hung in the air behind the warlord, like a thousand fragments of glass bound up with threads of light. Some kind of three-dimensional military diagram?

He cleared his throat. "Yesterday I received some very grave news: one of my Deathguards has apparently joined with one of your soldiers. If you have subverted him somehow, hijacked his programming, the Earth League will protest strenuously. Such mental attacks are specifically prohibited in the terms of our interim treaty."

Kiltik stiffened, though Sobel couldn't read any subtle change of expression on the alien face. "We have not broken the treaty terms. I myself received reports that one of our soldiers has deserted, possibly kidnapped by a Deathguard in clear violation of our no-prisoners protocol. Summon your cyborg back to base and release our captive soldier to us so that we can address the charges of desertion."

"I can't control or recall the Deathguard, Warlord." Could it be that this wasn't a Jaxxan plan? "It seems we both have a potentially embarrassing problem. For the past few months, my record here has been impeccable, thanks in large part to the Deathguard program. I can't have one of them shooting his own comrades and fraternizing with the enemy."

Kiltik's staccato coughs interrupted his train of thought. The Warlord composed himself with an effort, then added, "Jaxxans do not break ranks. Jaxxan soldiers are tightly trained. But this deserter was not a member of the soldier caste. He was a holystal imaginer who was improperly reassigned."

Sobel didn't understand half of what the Warlord had just said, but he seized on one detail. "So, you're saying you could be in trouble for this, too."

"I have been assigned to the Fixion Belt since the beginning of the war. Although I will not lose my position here, I would prefer to avoid an 'embarrassing problem,' as you so delicately put it. My superiors will never send me back to Jaxx." He broke off for a quick burst of coughing. "However, this war was getting tedious. What do you propose we do?"

The Commissioner hid his sigh of relief. "When I received the report, I immediately sent five special commandos to terminate the defective Deathguard. I assumed your deserter would be collateral damage."

Kiltik did not sound unhappy. "Then the problem is taken care of."

"Unfortunately, the Deathguard killed the entire team, with possible assistance from his Jaxxan ally. This morning I dispatched another seven on the same mission, but they are going to have a tough time behind your lines. If you send your own hunters, one of the groups should succeed."

The Warlord stiffened. "That is nonsense, Commissioner. A ruse on your part."

Sobel hurriedly continued, "This matter concerns both of us, Warlord, and it may require all our resources to put an end to it."

The Warlord coughed once before he spoke again. "The morale of our soldier caste will suffer when they learn of this, and henceforth they will doubt the veracity of our holystal projections that guide this war. I must ponder this further and consult my holystal, Commissioner. I will contact you shortly. Your line will be open?"

"Of course." Sobel used his sweetest-sounding voice, but as soon as Kiltik's image faded, he slammed his fist on the desktop.

—VIII—

They had been on the run for days.

Before he and Click set off again, Rader had insisted on burying the other scout he had instinctively killed. He remained tense, all of his sensors alert, knowing that the third recon scout would report to Base.

With the two soldiers buried, showing a last glimmer of responsibility, Rader had activated his helmet communicator and transmitted the location of the two graves. He added a brief message to let Commissioner Sobel know he was going offline and not to expect any further reports from the field, then he tore out the locator, disengaged the built-in comm, and told Click they had to move.

The Earth League would want to deactivate and analyze Rader. It was absurd to believe he could surrender, explain what he had done, and apologize to his superiors for his mistake. That wouldn't bring the dead soldiers back to life. Now that he had proved to be dangerously unreliable as a Deathguard, he would be "retired," and the Commissioner would quietly remove his name from the books.

And the Earth League would kill Click.

Addressing his own situation, Click was certain he would be decapitated in a public ceremony if he ever turned himself over to the Jaxxan military. They could not surrender to either side. Rader didn't know how much time he had left, but he refused to waste it. They were on their own.

On the day after Rader met Click, five Earth League trackers had found them, set up an ambush, and attacked. Click, the first to spot the trackers, set up a clumsy energy-web that knocked out one of the fighters. When the other four turned their weapons on the Jaxxan deserter, Rader let his Werewolf Trigger take over, and he eliminated them with professional efficiency.

More blood on his hands.

During Rader's training, the counselors had insisted that Deathguards had no conscience. Although he didn't think that was true, Rader did not let the guilt paralyze him. While he would not have chosen to kill other Earth League soldiers, they had given him no choice. The best solution to protect himself, and Click, and other soldiers, would be to avoid any further encounters.

—IX—

Commissioner Sobel's shuttle touched down on the Détente Asteroid's shared landing field, as had been previously arranged. It felt strange to be here at the same time as his Jaxxan counterpart. Uneasy, Sobel glanced behind him at the five specially chosen soldiers who rode in the shuttle—not as an honor guard, but as candidates for the unorthodox mission Kiltik had proposed.

It had taken Sobel some time to realize that the Jaxxan Warlord was serious; the idea proved that the alien military leader was in fact *alien*. Sobel would never have suggested such an insane approach, and yet ...

A joint team composed of both human and Jaxxan soldiers to hunt down and eliminate the two deserters as swiftly as possible? If it was a trick, then Sobel would lose five good fighters ... but he had already lost almost three times that many in his solo efforts to control the situation. He decided to risk it. This mess had to be cleaned up, swept under the rug, and the fewer people outside of Fixion who knew about it, the better.

Deathguards were the best fighters in the Earth League, although not necessarily stable or controllable, as Rader had proved. His hand-picked soldiers were specialists in their own right; Kiltik had chosen similarly talented Jaxxan hunters.

His five specialists crouched on the benches, anxiously shifting their laser rifles from hand to hand. The Commissioner had given them strict instructions not to open fire on Warlord Kiltik or any other Jaxxans when they disembarked on the Détente Asteroid. That would ignite a powder keg, and Sobel did not want to deal with the resulting paperwork.

As the door split open and the disembarkation ramp extended, the men jumped out and stood protectively beside their Commissioner. A line of warrior caste Jaxxans greeted them, and the two groups faced each other, as if daring someone to break the agreement.

Sobel said to his team with a scowl, "Enough posturing. We've got work to do."

An alien, obviously the Warlord, walked across the landing field, sliding through the line of stiff Jaxxans. Sobel actually recognized Kiltik after only two viewscreen conversations, picking out distinctive features on the alien face.

Kiltik bowed his head, bending his stalk of neck. "Commissioner Sobel?"

"Good to meet you in person, Warlord!" He reached out to shake Kiltik's brittle hand, but the Jaxxans reacted as if it were a hostile gesture. The air thrummed with building energy-webs, and the human specialists brought their laser rifles to bear.

But the Commissioner knocked the nearest soldier's rifle aside. "That's a friendly gesture among my people, Warlord. We're not here to kill each other now."

Kiltik stood silent, as if reading Sobel's emotions. "I sense hostility in you, but it is not directed at us. For the moment."

Sobel nodded. "I'm glad your empathic ability can break the ice."

The Warlord fought back a spasm of coughing. "Please pardon my cough—it comes from breathing this thin, dry air for years."

"No problem at all." The Commissioner gestured for his five specialists to follow him toward the normally empty embassy buildings. "Is the conference room ready? We've got important things to do."

—X—

For several days, Rader and Click made their way across the landscape, remaining hidden, staying alive, but without a plan. Each still possessed high-density ration packs, but the food would run out soon enough.

Despite the Deathguard's best attempts to remain out of sight, they were repeatedly attacked by patrols—both human and Jaxxan—eluding some, killing others.

He and Click sat together at night, quietly brooding, thinking of what they could do next. Night on Fixion was oddly different from how Rader remembered nights should be. The dark sky was strewn with brilliant clumps of asteroids from the Fixion Belt, glittering almost-moons that added to the feeble starlight. He didn't think he would ever get used to the low gravity, the thin atmosphere, the wrong constellations.

He would not see the skies of Earth again, no matter what. Even if he hadn't fallen in with Click, if he'd been a good and loyal Deathguard, he would have rampaged behind enemy lines until the alien soldiers destroyed him, or until his systems shut down from cascading failures in the cyborg process. What remained of his human body—wired up and intertwined with weapons and armor—could not withstand the shock for long. Maybe biological tissue rejection would get him, or faulty mechanical and electronic integration.

The Werewolf Trigger was oddly quiet inside his head, and he felt no compulsion to rampage among Jaxxans and slaughter them. Maybe that compass of violence had also gotten skewed, the neural hookups damaged somehow by his second thoughts. But no, it was more than that.

Each day, Click focused his thoughts and manifested the shimmering holystal. After watching his comrade's meditation, Rader had begun emulating the process as best he could. The Werewolf Trigger could send him into a murderous frenzy at any time, but he was learning to quell the urges. He hadn't known that a Deathguard could control the trigger—no one had mentioned it in his training.

Now, Click rotated and inspected the glowing image he had manifested, and even Rader could see the extreme changes in the crystal pattern. As his mistakes piled up and his options became more limited, the three-dimensional map of Click's life became more jumbled. The holystal was a sorry mess, a lump with no discernible paths leading into the future.

"We can't just stay here and hope no one finds us," Rader said. "We've got to get off of this asteroid."

During basic training with his squad mates, Rader had studied the layout of the Fixion Belt. He knew the handful of human outposts and remembered one of the first facilities the League had built here: an automated observatory on a small outlying asteroid, established before the initial encounter with Jaxxans. Observation dishes mapped the deep cosmos and monitored the Belt's other asteroids. Years ago, those telescopes had been the first to spot Jaxxan incursions into the asteroid belt, watching the aliens build their own bases on the handful of habitable rocks.

The observatory was out of the way and uninhabited, but with functional life support installed and left behind by the original construction crew.

"I know someplace safe. We'll have time and breathing space—if we can get there."

After Rader described the observatory, Click said, "But we cannot live there for long. It can only be a temporary measure."

Rader's voice was bleak. "My life is just a temporary measure. If we reach the observatory, maybe I'll stick around long enough to help you find a safer place. One step at a time. First, we've got to get from here to that little asteroid."

Click pondered for a moment. "If we need nothing more than an in-system ship to take us through the asteroids to the observatory, the Jaxxan base's landing field has many capable vessels. We could take one."

"I couldn't fly it," Rader said. "How about you?"

"That depends on the specific type of vessel. I flew several of those craft during my team's work on the System Holystal. We could try."

"We could try," Rader agreed.

Click looked across the landscape to where the distant Jaxxan base and its landing field glowed above the foreshortened horizon. Suddenly his holystal shifted, adjusted itself to the new reality—and one new bright spire emerged.

—XI—

Commissioner Sobel traveled in secret to a landing field near the main Jaxxan base, where he would meet with Warlord Kiltik. Together, they would unleash their special team behind battlefield lines to take care of the embarrassing situation before rumors could leak out.

Sobel could cover up the problem for another few days, but high command would know about it before long. He wanted to be able to announce that he'd eliminated the defective Deathguard before uncomfortable questions came down the pipeline. He didn't have much time. Although he had no understanding of Jaxxan politics or military protocol, he sensed that Kiltik felt just as much incentive and anxiety.

As he and the alien Warlord watched the ten human and Jaxxan trackers demonstrate their cooperative efforts, Kiltik startled him with an unexpected comment. "I have learned that your people call us 'cockroaches,' Commissioner."

Sobel tried to cover his embarrassment. "Roaches? Yes, I've heard that. It's just an Earth insect. There are some ... physical similarities."

"Not just an Earth insect, Commissioner, but one that is considered filthy, one that wallows in or feeds on garbage. In reality, the Jaxxan race is quite fastidious."

Sobel gave an unconvincing laugh. "I wouldn't worry about it. It's a common practice among grunts—er, lower level soldiers—to create derogatory names for the enemy. I'm certain your race does the same. Don't you have any insulting terms for humans?"

Warlord Kiltik twitched. "We call them *humans*. That is all the insult we need."

The ten-member hunter squad continued training. The human soldiers had already been briefed specifically on how to kill a Deathguard (details they would not reveal to their alien counterparts). The current exercises showed the team members how to effectively combine Earth League laser weaponry and Jaxxan energy-web techniques. Most importantly, they got used to working with one another. That was the big barrier to break.

Kiltik said, "I find it discouraging that ten trained fighters are necessary to combat two deserters."

"No one is more annoyed than I am, but those two have already killed fourteen of my fighters and six of yours. I should be proud of our Deathguard's fighting skills, but I cannot help but wonder if your soldier somehow corrupted him."

Kiltik choked his dry, rustling cough. "Who corrupted whom? Remember, Jaxxans are empaths. How can one of us possibly remain normal when constantly bombarded with your Deathguard's alien perspectives? Our deserter was already flawed, in the wrong place after being removed from the System Holystal project. Your Deathguard has irreparably damaged him."

A Jaxxan trotted up from one of the outpost buildings and handed the Warlord a small geometric crystal. Kiltik turned the object over in his hands, feeling the facets and reading its shape. When he finished, the crystal vanished from his hands.

"I have just been informed by my reconnaissance that the two deserters were spotted in the wastelands, moving away from the front. Then they vanished again."

Sobel frowned. "If we knew where they were going, our hunter squad could intercept them."

The Commissioner remembered visiting Rader in the med-center when he was no more than a few mangled lumps of flesh wired up to life-support; he'd had high hopes for his newest Deathguard. Now, he just wanted him removed from the equation.

He and Kiltik stood together, admiring their special team.

High above the ecliptic, bright starlight reflected off of the giant planes of polished cometary ice and majestic crystal spires being assembled there by Jaxxan imaginers and psychics.

The human military did not know the location of the System Holystal construction above the asteroid belt. Even if they did stumble upon the site, they wouldn't understand it. Warlord Kiltik did not understand it himself. Holystal interpretation was not the duty of his caste, but he trusted the skills and knowledge of those who manifested such a representation. They could read the lines of fate, the fractures and angles that showed which paths Jaxxans could take into the future.

Thousands of workers operated here in space. While high-powered imaginers used their mental powers to create holographic portions of the ever-changing structure, teams of builders pushed small chunks of orbiting ice and diverted comets to deliver the materials here.

The Jaxxan race now inhabited five star systems. In each one, a revered System Holystal such as this one guided their decisions. The Jaxxan deserter who had joined forces with the human Deathguard had once been a skilled holystal imaginer who could understand subtle nuances in the cosmic constructions.

Now the Warlord flew in a small observation shuttle, piloted by his chief adviser. It was part of Kiltik's regular briefing to plan the next week's tactics, but he was losing confidence in the adviser's recommendations. Any decent interpreter should have been able to warn against the current mess. The chief adviser knew his failing and desperately wanted to return to the Warlord's good graces.

The observation shuttle approached the gigantic holystal, and Kiltik marveled at its facets, saw the distant starlight that reflected from the shining surfaces. He realized that it had been a mistake to demote the holystal engineer and turn him into a mere battlefield soldier. Observing the facets and angles, the Warlord could see how easy it would be to predict a different future from all the complexity. Even his chief adviser now suspected that some of the deserter's contradictory warnings might have had some merit.

However, the deserter's actions were indefensible: collaborating with a human—and not just any human, but a Deathguard who was single-handedly responsible for the murder of dozens if not hundreds of Jaxxan soldiers! It was shameful, an embarrassment, and Warlord Kiltik needed the situation resolved. In that, he was completely aligned with his human counterpart.

Reticent and chastised, the chief adviser flew the survey shuttle in a tight orbit over the giant holystal. Kiltik remained silent, his disapproval hanging in the enclosed cockpit. The adviser devoted his attention to the kaleidoscopic facets, the ever-changing fissures, crystalline angles, cracks and impurities, each of which indicated a different future, a path of fate that must be heeded.

Finally, the Warlord expressed his impatience. "I am not sightseeing. I am here to ferret out information. You are my interpreter. If you wish to regain my respect, then find answers." He turned his polished eyes to the nervous chief adviser. "Look at the holystal, find the portions that are relevant to these deserters. I need to know what their plans are. Our hunter squad must know where they intend to go."

The adviser's voice was thin and warbling. "The holystal is still under construction, Warlord. Even if we find the proper facets, any answers are merely within a locus of possibilities."

"Then I need those possibilities. Narrow them down so I can make my decisions."

The chief adviser guided the survey shuttle over an expanse of stalagmite-covered ice and broken shards, a jumble that meant something to a Jaxxan properly versed in interpretation. "There, Warlord!" The adviser pointed to a flurry of cracks and warped transparency in the polished ice. "That appeared since my last visit here."

"What changed?"

"The deserters have made a concrete plan, which is reflected here. This allows us to draw conclusions."

Kiltik was careful not to praise the man too much. "How accurate can you be?"

"I have a … reasonable certainty." He was cautious, not wanting to commit to what might be another error. The chief adviser stared through the window port, assessing the ripples and distortion in the crystalline structure. "We cannot extrapolate far into the future, but I can project where they intend to go next."

Kiltik felt pleased. "If that information is accurate enough for our hunter squad to intercept them, then we won't need any further projections."

—XII—

With Click leading the way, they entered the hulking lump of buildings that was the Jaxxan military base—neatly organized but crowded structures, large and small, with flat walls slanted at hard-to-interpret angles. The buildings were dark, the passages between them narrow, the architecture strange and disorienting to Rader—everything based on oblique angles rather than perpendicular walls.

The Jaxxan military base, as with the human outpost on the other side of Fixion, had started out as a basic forward station, a testing ground for a possible colony, before the war broke out. But no hopeful colonists had ever arrived, and now the temporary city was a bizarre collage of trading posts, refectories, warehouses, arsenals, administrative hives, and command posts.

He and Click had to make their way through the middle of it at night, skirt any populated sections, and reach the landing field, where they hoped to steal a small in-system craft.

Rader used his suit sensors to scan for danger, while coaching Click in how to keep himself from being seen. Somehow, the alien couldn't grasp the technique of searching for cover. However, after countless switchbacks and false starts, Click had become lost in the tangled streets. He sounded dismayed. "I was assigned to the System Holystal project out in space. I spent very little time in this settlement."

Rader scanned ahead. "We'll figure out a viable route to the landing field." He and his companion moved from alley to alley until they had lost all sense of direction.

Disoriented and impatient, Click stepped into a wide intersection to get his bearings while Rader took a reading to determine how far they were from the ships. The Deathguard's sensors detected movement in the shadows, forms converging on them with high-sensitivity detectors of their own. He knew this wasn't right.

He heard a voice hiss, a *human* voice, here in the middle of the Jaxxan base. "That's him! The Deathguard—and the deserter!"

A laser rifle etched a molten line across the flat tan wall of a nearby building. Rader jerked Click back into the dark alley as a freshly formed green energy-web hurtled toward them. The shimmering threads sliced off the corner of a structure.

The hunters surged out of their cover, humans *and Jaxxans* tracking them together. Before Rader could grasp the implications, he used his laser rifle to kill one—a Jaxxan, he thought—and scatter the others. *One down.* Synthetic adrenaline juiced him, and he fell into full defensive mode. He dragged Click with him down to the end of the alley and blasted a hole through the thin wall so they could push their way into a side street.

They dashed through the maze of passageways, glad for the darkness. Deathguard reflexes kicked in, filling him with a sense of heightened danger. Without saying a word, Click ran along beside him, in shock. From behind, they could hear shouts and noises as the hunter squad continued their pursuit.

Rader was amazed to realize that the Earth League and the Jaxxan military had cooperated to hunt them down. It would take all his skills and energy to avoid capture and keep Click alive. He focused entirely on their escape.

Suddenly his insides jerked, and he felt pressure building up in his brain as the Werewolf Trigger activated: KILL. KILL.

"Click, get out of here!"

The Jaxxan stumbled next to him. "But where should I go?"

"I'm dangerous! Get away from *me!*" Rader shoved him off to one side, hunching over in his futile attempts to control himself. "Quick, dammit!" Click stumbled off, running but woefully clumsy.

The Deathguard's implanted weapons systems activated, his laser rifle became part of him, and his head exploded with red noise, the alarm voice pounding against pressure points in his brain.

The whole world around him became a target, and the enemy lost its distinct form. He didn't know for sure what it was he must KILL, but he had to KILL it anyway. The berserker alarm told him to.

Gripping his laser rifle with reinforced gloves, he leaped out into the street, taking pot-shots at buildings, shooting at shadows in windows. Rader's shout was amplified by his helmet speakers—and from his scream, the hunter squad pinpointed his location.

He looked ahead down an alley, studying details through light-amplification sensors. A vague memory jumped into his mind. Someone had gone that way, indistinct—the enemy? He bounded between the angled buildings, paying no heed to the movement behind him.

Rader breathed with mechanical rhythm, peering into the shadows with heightened senses. His cyborg systems increased his metabolism, supercharged what remained of his biological tissue.

A brilliant shooting star, a gift from the Fixion Belt, whistled over his head in a final flash of glory.

Rader leaped forward, unable to control his actions. He saw a Jaxxan ahead of him, running, stumbling along. A vague, distant voice tugged at the back of his mind, telling him that this wasn't the real enemy … but the Werewolf Trigger drowned the rational voice.

Click.

The lone Jaxxan let out a chitter of fear and ran along a perpendicular alley, straight toward the landing field, still trying to reach the ship they needed. He reached an open construction area where skeletons of oddly angled buildings stood among piles of naked plastic-alloy girders.

Rader launched himself into the construction area like a jungle fighter. Shadows surrounded him, but he paid them no heed. Ahead, he saw the alien, the enemy. Recognition flickered in his mind for a moment—but the clamor forced it away.

KILL

No!

Click stumbled among tangled wires and slabs of polymer concrete in piles for assembly crews. He stopped short against a half-constructed wall, wheezing in the thin air.

Rader stepped victoriously over a girder, then leaped down in front of the cornered target. He pushed the laser rifle close to the Jaxxan's large black eyes.

But the alien refused to use his energy-web. Click merely regarded the weapon's blunt barrel.

KILL KILL, the voice of the Werewolf Trigger insisted.

No! *No!*

Rader's will struggled against a fortune of scientific conditioning. He had to fire, had to destroy. The command pulled harder at his mind, building in intensity, tearing him apart.

KILL KILL

No!

The Deathguard swung his weapon up and went wild, blasting buildings, slicing through support struts, destroying anything but Click.

Jumping away, he charged back in the direction he had come—and ran abruptly into the hunter squad. They reacted, but the Deathguard was too fast. The Werewolf Trigger ordered him to KILL—and this time he didn't resist. He left two dead human soldiers and one Jaxxan in the wake of his fury, then dove into cover, racing through the construction site. *Four down.*

The six remaining members of the hunter squad took only a second to regroup. Leaving the three bodies where they had fallen, one of the Jaxxans motioned to the others, and they stalked after the Deathguard.

As soon as he escaped the scattered hunters, the Werewolf Trigger lapsed into quiescence, and Rader's thoughts, intelligence, self-control flooded back into his mind.

He heard shouts from behind as the hunters called to one another. They were still out of sight, but with his amplified senses, he could hear them split up to approach him from different directions. However, Rader had an advantage now as calm calculation returned to him. The others expected him to act like a rampaging berserker.

He had to damp his emotions, draw them back into himself so that his turmoil wouldn't become a beacon that declared his hidden presence to the empathic Jaxxans. Rader sought refuge in the darkness beneath an outside stairway, and his non-reflective, camouflage armor helped him melt into the shadows, turning him into a shadow himself.

He breathed methodically, forcing rigid control back into his body, imitating Click's holystal meditation. Click! He didn't *think* he had killed his comrade. Rader closed his eyes, ignoring the marching feet and hushed voices that hurried closer, then moved past him.

When the team had passed, he emerged from his sanctuary. Instead of pursuing the hunters, he crept toward the landing field and their way off Fixion. Click would have gone to the ships—he hoped.

Across twenty meters of open concrete, a small short-range cargo vessel rested, as well as six larger personnel transports and a bulbous fuel tanker. One lonely Jaxxan guard stood at the open door of the small cargo ship.

On the perimeter of the landing field, Rader spotted Click's ill-concealed form in the shadow of a building. At least the alien was trying. The Deathguard silently made his way over to his friend, keeping so well concealed that even Click didn't know he was there until the last moment.

The Jaxxan froze, then realized that he no longer sensed the raging, killing beast inside the Deathguard. Rader spoke in a whisper. "I'm in control now, but the rest of that squad is still after us. It won't be long before they realize I've doubled back. Let's get that ship!"

He knew that if they could get off of Fixion, they could lose themselves in the debris of the asteroid belt, travel slowly, hopscotch from rock to rock, and reach the observatory asteroid. Beyond that, Rader didn't care.

He brought his laser rifle up, aimed. "I'll get rid of the sentry."

But Click's bony arm stopped him. "Wait, there is a better way." He hunkered down and concentrated on the sentry. Even through his armor, Rader felt a tingle in the air; his sensors registered an energy buildup. A galaxy of lights flickered in the deep universe of Click's black eyes.

The sentry flailed his angular arms as a half-formed energy-web folded over him. The sentry clawed at the dimly sparkling strands, searching for his unseen attacker—a Jaxxan attacker.

Leaving their hiding place, Rader and Click rushed across the landing field toward the Jaxxan cargo ship. When Click spoke to the sentry, Rader was surprised to hear the menace in his comrade's usually timid voice. "Do nothing unwise, or I shall be forced to complete my web."

The Jaxxan guard did nothing unwise.

While Rader kept his laser rifle pointed at the sentry, Click scuttled forward and activated the hatch. "Can you fly this ship?"

The insectoid head bobbed up and down on its stalk of a neck.

"A hostage and a pilot," Rader said. "Good enough." He did not know what they would do with the sentry once they reached their destination.

Click chittered his instructions to the sentry. "You will fly on a random, evasive course. The humans have an observatory asteroid located on the far edge of the Belt. It must be in the database."

Rader detected movement in the construction area, the hunter squad picking up on them again. "They're coming. Get inside the ship—now!"

With a victorious outcry, the hunters charged across the landing field. Rader shoved Click through the cargo ship's open hatch as one of the human soldiers braced for a careful shot, but chose the wrong Jaxxan. He burned a large hole in the alien sentry's back.

As he tried to escape, Rader's left leg suddenly collapsed, and he sprawled on the ramp. The attackers raced toward them, shouting, and he rolled, trying to assess the damage, sure that a laser blast had cut through the armor, ruined his cyborg leg systems. Using his good leg, his elbows, and his gloves, he hauled himself to the hatch.

Click had turned back to help him, and an energy-web glittered against the hull, smoking and sparking. Rader yelled, "Leave me— get to the control room!"

Instead, the Jaxxan grabbed his arms, dragged him the rest of the way into the ship. As soon as he was clear, Click sealed the hatch.

Rader looked down to see how much damage the shot had done to his leg, but he saw no burned hole, no melted slag of armor or shorted-out cyborg parts. The leg had simply failed.

Click dashed away from the hatch and scrambled up a thin-runged ladder to the control deck. Rader called after him, "You *can* fly this type of ship, can't you?"

Click pointedly did not answer, and Rader stifled a groan.

The cargo ship rose jerkily, leaving behind a whirlpool of displaced air. The hunter squad watched in anger and defeat. After the vessel zigzagged in a drunkard's flight from the landing field, the soldiers watched the flares of its engines dwindle into Fixion's thin atmosphere.

The human captain stared at the sentry who lay sprawled on the still-warm pavement. "He's dead. We can't interrogate him for any intel the two deserters might have revealed."

The Jaxxan leader shook his head. "Not too late. We will implement a post-mortem interrogation."

He removed equipment from his belt pack—a probe, a diagnostic reader, two long wires, and a skull splitter. Jamming down hard, he broke the chitinous shell of the dead sentry's head, spreading the hard faceplates to expose the soft, contoured brain. "We should still be able to access the chemical memory of the last few moments he experienced."

The Jaxxan unfolded the screen, then dipped the sharp probe

wires into the dead alien brain. Static washed across the screen accompanied by surreal images, colored patterns, old memories. He worked quickly before the memory-storage chemicals dissipated, the neurons deteriorated.

He touched different sections of tissue with the probe wires, moving urgently, until he found a blurred image of Deathguard Rader and his Jaxxan companion. He zeroed in, turned up the volume on the receiver, and heard their words, relived their last conversation, studied everything they had said.

The Jaxxan captain got the information he needed before the chemical traces crumbled into disjointed fragments and incomplete sentences. It was enough. He looked up at his comrades. "Now we know where they are going."

—XIII—

"They got past *all ten?*" Sobel was still rubbing sleep from his eyes in front of the image of Kiltik.

The insistent call from the viewscreen had dragged him out of bed. He hadn't expected to be disturbed, but Sobel had given the Jaxxan Warlord his direct contact code. At first, the Commissioner thought he would be happy to receive the call regardless of the hour, expecting good news—but Kiltik had not told him what he wanted to hear.

"Yes, all ten, Commissioner. The Deathguard killed four of them and escaped with the Jaxxan soldier in a stolen ship. A very reckless flight, evasive action. They vanished into the asteroid field."

"Good riddance," Sobel muttered, but knew the problem didn't end there. Even if the two were never seen again—and the cyborg systems had to start breaking down soon—Sobel's failure to resolve the situation properly would be a permanent blot on his record. He couldn't just let the Deathguard die on his own. "This is a disaster, Warlord. We'll never be able to track them—unless you can guess their destination from the patterns in that holystal thing of yours?"

The Jaxxan's face was unreadable. "We have a clearer answer than that. Your Deathguard and my deserter tried to take one of the landing-field sentries hostage, but our hunter squad shot him inadvertently—a happy accident. Fortunately, one of my soldiers set up a mind probe quickly enough. We know the location of the asteroid where the two intend to go."

"Really?" Sobel didn't quite allow himself a sigh of relief. "Well, that's better than a complete debacle, but we have to act without delay. Let me send you two of my best fighter ships—ours are faster than yours."

"Accepted." An expression of what might have been humor crossed Kiltik's face, but then the alien broke into a spasm of dry coughing.

Sobel rolled his tongue around in his dry mouth. He had been asleep for only a few hours, and already his mouth tasted foul. "I'll get those fighter ships sent over right away—and please don't shoot at them! Then I'm going back to bed." He yawned, but felt no better for it. "Don't you ever sleep?"

"No."

"Oh … Well, I'll speak to you when I have something to report, Warlord."

"Call me Kiltik." The Warlord touched the screen, and the images of his fingertips were blurred. "Now that I have met you in person, I find this communication very unsatisfactory. I feel no emotions, which makes understanding more difficult. From now on, I would rather dispense with this apparatus and meet you face-to-face."

"That can be arranged—but let's hope we can wrap up this problem quickly." He blanked the screen, then established another connection. He spoke to a corporal in the fighter ship hangars, repeated his baffling instructions several times, then worked his way up the chain of command.

Sobel knew his bed would be very cold by the time he finally climbed back into it.

—XIV—

They flew away from Fixion, diving at breakneck speed and without a course into the scramble of drifting asteroids. Click quickly became adept at maneuvering the cargo shuttle.

"The military will be tracking us. We have to get far enough away," he announced over the intercom.

Rader still lay on the lower deck, trying to get his uncooperative

111

leg to function. He was sure the survivors of the hunter squad would be commandeering their own pursuit ships. Click accelerated as much as he could tolerate, and his tough alien body could withstand severe gravitational stresses. Rader's Deathguard armor protected him.

"Once we are in the densest portion of the Belt, I will cut the engines," Click continued. "Then our signature becomes identical to that of the other small asteroids."

Taking a moment to assess his own malfunctions, Rader propped himself against a bulkhead. The cyborg leg had suffered no obvious damage, but the neural pulses from his brain no longer made it move as he intended. Unavoidable glitches, the start of what would be a cascade of breakdowns, and he knew how to do only the most basic repairs. He breathed silent thanks that his systems had functioned long enough and well enough to get him and Click off of Fixion. Now, if he could only find a plan that would get his Jaxxan comrade to safety.

One problem at a time.

Working with enforced patience, still feeling the afterwash of the synthetic adrenaline that had poured through his systems, Rader removed emergency tools, cracked open the primary circuits, and performed a standard reset procedure twice before his armored leg would twitch again. He swung himself back to his feet and tried to walk. He took painstaking steps at first, then limped forward. The metal ladder to the upper deck proved quite a challenge, but he eventually made his way into the control chamber.

Click flew the ship among a cluster of high-albedo icy asteroids. To confuse any systems tracking them, he matched the orbits of random stony asteroids of approximately the same size as the cargo ship, and the glaring sunlight masked their thermal signature after Click shut down the engines.

"We wait half a day," the Jaxxan said, "then alter course slightly to take us closer to the observatory asteroid. We are patient."

"Yes, patient." Rader silently ran thorough diagnostic checks of his systems, his power sources, the alignment of neural conduits, and found many domino-effect malfunctions; his last battle and escape in the Jaxxan base had strained his components, running out the service life. "Take as much time as you need."

One way or another, he doubted he had more than a week. Click didn't need to know that, but his empathic senses would probably tell him anyway.

"With the ship's life-support levels, we can survive for three days. Breathe as little as possible."

Rader realized it was a joke. "Nobody's been to the observatory asteroid in ages. Better hope their systems are functional. We won't make it to anywhere else."

Click said, "We have nowhere else to go."

"That's the next thing I have to figure out."

While they drifted, Rader tried to implement repairs to his cyborg systems in order to buy a little extra time, but most of the systems were beyond him. And the failings were in his mental interface, not in the large-scale mechanics. He experienced a persistent headache that seemed to be growing worse. His eyesight suffered from double vision, as if the images from his real eye and artificial eye did not align properly.

For two days, they made their cautious, tedious journey across a stepping-stone course. Click monitored the cargo ship's passive sensors. They were surrounded by far too many data points, which was good—a swarm like identical needles in a very large haystack. "I see no indication that pursuers have followed us through the numerous blips."

Rader's hope grew as the image of the observatory asteroid grew on the viewscreen before him. It was a domed rock less than two kilometers wide, moving among the rubble in the Fixion Belt. In less than an hour, if Click kept up his improved navigational abilities, they would arrive.

Rader almost smiled for the first time since … since that final day with his squad mates. He should have died then, and *that* day could have served as his final flash of glory, not this awkward encore. With so much time to think aboard their ship, he could not escape the conclusion. Even after they reached the observatory, Click had little chance of going much farther. He had not managed to come up with a viable plan.

He felt dismayed that this abortive "second chance" as a Deathguard had accomplished nothing—not for himself, not for his people, not for Click either. It was just a delay. And when Rader's cyborg systems finally broke down, Click was not likely to last long alone on the observatory asteroid. He'd wait there until food supplies and life support ran out, like a man stranded on a desert island.

Short-term thinking. But it was better than *shorter*-term thinking. They were still alive. Rader had to hope they would find some other ship, or supplies … or a miracle once they got to the asteroid.

In the pilot seat, Click seemed satisfied. If he detected Rader's troubled thoughts, he did not show it.

As they made their final approach, Rader studied the enhanced images, saw the framework of bowl-shaped radio telescopes reflecting starlight, the automated tracking mirrors of optical telescopes gazing out into the universe to gather astronomical data.

And he saw the recently installed military fuel depot, large tanks of spacecraft fuel, as well as Earth League stockpiled missiles, a forest of javelin-shaped warheads ready to be launched. He stared, realizing that this asteroid was not as forgotten and abandoned as he had hoped.

When Click scanned the rear navigational sensors, his glassy black eyes clouded over. "Rader …"

Two pursuit fighter ships swept up behind them like cruising sharks. They came straight toward the sluggish Jaxxan cargo ship.

"I cannot accelerate enough to outrun them," Click said. "And we have very little fuel remaining."

Rader glanced at the type of ship, knew their capabilities. "Those are the League's fastest fighter ships. We don't have any chance of outrunning them."

When the pair of pursuers circled the cargo ship, Rader saw the Earth League insignia, but the image blurred and shimmered in his unfocused vision. The face that appeared on the comm screen, though, was a Jaxxan, demanding their surrender.

"Why don't they just destroy us from a distance?" Click said.

"They will want proof—or trophies."

The squad of hunters was composed of humans and Jaxxans working together; Rader wondered if the Earth League soldiers had orders to kill their alien comrades after a successful mission—especially now that they had seen the unexpected missile stockpile hidden on the observatory asteroid. Commissioner Sobel could not possibly want the Jaxxan high command to know about the depot.

"We cannot defend ourselves," Click said. "This cargo shuttle has no weapons."

Rader held his laser rifle. "We can defend ourselves."

A clang of metal thrummed through the hull as the two fighter ships attached to the Jaxxan airlocks. "I have sealed the airlocks and denied them access," Click said.

"They'll burn their way through." On the visual monitors he discerned a glow on the inner hull: one airlock being cut away by a powerful laser rifle, and the opposite lock rippling from a continuously applied energy-web. Even a Deathguard couldn't defend both hatches at the same time.

Limping on his faulty leg, aligning his weapons systems with the vision from only his artificial eye to minimize errors, Rader picked a defensible position at the entrance to the cargo ship's cockpit. He braced himself there, holding his laser rifle ready, his targeting sensors attuned. His artificial heart pumped nutrients through his cyborg and biological components, but the Werewolf Trigger remained silent. He didn't need it. Or maybe that, too, had malfunctioned.

Both hatches surrendered at the same time, and on the visual monitors he watched the remaining members of the hunter squad move with brisk efficiency through the corridors up to the cockpit. The humans were wearing mirrored armor, which would reflect the beam of his laser rifle.

"I'll take out as many as I can, but I doubt I'll get them all," he said. "Sorry we didn't make it all the way."

"We made it this far, Rader, and now we are dead." Click's voice was strangely emotionless. "But so are they."

Rader identified an expression on the alien face that no other human would have seen. Click punched a sequence into the navigational computer, and the observatory asteroid shifted its position in front of them. "Our engines cannot outrun the fighter ships, but we have enough power to drag them along."

Rader nodded approval. "A Deathguard's mission is to cause mayhem."

"Yes, I believe we have caused a fair amount of mayhem," Click said.

"I just wish we had accomplished something more than that." He wondered if the Commissioner would take the medal of honor away from his family ... but that would be admitting something had gone wrong.

The six members of the hunter squad advanced up to the control deck.

Rader darted a farewell glance at his comrade. After setting their collision course, Click crouched in motionless silence, not even trying to fight. Instead, he hunched over a shining image, studying his last holystal. The glowing shape was a dazzling, perfect sphere.

Rader took a quick breath. "What does that mean?"

"It means that we have run out of alternatives."

The hunter squad let out a chorus of shouts as they stormed the final corridor. Rader opened fire, placing a neat, centimeter-wide hole through the head of one Jaxxan.

Now the Werewolf Trigger clamored in his mind, but as he fired on the advancing squad members, his arm jerked and spasmed, spoiling his aim. The Jaxxans took shelter against door wells in the corridor, and Rader's energy blasts reflected off the mirrored armor, ricocheting down the hall. The fractured beams dissipated, but he kept firing.

Rader's leg gave out beneath him, and he tumbled over like a mannequin. He tried to aim his laser rifle as momentum carried his body in a clumsy roll, and he lay face up on the deck.

An energy-web hurled by the two remaining Jaxxans engulfed Click in luminous tangles. Click cried out as the web completed itself, but his words turned to scintillating shards of sound. His holystal dwindled to a last spark of light until that, too, vanished.

The human fighters targeted the Deathguard and rushed forward, while the Jaxxans ran past him, urgently trying to reach the shuttle controls in time. Rader stared at them through his visor: A band of humans and aliens working together, to destroy a human and alien who had dared to work together. He wondered if they understood the irony.

He looked past them to the cockpit to see the observatory asteroid rushing toward them. The cargo shuttle was going to crash into the spiny missile batteries instead of the telescopes ... not that it made any difference.

A short time was better than no time—and he had spent it with a friend rather than alone.

—XV—

Sobel grinned, ready to celebrate the news. "Well, Kiltik—we did it!"

"Yes, not even one of your Deathguards could resist the two of us." The Warlord sat across from him in the conference room on the Détente Asteroid. Kiltik had shuttled over to the Earth League embassy at Sobel's invitation, so they could await the final report.

The Warlord seemed troubled, however. The Commissioner would never have noticed it before, but now he could detect subtle differences in the alien's moods. "You don't seem as overjoyed as I expected."

"Perhaps I grieve for the loss of your … astronomical facility."

"Oh, that!" Sobel brushed the matter aside. "It was obsolete. We can always build another one—astronomy is low on our priorities."

"But it did provide a good hiding place for your weapons stockpile. Either astronomy is quite a volatile science, or your supposed observatory was merely a camouflage."

Sobel felt flustered and embarrassed, especially in his moment of great victory. "I could lie about that, but you'd be able to detect the truth, wouldn't you?"

"Yes." For his own part, unfortunately, Sobel couldn't tell whether the Jaxxan was lying. The Warlord said, "We will need to discuss this further—at the appropriate time."

"I'd be happy to talk about it with you, but right now, this calls for a drink! Would you care for some refreshment?"

The Jaxxan rattled his dry cough. "Water would be nice."

"Nothing more festive?" Sobel frowned. "As you wish, Warlord." He placed ice cubes in a glass and filled it from a pitcher.

Kiltik broke out in a spasm of raspy coughing. Sobel ran to help him. "You really should have that cough taken care of. Would you like one of my medics to check you out?"

The Jaxxan breathed deeply, expressing his thanks. "No, it would do no good. The dry air of Fixion has ruined my health. I have spent years in this climate—it is a wonder I'm still alive, so far from home." In a distant, dreamy voice, Kiltik described his warm humid planet with steaming jungles and crystal cities, where rain fell in syrupy drops and sluggish rivers were choked with sweet algae.

Sobel tried to picture it. "After our great victory over the two deserters, can't you use the political mileage to request a transfer back to Jaxx? For a short while at least?"

"I do not plan to report this matter to my superiors at all. I will be here for the duration of the war." He looked up. "How long are you to be stationed here?"

"I have a year and a half left of my three years."

"A year and a half." Kiltik sipped his cold water. "These facilities on the Détente Asteroid are used ineffectively." He paused for a long moment. "Would it be possible for me to visit you from time to time, friend Sobel?"

Still deciding what his celebratory drink would be, the Commissioner finally sat down with his own glass of ice water. "That could be arranged." He chuckled. "Friend Kiltik."

My first collaboration with Doug Beason started out as a lark. I was working as a technical writer at the Lawrence Livermore National Laboratory, where Doug had come to spend the summer as a visiting physicist. Up to that point, I'd had a few minor short stories published, as had Doug, but neither of us had broken into any professional sales. Being two aspiring science fiction writers in the same workplace, of course we had to meet.

We knocked around a few ideas and decided to write this story—just when Doug was recalled to Albuquerque, where he was stationed in the US Air Force. We sent partially completed drafts of the story back and forth through the mail (long before the days of compatible computer systems, so that each of us had to rekey the other's pages whenever they arrived in the mail).

We managed to place this story in the anthology Full Spectrum, *a major release from Bantam Books, which definitely gave us both a leg up in our careers.*

REFLECTIONS IN A MAGNETIC MIRROR

(with Doug Beason)

The Church questions whether this ""anomaly" is even alive. And if alive, we question whether it is intelligent. And if intelligent, we insist—without qualification—that it has no Soul. Man cannot create a Soul; that is for God alone.

— CARDINAL ROBERT K. DESMOND

As the deuterium passed through the opening, the discharge bombarded it from all sides. Electrons were torn from their nuclei, heating the fuelstuff in the plasma until the elementary particles fused together. The reaction sustained itself. Billionths of a second passed—an eternity to the plasma—while lasers delicately probed the inner workings of the maelstrom.

His own thought processes moving infinitely slower, Keller stood in silent awe, praying that it would *work*.

The particles bounced back and forth in the chamber, billions of times a second, unable to escape past the giant yin-yang magnets on either side of the Magnetic Mirror Fusion Facility. Long-range coulombic forces sculpted the plasma, creating swirling, complex interactions.

"And?" Keller asked.

The technician reached up to the screen directly in front of him, touching a blue icon that opened up to display two columns of numbers happily glowing green. "Everything's perfect, Gordon. Blessed be the Holy Laws of Physics."

Keller frowned at how the technician—all Californians, in fact—too often used his first name; especially in this, his moment of triumph after so long. He wanted to feel important.

In the background, filling the stuffy room with a much needed festive atmosphere, two operators hoarsely sang, "Fusion power, here we come!" to the tune of "California, Here I Come."

Then someone else called from behind another barricade of control consoles. "There it goes again!"

The singing abruptly stopped.

Keller reached forward to touch icons on the top two screens, opening up another numerical display while the second screen showed the data from varying perspectives.

"Glitches again!" the technician cursed. "But they're different from the last time."

The data repeated itself in oddly distorted cycles. The plasma seemed to be on the verge of blowing up as the instabilities on the screen grew, then decayed, as if a dancer were lightly touching the boundary of a dance-space, feeling her way. It seemed almost as if the plasma was testing its enclosure, exploring.

Keller stared at the screen, silently urging the anomalies to go away, but knowing they would not heed him. He wanted the experiment to be *over*, successfully completed at long last—he had driven so hard, worked his brain to the bone. And at thirty-three, he felt he was getting to be a little too old to be the proverbial whiz kid anymore. When they brought the MMFF online, the damned instabilities were always there ... but they were *always* different. Whatever the hell they were. He sighed and checked different readouts. In disgust, he walked to the windowless wall, wishing he could stare through the concrete cinder blocks to where, half a block away, a gigantic vacuum chamber held the eye of the storm, a sustained fusion reaction in a plasma confined by magnetic mirrors.

"But it *does* run? It's stable?" Keller asked without turning, sounding half-defeated.

"Sure, it runs. Close enough for government work," the technician answered.

Keller placed his hands behind his back and mentally tried to think of something historic or profound to say. "Good," was all he could manage.

This could prove to be extremely dangerous or extremely embarrassing. I don't want it to be either.

— CONFIDENTIAL MEMO TO LABORATORY MANAGEMENT, REGARDING THE MMFF ANOMALIES.

Keller shielded his eyes from the glaring, obnoxious lights. Three camcorders, eleven microphones, and sixty people crowded in a conference room that had been intended for forty-five, waiting for him to speak. Many of the reporters fingered their laminated temporary ID badges, looking with some concern at the dosimeters attached to them. Keller tried to kill the butterflies in his stomach. The DOE bigwig on his right grinned broadly and finally removed his arm from around Keller's back. Just before entering the crowded room, the DOE man had force-fed him some coaching for the cameras. "And for God's sake, don't *mumble!*"

The official held up his hands, quieting the crowd. "If you could please hold it down, Dr. Keller can say something about the Magnetic Mirror Fusion Facility." Silence was a long moment coming, but the DOE man finally continued. "Gordon, why don't you tell us what's so special about the MMFF?"

Keller leaned forward, cleared his throat, and tried not to look at all the faces looking at him. "Well, to start with, thank you for coming. This really *is* important, I think.

"The MMFF is the simplest design of all mirror machines: as you can see from the diagrams in the press kits, it's basically a long tube with a special type of powerful magnet on each end. The magnets act like mirrors, bouncing the plasma back and forth, confining it long enough so that fusion occurs. Once our yin-yang mirrors were perfected, all we had to do was turn it on. The MMFF doesn't have a lot of the instabilities associated with other mirror devices, such as the tokamak and spheromak machines."

The DOE official cut him off, interrupting with a large grin on his face. "And best of all, this machine uses *no* dangerous heavy elements such as uranium or plutonium. We all remember Three Mile Island. But TMI—and all other commercial nuclear power plants—rely on nuclear *fission*, rather than its opposite, nuclear *fusion*. With fusion power, five gallons of seawater could provide electricity for a town the size of Livermore for a week. Once we can bring MMFF sites up commercially, it's a no-lose situation."

The DOE man clapped Keller on the shoulder, then turned back to the audience. "Dr. Keller has been assigned to continue studying the MMFF, and he will release his complete findings at the November APS meeting in New York. To reiterate, the MMFF machine you saw a few moments ago is purely a feasibility study, but a study that has achieved the breakeven point in fusion energy. The next step is a facility that can be used for the *commercial* generation of power. And I'm sure we'll be asking Dr. Keller for his advice and assistance during the next phase of the project. And on that note, allow me to introduce Dr. Zel'dovich, the director of the MMFF-2, currently in the planning stages."

Scattered applause came as Keller turned, then was ushered away from the head table and into the background. He stood and watched, feeling sheltered and hidden by the other people. The fusion facility worked, despite the unexplained glitches, and he wondered if it was all over, if he had indeed completed the purpose of his life ... if the heaviness inside him would grow any larger. When he realized he wouldn't be missed in the conference room, Keller slipped away.

What is Life? What is Death? For that matter, how many angels can dance on the head of a pin? You can argue yourself silly, and I don't really care what the answer is. Right now, I want to know what the hell we should do about that Thing in there!

— DR. F. GORDON KELLER, MMFF STAFF MEETING

Keller stared at the small radio for a long moment, but ultimately decided to keep the house silent. Though he didn't particularly want to hear the depressing sound of the rain outside, he wasn't sure he was in the mood to hear music or another human voice, either. Keller slipped into his pair of faded, threadbare old brown cords and a lightweight cotton shirt—his "around home" clothes—but he couldn't shed the thoughts of his work as easily as he shed his clothing. He heaved a sigh.

Glitches.

He placed a TV dinner with a fancy-sounding French name into the microwave, carelessly jabbing at the timer pad. They had been so *careful* designing the huge magnets, the fusion chamber, the diagnostics. What the hell was going on? The plasma theorists were just as stumped as the computational physicists to explain the anomalies.

The microwave sent rhythmic pulses of electromagnetic radiation into his food, warming it. Keller muttered to himself that he would never have received a PhD in physics if he'd set up his plasma experiments the same careless way he cooked his food. But at least when he cooked a frozen dinner in the microwave oven, it left him with no surprises ... disappointment maybe, but certainly no surprises.

The anomalies just didn't make any sense.

He decided not to switch on the lights while he ate. He sat alone in the shadows, surrounded by the gray-washed dimness of the rainy windows. He stared absently at one of his son's crayon drawings attached to the refrigerator door with an old happy-face magnet. The drawing was somewhat curled around the edges and starting to yellow, but he hoped he wouldn't be able to notice that in the dim light. Three months—had it really been three months? He couldn't even remember if he had answered Shelley's letters.

It wasn't so long ago that she'd been the most important thing in his life; and when Justin was born, the little boy had taken over that special place in his heart. And what did Keller have now? The MMFF was online, and he finally had time to spend with his family ... time that had been so precious to him, so precious that he'd put his wife and son on hold just to complete the project—but now Shelley was gone, with Justin.

Some things just went wrong—there was nothing you could do about it, no equation you could solve, nothing you could explain with a simple, clear-cut answer.

But the plasma anomalies were a *physics* problem. They were solvable—they had an answer, an explanation. And if he didn't spend too much time wallowing in self-pity, he could probably clear his head and figure out some simple thing that was causing these anomalies, these embarrassments. He had a PhD—Piled Higher and Deeper, in layman's terms—which meant he was supposed to *know* something about physics.

That had been his scholarly battle cry for so long. *Get the PhD.* The incessant pushing, grinding out problem sets, spending long hours at the lab. It was the single most important thing in his life, with his entire world centered around that one goal: *Get the PhD.* He couldn't settle for anything less. And then, after actually getting the doctorate, it was as if all his personal drive had been snatched like a rug from under his feet.

He put down his fork and stared down at his wrists. Two slashes, running across the veins, had healed years ago to thin white scars, now almost invisible in the dim light by the dining room table. He'd spent so much time in the physics books that he couldn't even kill himself right; the cuts were supposed to be made *along* the vein, so that the bleeding would be more profuse. He knew that now. The shock, the jolting reality of obtaining his degree—getting what he wanted more than anything else in the world—had left him with nothing else to live for. At the time, it had seemed so coldly logical: he had achieved his one goal in life, and what else was there left to do? It sounded trivial now, but it did help explain his depression about finally completing the MMFF.

But what were the damned glitches?

Depression—it was such a nice excuse. He could still remember his mother, but at the time he had been too young to know what "cancer" was; watching her die had been a profound experience for him. One moment she had been lying on the white bed, as she had for the previous interminable weeks, connected to a wall full of electronic machines. An oscilloscope displayed patterns that showed she was alive.

Her suffering went on. The doctors all said she couldn't experience pain in her coma, but young Keller suspected otherwise. They said she couldn't feel the long, long time she spent on the machine, that it wouldn't be real to her. Keller had felt an urge to end it all for her, to *make it stop....*

But then one moment the machine had changed its mind and

pronounced her dead. His grandparents said that the Hand of God had reached down and taken her soul, but young Keller had seen nothing. Even now, Keller still found it difficult to understand, with the physicist in him trying to break down the entire experience into specific questions with specific answers.

What *actually* had taken place during those few seconds in the hospital room? What *actually* had been the difference between life and death? Just a tiny voltage differential across the brainpan?

He remembered the somber warnings from his electronics classes about the kid who had leaned over a bank of capacitors: a line had slipped, and the capacitors had discharged across his temples. The twenty microamps had been enough to short-circuit his head, killing him. Was that all life was, an electric field skittering around the contours of your brain? Was even the template of the brain, the body, just so much extraneous mass to hold a special electric field?

He switched on the light and switched it off again.

Glitches. Anomalies.

He decided to go back to the lab.

Before going to the MMFF control room, Keller walked down the deserted laboratory street past the trailers and other research buildings. Heavy equipment sat idle, sleeping, in wide roped-off lots near numerous construction sites. Keller stopped in front of the huge housing for the MMFF chamber, which rose into the darkness like an airplane hangar. Concrete walls three stories high plunged deep below ground to make the structure earthquake-safe. Girders strung with fog lights bathed the interior of the bay with an orangish-yellow light. Even at this hour of the night, a dozen workers kept their vigil around the armored hull of the MMFF chamber, an airtight cylinder over a hundred feet long, layered with thick sheet metal and bristling with diagnostic instruments. The great fusion chamber throbbed and pulsed, making thunderous sounds pitched just below the level of human hearing. Inside, held captive by two of the world's largest magnets, were temperatures hotter than the sun itself, powerful enough to melt through any metal known to man. He stared for a moment, then headed to the main building.

"We've tried *everything* to get rid of them, and at times we got some responses you wouldn't believe." The technician was packing up, getting ready to go home in the darkness and the rain. "You know, Gordon," he said with a lopsided grin as he looked over the readouts displaying the glitches, "sometimes it reminds me of my wife. Like we're dealing with something that's got a mind of its own."

The technician left, calling his goodbyes into the room. The new shift of technicians mumbled about the prospect of working the next eight dead hours of the night while the rest of the world slept. Keller smiled thinly, distracted. "Yes, like it has a mind of its own." He stared at the readouts for a long time, hypnotized by the wavering plots that sometimes displayed patterns, sometimes chaos.

He reached forward carefully without taking his eyes from the display screens. His fingers were shaking somewhat. Then he began to touch the controls, adjusting the laser probes. Injection on, and the m numbers ran up the scale; the plasma went through the sausage, kink, and firehose instabilities, all in sequence, all on the verge of getting out of control.

Injection off, and the sequence reversed ... then *repeated* itself—spontaneously. Like a code. Or was it only some weird sort of resonance?

Keller drew in his breath. He sat and tried to establish a link, any link, using anharmonic modes from the RF generator. It could almost be classed as communicating.

He caught himself. Communicating?

... The discovery at the MMFF facility opens wide a new door for the human race. It will force us to restructure our philosophy of the universe and life itself.

— EDITORIAL, PHYSICAL REVIEW LETTERS

The official lab spokesman looked good on TV, perfectly groomed, selected from the vast DOE complex as *the* man to best handle the explosive publicity. The late-night talk show host nodded soberly, hanging on to every word said by the panel of distinguished experts. As Keller watched, he knew the publicity generated by the televised discussion would bring out every nut, fruitcake, and religious fundamentalist who was offended by the suggestion that *something* was happening inside the MMFF. He had already taken his phone off the hook.

The host defused an argument among the "experts" and cut right through the static: "But *has* the Fusion Facility created life? Yes or no?"

The lab spokesman had been talking around the subject all night, and he finally looked as if he had been trapped. "We like to think of it as an unknown physical phenomenon which can spontaneously react to stimuli within correct statistical parameters."

The host rolled his eyes, and the lab spokesman responded a little too defensively. "That is a direct quote from Dr. Keller's recently published paper in *Physical Review Letters*. I'm sure Dr. Keller could explain what he meant to say—"

"Dr. Keller is not available for comment at your lab," the host snapped.

"Ah, yes." The spokesman brought his fingertips together. "He is a very busy man, and I assure you he is doggedly working on this problem."

"I'm sure he is," said the host dryly.

"But getting back to your question—and answering quite honestly—we just don't *know* what the phenomenon is. Granted, some do claim it's alive. But a simple virus is also technically alive. A better question would be: does it have self-awareness? These questions just can't be answered at this time.

"But the point is that *something* is happening in the chamber, something we can't explain. This was to be just a test run, a feasibility study to see if the MMFF would indeed perform as expected before we began full-scale tests. The experiment was originally scheduled to be shut down after three days of continuous operation, but, given the unusual anomalies, we have directed that the facility be kept running for as long as it takes us to understand what is going on."

The discussion grew more philosophical, with the lab spokesman dancing away from pointed questioning. It went on and on, growing fuzzy like a plasma … until the spokesman leered out at Keller, stuck his head through the TV set, and made a grab at him. Keller tried to run but his legs were stuck in a magnetic field and he couldn't stop bouncing back and forth and back and forth and—

Keller woke with a start. He blinked his eyes and realized he had fallen asleep, probably for more hours than he had slept the entire previous night. Keller glanced up at the television and saw that the panel discussion had been replaced by the climax of an Italian-made vampire movie on *The Late Show*.

A man—obviously the hero, obviously the vampire hunter—had pinned the king vampire in his coffin just before sunset. He held a wooden stake against the vampire's chest and made ready to strike.

Keller stood up stiffly from his chair, tried to straighten his shirt but then pulled it off instead, and shuffled over to the television. On the screen, the king vampire had awakened, glaring in melodramatic horror at his victorious adversary and the wooden stake, but then a calm, beatific expression of relief passed over the vampire's face.

"You are trapped, Count!" cried the vampire killer. The actor's lips didn't quite move in tandem with the English words.

"Trapped?" whispered the vampire. "I have been trapped for uncounted centuries. Trapped as what I am, unchanging, never to see the light of day. I have lived for so long that what you do to me is an act of kindness. I can no longer endure my life." The king vampire closed his eyes again and drew a deep breath. "Kill me."

Keller flicked the switch and shut off the television. "There, you're dead."

We do a lot of stuff here, so we always have protesters. But I'm getting tired of those nuts claiming we've got God bottled up in there. They're spooky!

— SECURITY GUARD, MMFF

With a sour and harried expression on his face, Keller wadded up the formal invitation and threw it at the motel room wastebasket. An invitation to speak to a Congressional hearing on the Search for

Extraterrestrial Intelligence project. SETI wanted him to talk about "communicating with alien beings"—they had their gall, especially now!

He flopped back on the hard bed. It probably wouldn't be long before the reporters found him again—Livermore had only a few motels, and those were used mostly by out-of-town job interviewees and DOE contractors. Judging by the stories they ended up printing in their newspapers, the reporters never seemed to listen to his answers to their questions anyway, but they were damned persistent in trying to track him down.

He knotted his fingers in the bedspread. He could hide from the reporters, the decisions, the publicity—but he couldn't hide from the problem.

The thing in the plasma had stopped communicating. Or rather, as the careful side of him liked to point out, the plasma "wasn't spontaneously initiating any controlled instabilities" anymore. The glitches showed it was still there, still living within the fusion chamber, staring at itself in the magnetic mirror. Like Alice unable to get into Wonderland.

Keller could not fathom why the thing didn't treasure every bit of communication, why it didn't eagerly anticipate every new mathematical challenge. It was trapped within its huge chamber, unchanging, unable to come out. It had nothing to do but listen, and talk.

The Congressional invitation caught his eye. He hated to talk in front of people. Yet, it was the most logical thing in the world for SETI to ask him to speak on their behalf, since he was the only human being ever to "successfully" communicate with an alien intelligence.

But what in the hell was Keller supposed to say to the SETI people? Should he confess that he'd always thought their project was basically a waste of time and effort? Sure, he believed there were other civilizations Out There, but the nearest star was five light-years away, the nearest galaxy 2.2 *million* light-years away—as the photon flies. How in the blessed world were you supposed to hold a conversation?

If they were to receive a message from Andromeda tomorrow, it would have been sent twenty thousand centuries before *Australopithecus africanus* had just begun to make his first tool, just begun to chase woolly mammoths while wondering why it was getting so cold even in the summertime ... and no one on Earth then had even the slightest desire to build a satellite antenna to listen for extraterrestrial signals. And if SETI were to acknowledge that message, how many millions of years in its grave would be the civilization that had initiated the conversation? It was all a matter of perspective on time.

And here he was, Dr. F. Gordon Keller, separated from an alien intelligence by only a thin wall of stainless steel, but he couldn't communicate with the thing either—and he didn't have the incredible time differential working against him. But something was very wrong with the creature in the plasma. It didn't seem to want to communicate anymore.

Then it hit him like a load of bricks falling on his head.

How many times did he have to stare at something before the obvious answer reached out and bit him on the ass? Time scales of tenths of nanoseconds were critical to a plasma: in a second, a plasma could undergo thousands of millions of interactions. A second to Keller would be *billions* of times longer to something that lived on a plasma time scale.

A strange sense of horror began to grow in the pit of his stomach, and Keller even found himself feeling sorry for the thing.

Imagine being *alone*, trapped inside the fusion chamber for what was—to the thing—an absolute eternity. Even when Keller was communicating with it, tapping icons on the touch-sensitive screen or rapidly keying in commands—centuries would have seemed to pass between each individual finger stroke. The thing had been alive and aware for a million centuries, without a break to the monotony.

Keller remembered his mother dying, in a coma "with no sense of time," connected to the life-sustaining machines as an oscilloscope displayed her life as a pattern on a screen.

Electrical patterns in a plasma. Putting it out of its misery would be like switching off a light. But he would be destroying the world's oldest living thing. He would be killing a living being.

A million centuries alone and in silence, without another living being to talk to. Something wrenched in his stomach as the implications pounded themselves home. The thing was immortal, chained to an utterly useless life, unable to die as long as the MMFF remained running.

He would be giving it peace. Something in the world deserved peace.

It was the dead of night, with only a skeleton crew in the control room. Nothing had changed for days. A security guard checked Keller's badge at the gate, and then another let him pass into the control room. He wasn't going to break in and shut down the experiment … he was going to *walk* in and shut it down. He would free the living being that had been trapped inside, bottled up for eternity by Keller's wonderful mirrors. He moved with brisk and determined steps to the MMFF control room. Every moment he delayed meant another year of suffering for the thing.

"No change, Gordon," one of the operators said, seeing him as he walked purposefully into the room.

Without acknowledging, Keller went to a vacant bank of computer screens and stared at the jagged display of glitches on one of them. Even as he stared, even as his heart beat, years were ticking away for the thing imprisoned in the chamber. It could only bounce back and forth and *exist* for millions of its years, unable to escape and see the world outside. Keller felt his eyes sting, almost with tears, at the unspeakable loneliness.

But what about himself? He'd thrown away his marriage working on this damned project, trying to push and work and *achieve* so that he could hold an accomplishment up before himself to prove that his life was worthwhile. Like his PhD, getting the degree for a trophy. Was he trying to commit *career* suicide this time? The MMFF success had been the pinnacle of his research, but the living thing he had created was unexpected, a blessing, a curse. Keller had hidden from the publicity, passing the responsibility to others. But no one else would see the responsibility he had now, the imperative goal to free the creature he had trapped between the magnetic mirrors. It was time for Gordon Keller to stop hiding.

Keller stared at the red switch. Emergency shutdown—the only hardwired switch in the entire computer-screen-driven control room. It would be simple. Keller held out the palm of his hand—the razor blade against his wrist, the oscilloscope in his mother's hospital room, even the stake on the movie vampire's chest.

With a quick thrust of his arm, he shut the MMFF down.

He would have more time for Shelley now, and Justin. He'd try to call her, and maybe—*maybe*—she would even admire what he had done, tell him he'd been brave. He could write a book, *Memoirs of a Modern-Day Frankenstein.* Or maybe Zel'dovich would consult him about how the next generation of fusion chambers could be built without spawning a new life form.

As it died, and before anyone could act or any alarms could sound, Keller thought he felt a tingling rush through his skin—a flash of dissipating electricity. But it was only his imagination, or just the release of some of the psychological weight on his shoulders. With a sigh, he slowly eased himself into a chair as the shouting started.

This story is full of ideas I had been playing with since high school, and I even wrote the first several drafts on my old Smith-Corona typewriter. With the scope and background of "Rest in Peace," I could easily have developed it into a novel, but I was still learning my craft by experimenting with shorter works.

After many iterations, I finally placed this novelette in one of the New Destinies *anthologies from Baen Books, my first sale to up-and-coming editor Betsy Mitchell—and I can't overestimate the importance of that. Betsy moved on to Bantam Books, where she offered Doug Beason and me a three-book contract after accepting our short story for her* Full Spectrum *anthology. After working with her on those collaborative novels, Betsy called me out of the blue and asked if I liked Star Wars, a conversation that resulted in my Jedi Academy trilogy (my first* New York Times *bestseller) as well as dozens of subsequent projects for Lucasfilm. Then Betsy moved on to Warner Books, where she bought my Saga of Seven Suns, which I consider my science fiction masterpiece.*

So when you read this story, think about the impact it had on my career!

REST IN PEACE

—I—

Every shadowy corner hides a thousand assassins.

Prez Siroth stopped suddenly in the darkness just inside the crumbling catacombs. He narrowed his eyes. He sniffed the air, drawing in the earthy scent of shadows, the lingering smells that would attract rats.

The guards quickly stumbled to a halt to avoid running into Siroth, then backtracked to form a protective ring around him. In the dim torchlight, Siroth could see that their eyes had gone wide. "What is it, my Prez?" asked the captain of the guard.

With ice-blue eyes, Siroth gazed silently into the broken tunnels for a moment longer. Wispy long hair hung to his shoulders, untrimmed. Sacks of grain had been piled up against the collapsing walls to shore them up against negligence. In the older sections of the tunnels, worn and fragmented flagstones lined the floors … but the newly dug catacombs offered only hard-packed dirt, which might easily muffle the footsteps of someone in hiding.

"Light two more torches." Siroth turned to glare at the fat, dirty man leading them deeper into the tunnels. "And if *he* makes a single unexpected move—slit his throat." Siroth's lips curved in a snarl/smile.

Rathsell, the fat man, tittered nervously. "You are too suspicious, my Prez."

"I have held my reign for *six years now*. You can never be too suspicious!"

"Nothing to fear from me, my Prez. Wait until you see what the children dug up. It's a great discovery!" Behind Rathsell's grin, Siroth could see the splotchy red of anxiety on the man's face.

"Children? I left *you* in charge of storing grain down here—"

"Oh yes, my Prez! But the children stay in here to kill the rats and to dig out more tunnels. You can be sure I gave them a sound beating when I learned they never told me about the vault they found. And then I came to you without delay!"

Siroth's voice was cold. "Why would you come to tell *me*?"

Caught off guard, Rathsell smeared his palms on his worn and dirty trousers. He wore no shirt to cover his folds of fat; a clean red barrette was clipped to his ear as an ornament. "I … um, well, my Prez, there are some who would pay great rewards for something like this …"

Siroth scowled. "What's so special about this vault?"

Fat Rathsell's eyes lit up, as if he was about to share the secrets of the universe. "It is from *Before*!"

"So are all the old buildings." The Prez sounded bored.

"But this vault is untouched!"

"If it isn't worth my while, I'm going to let Grull play with you."

A flicker of terror passed across the fat man's eyes, but he forced another smile. "It *will* be worth your while, my Prez."

Their footsteps suddenly became muffled as they passed from the last flagstones to the bare earth of the new tunnels. The shadows grew deeper.

"What can you possibly want with a reward? You already have more than you deserve here."

Siroth saw that fat Rathsell was struggling to put on his kindest face. "You may remember, my Prez, how ugly a woman my wife is, with three arms and all. With a nice reward, perhaps I can buy myself a prettier one. That's all I want with my humble life."

"Uh-huh," Siroth said.

Suddenly the Prez's heart twisted into knots, clenching and thumping as if choking on an air pocket. Pain shot through his chest, radiating like electrified wires from his sternum. He held his breath. He kept his face molded in a mask of self-control, showing nothing. Bloodwind roared in his ears; flecks of color tinged with black swirled behind his eyes. His mind began to pound, and he felt like he was rising, floating, swallowed up in a great maw more deadly than any assassin's knife. Siroth gritted his teeth as Rathsell led him onward, with the guards close behind. The Prez fought with himself not to stumble. He reached inside his tunic and massaged the long, lumpy scar in the center of his chest until the pain subsided.

Again? Already? he thought to himself. *I should have known a peasant's heart wouldn't last more than two years.*

The pain backed off again, momentarily tamed, and Siroth strode forward with a grim enthusiasm he hadn't felt in a long time. The undulating torchlight reflected off a metal door set into the left wall as they turned a corner. Rathsell made a show of opening the heavy door. The guards stood tense and silent. He gestured for Siroth to enter. "My Prez—?"

"No. You go first. Then three guards. Then I'll come. The rest of the guards will follow me."

Rathsell hastily agreed and entered the vault as pale light began to flow automatically from darkened plates along the interior walls. The guards uttered their astonishment as they followed. Siroth came next, trying to adjust his eyes to the light splashing on his face.

The Prez forcibly resisted expressing his awe. The glistening walls of the chamber were a polished white, cleaner than anything he had seen in his entire life. The faint, not-unpleasant smell of ammonia and chemicals floated just at the limits of perception, driving back the odors of dirt and mustiness from the catacombs. The floor of the chamber, though hard, somehow swallowed the sound of his footsteps as he walked farther into the room.

Most of the crowded floor space was taken up by eight oblong cases like crystalline coffins. Each contained a motionless human form. Siroth stepped cautiously among them, looking through transparent walls. The bodies inside seemed like wax sculptures, pale, not breathing ... dead? For an indefinable reason, Siroth didn't think so.

The guards stood in silent awe, and Rathsell rubbed his hands together in delight. The fat man ran mumbling among the machines along one wall, closely inspecting a series of lights lazily pulsing on and off, as if he knew what he was doing. Siroth didn't like the look of Rathsell's confidence. Beside each of the coffins squatted a bulky control box that appeared to monitor the unmoving figure within.

One crystal coffin had been positioned slightly in front of the other seven, and Siroth moved slowly toward it, running his fingertips along the polished surface of the glass cases. The central human looked like a god come to Earth: his perfect face was capped with delicately styled black curls, and his physique was large and muscular, seeming to radiate power, even helpless as he was. The Prez rapped his knuckles on the glass in defiance, to show his own superiority.

"Do you like that one, my Prez?" Rathsell said. The fat man's eyes gleamed and his chins bobbed in a disgusting way. "I can make him speak to you. Watch—he can talk even while he's asleep!"

Intoxicated with his own good fortune, Rathsell rushed to a console under a blank patch on the wall opposite Siroth. Making certain the Prez was looking, Rathsell singled out a large green button surrounded by inward-pointing arrows; it simply cried out to be pushed, and Rathsell obliged.

Images began to form within the depths of the screen, rapidly crystallizing into a picture of the eight sleepers—awake now—standing together in spring-green jumpsuits and each bearing gleaming eyes and a blank smile. The picture made Siroth think of the old family photographs that scavengers sometimes burned in their hovels because the fumes made them feel lightheaded.

The godlike man with the dark hair stepped forward, looking out of the screen with gleaming black eyes as deep as the universe. The Prez stifled a shiver.

"Greetings, men of the future. If you have come to witness our awakening, we welcome you in peace and friendship. You will not remember us, for we are merely dreamers and have left no record of ourselves behind."

The leader smiled, pausing for a breath. The others smiled as well. "I am Draigen, and these seven others are with me: a surgeon, an artist, an agricultural engineer, an historian, a singer, a mathematician, a writer. We come from a troubled time, with many needs and many problems. But we could see that this bureaucratic nemesis was dying at its core, strangled in its own red tape, lost within its own intricacies. Within a century, the serpent would have finished devouring itself. We had to *wait* until nothing would hinder us from doing what we had been called to do."

Siroth found the man's voice charismatic, dangerous. Draigen's words seemed laced with fever, and his dark eyes glistened. The other green-suited dreamers stood behind him as if in awe of their leader's vision.

"We collected our knowledge and all the tools we would need to reshape our world after the demise of bureaucracy—and came here to slumber for a hundred years. Now we shall help *you* to rebuild the world as it was meant to be, without opposition, without cruelty, with freedom and justice for all mankind!"

The tape finished, and the shining white wall absorbed the image. Siroth stood motionless, pondering, with a distasteful smile locked on his face.

He silently reached out to take a stainless-steel club from the nearest guard and hefted the heavy pipe in his hand. He stepped over to Draigen's case, looking down at the strangely impotent form of the dreamer. Siroth swung the pipe down, smashing the crystal coffin above the dark-haired dreamer's face.

The Prez smiled.

Siroth took a calculated breath before he went berserk, plunging from one case to the next, smashing them, swinging the club down to crush the monitor-computers, hurling the pipe like a spear through the screen at the far wall. He kicked at shards of crystal, dodging sparks and plunging through smoke.

The guards watched dispassionately. Fat Rathsell sobbed in horror, confusion, and genuine loss. He might have wanted to stop the Prez, but he dared not.

Panting, Siroth picked up the club again and casually handed it back to the guard. The rebellious pain behind his sternum returned, but he had more important things to attend to. He tried to ignore the pain, mentally and uselessly cursing his heart. But the pounding knives in his chest remained.

Siroth turned his cold eyes on Rathsell, motioning to the guards. "Take him away and execute him. For most vile treason!"

Rathsell's face blanched to a pasty white, as if his skin had just turned into gruel. The guards grabbed his arms and began to drag him out. The fat man struggled in disbelief and confusion, but his feet found no purchase on the polished white floor. The decorative red barrette dropped from his ear.

Siroth held up a hand. "But kill him *quickly*. That's his reward."

Rathsell made other sounds, but could form no coherent words.

In the shadows of the catacombs, haggard and dirt-encrusted children with eyes sunken from near starvation watched Rathsell's plight, and snickered.

Forgetting all else, Siroth stared down into the crystalline case containing Draigen's body. Tiny flecks of broken glass frosted the dreamer's brow like snowflakes, but otherwise the body was unharmed. The Prez reached out to touch Draigen's large, muscular arm, admiring the lean body. The mold for this one had been shattered long ago in the holocaust.

Rathsell's screams reverberated through the winding catacombs, then abruptly stopped.

The convulsive pain in Siroth's chest took a long time to subside, but he managed to smile as he ran his fingernail on Draigen's motionless breastbone. "Such a helpful dreamer. I may be able to use you after all."

—II—

Deep in the Prez's chambers, the blind old man sat in front of a crackling fire, letting the warmth bathe his face. He heard one branch, somewhere near the back, settle heavily into the ash. The wood snapped and sputtered as it burned. It smelled a little green.

He felt a disturbance in the room, the barely noticed shifting of air currents. He tensed, trying to restrain his smile. "You sound weary, Siroth."

He heard the Prez slap his hand down on the tabletop in exasperation and defeat. "Dammit, Grull! How did you know it was me?"

"Your breathing is very distinctive. Look on the tabletop at the new device I designed."

The Prez looked at the scattered papers on the table. Grull stood up from the chair by the fire and unerringly found his way over to Siroth.

"See, the loops fit around the victim's fingers, toes, wrists and ankles, and are then attached to those wheels of varying sizes in such a way that merely by turning the wheels we can wrench every finger, every toe out of joint, one by one, until we have achieved the desired results."

Siroth nodded. "You still have trouble closing up your circles, Grull." He dropped the sketch back on the tabletop and went to sit in the old man's chair by the fire. The Prez cracked his knuckles as he watched the firelight. "What happened while I was gone?"

"Well, the fukkups staged another revolt, trying to break out of their pen and clamoring to be freed, again. They said they wanted to see you."

"And?"

"Three of them seemed to be the instigators. I had them strung upside down over the pens and then burned alive. The rest calmed down."

"Anything else?"

"Well, two men rode up, emissaries from Prez Claysus."

"That water-spined fairy!" Siroth snorted.

"Remember Praetoth, the architect who rebuilt your castle when it collapsed two years ago? You've still got him in the dungeons, you know. It seems the home of Prez Claysus has likewise fallen in on itself, and his emissaries are 'honorably requesting' that we should work together for the common good of all. Claysus wants to borrow our architect."

Siroth laughed. "That sounds exactly like him! Have you replied yet?"

Grull smiled broadly. "I tied the emissaries backwards on their horses with their own entrails, and sent them back."

"A straightforward enough answer."

Grull made his way back to the chair beside the fire, found that Siroth was already sitting in it, and scowled as he paced the room instead. "So what did Rathsell want?"

The Prez briefly explained about the vault from *Before*, the dreamers, and how he had destroyed the apparatus.

"A wise decision, my Prez. We don't want any empire-building dreamers from *Before* ruining all you've done. Everything in that vault should be burned."

"No." Grull detected a pensive note in Siroth's voice, though he could not see the expression on the other's face. "I have saved them, especially their leader. I want his heart. And you can have his eyes."

Grull bit his breath back, stunned. Siroth rarely surprised him anymore.

"Doctor Sero has given me one new heart, but it is already dying. And now, with this godlike dreamer's heart … I will be *strong*! You should see him, Grull! He's perfect. Up until now you said you wouldn't have new eyes if they had to come from a peasant, or from a fukkup who had five or six extra eyes. But now it's *perfect*! You'll have your sight back, Grull. After sixty years."

The blind man sat in silence, thinking about sight and Siroth's not-quite-correct reasons as to why he had denied new eyes before. Grull had lost his sight during the holocaust, six decades before. He had never looked upon what *After* was like. He wasn't sure he wanted to.

—III—

The dark-haired dreamer lay on the surgical table, stretched out like a mannequin as Doctor Sero inspected him disdainfully. Rigor had shut Draigen's black eyes, trapping his Utopian visions beneath the thin lids. Later, before the body could begin to spoil, the doctor would have to cut those eyes out and preserve them for Grull.

Siroth turned his head and sat up on another surgical table beside Draigen's. "Are you about ready, Sero?"

The doctor looked up from his assortment of medical tools, staring with swollen, bug-like eyes. "Yes, my Prez."

"And you *will* be successful?"

"I was successful the last time. You're a quick-healer, Prez Siroth. I explained it all to you before—the chromosome-scrambling viruses that filled the air after the holocaust poisoned our gene pool. Most of the aberrations turned out like the fukkups, but what went wrong with them, went *right* with you. You know what happens whenever you get injured." The doctor's voice betrayed his own lack of interest in the lecture, in the upcoming operation, and in the Prez himself.

"I've been practicing this operation for the past week. Out of ten tries, three have survived. All three were quick-healers."

Sero ran a finger along the scar on Siroth's bare chest, thinking how much it reminded him of an artist's signature on a masterpiece. His father had been a great surgeon from *Before* who had taught

Sero from the books and implements found in the old buildings. But his father hadn't been good enough to heal himself of his own death wound. And now Sero had to discover all the lost surgical arts by hit-or-miss vivisection.

The Prez narrowed his eyes and reached out to snatch the doctor's fingers away from the old scar, holding them in a brutal grip with his clenched fist. "Grull will be here with my guards during the operation," he hissed.

"My father used to say a surgeon's hands are sacred things, never to be touched by another," Sero said almost offhandedly. "My dear Prez, if I saw you were about to die during this operation, I'd plunge a scalpel deep into my own throat, rather than let Grull touch me."

Siroth stiffened, and the doctor pushed him flat on the table. "But *relax*, my Prez. When you awaken, you'll have the heart of the biggest dreamer of all!"

His eyes took so long to focus.

An apparition stood in front of him, dressed in the spring-green uniform of the dreamers. Draigen! No ... one of the others on the tape, one who had lain sleeping at the far end of the vault. The dreamer's eyes were filled with tears and rage. "Why? *Why!*"

Siroth then saw Grull beside the dreamer, and he began to suspect that the apparition might be real after all.

"Guess who woke up," Grull said.

Siroth passed out again.

Grull took the arm of the seething dreamer, turning him away from the unconscious Prez. Blood still spattered the operating room, smeared into the wood with wet rags but not quite cleaned after the operation.

"Come along now. Let's have a chat." The blind man leaned heavily on the dreamer's arm, hoping to calm the other man. Grull guided him down a corridor where smoky torches had long ago replaced broken fluorescent lights.

"What's your name, dreamer? I am Grull."

The old torturer could not see the tears drying on the dreamer's cheeks, but he could feel the breath of the man's answer on his own face. "Aragon."

"How come you're still alive, Aragon, when none of your other companions woke up?"

"All our stations were monitored by delicate computer systems, with triple-nested backup functions. It's more of a surprise that no one else survived." Aragon took a deep breath, and Grull felt a faint shudder pass through the other's body. "My station was at the far end of the vault. Maybe your paranoid Prez had exhausted himself by then."

They said nothing more until they emerged into the open air from Siroth's great square castle that bore the crumbling words *First National Bank* across its façade. They walked through a courtyard and Aragon stopped short, but Grull pulled him over to a stone bench in the sun. The stunned dreamer didn't resist.

The *First National Bank* castle rested at the top of a gentle hill, just high enough that the view stretched out to engulf the ruins of a city below. Streets had turned into lawns; roofs and walls had collapsed. An accidental forest of fast-growing, genetically engineered trees had grown up alongside the buildings.

The blind man let Aragon stare speechless down at the dismal panorama for long moments. The dreamer finally managed to choke out a whisper, sounding betrayed. "How long has it been?"

"Sixty years." He sat down on the cold stone seat and patted it, motioning the dreamer to join him. "I was too young to remember much about those few hours of madness when *Before* turned to *After*. Somebody screaming 'Get To the Shelter! Get To the Shelter!' Something exploded in front of my face, spectacular, searing white fire, sort of a grand finale to my eyesight.

"I was eight years old. For a little while I lived on whatever I could find. Then a religious cult, 'The Apocalypse Now,' found me and took me in. They believed they had been chosen to rebuild the world exactly as God intended it to be, to the death of all nonbelievers. And here I was, a blind child who had miraculously survived the holocaust. Perfect prophet material."

He shrugged a little to himself, and had no way of knowing whether Aragon was paying attention. "But I never turned out to be what they wanted. I was smart enough to know I'd never make it alone, so I played along with them. The Apocalypse Now treated me with respect—they all died by the age of thirty from cancer or genetic defect, but I just kept getting older.

"The fukkups were being born then, every one of them with the wrong number of arms, legs, even heads. Something about the war, biological weapons rearranging everyone's genes. Most of the mutants were so messed up they died anyway, or the mothers would throw them away, or kill them—but some survived. At first they must have hidden in the ruins or in the burned-out forest, horrified of themselves and the others of their kind. But then they started banding together, venting their anger at the normals. You know, terrorizing the countryside, mutilating people to look like themselves.

"Of course, I had a distorted view of it all, living in the Apocalypse Now. But there were plenty of other hunter groups, or communes, or scavengers, and they all came together for defense under a new leader, the Prez. Prez Mecas, Siroth's father, managed to unite his realm with a few other Prezes and with the Apocalypse Now. Together, they managed to cut the marauding fukkups to pieces. Now we keep them all in a huge corral where they can rot on their feet for all we care. Sero uses them for his experiments, or Siroth plays with them on hunting games now and then. They've been made pretty much harmless."

Aragon didn't seem to know which expression to keep on his face. He sat silent, stunned, as if looking desperately for some way to survive his despair.

"After the fukkups were brought under control, the Prezes took to fighting among themselves—assholes, none of them had any *real* concept of leadership. Any given Prez might last a year or two before he was assassinated. Prez Mecas was a lousy dictator—didn't know how to hold people in fear of him, never listened to anyone's counsel because he was too busy with his own pleasure. He didn't know how to be careful.

"I had become Master Torturer of the Apocalypse Now. I went to his son Siroth because I knew I could train him to be a real Prez. We trapped Mecas in his chambers, tangling him in his own sheets, and fed him to the fukkups. Siroth didn't show any regret whatsoever. I knew he would make it, then. Love is one thing a Prez cannot have."

"A good leader should love his people above all else," Aragon muttered, but he seemed too stunned to begin an argument. "My God, the mess we left behind was the Golden Age of Mankind."

Grull frowned. "How can you possibly call *Before* a mess, compared to what we have now?"

"We still had plenty of problems. I kept finding perfect solutions to them—but people wouldn't *listen*. They said my solutions were 'wildly unrealistic' and that I should come down to the Real World. I never found their Real World—I found Draigen instead."

Grull detected bitterness in the dreamer's words, but they took a subtly different tone, as if Aragon were no longer speaking from his heart, but from a speech Draigen had given. He heard the dreamer stand up and shout toward the ruins at the bottom of the hill. "We understood things nobody else did. We could plan ahead. We could see the wisest things to say and do—but everyone was so bogged down with whether the books balanced, whether they would get the promotion, what kind of deodorant to use, what to cook for dinner ... they never learned to understand life. We *understood* it!" He turned back to Grull, sitting motionless on the stone bench.

"I became an agricultural engineer, a damn good one, to solve the world's food shortage—and you know what? Nobody *wanted* me to! All the money spent to bring huge tractors, better seed, and fertilizer to poor countries—and the minute we turn our backs the savages let our shining tractors sit there unused while they go back out in the fields with their oxen and scratch plows, because 'that was the way their forefathers grew the crops.' Nobody seemed to remember that their forefathers died of malnutrition. They *wanted* to starve! How can a perfect solution work if people don't cooperate?"

"People, by nature, don't cooperate," Grull muttered.

"The seven of us under Draigen cooperated," Aragon said defensively. "All lonely revolutionaries, totally devoted to saving the world ... but the world wasn't ready for us. Draigen had his dream. We were to make the world pure and good and right for all mankind. Why didn't anyone else want it that way? How can I carry on that great vision by myself?" he moaned.

Grull directed his sightless eyes into the breeze. "Now do you understand why Prez Siroth could never let your group wake up?"

Aragon shuddered, as if suddenly remembering who Grull was. The old man let the dreamer sit in an uninterrupted, awkward silence, waiting for him to deal with his churning emotions. Aragon surprised the blind old man by sighing in apparent defeat.

"Your Prez has taken Draigen's heart. And now you're going to take his eyes. Isn't that enough?"

Grull found himself thinking back to the dim childhood memories he normally kept tightly locked away, answering a different question. "My mother had a large flower garden filled with roses and snapdragons. My father took me to the big city once … I can still feel how *tall* those shining buildings were." He fell silent for a moment, then. "Yes, I would like to see again. But I doubt Doctor Sero is capable of performing the transplant."

Aragon looked at him, raising his eyebrows. "Surely if this surgeon can transplant a heart, he can give you new eyes?"

"Siroth is a quick-healer. Sero could probably have *dropped* the heart into his chest and he would have survived. I am just a blind old man."

The dreamer smiled, and Grull could smell a strange excitement in Aragon's body scent. "Vesalius, the surgeon with our group, could have performed the operation easily. Too bad your Prez killed him. But we still have our medical knowledge in the vault, in a place even Siroth couldn't harm. That way we can be of *some* use to the world. Your Doctor Sero can study it.

"I want you to *see* what you've done to our Utopia."

—IV—

Aragon wandered, absorbing the immensity of *After* and feeling like a glass Christmas-tree bulb that had just been stepped on.

He went alone through the ruins, gazing at unrepaired buildings poised on the verge of collapse.

He went to the fukkup pen, where living lumps of twisted flesh screamed for their freedom, or at least an end to agony.

He returned to the smashed vault where all his dreams lay destroyed, and he wept.

The dreamer came to Siroth, now almost recovered from his surgery. "Prez Siroth, I have a few things I wish to say to you."

The Prez scowled with a "here it comes" expression on his face and sat up in his bed, waiting in silence. Aragon sighed, then sat down. "But they are hateful things, and better left unsaid. Hate destroys, and enough has been destroyed already. It is better if I just forgive you."

Siroth almost choked in surprise. "*Forgive*? You're a coward."

The dreamer looked at him for a long moment, holding the other's disturbed gaze. "It was the bravest thing I could have said."

Siroth tried to get out of bed. "I can still kill you, dreamer!"

"Then you are hopelessly lost." Aragon stood firm. Siroth looked uncomfortable. He ran his fingers through his silky-fine blond hair.

"Where's Grull?"

"He is with your Doctor Sero ... receiving Draigen's eyes, remember?"

The Prez's face purpled with rage, and he swung himself out of bed. "What? He would leave my realm without someone in charge?"

"You were almost recovered."

"I need his counsel!"

"Think for yourself, Siroth."

The Prez sat back down on the bed, laughing darkly to himself. "And what do *you* want, dreamer? My lands? To be Prez yourself? Now's your perfect chance—Grull is gone, and I'm weaker than I should be. Go on, kill me! Make yourself Prez, and see how long you survive."

"No. With Draigen and the others gone, our dream is dead."

"Then what *do* you want?"

"I want you to change."

Aragon could see that had some effect on the other man, and he quickly continued. The Prez looked baffled, but not quite impatient. "Maybe I can make some small difference by myself. Have you ever walked out among the people? Actually *been* with them?"

"Too dangerous."

"How can you know what's going *on* out there?"

Siroth shrugged. "My guards report back."

Aragon sighed. "It isn't the same. Do you know that the old buildings are rotting, and another one collapses almost every other week? Do you know the horrors in that place where you keep the mutants corralled like so many animals? How they scream in agony, tear at each other, kill to eat the slop your guards throw at them, crying for freedom with even their dying breath!"

Visionary fire burned in the dreamer's eyes as his anger rose. "And the *people*, Siroth! Children *live* down in those filthy catacombs you found us in! Families starve because they cannot grow enough food. I have even seen evidence of cannibalism!"

"So what?"

"Don't you care?"

"No."

"Siroth, you must change!"

"My system works. I've been leader here for *six* years, with Grull's help. How would you change me?"

"Feel some compassion for the people you rule. They are your subjects—you should care for them!"

The Prez's voice was sour. "They don't care for me."

"If you were kind, and beneficial, seeing that their children are fed and educated, that their homes are repaired—Grull tells me you have a master architect in this castle, but you keep him under house-arrest! What good is he doing here?"

"I think you're retarded, and you understand nothing! You want to make me into another jelly-spined Prez Claysus!" Then Siroth laughed. "I wish you had met my father, dreamer—then you wouldn't think I'm so bad!"

Aragon raised his eyebrows, trying another tactic. "In those six years, how many assassination attempts have been made on you? How many?"

"Too many to count. But I *survived*—that's all that matters."

Aragon continued to press. "Grull says that Claysus has held his lands for eight years now. How many attempts have been made on him?"

Siroth looked up, frowning. "None ... but then I cannot be completely sure."

Aragon folded his arms in triumph. The Prez looked upset and stood up to pace the room, rubbing his hands together as if he were trying to get rid of something. "I'd rather trust what Grull has always told me."

"Grull showed you only *one* way—the only way he knows. But I'll teach you others, and I will make you change."

Siroth scowled, but refused to face the dreamer, continuing to stare into the fire. "*That* is exactly why I wanted to kill your group."

The wooden door smacked against the wall of the Prez's chambers as a guard burst into the room. "My Prez! The fukkups are going wild! It's bad this time. They already killed two guards, and they are smashing the fences in the corral!"

Siroth paled in alarm, and his eyes flickered from side to side as if searching for Grull. But only Aragon stood there, letting a trace of his self-satisfaction show through.

"*Try* it my way, Siroth, and I'll show you it can work! It's obvious Grull's solution has no effect."

"And if it doesn't work?" The Prez scowled.

Aragon nervously raised his head high, looking proud. "I'll stake my life on it!"

Siroth laughed in delight. "Now *that's* what I like to hear! All right then, come on—I want to watch this!"

Breathlessly, Aragon turned to grab the guard's arm and began to pull him toward the door. Siroth quickly dressed, flailing into a threadbare robe to cover the scars of his recent surgery.

The mutants silenced themselves with a hushed grumble as Prez Siroth arrived. They pushed closer to the spiked fence, leering, some drooling from mouths crowded with two tongues. And these were the ones that had survived birth.

Aragon could not force away his revulsion and broke out in a thin sweat as he pondered how Draigen would have dealt with such a situation. The Prez stood calmly, surrounded by his guards and looking around with his sharp cold eyes. He seemed curious and oddly satisfied, as if pleased that he could try a truly unexpected leadership tactic and possibly get rid of the dreamer at the same time.

Aragon swallowed and finally spoke. The fukkups quieted as his voice drew strength. "Who speaks for you? Do you have a leader?"

The mutants milled about, but did not answer. Then Aragon remembered what Grull had done to the leaders during the last insurrection.

"All right, then we speak to all of you. You are clearly

dissatisfied here—Prez Siroth offers you an alternative." He took a breath and then spoke rapidly, anticipating that the Prez would stop him at any moment. "We will release you, give you your freedom— but you will have to *work*. Many of you have committed grave crimes against humanity, but we feel you have served your punishments. Up until now, we have used our own provisions to feed you—once freed, you will have to fend for yourselves. You will have to repair the old buildings for your homes. You will have to work the land, grow crops." He hesitated, thinking of the unfairness, but realizing Siroth would have to gain something other than a clear conscience from the bargain. "And we will let you keep *half* of your produce for yourselves."

The fukkups stood stunned for an instant. Siroth waited, glanced at his guards, and firmly believed the dreamer was sticking his head more firmly on the chopping block. The Prez picked up the speech as the mutants began to cheer. "*But*—this is a trial period for you. The fate of all your children depends on how you behave during the next few weeks." His voice was as hard and as sharp as a razor. "If *any* one of you harms a man, in *any* way, or does damage to property, or tries to flee—you will *all* be returned to this pen, never to be released again!"

Aragon spoke up quickly, shouting into the brief lull. "But you have nothing to fear if you're willing to work for your freedom. Isn't it better to work the land, produce food for everyone, than to rot here? Those are the terms—do you agree to all of them?"

Wild cheering almost deafened him as all the mutants clamored at once. He smiled at the Prez. "See, they're satisfied."

"You may very well have just sealed our doom. We still have to see if they'll keep their word." Then Siroth watched them with his darting eyes, and he let another smile steal across his face. "But just to make sure, I'm going to have you go live with them, without protection, for the first few weeks."

Siroth's smugness was squashed when Aragon calmly said, "All right."

—V—

Grull tried valiantly to be patient, commanding his fingers not to fidget. For days Doctor Sero had been cutting away his bandages, one by one; and now the old man could see grayish light behind his wrappings. To him, this was even worse than blindness, because now he knew his eyes might work.

The old man sat on the cold stone bench in the courtyard. The shadow of the *First National Bank* castle stretched out over him as the sun fell behind the building. He could sense Siroth beside him as Doctor Sero fumbled with the last bandages, removing one thread at a time. Impatiently, Grull slapped away the doctor's hand and ripped off the bandages himself.

After sixty years, he couldn't possibly have remembered what sight was like. Now even the blurred images shone with wonder as his aching mind tried to take in six decades' worth of light. The deepest shadows were blindingly bright. His thin but strong hands instinctively reached up to cover Draigen's eyes, *his* eyes now, but he drew them away, wanting to see more.

The forms and shapes slowly focused themselves, but he didn't know what he expected to see. He remembered only scattered visions from his childhood, the flower garden, the shining city with sky-scraping buildings of steel and glass. Grull blinked several times, and each time the world became clearer. Then he looked down upon the ruined city, the broken buildings, the weeds pushing up through crumbling streets and sidewalks.

The vision became indistinct again as his new eyes filled with water. Funny, he had never thought that simple tears would ruin anyone's eyesight. He blinked several times and tried to force his breathing to follow a slower rhythm. He had *never* guessed the effect would be this profound, and it embarrassed him.

Grull sat in silence for a long, long moment, and then turned to the man he recognized to be the Prez. "We really made a mess of things, didn't we?"

The guards looked askance at Aragon—dirt-smeared and clothed in the torn rags of his spring-green jumpsuit—but they moved aside to let him enter Prez Siroth's chamber. Two of the guards accompanied him, but Aragon smiled with self-satisfaction and ignored them.

Siroth looked up from the old-fashioned mousetrap he had been playing with on the table. Sunlight slanted in through the narrow and drafty windows of the chamber. "I'm surprised to see you still alive, dreamer. You didn't strike me as someone who could handle much hardship." He lifted the thin metal bar against the strong pull of the string, and let it fall shut with a loud snap against the wood. "You smell like shit."

"That's what I've been living in for the past week." Aragon looked tired, and hungry, but beatifically satisfied. The gleam of despair had faded from behind his eyes, to be replaced by the barest shadow of the visions that had haunted Draigen's eyes.

"I'm not a great leader who could have changed the world, like Draigen was. But I *am* an agricultural engineer! This is what I was trained for—to improve your godawful methods of farming. You don't have enough people to adequately work all the available land, and right now you split your fields in half, working one side and letting the other lie fallow for a year. With the mutants, I am showing them how to take the simple step of dividing the fields into thirds, plant grain on one third, legumes on another, and leave the last one fallow—just think of what a difference it can make! And there are efficient ways to use the fertilizers you have—just dumping manure all over the place isn't going to solve anything, you know. I can change that, too. Fewer people will starve."

Siroth pressed his fingertips together and turned to face Aragon. "And what do the fukkups have to say about all this? Have you been whipping them yourself? How do you expect them to obey?"

"When you treat them as human beings, Siroth, tell them the *reason* you're doing something and *show* them how it will help them —they work by their own free will. You can ask your own guards: in the first week, the mutants have not done a thing even your paranoid watchers could call dangerous.

"If you play this thing right, Siroth, your subjects will stop hating you. It's the difference between being a dictator and being a king."

Siroth raised the mousetrap again, let it snap down, almost catching his own finger. Dangerous. Playing with a dangerous toy, like this dreamer who was disrupting Siroth's philosophy by damnably proving an unconscionable theory, that the methods of leadership could still function the same way they did *Before*.

"I am impressed, dreamer. I'll admit that. I wish I could talk to Grull about this." But now Grull was gone as well, all because of this dreamer, and the other dreamer's eyes.

Cleaning, fixing, watching, polishing. Grull saw to it the *First National Bank* castle was repaired, loose stone replaced, new mortar added. He cleaned the interior. He removed all the weeds from the courtyard, and swept the flagstones at least once a day. He watched the fukkups as they tore down the fence surrounding their former pens and began to plow the land according to the guidelines Aragon had given them.

Siroth joined him, standing with folded arms and staring down the gentle hill at the remnants of the city below. Grull knew the Prez had come, but he waited for Siroth to speak first.

"Would you ever have believed the fukkups are actually keeping their agreement?" Siroth snorted a little, but to Grull it sounded somewhat forced. "They're working harder than any of our farmers. The food supply should be drastically increased from last year. I'll have to see to it that the children dig out more tunnels for storage."

Grull wanted to answer, but couldn't think of anything to say. He did notice that the stone benches could use a little more polish. And dust had begun to collect on the flagstones again. Siroth continued awkwardly. "The fukkups haven't even caused trouble, Grull. I hear they're building their own little village in the forest. Why would they build new homes when it's so much easier just to repair the old ones?"

Grull sighed and turned to look at him with Draigen's dark eyes, oddly set where the glassy blind ones had been. "That's good to hear, my Prez. But for some reason state matters don't interest me much anymore."

The old man still had trouble correlating facial expressions with emotions, but he believed Siroth looked shocked by his comment. He tried to justify what he had said. "I'm an old man, Siroth. For sixty years I have meddled in political affairs, and now it's time to leave them to someone else. I might relax, and even enjoy my life for a change."

He found his broom and vigorously began sweeping out the cracks in the flagstones.

"Grull," Siroth sounded almost concerned, "Aren't you getting a little carried away?"

The old man paused for a moment. "Nonsense. I didn't wait sixty years to see an ugly world." He replaced the broom and started to walk away, mentally dismissing the Prez.

"Where are you going now?"

"I think I want to plant a flower garden."

—VI—

The army of Prez Claysus arrived swiftly, and unexpectedly, with barely enough warning for Siroth to take even the simplest of defense measures. The castle gate was barred, the guards were mustered—but not much else could be done. Claysus's soldiers stood waiting on the long hill.

Furious, Siroth stood beside the dreamer on the balcony, glaring at the opposing army. He turned red in the face, and his fists clenched convulsively, as if he were desperate to strangle something other than his knuckles. "All these weeks I've been doing *kindhearted* things—" he almost spat the words, "and the wimp has been gathering up an army against me! Because of *you* I'm going to be defeated by a jelly-spined pansy!"

Aragon seemed confused, and Siroth felt a little satisfaction through his despair. "But you told me Claysus is a kind, gentle humanitarian—"

"He *is*, dammit! That's why I never expected this!"

Outside the castle, one man strode forward from the body of the army, Prez Claysus shouting so that Siroth could hear. "Prez Siroth! You are vile and inhuman—and I can no longer tolerate your foul ways! I will tear your castle apart brick by brick and take the architect by force! Then you'll atone for your hideous actions. It's going to take a lot to avenge the murder of my peaceful ambassadors!"

Claysus drew a weapon from his side, a kind of spiked club which looked too heavy for him to use. The other Prez held it out threateningly as his army fidgeted.

Aragon looked at Siroth. "What has he got against you? What 'ambassadors' is he talking about?"

The Prez sighed. "His castle collapsed about a month ago. He sent two ambassadors to ask if he could borrow my architect."

"And?"

"And Grull slit their bellies or something, then sent them back to Claysus still bleeding."

The dreamer's face suddenly turned greenish. "But they were *ambassadors*! They had diplomatic immunity!"

"Not in my lands they don't."

Aragon sat down weakly. "Siroth, you must change your ways!"

But the Prez unleashed his anger. "And these past weeks, if I *hadn't* changed my ways, if I *hadn't* been kind and nice and good, if I *hadn't* let my guard down—"

Siroth stopped abruptly, staring out the window as he caught a glimpse of something in the forest. His eyes widened; his jaw even dropped a little bit.

From out of the wood emerged dozens of horrible misrepresentations of the human form, each with the wrong number of arms or legs or heads—and they were armed with pitchforks, rakes, hoes, scythes, anything they could find.

"Dreamer," Siroth whispered, "I think you'd better see this."

The fukkups marched slowly out of the trees, determined and numerous enough to surround Prez Claysus's startled troops. They did nothing, standing motionless, but threatening nonetheless. One of them, a two-headed man with one arm, cried out in a guttural voice that echoed oddly from his twin throats. "We will fight to defend our Prez!"

Siroth stood absolutely stunned, and his lips began to work seconds before his voice box did. "They're willing to fight for me! For me!"

Aragon laughed in delight. "Of course they are! You freed them. You showed them you *can* be kind, and they're expressing their appreciation."

Prez Siroth stood speechless for a long moment, watching the commotion in Claysus's ranks as the soldiers realized what the mutants were doing. He began to chuckle loudly. "Hah! Now I can crush him! With the fukkups and my guards, we can wipe out Prez Pansy once and for all!"

Aragon leaped to his feet. "No! No, that's not the *point!*" The Prez whirled in sudden rage again, looking as if the dreamer had gone insane. "Look, Siroth, it doesn't matter if you can defeat him or not! The point is you can do this *without* fighting!"

The Prez's scowl became even more unpleasant; but Aragon persisted. "Those mutants are standing up for you because of how you've changed! If you're a *real* leader, you won't have to resort to war."

"And how else am I supposed to get rid of Claysus?"

"You're the Prez. Solve it yourself, or else you've learned nothing."

Siroth's forehead wrinkled as he thought, anxiously looking around the room for someone to help him. "You expect me to give up Praetoth willingly? After all this?"

"And that will atone for what you did to the ambassadors?"

"Yes!" Aragon stared at him relentlessly, until the Prez looked away. "No. I will also send along some of my men to help him rebuild."

"You could offer to supply some of the materials ..." the dreamer suggested.

"Enough!" Siroth shouted, and Aragon decided not to press home the point. For a moment, he thought of Draigen's heart still beating after all, even in the chest of someone like Prez Siroth.

—VII—

Grull wandered in the courtyard, drifting gently through his vast flower garden. Everything had grown up tall and beautiful, in full bloom around the castle. He tended the flowers meticulously, pulling up a weed from between two brilliant orange snapdragons, humming to himself unconsciously.

He liked being alone. He knew Siroth was inside somewhere mediating a dispute between two mutants, but that didn't matter to him. Grull turned to look and noticed Aragon in the courtyard, sitting on one of the stone benches in his faded spring-green uniform, staring empty-eyed off into the distance. Grull followed the dreamer's line of sight, looking at the city and smiling faintly. Many of the buildings had been repaired and cleaned up, or torn down entirely. Grull decided he liked the encroaching forest after all. One of these days he was going to find a stream, and try fishing.

The old man bent down to inspect his rose bushes, and saw one bud just starting to bloom. He looked up at Aragon again, then at the city, then at the fukkups working the fields.

Grull snipped off the bloom and walked quietly over to Aragon, getting his attention. He extended the rose toward the dreamer's hand.

This story is darker and edgier, as well as more political, than my usual fare. But sometimes you need a good dystopia.

The expectations we place on our politicians seem impossible for any person to achieve. A candidate needs to be all things, know all walks of life, understand every segment of his constituency. How could one person achieve so much, without a little help?

JOB QUALIFICATIONS

Candidate Berthold Ossequin—the original—never made a move without being advised or cautioned by his army of pollsters, etiquette consultants, and style experts. Whether in public or in the privacy of his family estate, his every gesture and utterance was monitored. The avid media waited for Berthold to make any sort of mistake.

Elections would be held soon, and he must be absolutely perfect if he wanted to become the next Grand Chancellor of the United Cultures of Earth. According to surveys, he did have a slight lead over his opponent, though not enough to inspire complete confidence.

Berthold sat in an overstuffed chair that vibrated soothingly to calm him as he prepared to give a dramatic and insightful speech that his team had scripted for him. From rehearsing the speech before test audiences, the candidate knew where to modulate his voice and which points to emphasize in order to guarantee the strongest emotional impact.

Two young women, one at each hand, worked vigorously to trim his cuticles, file his nails, and give him that perfectly manicured appearance. A stylist worked with his bronze-brown hair and fixed every strand into place. Dieticians made careful recommendations about the foods Berthold should eat. Style experts met for at least an hour each evening to plan the candidate's wardrobe for the following day. No one could ever find fault with his appearance.

His stomach ached from eating too large and too rich a meal the night before, against the advice of his dieticians. He reminded himself to be careful with his facial expressions today, since a twinge of indigestion might show up as an inexplicable frown.

Berthold glanced up from the speech notes, looking at his chief advisor, who waited beside him. "How are the others coming, Mr. Rana?"

Rana nodded. "Precisely on schedule, sir. The others will be ready when they become necessary for your campaign."

The lash struck with a bite of electrical current that produced a fiery sting. Though the high-tech whip caused no actual harm, Berthold 12 felt as if his skin had been flayed. More misery, the same as the day before, and the day before that.

Fingernails cracked and bleeding, he stumbled under the heavy rock he carried while the hot sun pounded down. He could smell rock dust and his own sweat, heard the impatient shouts of the guards and the groans of other slave-prisoners. His mind ached, and Berthold 12 drove back the myriad shouted questions that hammered through his head. *Why was he here? What had he done?* The injustice burned like acid within him. *Why do I deserve this?*

Up and down the winding jagged canyon, layered limestone walls crumbled like broken knives. Work teams moved sluggishly, carting loads of quarried stone. Berthold 12 knew that machinery existed to do this sort of work, robots and automated conveyers could have taken away the rock. But this labor site wasn't about efficiency; it was about misery and punishment.

When the electrical whip snapped again across his shoulder blades, Berthold 12 dropped the rock and collapsed to his knees. The guard's hover platform came closer, and the armored man loomed over him. Beneath the polarized helmet, Berthold 12 could see only the guard's chin and a smile that showed square white teeth. "I can keep whipping you all day if that's what you want, prisoner."

"Please! I'm working as hard as I can." His throat was raw, his body a living mass of aches. "I don't even know why I'm here! I don't remember anything ... but this."

"Perhaps you committed the crime of amnesia." The guard chuckled at his joke, then threatened with the electrical whip again. "If your crime was bad enough that you blocked all memory of it from your head, then you probably don't want to remember."

Berthold 12 used his reserves of energy just to get back to his feet. He picked up the heavy limestone slab before the guard could lash him again. He could not recall any day that hadn't been this litany of labor and torture. He didn't know when this awful part of his life would end.

The greasy smells and comfortable bustle of the Retro Diner always made him feel at home. Berthold 6 stood by the heat lamps, adjusted his stained white apron, and pulled out a few guest checks. He quickly added up the totals while the short-order cook slopped extravagant nostalgic breakfasts onto warm plates and set them on a shelf. Low-carb pancakes and waffles, minimal-cholesterol eggs, reduced-fat bacon and sausage; such dietary innovations had made the traditional American breakfast into something the trendy customers could once again consume with great gusto.

The Retro Diner, modeled after popular eating establishments of the mid-twentieth century, had silver and chrome fittings, stools and booths upholstered with red naugahyde, table surfaces covered with speckled Formica. The menu featured re-creations of classic products. Many patrons got into the spirit by dressing up in old-fashioned costumes and smoking non-carcinogenic cigarettes. The place had a neighborly feel to it, a celebration of more innocent times. Berthold 6 felt right at home. He wouldn't have wanted any other job.

Carrying his loaded tray, Berthold 6 made a slight detour to snag the pot of coffee—weak, bitter, regular coffee, not one of the dramatically potent gourmet blends. "Here comes some morning cheer for you and your family, Eddie."

"Hey, Bert," said the jolly old man lounging back in his usual booth. "The waitresses around here are getting uglier every day."

"Yeah, but the waiters are certainly looking fine."

As the man grinned at the good-natured response, Berthold 6 delivered a stack of strawberry pancakes topped with a swirl of whipped cream, which looked like the eruption of a fruity volcano. He gave a cherry cola to the freckle-faced boy who sat next to his grandfather, refilled coffee cups around the room, then scooped dirty dishes from an unoccupied table into a bus tub.

Berthold 6 enjoyed working with regular folks. He liked serving people. He didn't earn much money, but enough to get by (though he wished some of his customers wouldn't *tip* like it was still 1953). He'd had a busy shift today, and tomorrow was his day off. Since he had no major plans, he thought he'd spend time with a few friends, talking, drinking beer, maybe watching sports or playing a game or two. Berthold 6 wasn't unduly stressed with the nonsense of unattainable goals or unrealistic ambitions. He was just an everyday guy, working an everyday job. A simple life.

"Order up!" the cook called with a clatter of dishes as he set the next breakfast under the heat lamps.

Before he was escorted off to a glamorous banquet, Candidate Berthold received Mr. Rana in his dressing chambers. The chief advisor brought documents for him to approve and sign. "This will take only a few moments, sir."

Berthold glanced down at the papers, shuffling from document to document. "Each one needs a signature?"

"Yes."

"Have they all been read for me?"

"Yes. And all necessary changes have been made."

"And do I agree with everything they say?"

"The statements are very much in line with your platform, sir." Rana formed a paternal smile. "You are, however, welcome to read any of them you like—in fact, I encourage it. The experience would be valuable for you."

Candidate Berthold gave a dismissive wave. "That won't be necessary. I'm already tired of the incessant paperwork, and I haven't even been elected yet." He laboriously began to sign each one. "I'll have plenty of time to learn after I get into office."

His head felt as if it would explode from so much information, but his passion for the material did not wane. His brain swelled with facts until all the bones of his skull—twenty-two bones in all, fourteen facial bones, eight cranial bones—seemed to pry apart.

For years Berthold 17 had been studying all aspects of medicine, from surgery to physical therapy to microbiology to anti-aging research. Even with proven teaching aids and somatic memorization devices, he struggled to remember the components of the human body and all the diseases and maladies that could afflict it.

He would be taking his exams in three days. His future depended on his performance for those vital hours.

Not that he had any doubts. He had been born for this. The prospect was daunting, but he always liked challenges. Upon first entering medical school, Berthold 17 made up his mind to become one of the best doctors ever. The higher the hurdles, the more effort he put into meeting them. He took great satisfaction in a reward that he'd *earned*. He had painted his own finish line and would never look back over his shoulder until he had crossed it. "Good enough" was not in his vocabulary.

Berthold 17 hit the books again, studying, studying. It would be a long night....

Meanwhile, in another campus library in another state, Berthold 18 sat surrounded by legal tomes, equally convinced that he would pass the upcoming bar exam with flying colors.

They were all dying of Ebola-X.

Berthold 3 could do nothing to save the afflicted villagers, but he forced himself to remain at their sides and comfort the men, women, and children in their final hours. He prayed with them, he listened to them, he comforted them. Not being a doctor, he was unable to do anything else ... and even the doctors couldn't do much.

Ebola-X, a particularly virulent strain of the hemorrhagic plague, had been genetically engineered by a brutal African warlord who, upon being deposed, had unleashed it among his own population. *As if their lives weren't already difficult enough*, Berthold 3 thought.

The villagers had impure drinking water, no electricity, no schools, no sanitation. Thanks to a persistent drought, almost certainly caused by the government and its shortsighted agricultural policies, the locals had lived on the edge of starvation for years. Immune systems and physical strength were at their nadir. When the Ebola-X arrived, it mowed down the village population as easily as if it were a jeep full of machine-gun-bearing soldiers. The thought of their situation tugged at his heartstrings. How could a person hold so much pain?

The hot and stifling hospital tent reeked with the stench of sweat, vomited blood, and death. Berthold 3 still heard every gasp, every moan, every death rattle. He sat quietly on a wooden stool, looking at the strained, pain-puckered face of a young mother. He read soothing passages aloud from the Bible, but he didn't think she could hear him or even understand the flowery English words. But he stayed with her anyway, changing the moist rag from her forehead, holding her shoulders when she needed to roll over and vomit.

The woman seemed to know she was dying. She had communicated with him about her three children, and Berthold 3 promised to look after them. He brushed her wiry hair, cooling her forehead again. He didn't have the heart to tell her that the children had died two days earlier.

Exhausted medics moved around him like zombies. They had too little medicine, certainly nothing effective against this epidemic. Berthold 3 tried to take as much busywork from the doctors as possible; he felt a calling to do his part, any part, so long as he helped these people. He had some first aid training, but the bulk of his schooling had prepared him to be a missionary, not a medic. Perhaps if he'd known ahead of time, Berthold 3 would have learned more practical skills. Even so, he wouldn't have turned from this obligation. In his heart he wanted to be here, wishing only that he could ease their suffering more effectively.

The dying woman reached out, her hand extended upward as if trying to grasp the sky. Berthold 3 took it in his own hand, folding his palms around hers and pressing her clenched fist against his chest so that she could feel the beating of his heart. She breathed twice more, arched her back, and then died.

Berthold 3 said a calm prayer over her, then stood. He had no time to rest, no time to grieve. He dragged his wooden stool over to the cot of the next patient.

Red tape. Bureaucracy. Incomprehensible forms in triplicate. Revisions to revisions to procedures that had already been revised repeatedly.

Job security.

Berthold 10 could not pretend his job was interesting, nor could he console himself with the thought that it was necessary. But it was a career, and he was good at it. Few people were so careful or detail-oriented; some of his coworkers called him anal retentive.

He sat in a small cubicle like thousands of others in this governmental office building for the United Cultures of Earth. Berthold 10 processed forms, input data, tracked regulations, and submitted comments and rebuttals to his counterparts in rival departments of the government in other cities around the world.

He was content to be sifting through paperwork in his own tiny cog in a single component of the sprawling wheels of government. It was good to have an understanding of how the details worked, instead of just the Big Picture, which the career politicians saw. Berthold 10 had no aspirations of running for office or being a great leader. He kept his sights on a shorter-term desire for an increase in pay grade. And he was sure to get it, with only a few more years of diligent service.

When the Urgent communiqué appeared in his IN box, Berthold 10 didn't at first pay special attention. Urgent matters went into a separate stack and he generally made an effort to take care of them first. But when he noticed that this message was addressed to him personally, from the office of the candidate, he read it with puzzlement, then amazement.

He was summoned to the candidate's mansion at a specified time and date. Berthold 10 looked around his drab cubicle at the never-changing piles of never-changing work. He didn't know what all this was about, and the letter did not explain. Official escorts would arrive to escort him. He smiled. At last his life was about to become more interesting.

With Mr. Rana beside him to operate the apparatus, Candidate Berthold cradled the head of the final clone in his lap. The man still twitched and struggled—Berthold had forgotten which number this was—but the clutching fingers could not remove the electrodes and transmitters pasted onto his temples and forehead.

"I'm glad this is the last one," the candidate said. "It's been an exhausting day."

One of the clones had struggled violently when the guards brought him in, forcing them to break his forearm. The snapped ulna—ah, the medical knowledge was coming in useful already!—had been unforeseen, but not necessarily a bad thing. In his pampered life Candidate Berthold had never experienced a broken bone; now, after absorbing the clone's experience, he knew what it felt like.

Memories and thoughts continued to drain out of the last clone's mind like arterial blood spurting from a slashed throat. The candidate held his duplicate's shoulders, felt everything surge into his own brain. What a difficult and painful life this one had lived! But the experiences certainly built character, giving him a firm moral foundation and impeccable resolve. It would be an excellent addition to Berthold's repertoire. Each detail made him more electable.

Since worldwide leaders guided so many diverse people, the citizens of the United Cultures of Earth demanded more and more from their rulers. To win a worldwide election, a candidate needed to demonstrate empathy for a multitude of different tiers of voters, from all walks of life. He had to be both an outsider and an insider. He had to understand privilege, to grasp the overall landscape of the government as well as the minutiae of how the bureaucracy worked. He was expected to have a passion for helping people, a genuine heart for the common man, and a rapport with celebrities and captains of industry.

Such expectations were simply impossible for a single human being to meet. Fortunately, thanks to the mental parity of clones, men such as Berthold Ossequin—and quite certainly all of his opponents—could live many diverse lives in parallel. The clones were turned loose in various situations where they gathered real-life experiences that went far beyond anything Candidate Berthold could have learned from teachers or books....

The last clone spasmed again, and his face fell completely slack, his mouth hung slightly open. His eyelids fluttered but remained closed. A few final, desperate thoughts trickled into Berthold's mind.

With a satisfied sigh, he peeled off the transmitter electrodes and motioned for the guards to carry away the limp body. All eighteen of the clones were now vegetables, empty husks wrung dry of every thought and experience. The comatose bodies would be quietly euthanized, and a newly enriched candidate would emerge for the final debates before the elections.

Berthold stood from his chair, completely well-rounded now, full of vicarious memories, tragic events, and pleasant recollections. The chief advisor looked into Berthold's eyes with obvious pride. "Are you ready, Mr. Candidate?"

Berthold smiled. "Yes. I have all the background I could possibly need to rule the world ... though once I get into office, we may decide to continue my education in this manner. Are there more clones?"

"We can always make more, sir."

"There's no substitute for experience."

Berthold stretched his arms and took a deep breath, feeling like a true leader at last. He issued a sharp command to his staff. "Now, let's go win this election."

Sometimes odd opportunities just appear out of nowhere—and as a writer, I usually accept the challenge.

I was asked to contribute a new story for a charity anthology about … teddy bears. How was I going to write a science fiction tale about a cute, cuddly, childhood artifact passed down from generation to generation, just smothering the ragged lump of fluff with love. Where's the drama in that?

In this case, an alien invasion helped.

REPOSITORY

Images evoked from an age-yellowed photograph, taken in 1939, now hidden among other childhood memories in a box garnished with cobwebs. The photograph is framed in wood, but the glass has broken long ago:

I doubt she'll let anything replace that tattered rag doll she lost." Elizabeth's father frowned at his wife, waiting to be convinced.

"Don't worry, John. With all the love and effort my mother put into making that Teddy Bear, she'll like it."

And when Elizabeth held the Teddy Bear for the first time, her exclamation of delight brought white-hot satisfaction to her parents.

"What's his name?" Elizabeth cried, as if she could not be close friends until she had been properly introduced.

"Morton," her father said. "That's a good name."

She hugged his clean brown fur, smelling the fresh material. She ran her finger along the seams, along his black button eyes. "I want my pitcher taken with him!"

Elizabeth slept with Morton, ate with Morton, traveled with Morton, talked to Morton. And the Teddy Bear accepted all the love she could give, uncomplaining.

"I'm going to love him forever and ever!" Elizabeth said.

"Or at least until you have a little girl of your own," her mother warned.

A scrapbook, filled with glossy black-and-white photos (circa 1960) taped in place with yellowed cellophane tape:

"She never lets go of that Teddy Bear of yours," Kristin's father said. "I don't think it's good for her to be so dependent on a stuffed animal."

"Don't be such an adult, Frank," Elizabeth chided. "Morton's the best friend I had when I was a little girl. We all need someone who's always there, someone who doesn't judge you or expect anything of you. Morton just sits there and takes all the love Kristin wants to offer. She'll outgrow him … I did."

In a white-enameled child's rocking chair, Kristin swayed back and forth, hugging her Teddy. And Morton soaked it up like a sponge.

A picture is worth a thousand words, and a thousand pictures tell the saga of a child's early life. Full-color polaroids lay scattered next to the granola on the apartment's only table:

"That ratty old Teddy Bear of yours smells worse than a mortuary. How come you gave it to her, anyway?" Bethany's stepfather asked.

"I have a right to be sentimental at times, don't I?" Kristin snapped. "And we can't afford to buy her a new Cabbage Patch doll. She'll be satisfied with him—Morton never let me down when I was Bethany's age. I gave him all the love I had."

"I hope you've still got some left for me." He grinned and reached for her, but Kristin avoided him, refusing to answer.

On the terrace next to all the other identical terraces in the subdivision, Bethany clung to her anchor of stability. Much of Morton's fur had been worn away over the years, and his button eyes had been replaced several times … but Bethany told him she didn't mind. Morton was her one true friend.

She held him tightly and looked up in awe. Strange lights were coming down from the sky.

Report from Zaxxaj invasion fleet, after contact with large aggregate of earth dwellings:

The Zaxxaj oozed over the rubble, a cloud of black electric fire, extending parts of herself like purple-blue bolts of lightning. The glimmers of consciousness she had detected here had been tied to primitive thoughts connected with solid objects. Upon her landing and first tentative gropings of destruction, the Zaxxaj barely noticed the solid projectiles the former inhabitants had launched at her. But after she had sizzled hundreds of thousands of their minds, she began to realize that these had been weapons, and that the inhabitants had been trying to damage her.

This delighted the Zaxxaj and rekindled her dynamo of hatred and fear.

She began to think her report to the main fleet. By feeding fear, hatred, and paranoia into the scattered life forms, the Zaxxaj had overloaded their minds without difficulty. They had no defense against a being that was a roiling mass of self-nourishing hatred, fear, pain, lust, paranoia. The Zaxxaj had not intended to conquer at first, but the fleet could not resist the ridiculously trivial victory this world offered.

She extended herself over the broken ruins of buildings, and sensed something that caused her black static to turn an alarmed purplish color. The Zaxxaj felt no consciousness here, nothing alive, nothing that could be a threat to her alarm. They would drag her over the Sun's magnetic poles and feed on her torment if she did not investigate.

The Zaxxaj thought away the piles of shattered stone and buckled wood, flinging aside the twisted ruins of a terrace railing and blasting it into a jet of incandescent fire. She ignored the crisped remnants of former inhabitants and uncovered *Morton*, whom the Zaxxaj saw as a talisman, a foul repository of deadly emotions. Her black electric fire glinted off Morton's button eyes.

Contact with the hate-being, the Zaxxaj, triggered the release of all the happiness the Teddy Bear had absorbed over three generations. Morton shouted happiness and love at the Zaxxaj, pummeling her with an armada of devotion, clawing her with talons of joy and peace.

The Zaxxaj shrieked and shriveled into an electric lavender color, trying to fend off the blows of compassion by blasting weapons of hatred and fear at the Teddy Bear. But Morton had no consciousness and acted only as a repository, a battery charged by love, releasing all the affection he had stored.

The Zaxxaj moaned as she dispersed into a pale pink mist, wafting over the destroyed city. And instead of weakening with the love he expended, Morton grew stronger, following the Zaxxaj's transmissions back to the Queen Cluster of the fleet.

The rosy aurora of the dissimilated alien ships hung in the skies of Earth for nearly a month, creating breathtaking sunsets for the survivors who could look up at the sky without shutting their eyes in terror. The survivors clung to each other to strengthen their own defenses against the lingering fear.

And now ... a story about SEX! Well, not entirely, but that did get your attention.

"One Night Stand" is more adult than my usual fare. Most of my work doesn't go farther than PG-13 in either sex or gore, and this was my first story that axctually pushed an R rating (so consider yourself warned if you're overly sensitive). And I wanted to see if I could write a sex scene.

There have been many stories about a guy who picks up a mysterious, exotic woman in a bar and gets much more than he bargained for. This one has an unexpected twist and, I think, a poignant message about loneliness.

ONE NIGHT STAND

How about: Hi, I'm Gabe. What's your name?

Feeling like a hunter, he stopped at the door of the cocktail lounge, mimicking an air of confidence. The bar stood nearly empty, serving only a few motel guests who weren't ambitious enough to go anywhere else on a Tuesday night.

He looked around in the dimness, praying that he wouldn't see anyone else from the Conference. Everyone attending the meeting was staying at the same motel. How could he, Doctor B. Gabriel Stockton, live with the embarrassment, the sidelong glances? How could he stand up and give a paper on "Time-Correlated Neutron Pulse Trains" if someone saw him in the motel bar the night before, looking for a pickup?

How about: You remind me of someone I once met—don't I know you?

Gabe wished he had the money to rent a car, not that there was much to see in Albuquerque anyway. What would he say if he did find someone—let's take a bus back to my place? Real macho stuff, all right.

He walked into the lounge, looking for prospects. He felt all eyes on him briefly, sizing him up, seeing through to his soul, exposing the real reason why he had come into the bar.

How about: Come here often? I'm just in town for the Conference on Subcritical Reactivity Measurements.

For a moment he thought it was his own paranoia, his own uncertainty, but the sensation of being probed increased, as if something brushed light fingertips across his brain. He felt his skin crawl, but then it stopped.

How about: Can I buy you a drink and sit down for a while?

Gabe saw her sitting off at a small table next to the Big-Screen TV that showed a videotape of the last Super Bowl. She looked directly at him, and did not flinch when he glanced in her direction. The woman raised her eyebrows. Gabe found himself walking toward her before he could think about it, before his anxiety could reassert itself and make him flee the bar after all.

She got up from her table and took a few steps, then silently indicated two isolated stools along the bar. Gabe felt his pulse begin to race. His heart made a hollow thudding noise in his chest. It felt like a dream—nothing could be this easy.

In the uncertain light of the lounge she looked odd, the angle of her eyes, the set of her cheekbones, even the way her hair moved when she turned her head. But as she stepped closer to him, Gabe saw how wrong his first impression had been. Her clothes shifted as she moved, letting the blue taffeta blouse insinuate breasts that were "just right"—not huge balloons, but not bee-stings, either. She wore soft, tight jeans faded to a pale blue; they clung to her hips as she walked. Her hair was so intensely black that it gave off an electric bluish glow. She looked Indian, but different somehow, very different.

How about: I don't have the slightest idea what to say?

"I'll have a Tecate. Dressed," she said, half to him, half to the bartender. The way she said "dressed" sounded provocative. With a dry throat, Gabe ordered one for himself.

He turned and sat down beside her, trying to think of something clever to say. She extended her hand, showing nails that had been painted a lustrous sapphire.

"I'm Stella," she said.

"I'm Gabe." He shook her hand in a businesslike manner, realized what he was doing, and allowed the grasp to linger. Stella didn't pull away.

"Three bucks." The bartender set two Tecates in front of them, deftly sliding bar napkins under the red aluminum cans; he brought out two wet glasses rimmed with salt and topped with lime slices.

Above the bar, a small sign stated baldly, "Tipping is not a city in China."

Gabe fumbled with his wallet and pulled out three singles. The bartender flicked his gaze at Stella, looked back at Gabe with the faintest of smiles on his lips, then took the money and turned toward the cash register. Gabe felt his ears turning red.

"It's okay," Stella said.

He looked at her and smiled, trying to feel at ease. Someone got up and played the jukebox, drowning out the old Super Bowl videotape. "Of course it is."

God, she was beautiful—he had never before seen a woman who struck so many of the right chords. Uncanny. Already, he felt lead bricks in the pit of his stomach. Time seemed to be moving too slowly, and too recklessly fast.

Stella shifted a little on the barstool, looking at his fingers. "I see you're not married, Gabe," she said matter-of-factly. "Don't you get a little lonely sometimes?"

"That's right," he answered, puzzled. He almost launched into a confession-style story of his life, but then decided that Stella had summed it all up nicely in just those few words. "Not married, but I just get a little lonely sometimes." No adultery, no cheating, no breach of faith—just too damned devoted to his work to have time for a wife. Gabe kept his body in good shape and, despite a receding hairline in front of curly brown hair, women did find him attractive —when he got up the nerve to go through the whole barroom courtship ritual. But that took so much emotional energy that he didn't have stamina left for his research. "I just get a little lonely," he repeated to himself, perhaps defensively.

He couldn't bear to ask Stella what she did, where she worked, what her hobbies were—all that was too blasé. And he didn't want to upset the eerie sense of communication he felt with her. He sipped at his beer, trying not to drain it too quickly. He felt obligated to spend a certain amount of idle time with Stella, getting to know her, feeling the waters. She finished her own beer, seeming to enjoy just sitting next to him.

"I'm here for the conference," he said abruptly.

"Of course you are." Stella stood up from the stool as if she hadn't heard him and held out her hand. "Shall we?" Her voice was low and seductive, and she began to walk toward the door without waiting for him to respond. Gabe blinked and followed her, barely able to believe what he was doing. He felt his chest grow tight, and adrenaline started to flow like a locomotive through his veins.

Gabe and Stella walked side by side, and she matched her step to his as they left the cocktail lounge. Gabe didn't even notice if the other people stared at them or not.

Outside, a freakish August thunderstorm had slicked down the pavement, filling the air with a fresh dampness. At the edge of the parking lot a cyclone fence blocked off the steep drop to a concrete drainage ditch. A narrow stream of water trickled into an unseen drain. Winking traffic lights and a chain of car headlights made the Interstate look like a conveyor belt for moving automobiles. Above them, the sky had cleared, and a billion stars stabbed through, visible even over the pinkish-orange streetlights.

"My room's in the annex. Over there." He pointed, mumbling his words.

Stella looked up at the sky and stopped for a moment. Gabe thought he detected an expression of longing and despair on her face, that her features flickered for just an instant. She seemed to be expecting, hoping to see something there, but when Gabe looked up, he saw nothing.

"I used to know all the constellations," Gabe said, still trying to be conversational. His comment distracted her, and it was as if she let a mental drawbridge down for a brief flash.

The ship sang, then screamed, as it skipped across the atmosphere like a hot stone. The shielding turned cherry red, dripping and bowing into the air. She had no control whatsoever. She had come here only to scoop up some oxygen—and now the ship would crash. She would survive, of course, but the ship … the ship …

It seemed to be a cross between a vision and a thought, plowing through Gabe's head like a bullet. And then it was gone, leaving only a vivid afterimage, as if someone had popped a flashbulb in his face. He blinked his eyes, baffled and confused.

Stella tugged on his arm. "Come on." She flashed a dizzying smile at him. Unable to ignore her, he stumbled after her.

They entered the motel annex, and Gabe forgot to hold the door open for her like a gentleman. He fumbled the room key out of his pocket and tried not to let Stella see him glance uncertainly at the engraved room number. The hall looked like one of those infinite optical illusions: doors next to identical doors next to identical doors, stretching out until they vanished in the distance.

Gabe stopped in front of his room, muttering a prayer of thanks as he managed to insert the key without looking like a klutz. He opened the room, making a grandiose gesture for her. "After you, Madame."

Stella smiled and entered. Gabe paused a moment, feeling a twinge of guilt. He didn't even know Stella; he knew nothing about her, nothing about her personality—but he was attracted to her, powerfully. He convinced himself that this was actually more honest, in a way—this was sex, pure and simple. No airy thoughts about love or commitments or the future, just that animal thing, the overblown hormones that clamored for attention once in a while.

Will you still respect me in the morning, Stella?

He closed the heavy door, and Stella slipped behind him to snap the deadbolt, displaying the "Do Not Disturb" sign. Gabe had left the air conditioner on, trying to combat the desert summer, and now the room felt cool and smelled metallic. His suitcase lay open on one of the two double beds, and some of the notes and viewgraphs for his technical paper lay scattered on the room's "courtesy" table. Gabe moved past Stella and turned on the motel's tiny clock radio, looking for a soft-rock station, but he found only static, though the reception had been clear before.

Stella switched off the radio with one blue-nailed finger, touching his hand. She turned to face him, resting her palms lightly on his arms.

"So, Stella, just what did you have in mind?" he said, trying to sound playful, but the words came out thick and nervous.

She was shorter than he by a few inches, just like in the movies. As she lifted her head, he looked down into her eyes, dark eyes, so deep and black they seemed to contain a galaxy of distant stars. He ran his fingertips on the ebony strands of her hair. It felt almost alive.

As if she could restrain herself no longer, Stella suddenly flowed into his arms, nuzzling his neck and brushing the top of her head against his cheek. She pushed her breasts against his chest, her abdomen against his groin, even her thighs against his legs, acting desperate to be touching him as much as she could. He brushed his lips across her hair, and Stella turned her face so he could kiss her, first lightly and tenderly, but then deeply, faster. Her breath was hot as he breathed it into his mouth.

Stella's hands were deftly working at the knot of his tie—a tie? Why in the world had he worn a tie? The thought bothered him a moment, and then he was running the palm of his hand up and down the back of her blue taffeta blouse, touching the soft fabric, adding just enough pressure to feel her back, the thin bumps of her spine. The blouse rode up a little and he touched the warm, smooth skin above her waist. He let his fingertips linger a moment, and then he dropped his hands down to her faded jeans. He brushed his legs against hers, swaying, grinding hips together.

Stella let his tie fall to the floor and undid the buttons of his shirt with the back of one fingernail. She slid her fingers across his chest, then into his shirt, feeling the thin, wiry hair over his heart

He hiked up her blouse, running both hands across her skin, up and down her back, across her shoulder blades, noting delightedly that she wore no bra. Then he reached forward to take one of her breasts in his palm. The warm, pliant flesh seemed to vibrate under his touch, but her nipple was incredibly hard, almost crystalline, with a sharp end. Gabe touched it with his fingertips, curious.

Then Stella reached down his pants, grasping his cock firmly in one hand while she rubbed it against the cloth of his shorts. An orgasm rushed up on him, and Gabe had to clench his teeth and shut his eyes to hold it back, breathing tightly as he concentrated.

Somehow his shirt had come off, and Stella unzipped his pants, dropping them down around his ankles. Her hand kept working behind the elastic band of his briefs, and then she pulled them down as well. Gabe tugged at her blouse, and she obliged by slipping it off her shoulders. Stella's breasts rose flawlessly from her chest, golden and perfectly formed as any centerfold's—but the nipples were a bright sapphire blue, transparent and sharp, like shards of a glass bottle.

He tried to say something, almost succeeded, but Stella crouched and, breathing rapidly, drew her tongue along the inside of his thighs, kissing, brushing the tip of his stiff penis.

Other images exploded in his head.

She lived by the smoldering, radioactive wreckage of the ship. The ship was everything. The stardrive could pull along the other minds, Touching, to keep her company on the long, long journey. But the ship had died, severing her from the others.

The pueblo-building people of the desert mountains came to look at first, but soon they learned to shun the place, leaving her even more alone.

She spent decades salvaging the dead metal bulk until she finally pieced together a functional transmitter. Her cry for help went out into the void between the stars. They would send someone to rescue her, she had no doubt. But it would take thousands and thousands of years for them to reach this distant planet.

"What are you?" Gabe tried to ask, but she rose to her feet, rubbing against him deliciously. Stella brushed her soft breasts with the sharp nipples against his skin.

"Don't worry about it," she answered "I won't hurt you."

She wriggled out of her jeans, leaving them where they lay, and a moment later she removed her thin web-like panties as Gabe stepped out of his own pants.

Stella clutched the bedspread and, with one flick of her wrist, she pulled it completely free of the bed, exposing the cool sheets. She sat down on the mattress and held out her hands.

Gabe almost took a step backward. He tried to close his eyes to think, to turn away for just a moment, but his arousal was at its peak. It was so easy to ignore his clamoring questions, to push them to the back corner of his brain. Fun first, think about it later. Sometimes the universe played strange tricks that couldn't always be explained. He could feel his heart beating in his throat. He noticed the prickle of sweat on his skin. Fear? Awe? A little of both.

But desire rose from his solar plexus, numbing everything, and his body convinced him to ignore better judgment.

Gabe slid next to her on the bed, and she lay slowly back. They remained next to each other for a moment, belly to belly, kissing passionately, just feeling the naked skin where it touched. Gabe's every neuron felt on fire, reaching for more.

She hooked one leg over his hip and reached down with her own hand to grasp his penis, guiding it between her legs. An icy trickle ran down the center of his spine. He felt as if he had been sucked into a glove of wet velvet, enfolded by fleshy damp lips ... with only the faintest suggestion of teeth somewhere deep inside her.

Waiting. Waiting as the years, the decades ticked slowly by. She studied, she observed, but centuries passed before she learned how to look like the pueblo-building people. It was so different, because she was so different. But at last she walked among them, hidden and unable to express her unspeakable boredom and emptiness. Their history changed before her eyes. She waited for the ship to come.

Stella rolled on her back, taking Gabe with her, keeping him deep inside her. He began to move back and forth, rocking his hips; she shuttled her hands up and down his back, squeezing his buttocks, increasing his rhythm. She closed her eyes and seemed to melt further back into the pillows, lifting her legs up, spreading them wider in an attempt to draw him deeper.

The air conditioner whirred to life by itself. Gabe breathed heavily, rapidly, as their sweat ran together. He drove his abdomen against hers, pressing his body down to feel her breasts against his chest. The shards of her nipples scratched his skin, leaving fiery red welts in parallel tracks. He tried to ease off a moment to quell the rising orgasm deep in his groin, to savor it. But Stella would not let him, making him go faster and faster, with a rising frenzy.

When he reached the peak where he knew he could no longer stop the feeling, he abandoned himself. He thrust into her with rapid, staccato strokes, but the orgasm continued to build, intensifying, rising far beyond anything he had ever experienced before. Every nerve was pulled taut with pleasure, tightened into thumbscrews of ecstasy, stretched even further until he could no longer tell the difference between orgasm and pain. Then he came explosively, releasing everything and laying his mind open to an alien mental barrage from Stella, a final surge that made the pieces fall together. As if out of the corner of his eye, he saw a shadowy and powerful thing with many insectoid appendages. As he plummeted back down, exhausted and breathless, Gabe thought he heard Stella emitting an eerie, insect-like hum from suddenly brittle lips as she experienced her own orgasm....

"What we did," Stella said later, "is the only way I can cope." She gracefully slid off the bed, lifting the sheets from her sweat-glistened body. Gabe thought he saw a viscous tear hanging in the corner of her eye.

He lay exhausted, listening to his heart pound, feeling as if every nerve in his body had fissioned. Stella began to dress, sliding into her tight jeans, pulling the blue taffeta blouse over her head. Her hair moved back into place by itself, until it didn't even appear tousled. She moved slowly and carefully, unhurried.

Stella came back to him, and for an instant he was afraid she would do something to him, either kill him or erase his memory because he knew her secret. But she merely kissed him again on the lips, and then glided toward the door.

"I just get a little lonely sometimes," she said, and left.

Gabe closed his eyes for a moment, feeling the sweat dry on his skin and the itchy fire of parallel red scratches on his chest.

After a long time he got up, stretched his sore muscles, and went to take a shower.

My artist friend Jeff Sturgeon has spent years creating fabulous paintings on burnished metal, a sequence depicting an imaginative future history, "The Last Cities of Earth." It's a post-apocalyptic scenario set after the eruption of the Yellowstone megavolcano altered the Earth's climate forever, rendering the surface uninhabitable.

But disasters won't stop intrepid humans. Given a fair warning of the imminent disaster, humans developed new technology to lift the greatest cities into the skies, where they exist as floating islands. Different cultures spring up, and each of the floating Last Cities has its own story.

Jeff worked with a group of his writer friends—including me—to chronicle the stories of these cities. Jeff showed us the sequence of marvelous paintings, city after city in the sky, which evoked many plot ideas.

The painting of Las Vegas captured my attention the most, and it had the added story potential of nearby Hoover Dam. And pirates. I collaborated with Sam Knight on this one.

FOLLOWING ICARUS DOWN

(with Sam Knight)

In the golden rays of the setting sun, Aponivi climbed onto the balcony rail of the second largest tower, wavered, recaptured his graceful balance, and did what no one else in Vegas Station would have considered.

He jumped.

A startled cry from somewhere within the crowded, glittering casino behind him was lost to the rushing wind as he plummeted, headfirst, toward the jutting spires far below. The outer wall of the needlelike tower flowed beside him as he dropped. He felt the gentle nudge of the great city's antigravity generators pushing him outward, away from the immense floating construct they supported high in the air. As the smaller spire loomed below, threatening to impale him, Aponivi spread his arms and legs, lifted his head, stretched his membranes … and caught the breezes.

His people believed that wind flowed through their veins, as much as blood did.

Aponivi soared out over the sharp skyscrapers, away from the floating city and toward the warm sun. The late afternoon sky, unusually clear of murky clouds, let the golden rays shine across the desert to the canyon walls beyond the Hoover Dam. There, the sheer rock caught the light, calling to him, reminding him of home.

The temperate air felt good as it stretched taut the skin connecting his arms to his sides, turning the membranes into wings.

He flew for miles, toward the immense reservoir created by long-lost aspirations and the clifflike concrete wall, like a gate against a barbarian invasion.

He smiled. His father and his teachers had told him many legends, stories, and possible histories of the human race, long before the eruption and disaster changed everything....

As Aponivi passed over the water held back by the titanic dam, the cooler air made him adjust his glide angle so he would not lose altitude. He lowered his legs to catch the air with the membrane between them, slowing and lifting him at the same time, and he veered to the right to bring himself back over the dry, rugged land.

He rode the warm updraft from below, and with a joyous heart, he let it carry him upward into the sky instead of deep into the canyon as he'd originally intended.

As he turned back into the sun, he thought of the myth of Icarus, another fascinating story he'd collected only last year when his airship had docked at UC Tower. Aponivi understood the human desire to soar high enough to touch the sun, and he was still human ... mostly. Being a glider, bound to the whims of the winds, he sometimes wished for true wings, strong wings, that could carry him anywhere, maybe even closer to the sun.

But for now, this was more than enough. This was everything. This was what a Weather Mage lived for.

The other crewmembers on the airship could spend their leave and money inside the flashing casinos or dim-lit brothels, but Aponivi relished the warm air under his wings and the warm sunlight on his face. Both things were rare in this world of cold storms. He took a moment to cherish it all.

As he flew over the perfect gray curve of the battered dam, preparing to dive into the river canyon below it, something gave him pause. His sensitive membranes were vibrating, a faint change in the air, but it was not the normal vibrations by which he judged the environment around him. No, this was not a natural sound of the desert and sky, but rather a rising and falling rhythmic thrum that should not be there.

He scooped his arms and slowed his glide. Then, spreading his fingers wide, he exposed all of the sensitive webbing, the better to feel details. Something was happening down by the lake, the dam.

The vibration came from below. The steady flow of water over the spillways to either side of the dam filled the air with a fine mist that turned into rainbows as he circled, but the mist and the roar also masked the strange thrumming.

Aponivi turned in a wide circle, studying the dam like a vulture investigating a carcass. The upstream side of the dam, which held back the great lake it had created, had only air and water, and Aponivi could discern nothing unusual there. The western, downstream side glowed amber in the setting sun, magnificently haloed in rainbows and reflecting light back up the canyon, removing all but the deepest shadows. Even with his eyes, which were much more acute than any normal human's, he saw nothing out of the ordinary.

But the strange vibrations grew stronger as he circled lower.

At the edge of the waterline, near the central point of the graceful curve of concrete, he spotted a white bloom of disturbed water, something splashing on the glass-smooth lake.

As he turned his attention, Aponivi felt a sudden, quick spike in the vibrations, a threat, and he instantly reacted. He twisted away just as a deadly arrow streaked past him, hissing as it went by. The razor-edged point missed him by only inches. It had not been a warning shot.

Trying to put immediate distance between himself and whomever had shot the arrow, he banked away in his glide. Something was out there, in the air above the dam, unseen. Someone had attacked him! Maybe it was a camouflaged ship of the Ghost Fleet … but why would they fire on a Weather Mage? He was flying alone, no threat to them, and his people were neutral among all the airships and the floating cities. The Mages were regarded as invaluable, often even sacred, to the airship captains and crew who needed them as scouts.

Sensing another change in the air, Aponivi dove to avoid a second arrow that flew past him. He still couldn't see the ship, but they were firing on him, trying to bring him down.

If this invisible airship was merely stealing a resupply of fresh water from the reservoir, they could have done it anywhere on the lake, not so close to the dam. No one would have needed to fire upon him, but they had tried to kill him! They were up to something terrible. Perhaps they were readying an attack upon Vegas Station itself.

He needed to get out of here, back to Vegas Station. He needed find his own captain, warn—

A third arrow whistled toward him, and Aponivi twisted to the right so that the deadly projectile streaked past his ear—but before he could exhale in relief, the next arrow sliced though his left wing membrane and nicked his arm. Pain flared as the wind tore the wound even wider, ripped the thin, sensitive skin.

Aponivi dropped rapidly, drew his wounded arm close so he would fall in a tight spiral, while he tried to control the descent with his legs and good wing. As the vast dark lake rushed up to meet him, he folded himself up, braced himself, and dove into the icy water. The impact jarred him, and he lost his bearings, but his light frame quickly bobbed to the surface. He gasped for breath, coughing.

The lake's frigid water numbed the immediate pain, but he knew the tear in his wing was bad, a widening hole that would keep him from flying ... perhaps ever. He kept his arm tucked close to his body. The only way such a tear would ever heal—the only way he would fly again—was to protect the membrane, keep the tear from ripping wider. If he did not get help, he would never soar on the winds, never glide with the freedom of a Weather Mage.

First he had to get out of here, find safety and shelter. A place to hide. Someone had tried to kill him!

He heard a splash in the water, not far away, someone coming close. His mysterious attackers were not satisfied with merely knocking him out of the air. They had spotted where he'd crashed into the water.

Taking a deep breath, Aponivi dove under the water, using his leg membranes like a fish tail to propel him down and down. A Weather Mage belonged in the air, but for generations his people had sustained themselves by fishing out in the desolation, and water was not unknown to them.

Trying to outwit his attackers, he swam deeper and moved in the direction from which the mysterious arrows had come. With the powerful boost from his leg membranes, he nearly reached the dam barrier before his breath gave out. A Weather Mage's lungs could subsist on the thin air of the highest reaches of the sky, but he still had his limits.

Desperate for air, Aponivi let himself gently float up to the surface. Though he was starving for air, he forced himself to be calm, careful not to break the water hard. He didn't dare make a splash in the deepening twilight. Letting only his face emerge, he took a slow breath and looked up into the sky above him. It shimmered, ever so slightly, in the last fading light. Directly above the dam, not much more than a blur, he could make out the shape of an airship floating thirty feet overhead, but it was indistinct ... camouflaged.

"He has to come up for air sooner or later," a muffled voice said from seemingly out of thin air.

"Maybe he's dead."

"No. Those Weather Mage scouts are tough bastards. Hard to kill. They might look scrawny, like they'd snap in two, but they don't. They're strong as hell and twice as dangerous. Keep your eyes open. No witnesses, no warning. He could fly back to Vegas Station in time to cause us trouble."

A deep voice chuckled. "I've still got more arrows, boss."

Aponivi took a full breath and calmed his pounding heart, then slipped back under the water, trying not to think of his wounded wing. His light, lean body couldn't stay submerged in the deep cold for much longer. He had to get to the dam, or to the rocky shore.

As he stroked through the chill, dark water, he detected the strange vibration here, too, even stronger than in the air. As cautiously as he could manage, Aponivi swam in an arc until he located the vibration. Gently drifting up for another lungful of air, he paused to listen again.

This time he heard no voices, but that did not mean he was safe. The Ghost ship must still be there.

Tucking his wounded arm against his chest, he swam toward the vibrations. His legs and his good arm began to fatigue, and he needed to get out of the water as soon as he could. But the attackers were still out there.

Who were they? What kind of people would not only fire on a soaring Weather Mage, but would do so with contempt? And what were they doing in their camouflaged airship? *No witnesses, no warning.*

Aponivi had to find the answers ... but he had to survive first.

His strokes became more labored, but he continued moving toward the source. The vibrations became louder, stronger, until they were nearly unbearable, suffocating. The pressure waves not only affected his sensitive skin membranes, but his ears as well. He surfaced again, no longer worried about the sound of a splash over the noise, but the mysterious attackers in their airship could still spot him in the waning light.

His head broke water mere yards from the great concrete barrier of the dam. It held back the entire lake like a gigantic fortress wall. From this low angle in the water, he now spotted something he'd not been able to see when he'd glided overhead. A tight group of men were gathered on top of the dam, twenty-five feet or so above the waterline, and they were partially hidden by some kind of stealth technology. The strange camouflage field erased the people from the waist up, blending them with the sky as if they'd been cut in two, and he could see only their legs walking. Two more people hung in rope baskets just above the water.

From above, when he'd soared overhead on his other flights, this part of the dam had looked like much of the rest, where chunks had broken away, damaged by time and environmental upheaval. Here from the waterline, though, he could see that this part of the dam was actually whole, and sturdy.

These people were doing something to the dam itself. Considering that they had shot him out of the sky to hide what they were doing, to prevent him from warning Vegas Station, he knew immediately that he had to stop them. That was all the answer he needed.

His sharp eyes focused on the figures. These men did not wear the type of uniform he had seen on formal airship crews. Their piecemeal clothes were instead ragged and worn, in the way of scavengers and pirates, people who seemed more at home in the surface desolation than in the floating cities like Vegas Station.

Suddenly the vibration stopped, and Aponivi's ears rang in the oppressive silence.

One of the dangling men shouted up, "That's it! Bore hole is finished!" He held a piece of equipment in his arms, like a strange cannon loaded with a heavy spearhead. Someone on top of the dam began pulling it up by an attached rope.

"Ready for the payload! Lower it down," called the man hanging in the other rope basket. "And be careful—unless you actually believe the new stuff is completely stable!"

A ripple of nervous laughter answered him.

As the camouflaged group on top of the dam lowered something down, the two dangling men shifted positions, spreading apart. From the waterline, Aponivi saw that they had drilled a hole in the concrete wall—that was the vibrations he had heard. The bore hole was deep and wide enough to stick an arm into.

Now a package was lowered down to the men in the rope baskets, a long and narrow oilskin bag shaped to fit into the newly made hole.

"I can't see a damned thing," one of the dangling men complained. "It's too dark already."

"I told you we should have done this earlier," answered a half-visible man up on the dam.

"Shut up and send down the torch! Let's ignite this and get away from here. We'll watch the show from above."

In dismay, Aponivi realized they were trying to blow a hole through the dam and the satchel was apparently filled with explosives! He had no idea why anyone would want to do such a thing, but as the fuse was lit, he had no doubt.

He stroked backward to get away from the area of the blast, but he had no place to go. Fortunately, the sinister men were making so much noise of their own, they did not hear his splash.

The two dangling men frantically pushed the lit fuse inside the bag and knotted the top, then shoved the entire oilskin satchel farther into the hole. The second man tamped it in with a stick, pushing it as deep as it could go, while the other began filling the rest of the hole with mudlike cement or epoxy from a bucket hanging on another single rope.

"Done! Pull us up!" The first man tried to climb up the rope as his companions above started hauling him.

The other man tamped down the mortar one last time, then tossed his stick into the water below. "Hurry!" He tugged on the rope and began climbing rapidly up the concrete wall of the dam, like a fish on a line.

The camouflage field suddenly vanished, and the entire sabotage crew was revealed. Together now, they ran along the top of the dam toward a rope ladder that appeared as if by magic, falling out of the shimmering blur in the sky above. The Ghost ship was still enclosed in its stealth shroud.

"Full speed!" a voice called from somewhere above. "We've got less than five minutes!"

The men hastily seized the ladder and began scrambling up to their hidden airship, one at a time in a frantic rush. Even as the last man grabbed hold of the ladder, the invisible craft began moving away, pulling him along as he hopped on one leg.

Unseen in the cold water, Aponivi looked from the dangling airship ladder crowded with climbing figures to the dark spot on the dam wall, where they had patched in the explosive. His instinct told him to swim to shore with all possible speed, to scramble up the rocks and get as far away from the blast as he could, limp up to higher ground. Five minutes? The crude fuse could not be very accurate, but if the explosive technology was anything like the stealth field these pirates used....

This was about more than just saving himself and getting away from the blast. What would his father and his teachers say? Aponivi knew that if the already-damaged dam were breached, the seismic spilling of the enormous reservoir would cause incalculable harm. Yes, Vegas Station levitated safely above the ground, but the epic flood would obliterate the fledgling settlements that had just started to spring up along the river, kill all the people who were now living down there, just barely eking out a living. If the dam broke, how many would die? And for what purpose? The aftermath would damage all trade and disrupt the vital routes. Was that what the marauders wanted?

Five of the saboteurs were still climbing the ladder up into the invisible shroud, swinging wildly as the camouflaged airship began to cruise away from the dam. The other men had already vanished onto the floating vessel.

Aponivi felt a surge of renewed anger. These people had shot him out of the sky. He would not let them succeed in this barbaric attack. Setting his jaw, he made a decision that might cost him his life, but in exchange for so many, his life—and his death—would gain great value indeed. He was a Weather Mage. He remembered everything his mentors had taught him. Their honor code was as strong as the wind.

He could not let this go.

With powerful strokes, blocking out thoughts of the increasing damage he was doing to his wounded membrane, he shot forward to the dam. He no longer bothered to remain hidden as he swam. There was no time to cover the sound of his splashes.

An angry voice called down from the cloaked airship above. "What's that?"

"It's that damned birdman!"

Reaching the huge cliff of concrete, Aponivi pumped his legs to hold him afloat. He pushed his torso far enough out of the water so he could reach the plugged hole.

"He's going after the charge!"

"Dammit! Archers!"

The mudlike epoxy or cement they had used to seal the hole was already hardening. Aponivi's good arm, fatigued from all the swimming, was so weak he could barely raise it over his head, let alone dig at setting mortar. His long fingers scraped at the partially dried mud, but he couldn't clear enough of it. His hooked nails bled.

"Take him out."

Once exposed to the air, the torn wound in the membrane burned with pain. As he lifted his arms to claw away at the setting mortar, he felt his thin, sensitive skin rip even more, widening the wound. But there was no point in nursing the tear. With a grimace, Aponivi raised his other hand, using both to dig.

Inside the bore hole, the fuse would be burning down. Five minutes? How much time was left? He gritted his teeth and ignored the cutting pain to claw harder, faster, tearing his nails in the setting mortar. He grunted, kicking his legs to remain above the water.

With a sharp report, an arrow struck the wall just to the left of his head. The sharp steel tip sparked against the concrete, a brief flare in the thick shadows of evening. He closed his eyes and kept digging.

As he pushed his arms deeper into the clogged hole, his fingertips brushed against something that felt more like oilcloth than rock.

He managed to hook another long finger into a chunk of the hardening mortar and broke out a large chunk that fell into his face. The heavy shard smashed his nose with a flash of pain, and his nostrils filled with the quick smell of iron.

Another arrow ricocheted off the concrete just to the right of his cheek. The next one might strike him between the shoulder blades.…

His muscles were all lead and pain. He couldn't keep pumping his legs. He couldn't keep digging, but just when he thought he couldn't pull for one second more, he snagged the knot at the top of the oilskin sack. He grabbed it and pulled, dragging the sack partly out of the hole, then he let himself slide back. Gravity would do the rest of the work.

An arrow pierced his other wing as he fell away from the dam, tearing the membrane as he let out a thin scream of pain, but the prize was in his hand. He fell, taking the knotted sack with him into the water.

"I got him! He's done now!"

"He got the damned charge!"

Aponivi sank into the water, floating, vulnerable. With his torn fingers, he yanked at the knot, tugged and tried to untie it, but his hands were bloody, and the tight oilskin folds refused to yield. He submerged it, but the water would never extinguish the fuse. The bomb would go off at any time. He didn't even know what kind of explosive it was.

Even if he managed to get far enough away to save the dam wall, the blast would tear him to shreds.

Aponivi kicked away from the wall, hugging the package close. His ruined wings were agony, and he felt numb and sickened with the knowledge of how badly he was hurt. Even if he got away, he would never recover from this, never be whole again. But his first mission was to stay alive, get away so he could report to Vegas Station, warn them of these terrorists, even if he stopped the bomb this time.

He had to survive the next minutes.

An arrow pierced the surface above him as he swam, plunging down like a viper, but it missed him in the water. These marauders had casually fired upon a Weather Mage. Aponivi hadn't attacked them, hadn't threatened them, hadn't even seen them. Weather Mages didn't attack others. They were as calm as the winds, as open as the skies. Aponivi likely would never have realized what they were doing had they not shot at him.

But the hatred of these people seemed to run deep. Maybe they were just murderers and did not give bloodshed a second thought. They had no concerns about blasting the dam open and sending a deadly flood-hammer across the settled lands.

More arrows hit the surface, but he swam deep with his dangerous package, and the water stole the weapons' efficacy. The men on the airship had to know they couldn't harm him. Why were they wasting arrows, as if driving him away?

Thirty feet from the dam wall, he finally surged back up to gulp a breath. As he flung cold water out of his eyes, he spotted the last man on the rope ladder still struggling to board the invisible airship—directly above him. The rest of the craft was hidden behind the stealth field. Several more arrows peppered the water around him.

He realized they were trying to keep him away, even if they didn't kill him. He had the sack with the explosives, and he didn't know how powerful the blast would be. But the lumbering Ghost ship had drifted over the lake, where Aponivi was. The airship moved, trying to gain speed.

He realized that the magnitude of the bomb's destructive power had to be incredible, since no mere blast could crack open the behemoth of Hoover Dam. What kind of technology did these people have? Once the bomb did explode, it could well take out the nearby Ghost ship, even in the air above.

Grim satisfaction crept over Aponivi's face as he realized what he could do. This would be better than just sitting under the cloaked airship.

Diving deep with his burden, swimming down until the pressure squeezed his eardrums, Aponivi tumbled in the water, reversed direction, and raced toward the surface hard as he could. He used his membranes to push against the water, not caring how much more he tore them. Accelerating, rising, it was like flying again. When he broke the water, he shot into the air like a cork popping from a bottle. In the brief moment of weightless freedom, he kicked desperately, using his ruined wings to gain even a few feet of additional altitude.

Right overhead, hands seemed to magically appear around the last man climbing the ladder. The upper half of his body vanished as his crewmates hauled him aboard.

At the apex of his jump, Aponivi flung the wet oilskin package after the man's feet. And then he fell away, dropping back down to the lake.

The plunge seemed slower than any glide he'd ever done. Two

more arrows whistled past him just as he saw the charge vanish into the camouflage field.

Aponivi struck the water with his back, landing hard. Two arrows from the shower of projectiles bit him, sliced past as he fell beneath the surface, sinking to imagined safety.

There was nothing more he could do. The airship was gliding away from the dam, gaining altitude.

He surfaced, ignoring the burning pain of his numerous wounds. He struck out for the shoreline and the concrete dam, dredging more energy from his exhausted muscles. He noticed with odd detachment that an arrow protruded from the meat of his arm, and without thinking, he grabbed the shaft and snatched it out. The cold water did little to lessen the ripping pain. Discarding the arrow, he began swimming again. He no longer even felt cold.

A surge of light from above was like a flash of rare sunlight reflecting from a mirror. An instant later, the shockwave shoved him under the water. He stayed under as the roiling fire and debris swept over the surface, and then flailing, he swam up to air again. He broke the surface to see the flaming airship, its camouflage gone, the ungainly and mortally wounded vessel slowly falling to the lake. It was a large, hodgepodge marauder, flying no colors that he recognized. Debris rained down, components of the levitation engines, great hunks of the hull, flaming support struts. Burning human figures also tumbled out like debris.

Better the pirate airship was destroyed than the dam.

He began swimming again, sluggish with pain, bone-deep weariness, and shock. Only now did he feel the drag of another arrow shaft, and he found another projectile stuck into his thigh, but not deep. He plucked it out, as if it were no more than a splinter. The flames of the burning, crashing airship lit the water, and he could see a swirl of blood surrounding his pale body, leaking from all his wounds.

It didn't matter.

He drifted, floating, imagining himself aloft on an open breeze, free and weightless. On normal days, the skies were much warmer, and smelled of flowers and fruit.

Aponivi nearly lost consciousness, ready just to fall ... just to sink, but he shook his head and forced himself to swim farther, aiming for the rocky shore at the far end of the battered dam. The dusk had deepened to the edge of full night by the time he reached the smooth, water-stained rock where the concrete ended and the natural shore began.

The Hoover Dam had been damaged by time, nature, and the apocalypse from the great eruption. The titanic structure might not last for centuries more, but it would endure for a few more years. For today. Thanks to him.

At the edge of the concrete dam wall, he found stairs leading down to the waterline, an ancient maintenance access from the old road across the dam. He pulled himself up, staggering one step after another, climbing to a flat landing where the stairs turned to go someplace higher. He collapsed on his back, gasping, and looked up at the stars that had come out between patches of returning clouds.

Aponivi was glad to see the stars. They were so rarely visible from the ground.

He remembered a flight as a young boy, when his father had taken him above the near-perpetual storms to see the stars. So bright and clear, so pure and pristine, they made his heart hurt to look upon them.

He paid no attention to the burning wreck of the Ghost ship he had destroyed. Flames still roiled across the floating debris, orange and sputtering on the surface of the water.

As he huddled on the landing, throbbing with pain from a dozen wounds, a chill wind brought cold mist from the spillway across his body. He closed his eyes, listening to the distant roar of the spillway waterfall, and just waited for his spirit to join the stars cycling endlessly in the heavens above.

Voices woke him, nearby voices and the sound of splashing water.

"I know he went this way," one said. "I saw him. Bastard!"

"He could be anywhere, boss," another responded. "We should get out of here while we can. Vegas Station might've sent flyers out to investigate already."

Aponivi couldn't make himself move, as if parts of him were already dead. Collapsed on the landing halfway up to the roadway above, he managed to roll on his side and look out across the dark lake. Two forms, clinging to floating debris from the doomed airship, were approaching the shore.

"He took my ship! I'll kill that flying freak. I'll kill every one of those damned birdmen!"

Aponivi just wanted to close his eyes and be done. He heard the man's words with his heart, and he believed them. This murderous man had shown no compunction about shooting at an innocent, neutral Weather Mage out on patrol. The evil airship captain would do the same to any Weather Mage he encountered, Aponivi's people, his family. The man's hatred was irrational and deep. If the man lived through this night, he would kill more.

He had to be stopped.

Rolling to his belly, Aponivi used numb and bleeding hands to force himself up, to stand upon numb feet. His wounds, the only things he could truly feel, ached like cold fire. Reaching inside himself, he focused on the sensation and pulled himself out of his torpor. He lowered his head, turned away from the stars he wanted so desperately to join.

He was not done here. Not yet. Not with that violent man still out there.

With no weapons and no strength, a creature of the sky with clipped wings, Aponivi's only advantage over these men was that he could see in the night better than they could. He had to find a way to use that before his body failed him.

A clack and scrape below told him the men's improvised debris raft had reached the shore edge of the dam wall.

"Up there! I see him on the steps!"

Realizing he stood silhouetted against the sky, Aponivi hobbled up the second flight of stairs from the landing. Many of the steps were broken and missing after so much time, and he stumbled to his knees more than once. A warm streak ran down his arm and leg, and he realized it was blood mingling with the water on his skin. His torn wing membranes opened up like a gasp of pain each time he reached out to catch himself, but he pushed on.

A Weather Mage was meant to fly, and now he was trapped here on the ground, just out of the water. He would rather have faced a terrible storm.

At the top of the landing, he found an open expanse partially covered in the hard black paving the ancient peoples had used on their roads. Aponivi searched for any place to hide, any weapon or tool he could use, but his vision was obscured by the spillway mist that rose high into the air around him.

He turned toward the roar of the artificial waterfall, where the lake overflow gushed and drained around the dam to the river below. A force of nature, a different kind of explosion than anything the Ghost ship marauders could create. Maybe that was a weapon he could use….

He stood on top of the dam, well above the lake surface on one side of the concrete wall and the sheer drop-off and spillway to the canyon on the other. Behind him, the men were still climbing the first flight of stairs, panting and cursing as they reached the landing where Aponivi had held onto a peaceful moment and stared at the stars. He could hear their voices but could no longer make out the words over the spillway's crashing water.

Aponivi stood tall against the sky where he knew they could see him, luring them. The vile airship captain spotted him, shouted. Aponivi moved, trying to outrun the pain as well as the men in pursuit. He headed toward the spillway.

Jagged stones tore at his feet, shoving aside the numbness. Limping, leaving a trail of blood, he looked back only once to make sure the men still followed, then let himself become lost to them in the misty air.

In the smokescreen of the spillway spray, he slipped away from the cracked roadway and worked his way to the very edge of the drop-off to the deep canyon downstream of the towering dam. Here, the roar of the overflow water was deafening, the cold spray thick and blinding, like a dense fog. With his sharp eyes, he kept watch for his pursuers.

He had circled overhead many times, looking down like an angel on the crashing water, the tumbling and graceful gush that thundered down into the canyon. He had never come this close before, though. The sheer force of the spillway made the ground tremble beneath his feet.

When shadowy figures came closer, hunting him, he watched them stalk forward, but they continued moving along the remnants of the road. All but blind in the night and deafened by the roaring water, they did not even look his way.

Aponivi stooped and picked up a fist-sized rock. His nails were cracked and torn, and his arm throbbed with pain from the arrow wound and the torn wing membrane. He hurled the rock at them, missed.

The two men spun in his direction, and he saw that they brandished clubs or swords, some kind of weapons they had salvaged from the crash. They came closer, taking each step cautiously as they tried to find him. Aponivi waited.

They hesitated, aware of the danger he might pose. One bent down and scrabbled around on the ground before grabbing a rock. He flung it in Aponivi's direction, but it missed by a wide margin.

Warm blood dripped down Aponivi's arm, thick and wet, but it cooled by the time it reached his fingers. He could feel his time waning, his strength, his soul. These men only had to wait him out. Did they know that? He fought the urge to slump to the ground and just give up.

Instead, he picked up another rock and threw it. This time, he grazed the shoulder of the airship captain. Cursing, both men turned, more accurately facing him now. Aponivi heard angry voices but could not make out the words. He didn't need to. They were closing in on him. He threw another rock, but his arm was shaking. The effort nearly made him collapse. His head spun.

As they closed in on him, though, he stumbled to the side, camouflaged by the spray and the darkness. He was sure they could neither see nor hear him. With awkward movements, Aponivi circled behind them, tripping on unsteady feet. When both men stood between himself and the spillway, looking for where he had gone, Aponivi crouched, mustered the last of his strength. They were at the edge, looking toward the spillway below, trying to find him.

Instead, he found them. Aponivi charged, his arms wide, his tattered membranes like scoops to catch them both.

The marauders turned at the sound of his bestial roar, which was loud enough to be heard over roaring waterfall, but they were too late to do more than scream. The demonlike shape of the altered human flung himself out of the mist, wrapped them in his wings. He carried them over the edge and into the abyss and the embrace of the colossal waterfall.

Aponivi flew again, for one last time.

The morning was cloudy and cold, but the water was even colder as Aponivi's crew pulled him from the sandbar where he had washed up, a mile downriver.

He heard their words from a distance, familiar voices in an endless roaring nightmare. They talked as if he wasn't there, and he could barely cling to the last thread of consciousness. They said his wings were completely gone, they speculated he wouldn't live, they muttered disbelief and admiration over his single-handed victory against a ship of the Ghost fleet. Other search parties had been dispatched from Vegas Station.

But none of it mattered.

Aponivi closed his eyes as he felt his body lifted up, taken somewhere. He had already known he would never fly again, but that was all right. He remembered the story of Icarus, the tale his father and his teachers had told him again and again, and he finally understood something else about the story, something a man named Wilde had written about Icarus.

"Never regret thy fall, O Icarus of the fearless flight
For the greatest tragedy of them all
Is never to feel the burning light."

Aponivi had flown for all his life, something so few others would ever do, and he had flown one last, vital time. He had sacrificed everything for the lives of others who would never know. Countless others. The great fortress wall of the dam remained, and would remain, with the huge, light-filled city of Vegas Station hovering nearby, high overhead.

He felt the pure, burning light of the sun behind the ubiquitous clouds. It shone down upon him in approval, calling upon Aponivi to join the sun, to soar in the heavens, burning bright.

What more could anyone ask for?

As any pet owner knows, when you get a new male kitten or puppy, you have him neutered. It helps manage the animal's behavior, and the vet will tell you that it keeps him happier.

What if someone tried to control people that way? Keep a restless portion of the male population docile and remove their aggression by routinely neutering them when they reach puberty?

Who would do that and why? And what would one of those neutered young men think about the loss of emotions and sensations he will never know?

Asking the questions, world building, asking more questions, adding characters, all resulted in this story.

NEWTS

During what should have been the ring colony's Independence Day celebration, the mood in the family habitat was somber. Rex Hollings stared through the viewing window toward the pastel clouds of Saturn. Thanks to the mellowing influence of his implant, he wore a placid smile, aware of and yet immune to the misery and dread all around him. The others were incapable of being so stable in a time of crisis.

Rex admired the planet's gentle beauty. The majestic ring arced up and caught sunlight, glittering with a spray of rocks where the tightly knit group of Worthies had built habitation modules, storage depots, greenhouse domes. All those artificial structures should have formed the backbone of a carefully engineered society. A magnificent colony. Standing alone, Rex considered the grand aspirations of visionary Ardet Hollings, who had founded the Worthies.

Now there were three empty seats at the dinner table. All families had suffered similar losses in the recent space battle.

As the emotional currents moved around him, Rex imagined himself as a rock in a fast-flowing stream, as in the library images he liked to view. Images of natural beauty were the only parts of Earth that Ardet had allowed them to see, claiming that everything else was too corrupt. He found the lovely landscape scenes very soothing, the rushing waters, the crashing ocean waves, the silvery waterfalls. Rex had never visited Earth, and he never would, especially not now.

Though he could not personally experience extreme moods, he still recognized the agitation from his mother and his two sisters-in-law. It was like learning a foreign language. Even little Max was affected by the tension; the boy clung fussily to his Uncle Rex, who was two years younger than his father. Rex picked up his unsettled nephew, whispering soft words that soothed him. Max stopped crying, giggled once, then played with his uncle's hair. They both looked out the window. "See the planet? Isn't it pretty?" As a firstborn, Max would never be subjected to the implant, or the operation. If Rex hadn't been so calm, he might have envied the little boy.

Mother emerged from the kitchen unit, forcing a bright smile. She looked wrung out and pale, overworked, overwhelmed, but not willing to surrender any ground to Fate. She would keep doing what she must, regardless of the circumstances. As the wife of Ardet Hollings, she had always been an excellent example for other Worthy women to emulate, filling her role, doing her tasks, never overstepping the boundaries. Rex thought she was perfect. Even knowing the terrible things that had happened to the colony, and what they could expect from the Earth military forces, her job was to manage their home and keep the family unit intact. Mother would die before she gave up any of those tasks, no matter what outside threat might be coming their way.

"Today is our special day, so we have a feast. Twenty-one years ago today Ardet led us away from Earth and brought us here to form our model society." She said the phrases she had memorized. Her husband had written the original Independence Day speech, and the words had become canon. "We came here to find peace, despite the hardships we knew we would have to face and without interference from outsiders."

Rex intoned the benediction along with his two sisters-in-law, "Peace despite hardship." He handed the now-happy toddler back to Ann, tapping Max on the nose and making him giggle one last time before the meal.

Mother brought out platters of fresh vegetables grown in the greenhouse domes. At the end of his shift that day, Rex had brought home the best from the harvest, far more than they really needed to eat. There were ears of bright yellow corn, bowls of green beans, leafy salads dressed with spicy herbed sauces. Tofumeat added extra protein.

With all greenhouse systems perfectly functional, at last, the productivity in the domes was enough to feed a population beyond even Ardet's greatest dreams—and now that so many colonists had died, there was extra food for the table. *Silver linings.* Rex smiled at the thought. He served himself sliced tomatoes so red they made the eyes ache.

"There isn't much reason to celebrate," grumbled Ann as she took her seat next to one of the empty spots. When Max fussed, she set the toddler on her knee and absently shushed him. Rex offered to take the boy, but Ann shook her head.

Mother would not let anything derail her purpose. "It is still our Independence Day. We have always celebrated it, and we'll do so again this year. Our men would want it that way."

"Who knows what will happen next year?" Rex said, meaning to be optimistic. He let events flow toward him and accepted whatever came. He, like so many others of his generation, was kept on an even keel, cooperative, causing no trouble. Ardet had wanted it that way.

Instead, his comment stung the others there. Rex could see expressions fall and felt their turbulent anxiety: grief for lost husbands, fear of the inevitable end of their way of life, anger at the enemy that had robbed the Worthies of their future. No matter how brave their deaths had been while standing against the invaders, the men were still dead.

"I'm ... sorry for what I said. It was insensitive."

"That's all right, Rex. You can't help it," Mother said.

Dark-eyed Jen, the widow of his brother Ian, took a seat across from Rex, moving as if in a daze. She had full lips, a lush figure, and a once-sparkling personality that had made her an extremely desirable mate. Ian had been the envy of many Worthies when she'd accepted his proposal of marriage, and Ardet himself had blessed the union. Rex had been very pleased for both of them, hoping they would have many children ... but there hadn't been time. He could sense Jen's sorrow at that now, the suffocating weight of lost opportunities.

It all flowed past him. He was a rock in a stream. That was as much as the implant, and his altered body, allowed him to be.

Since Rex was the only "man" there, Mother asked him to say a brief prayer for Lee and Ian, as well as their father and all of the fallen heroes. Rex mouthed the memorized words in his thin, piping voice. Then they all joined in an uninspired but adequate recitation of Ardet's traditional Independence Day benediction. When he finished speaking, everyone murmured, "As Ardet said."

Giving him a shy smile, Jen served Rex one of the ears of corn, took a smaller one for herself, then passed the plate down to where Ann was struggling with Max while scooping up some beans. Ann had a round face and curly brown hair. When her husband was still alive, she had kept herself beautiful for him, but in the months since Lee had fallen, she'd had little opportunity to do so, especially with caring for Max.

Rex knew that Ann struggled to be strong, to follow Mother's example; Worthy women were groomed to be exceptionally competent in their well-defined areas of responsibility, and to rely on the men to fulfill their own duties. But not even Ardet, with his grand dreams and detailed societal models, had envisioned the possibility of an entire stratum vanishing practically overnight.

Ann asked, "How soon do you suppose the DPs will be here?" She spoke as if it were casual mealtime conversation, though Rex could hear the tension, like brittle glass in her voice.

"I'll have no such talk at the table." Mother passed the salad bowl around again and urged them to eat. "This isn't the time for it."

"I'm afraid," Jen said in a small voice, looking directly at Rex. He glanced away, knowing what she wanted from him but unable to give it. He felt so sorry for her.

The Democratic Progressives had dispatched a retaliatory force to crush them, and everyone knew it was only a matter of time. The Worthies had already sacrificed all their fighting men against the first small exploratory force that had come to Saturn. Ardet, Lee, Ian, and the other men in the Worthy settlement had defeated the enemy that day, but at incredible cost to themselves. The remaining colonists would have no chance when Earth's reinforcements arrived at Saturn. For months now, Rex had felt the uneasy panic wafting among the colony survivors like the wind from a laboring air recycler.

But he remained calm. All newts remained calm. Ardet had thought it for the best.

After the meal, his belly full, Rex helped out in the kitchen unit, cleaning dishes, recycling scraps. Though Worthy men did not do such work, newts were allowed to perform some duties traditionally reserved for women. Besides, Rex had designed or refined some of the household recycling systems himself, and he knew how to keep them functioning at peak efficiency.

Jen offered to help him while Ann and Mother played with Max in the main living area. One of Ardet's old recorded speeches played on the screen; crowds of exuberant new colonists cheered, giddy with their recent separation from Earth and assured of a bright future if only they followed the rigid Worthy plan.

Jen stood uncomfortably close to Rex in the cramped kitchen unit. He used a squeegee to scrape food into a compost-recycler and stored the serving plates in the sanitizer, which used water reclaimed from the abundant ice in Saturn's rings. For a while, she made light conversation, though he could hear a deep and desperate huskiness to her voice, a longing and a need. After a long pause, Jen said in a very low whisper, "Rex, I ache every time I see you. Do you know how much you remind me of Ian? You look so much like him."

"I *am* his brother. We've always looked a lot alike."

She slipped her arms around his waist. "Face me."

He felt awkward, interrupted in his work, but he dutifully turned. He looked at Jen's oval face, her delicate chin. Both of his brothers' wives were beautiful women, yet Rex felt no desire for his sisters-in-law. Still, he loved them deeply. Jen must have seen it on his face. He stroked her hair, trying to calm her, as he had done with Max.

Growing bolder, she pressed her soft breasts against his chest, then tilted her face. She kissed him, at first tentatively, then ferociously. Her lips were moist and pleasant, warm, wanting more than he was capable of giving. "I miss him so much, Rex. I'm so lonely."

"We're all lonely." He gently extricated himself, patted her on the shoulder, as a brother would, and reminded her of what she already knew. "I'm not entirely like Ian. I'm missing some of my parts."

Though he had not intended to upset her in any way, he experienced her reaction like whitecaps crashing against a sea cliff. *Another library image from Earth* … Rebuffed, Jen backed to the door of the kitchen unit. He could not experience the same reactions, with all the highs and lows of passion clipped from him, but he very much wanted to understand. "I'm sorry," he said automatically, hoping it would defuse the tension simmering in her. "Don't be angry."

Dark hair swirled around her as she tossed her head and looked at him with a flicker of … disgust? "How can you keep us safe from the DPs? They're coming! You know what they're like. They'll destroy us all."

Rex blinked at her, struggling to quell the situation. Yes, he had heard Ardet's speeches on the evils of Earth, the manic greed and violence of the Democratic Progressives. Rex, born here in the new colony, had never experienced Earth except through his father's harsh descriptions, but he believed the stories of a lawless society in which no member knew his or her place. After great struggle and persecution, the Worthies had broken away from that, coming far enough out here into unclaimed territory that they could achieve their potential, following Ardet's social map. Rex was part of that; they all were.

"We all have our tasks, Jen. I'm a newt. You know that being a fighter—or a lover—is not one of my duties." He offered a comforting smile. "I can do many things, Jen, just not what you're looking for right now." Rex squared his shoulders, as he had seen his brothers do. "But if we don't stay the course in our darkest hour, then we dishonor Ardet. He gave us our instructions. If we cast them aside now, then we are no better than the people from Earth."

It was an intellectual argument, the kind Rex was best at, and he could see that it did not convince Jen's heart. After she left him in a swirl of anger and fear, he went back to finish the kitchen chores by himself.

The handful of intact Worthy men insisted they would go down fighting for their principles, their way of life. Rex was physically, and chemically, prevented from feeling the same passionate resolve, but he could admire their determination, their bravery, their refusal to give up. He was sure Ardet Hollings would have been proud.

Shortly after their independence day, Rex and a dozen newts were removed from their daily assignments and sent out into the space rubble field with Commander Joseph Heron. Heron was old, scarred, and impatient, one of only twenty-three male survivors of the initial battle against the Democratic Progressives. Listening to him rail against Fate, Rex wondered if Heron had spent the last several months wishing that he too had died in the conflict. But if he had, who would defend the Worthies against the decadent and despicable DPs?

From the time he was a child, Rex had been trained how to suit up and how to perform outside functions. He was perfectly capable of performing tasks out in hard vacuum, as were his fellow newts. They were well-educated, even-tempered workers who remained unruffled in a crisis. They would complete their tasks as required, no matter how anxious and uptight Commander Heron and his desperate soldiers might be.

Scouts had already combed the space battlefield for any wreckage they could salvage, but Heron insisted on trying again and again. The vagaries of gravity in the rings churned up new discoveries, like repressed emotions coming to the surface. Rex was sure nothing remained to be found, but the commander had nothing to cling to but dogged optimism. Rex was surprised, and pleased, when the searches paid off: Far from where anyone expected gravity and momentum to have carried it, they discovered a nearly intact DP ship.

Leaving Heron in charge was yet another example of Ardet's great wisdom: No newt would have bothered to keep searching.

"This is our greatest break yet, men," the commander said over the suit intercom as their shuttle approached. Heron allowed only a small touch of irony when he said "men." His voice held an edge, as if anger could inspire the newts to greater dedication, but the implants continued to keep them controlled, calm. It was the most reasonable way to get a tough job done. After the Worthies' early years of near-starvation, Ardet had based much of his plan on that basic idea....

Heron named the wreck *Flying Dutchman* after an old Earth ghost story. The *Dutchman*'s hull had been breached in several places, venting its atmosphere and killing the small crew. When their shuttle circled the derelict, Rex studied the configuration, making mental notes about what needed to be repaired. Decades ago, when leaving their tainted planet behind, Ardet's followers had purchased brute-force commercial vessels to haul people and equipment on a one-way trip to Saturn. This DP exploratory ship was faster, its lines sleeker, its potential greater than anything the colonists had used.

When the shuttle docked against the *Dutchman*'s cold hull, Heron addressed his men and the newts. "Inside this wreck, there may be energy weapons, explosive projectiles, something we can use. It's my aim to get this vessel up and running. Then we'll have five ships, and we can make a good accounting of ourselves when the DPs come."

"Can we even understand the systems, sir?" Rex asked. "This technology far surpasses what we're used to."

The older commander turned to him. Behind the reflected glimmer on the curved faceplate, Rex could see his frown. "Just because you don't have any balls, doesn't mean you don't have any brains. I'm counting on you to figure this out, Rex. It's the only way we can survive."

Rex didn't think they would survive in any case, but he made no further comment. The other newts waited to receive instructions.

After they broke into the *Dutchman*, the salvagers separated into teams and methodically moved from deck to deck. They discovered the iron-hard bodies of six DP soldiers, expressions frozen as if surprised that a tiny group of isolationists had fought so bitterly against their impressive ship. Two of Heron's men let out defiant cries of triumph; the others were queasy and silent. The newts were put on corpse detail, gathering and ejecting the dead soldiers. They didn't mind.

On the bridge, Commander Heron and his men studied the dead ship's systems. Rex stepped up to the engine controls and navigation modules, and peered down to read the labels on each station. He knew how to fix familiar systems—recyclers, irrigators, and lighting—but these looked different.

"Don't just stand there and make this place crowded," Heron said. "Not much time left!" The other newts spread out and began to make repairs.

With so many unknown factors, the Worthies had no way of determining exactly when the retaliatory ships would arrive. After receiving distress signals from the battle in the rings six months ago, Earth should have taken at least a month to gather a new fleet, which would take five or more months in transit. But if the DP military had modified their engines, improved their speed or fuel efficiency, they could fly to Saturn more swiftly than expected.

By any calculation, the DPs could be here any day.

Rex used a circuit mapper and command-train isolator to check the station panels, one row after another. He documented which modules were functional and which needed to be routed around or replaced. Even if the *Dutchman* were completely repaired, though, the new DP ships were bound to be far superior.

That first engagement had been unintentional, at least on Earth's part. The Democratic Progressives had sent an exploratory force through the solar system, mapping resources, choosing possible locations for new colonies and outposts.

"It's what so-called 'progressives' do," Ardet had said in a speech to every member of the Worthy colony. "They spread, and exploit, and take what they want. We cannot let them steal our homes! We dare not let them disrupt our grand experiment. We must prove the strength of our principles." His voice grew deeper and more powerful; it had been so stirring that Rex found himself moved in spite of the implant. "The DPs are barbarians—they will pillage, and rape, and destroy everything we hold dear!"

The Worthy men had howled, the women had cringed, and the newts had listened carefully. The men gathered every possible ship, cobbled together anything that could be used as a weapon, then set an ambush in the rings to protect their way of life.

The DP exploratory force had come to Saturn with escort ships and scientific vessels, intending to use the plentiful ice in the rings to replenish their fuel and water supplies. Rex had studied the records of their arrival, and (as far as he could tell) the DPs had taken no aggressive action; it seemed possible that they hadn't even known about the tiny hidden colony. But fiery-eyed Ardet called it an incursion, a criminal trespass by plunderers. After overcoming birth pains and terrible difficulties, the colony had begun to thrive, exactly according to the design. They wanted nothing to do with the people of Earth.

The DP scientists and pilots were astonished when the Worthy men attacked. Though the DP exploratory fleet was not a military force, they had fought back, killing most of the young men and Ardet Hollings himself before being destroyed themselves.

"Nothing here we can't fix," Commander Heron said, rapping on the arm of the captain's chair. "We can get the *Dutchman* flying again!" He looked around the bridge as if expecting the newts to cheer, but they continued their tasks with silent efficiency. He turned to Rex. "*You*. You're Ardet's own son. Doesn't anything get you riled up?"

Rex shrugged in his bulky suit. "That's not possible, sir." He reset a panel and was gratified to see that all systems were now functional. "But I do my job to the best of my abilities. Is there something inadequate about my performance?"

Discouraged, the commander let out a long sigh that was audible across the helmet radio. "We won't be able to last five minutes against the forces from Earth."

Back at his familiar work in the greenhouse domes, comfortable with the routine despite the imminent arrival of the DPs, Rex was glad to be doing something worthwhile. "There is no more glorious work than providing food for our people," Ardet had said to all greenhouse workers. And since Rex also worked on the illumination and irrigation systems, he felt he was doing even more than his part. It gave him a warm satisfaction to know he fit in so well.

Overhead, bright stars and outlying ring fragments moved like fireflies. Some of the women harvesting produce looked up nervously, as if expecting them to be braking jets from Earth ships; Rex saw only lovely lights as bright as diamonds.

He hummed a tuneless song to relax himself, though the implant did most of the job. Crews of newts and women picked ripe vegetables and fruits, never letting anything go to waste. The recycled air smelled fresh, moist, mulchy. Overhead lamps poured out warm, buttery light to nourish the plants. Coming around the gauzy limb of Saturn, the sun also rose, adding its distant light and life. Bees transported from Earth buzzed around the flowers, sexless drones doing their work for the betterment of the hive.

Two years ago, encouraged by his father, Rex had improved the hydroponic trays and then the nutrient-delivery irrigators in the planted rows. Now he drew a deep breath and sighed as he looked out at the colorful patterns of growth, all the shades of green. Each species was planted in the proper order for optimal food production, everything in its place, everything productive. Ardet Hollings had been such a genius.

Rex ruffled his fingers through the velvety leaves of enhanced strawberries. Ripe and red, they would make a sweet dessert; perhaps Mother would serve some tonight. She had been more extravagant with her cooking in the past few weeks, as if to reassure everyone that nothing was wrong.

As he moved the leaves aside, Rex spotted a darting lizard. The original colonists had brought no large animals with them from Earth, but along with the bees they had released numerous small animals such as birds, shrews, and tiny lizards. The birds and rodents had died; only the lizards had survived, and thrived, finding an entire ecological niche for themselves.

Rex tried to catch it, but he wasn't quick enough. The lizard vanished among the strawberry plants, showing only a flicker of a tail that was a different color—obviously broken off and then regrown. Lizards had that amazing regenerative ability. Rex went back to his work picking the berries.

In the beginning, Worthies had planted only the fastest growing and highest-energy-density foods, then used reprocessing chemistry to break down even the waste vegetation into edible mass. They'd had nothing else to eat. Because of Ardet's innovative survival measures, that crisis had passed when Rex was just a child, and now the Worthies had the luxury and the inclination to plant decorative flowers and ornamental shrubs from stored genetic samples.

This place had become a home instead of just a subsistence colony. But it wouldn't last.

In their fourth year away from Earth, one of the three primary greenhouses had failed; a piece of rogue stony debris thrown from an impact in the rings had sailed at high velocity into the armored dome, shattering several panes and hemorrhaging atmosphere. Most of the air gone, the temperature plunged, the greenhouse was sent into an unstable wobble. Seven people died, and all the plants perished—one third of the crops to feed the settlement. Adding to the disaster, a blight had swept through the corn crop in one of the other greenhouses, decimating that harvest as well.

On the relatively new colony, their survival had already been hanging by a thread. Most of their preserved supplies were already gone. Devastated by the loss, the Worthies watched their perfectly planned future crumble. Though workers scrambled to build another greenhouse dome and create subsidiary growing areas, they faced the very real prospect of dying—or returning, beaten, to repressive Earth.

Ardet rallied them. "Return is never an option! We have fought too hard to establish a perfect society. I have provided the road map. Do we dare take our children back to that hellhole? How could we betray them in such a way?" He had lifted his young son Rex for all his followers to see. Now, when Rex watched the tapes and studied his father's words, he was glad that in his small way he had helped Ardet make his point. "We have given our citizens their places, defined their roles, offered them security instead of cultural pandemonium. Men and women fill the niches for which they were bred, without the confusion of too much freedom and too many pressures." It was a famous speech that all students were required to memorize. In the recording, the people were bleak, gaunt, and hollow-eyed—with fear, as much as from hunger.

After the greenhouse failure, knowing they would barely have enough to eat for the next few years, Ardet had assessed the big picture and repainted his grand social landscape. "As Worthies, we must watch ourselves. We did not ask for an easy life, nor will we ever have one. Our population must always be carefully controlled. We will grow, and we will triumph, but out here we must do it in a properly planned fashion. This is not Earth."

"Peace, despite hardship," the crowd had mumbled.

"Thus, for the time being, we must stabilize our population. We must shore up our society, keep our roles intact, keep our people happy. We cannot have strife, nor can we have uncontrolled breeding. Thus, as a gesture to strengthen all of us in our resolve, we must make sure that no more than two children in each family will reproduce."

This announcement had been met with dismay, since Worthies had, until now, been encouraged to have large families in order to increase their numbers. The people muttered. "Most of us already have more children than that, Ardet. Do you ... want us to kill them?" someone asked from the audience. Watching that interchange over and over, Rex was sure that the questioner would have done it, if Ardet had asked.

Their leader shook his head and gave a broad, paternal smile. "Of course not. We love our children. They are the building blocks of our great society. But, we must use them with great care, to a noble purpose." Ardet had looked at them all with his intense visionary glare. "While I am confident we have the strength to survive, this crisis is only an example of our possible tribulations. By our own design, we are in a new situation here at Saturn. We came to escape the anarchy and gluttony of Earth, and to do that we must change ourselves ... and that is a good thing, though it will be hard.

"For this generation, we must take interim measures. Difficult measures, but vital ones. After the first two children, our extra sons and daughters will remain important parts of our perfect society, but they will also make the sacrifice so that we can remain strong and stable." He had looked at them all. Rex still felt a chill when he recalled the historical tapes. "They must be neutered."

As an educated adult, when Rex considered the details of the solution, he didn't think the mathematics worked out. Neutering the additional children had not decreased the number of mouths to feed. But, as became clear later, that had only been the first part of Ardet's brilliant plan. Using the greenhouse accident as a springboard, he had led his people past another watershed, pushed his new society to an entirely new level.

Because he was their leader, because his followers would do anything he asked, they had not argued. To show his sincerity, Ardet had won their hearts by offering up his own young son as the first to be castrated. Rex was told again and again what a great thing he was doing, though being only four years old at the time he had understood nothing about what was really being taken from him.

After a large group of children was neutered and properly raised —girls as well as boys—Ardet had quietly revealed his deeper motivation to create an entire layer of society without aggression, without destructive competitiveness. Newts were cooperative and friendly, productive, and completely reliable, if not ambitious; the boys being the most prominently changed. The castration itself was not sufficient for Ardet's purpose, though. With carefully metered implants, the newts remained on an even emotional footing, causing no trouble. Each family was allowed two viable children, and the rest became a new caste, the strong and stable foundation for a great Worthy civilization. Rex had listened to the rationales over and over. He thought it was breathtaking....

Now, as Rex and the newts continued their work in the greenhouse, the women reacted to a signal piped in over the dissemination channel. The words were spoken in a crisp voice with just a tinge of fear. "An outpost on the fringe of the outer ring has picked up radio chatter, and long-distance sensors have just discovered the Earth military force on its way. The Democratic Progressives will arrive at the rings of Saturn within a week, two at the most."

Hearing this, Rex missed his brothers more than ever. He had never understood them, but he loved them nevertheless. In their youth, Lee and Ian had fought and wrestled with each other, so full of life. Fairly bursting with energy, they had always exhausted their little brother. They had tried to include Rex in their roughhousing play, but even as a boy he had never enjoyed it—due more to the implant than the actual neutering. What if he had been more like them?

As he finished filling his container with strawberries, Rex looked up through the transparent dome. He thought about Jen, desperate for him to be something he wasn't, then felt sorry for Ann and her little boy. For their sakes, he tried to imagine himself in a Worthy soldier's uniform. What if it came down to that?

Would he grab a projectile repeater rifle and stand at the habitat doorway with Mother, Ann, and Jen behind him? Snarling, would he point the hot barrel of the weapon toward oncoming DP invaders, scream like a madman and blast away one enemy after another? Maybe he would use the weapon as a club if he ran out of ammunition. He would bare his teeth. He would claw at them with his hands. The women would treat Rex as a hero, a savior. Then he would hop aboard the *Flying Dutchman* and streak off into space, using the ship's weapons to destroy more of the DP attackers. He would make them pay dearly....

Rex wiped away the faint sweat that had broken out on his forehead, shaking his head at the strange ideas. The implant struggled to banish the thoughts as fast as they came into his head. None of it felt like something he could do, something he *should* do. Rex was a newt, with his specific role to play—just like every Worthy. Ardet would have been gravely disappointed to learn his son had even entertained such fantasies. It was not at all what the great leader had designed newts to do. They served another purpose.

Rex emptied his container of strawberries, then went to pick soybeans. Even after the women had rushed off, he and four newt companions stood together chatting. Their conversation didn't touch on the approaching Democratic Progressives. Rex was confident that everything would work out for the best.

The family huddled together in the living quarters for their final hours. Rex held a squirming Max as he stood at the window, but even his uncle's attentions could not calm the boy against the palpable storm of panic. Rex felt the boy's misery and held him close, but they could not help each other.

Intellectually, he knew their dire straits, though the implant worked overtime to keep him quiet and anchored. Now he needed it more than ever. With a glance at the pale, wide-eyed faces of his mother, of Ann and Jen, Rex wondered if they envied him his calm.

With Max clinging to him, he pondered what it might have been like if he'd had a child of his own. If things had been different, would he have felt the longing to reproduce, the endless ticking of a biological clock?

Rex kissed the toddler's cheek, then looked toward the upswept rings, where he could see the glimmers of inbound DP ships. Some families were using telescopes to watch the defensive measures Commander Heron was struggling to implement. Rex saw all he needed to see with his own eyes.

Each weapons launch, each explosion, was a tiny spark. The Earth forces had come with more than a hundred fully armed military vessels, more than enough to overwhelm any resistance the Worthies could mount. Even so, Heron had taken the *Flying Dutchman* into battle; the other intact men had a few ships, little more than tiny cargo shuttles loaded with explosives. They faced off against the DPs in a brave but hopeless last stand. Fifteen newts had been recruited to man some of the defensive posts, but the Worthies did not have enough weapons for them. Rex wondered if his neutered comrades were experiencing any fear in their extreme circumstances. Was this what Ardet would have wanted them to do?

As they approached, the DP ships issued numerous warnings —they sounded like pleas—for the Worthies to stand down. From listening to the battle chatter, it seemed to Rex that the enemy fired only after Commander Heron had launched his weapons. Once the battle began, however, the DPs quickly obliterated the resistance.

The Earth ships were visible now as distinct blips closing in on the isolated colony. There seemed to be as many hospital ships as armed military vessels. Decoys? With their superior forces, why would the DPs expect so many casualties? And if they meant to slaughter the Worthies, why bother with medical aid?

"We do not intend to harm you," said a strangely accented but gentle-sounding voice over the dissemination channel. A *female* voice, in command. That startling fact alone demonstrated to Rex how different these invaders were.

"They're lying," Ann growled. Now she tried to take Max, but the boy clung to his uncle. Rex soothed him, and Ann withdrew to her terrified pacing.

As the DPs passed the outer supply depot, it exploded, booby trapped with proximity bombs. Flying shrapnel tore open one of the Earth battleships. Rex knew that the depot had been manned by two newts assigned there by Commander Heron.

Tears streaked Jen's lovely face. "That one was for Ian," she whispered, her voice cold and bitter.

Mother sat grimly in her favorite chair. "At least the damned Capitalists won't be able to take our supplies."

"Cease your resistance!" The female commander's voice sounded sterner now. "We cannot allow you to threaten peaceful ships. After you are disarmed, you will be given an opportunity to explain yourselves and air any grievances in world courts. But we must protect ourselves."

"Then stay away!" Jen shouted. Her once-luxuriant dark brown hair was stringy; her eyes grew red as she kept crying. Rex was sure his brother would still have found her beautiful.

When the ships surrounded the habitation complex, there were no more flashes, no more desperate attempts to block them. The crackling accented voice continued, "Please stand down. We do not wish to hurt anyone else. We will not harm you. You have our word."

Jen moaned from the other side of the room. "They're going to kill us all! They'll drag us back to Earth and make us their slaves." Ardet had painted that picture many times, convinced his followers what monsters the DPs were. Rex couldn't let himself believe that his father might have distorted the truth, exaggerated the threat.

Little Max continued to squirm, and Rex set him down. "It's already over."

Ann glared at him. "Don't you even care? Don't you realize what they'll do to us?"

Reaching an impossible decision, Mother disappeared into the sleeping quarters, then returned holding a heavy pulse rifle. Both Ann and Jen saw the weapon and cringed. Even Rex could barely cope with his surprise.

Ardet Hollings had wanted a peaceful society. He had reconfigured the human structure to guarantee there would be no conflict, only order and productivity. By using his followers as human building materials, by creating the unshakeable and diligent newts to be the backbone of a strong and satisfying life, he had intended to make such weapons unnecessary. The pulse rifle had no purpose other than to shed blood.

"Mother, we can't do that! It is forbidden," Ann said, though her voice held a rough hunger. Rex could see the raw conflict in her mind.

"The men are our defenders," Jen said.

"All our men are dead," Mother said. "We have no choice. We have to defend ourselves." She lifted the weapon, and it was obvious she already knew how to use it. Rex wondered where she had gotten the practice, why she had ever considered it necessary. "Unless Rex will do it."

She held the pulse rifle forward, and Rex found that he was unable to move. "I can't. I'm a newt. Our father made it so—"

"Do you believe in Ardet's teachings? Do you truly trust his words?"

He shied away from the weapon, shaking his head. "The implant, the operation—our father forced me not to be a man. How can you demand it of me now?"

"Because times demand it." Mother's eyes were sharp and hard. "You know what you have to do." She placed the rifle in his hands. It felt heavy and cold. He stared at the firing controls.

The DP ships clustered around the colony domes and locked themselves down. Rex's family members all jumped upon hearing a loud thump as the invaders forced open the access airlocks. "They're coming!" Ann said.

Rex stood with the rifle like a dead weight in his arms. Yes, he did believe what Ardet had told them. He had listened to all the speeches, enough to memorize most of them. He knew what the Worthies stood for. He accepted everything Ardet had claimed, though the actions of the DP invaders were not what he had expected.

The implant helped him to consider his thoughts, to see them objectively, without the disturbing backwaters and eddies of unruly emotions. He had no testosterone-induced distractions, no aggression, no wild mating drive. In this impossible situation, only the newts among the Worthies could remain solid and true to Ardet's principles.

Yes, he believed. He knew what his father would have wanted of him. Ardet had made it plain in his teachings, in his speeches, and in his actions. How else could Rex accept what had been done to him?

Mother looked at her only remaining son, her face full of emptiness. Jen and Ann stared at him, perhaps seeing echoes of his brothers.

The female DP spokesman broadcast another message. "You will not be harmed. You will be taken care of. If some of you wish to come back to Earth, we will arrange safe passage."

"Don't believe them," Jen cried. "They're barbarians."

Heavy footsteps came down the halls. Rex stood like a rock in a fast-moving stream, feeling the weight of great events all around him. He was a Worthy, a vital component of Ardet's vision. He had his role, he was a newt. He believed in what they stood for.

The pulse rifle in his hands was armed. The DPs were coming closer.

He set the weapon aside. Behind him, someone moaned in fear or disappointment. Mother, perhaps?

If he truly believed in his father's plan, then he had to accept what he was—and what he was supposed to do.

Newts were made to be teachers, listeners, faithful workers, a stable class without violent tendencies. If Ardet had wanted his son and all those like him to be heroes, he would never have cut them off at the … knees. Rex didn't need the implant to tell him that this was for the best.

As the DP consolidation parties moved toward the family habitat, Rex faced them. He experienced no despair or panic, neither elation nor fear. Just an unending sense of calm …

A time-travel story—the possibilities are endless!

When I read Ray Bradbury's "A Sound of Thunder," I was utterly captivated by his argument about how cascading tiny changes that would irrevocably alter the future. So captivated, in fact, that he basically ruined time-travel stories for me! How could a character go back centuries and traipse around, interacting with peasants and kings, and not dramatically alter the future?

But, I thought, what if you didn't go back centuries or millennia? What if you only went back a day or two and had a chance to fix a mistake or prevent a disaster that just happened yesterday? What sort of organization would do such a thing? And why? This story follows similar themes and ideas to my Alternitech stories.

Don't worry, "Entropy Ranch" has neither cowboys nor horses.

ENTROPY RANCH

Dallas Morning News, May 20—

A single-engine plane collided with a DC-10 jet during takeoff from DFW airport Tuesday, killing 93 people. The pilot of the Cessna 172, Lawrence Stilwell, 42, of Dallas, apparently received conflicting instructions from the control tower and was unable to avoid the collision. The crash killed Stilwell and 92 passengers on the DC-10."

< pause > < rewind > < play timeloop B >

Dallas Morning News, May 20—

"A single-engine plane narrowly missed collision with a DC-10 jet during takeoff at DFW airport Tuesday. Looking shaken, the pilot of the Cessna 172, Larry Stilwell, told reporters after the incident, 'It was real close. I got clearance from the tower the same time the jet did.' This is the third such near miss in four months at DFW, and the National Transportation Safety Board plans to investigate. 'I paused for just a second,' Stilwell said. 'Somebody had put one of those religious pamphlets on my pilot seat and I took the trouble to throw it away. Maybe it was a miracle, or maybe just a coincidence. You tell me.'"

Green-uniformed bellmen hovered around the hotel entrance, ready to pounce on anyone carrying luggage. Jersey glanced again through the angled glass of the revolving doors. If the shuttle-bus didn't come soon, he'd be late getting to the Dallas Convention Center.

He dutifully snapped open his briefcase to check the sheaves of Grovemont Industrial Gloves leaflets, computer printouts of permeability characteristics, and a stack of business cards held together by a red rubber band. Killing time.

Jersey withdrew the Hi! My Name Is: badge from the conference and pinned it on. They had gotten the first name wrong, again. Edmond Jersey, not Edward Jersey! Why do people always assume that someone named "Ed" is a -ward and not a -mond?

It would have felt so good to shout at the convention registration clerk, but Jersey calmed any such response before it could jump out of his mouth. Another dagger-headache threatened to take center stage in his brain pan. It was their mistake, not his, right? Jersey had taken the badge in silence as he wandered off into the vast convention center crowded with other industrial hygienists, posters, and exhibits.

Now, the following morning, he sat waiting in the hotel lobby. The A shuttle bus supposedly showed up every fourteen minutes; and he had been sitting there for eleven.

With a snap of his wrist, he dusted a comb through his thinning brown hair and adjusted his tie. Jersey still didn't feel comfortable in a suit, but he did his best to keep up the corporate image. The conference schedule had some interesting papers being presented in the third session, but Jersey would have to man the display table in the Exhibit Room. Time to pay his dues, to banter statistics, to coax new customers, and to give the good old Grovemont Gloves cheer.

He pressed his briefcase shut and stood up, brushing the seat of his pants. Better wait outside, he thought. He eased his way through the revolving door under the Hilton's wide awning. One of the green-uniformed bellmen moved toward him, but Jersey ignored him.

When the shuttlebus had missed its scheduled rounds by a full minute, Jersey scowled, but he quelled the annoyance. It doesn't matter. Damned if I'm going to be an ulcer candidate before I turn 33.

But the conference did start promptly at eight. He looked at his watch again.

One of the fat yellow buses pulled up to the curb with a groan of brakes. Jersey hustled toward it until he saw the bright "D" in its window. Wrong shuttle. With an effort, he made his face become calm again. He wouldn't risk bringing on another dizzy spell. They had been getting worse and worse over the past month, and Jersey didn't want to look like a fool by fainting to the sidewalk in front of everyone.

The traffic light changed at the corner, and other cars came flooding past the hotel. He could hear the D bus revving up. Its doors hissed shut, like a monster gobbling prey. The muggy air smelled of oily exhaust.

Bright blue-mirrored skyscrapers clustered around the downtown, peeking over the older buildings that still remained like fossils in limestone. Across the street from the Hilton stood a three-story-high Cokesbury Bible bookstore, flanked on either side by a pawn shop and "ABC Bail Bonds—Guaranteed!" Jersey smirked. Here, in the very midriff of the Bible Belt filled with this 'holier than you-all' attitude, what God-fearing Texan could ever possibly need "Bail Bonds Guaranteed"?

Out of the corner of his eye, he saw a plump fiftyish woman. She wore a baggy print dress that obliterated all sexual details, and under one arm she carried a stack of printed leaflets. Her face bore a beatific yet militant smile that said "The Lord is my Shepherd, and don't you forget it, buster!"

Jersey looked away quickly, trying to avoid her gaze, but she came toward him anyway. At another time he might have bantered with her, but not this morning—he had to save his rhetoric for potential customers, not waste it on a salvation zombie. He made up his mind to cross the street and look in the window of the pawn shop until the bus came.

He didn't look, didn't pay attention to where he was going as he flashed a glance behind him at the woman. The street seemed clear, and he clutched his briefcase as he scuttled around and in front of the waiting D bus, directly into the path of the second bus swerving around.

Jersey turned, had time to gawk at the giant yellow-and-black wall of metal slamming into him. He felt his nerves suddenly disconnect, as if short-circuited. No pain came into his head, but he sensed dozens of bones breaking at once—his arms, his rib cage, his skull. Then his vision turned all red, as if his eyes were filling with blood from the inside.

< pause > < rewind > < play timeloop B >

Out of the corner of his eye, Jersey saw a plump, fiftyish woman dressed in a baggy print dress. Under one arm she carried a stack of printed leaflets.

He quickly tried to avoid her gaze, but she came stumping toward him anyway. *Oh, not this morning!* he thought, wondering if he could dodge back into the hotel. He flicked his eyes back and forth. It might be easier to go across the street, stand by the pawn shop—a good Christian lady would never be seen by a sinful establishment, would she? Jersey made up his mind instantly.

"Wait!" she called. "The world is coming to an end!"

He turned his head and quipped back, "Yes, and I have soooooo much to do before it does! Can't stand around talking!"

Hah! Got off a zinger! He snickered and skipped out into the street, directly in front of the accelerating D bus. He missed the curve, stumbled, and pinwheeled his arms, trying to back up. Jersey saw the bus driver's head turned away, chatting with one of the passengers. Jersey dropped his briefcase. The giant vehicle looked like a prehistoric monster rearing up as it struck and rolled over him.

< pause > < rewind > < play timeloop C >

"Wait!" she called, "The world is coming to an end!"

Jersey groaned to himself. Couldn't she see that he didn't want to Know The Lord at eight o'clock in the morning? He scuttled toward the street. Maybe if he cut across against the traffic, she'd give up and seek easier prey.

The street seemed clear. The D bus began to move, lurching forward as it gained momentum. The woman hurried desperately, reaching out to clutch his arm and scattering a few of her leaflets on the sidewalk.

Startled, Jersey looked at her hand on his arm and glared at her. "Do you mind?"

The woman seemed surprised at her own action and quickly

released him, abashed. "I ... I'm sorry, sir. Sometimes I get a little carried away in the service of the Lord. I just wanted to have a word with you."

"Kindly keep your words to yourself." He didn't like someone intruding upon his morning. Now he'd probably be annoyed for hours.

He stepped off the curb, almost walking into the D bus as it passed. The bus driver honked at him in annoyance, then pulled out into the traffic.

With relief, Jersey saw the A shuttlebus arrive in a hissing of air-brakes and a belch of oily smoke. The missionary woman dropped back, and he was surprised she gave up so easily.

But as he grabbed the rail of the bus, Jersey felt a painful blackness swimming up between his ears, like a crowbar on his temples. A deep-seated sickness clawed its way from his heart and his solar plexus. He thought he was going to vomit. Disorienting pain burst from all the nerve endings in his brain.

Oh, not here, not here!

He slumped and sat down heavily on the steps of the bus. His face turned a discolored white, like a melted vanilla milkshake. "Hey man!" the bus driver said.

The missionary woman stood over him, looking astounded and concerned. She moved quickly, holding his chin, peeling the eyelids back and staring at his eyes, his pupils. She held his wrist as an expert would, taking his pulse. With the back of her hand, she felt his forehead.

Then all the pain and dizziness passed, as it usually did. The woman's appearance changed, a mask dropping back into place. She returned to her role as a formless old Bible-thumper. "There, there," she said. "Maybe you'd best just go lie down?"

Jersey thrust her away and stood up again, blinking and embarrassed. "Just moved too fast, that's all. Now please leave me alone."

She frowned, but dropped back. Jersey made his way to an empty seat. He closed his eyes and breathed deeply, in and out, as the bus pulled away from the hotel.

Jersey tugged his tie loose as he fumbled for the hotel room key in the pocket of his slacks. Thus ends another typical day at the convention. The suit jacket hanging over his arm steamed with perspiration in the afternoon heat. The Hilton had no swimming pool, only a couple of hot tubs on the roof—ninety five frigging degrees outside, and they had a hot tub.

Inside, the maid had shut off the air conditioner. He tossed his jacket on the bed. Jersey rubbed his temples, feeling the aftermath of hour upon hour at the Grovemont Gloves booth. He arranged and rearranged the colorful brochures. He plied the customers like an old carny huckster, holding forth his computer printouts of comparative permeability characteristics as if they were sacred scrolls. During a self-imposed break, Jersey wandered around the other exhibits, picking up a plethora of free pens, kitchen magnets, key chains. The spoils of war.

Jersey unbuttoned his shirt. Tonight, the conference would be having their banquet—Texas-style barbecue, of course. He could find dozens of better barbecue places up and down the street, within walking distance from the hotel. But he had come to the conference to enjoy himself—and everybody else would be going to the banquet.

Then he noticed the neat white envelope on the bed, propped against the pillow.

For a moment, he felt a touch of amused annoyance. Probably one of those 'thank you for staying at the Hilton' cards. He snatched up the note, then sat on the bed, puzzled.

The letterhead said simply, Entropy Ranch. His mind pondered the ludicrous notion, as if redneck Texas ranchers concerned themselves with 'entropy.' The note was handwritten, careful and neat, and made out to him personally. The paper itself smelled of faint perfume.

"Dear Mr. Jersey,

We would like very much for you to visit us this afternoon. We are concerned about the dizzy spell you had this morning on the bus. This is not a sales pitch—it's a personal invitation extended to you alone. Please take the time to come."

No signature. The only other thing he found in the envelope was a map.

The teeming madness of the Dallas freeway system finally fell behind, and all of Texas seemed to spread out in front of him. Ranch houses, fields, the roadside dotted with mesquite, corn flowers, and occasional stands of live oak and cottonwood. He drove with one hand on the steering wheel of the rental car, one hand holding the sketched directions.

How the hell had they known? Jersey didn't know whether he felt more amazed or frightened. It took him nearly an hour and a half to get to the last turnoff, a thin unpaved road branching off from a county highway—unmarked, and not much different from similar roads he had been passing for a dozen miles.

The rental car trundled along the gravel, raising dust. Jersey glanced at the odometer, ticking off seven-tenths of a mile as mentioned on the map. An alfalfa field spread out on either side, heavily overgrown with weeds. The unpaved drive hooked around a slight view-blocking hill, and then Jersey saw a barbed-wire fence and an ornate wrought-iron gate. Red-brick posts flanked the gate on either side.

Down the driveway, a large, well-kept farmhouse towered like something out of a Faulkner novel. Three cottonwood trees spread voluminous boughs in a protective shell around the house.

Jersey pulled the car to a stop outside the gate. He took his keys and stepped out of the car. How did they know? Why did they pick him? What did they have in mind?

Barbed wire stretched out for half a mile in either direction, enclosing nothing of significance, as far as Jersey could see. Several signs hung from the fence, alternating between KEEP OUT and NO TRESPASSING, in a typical Texan welcome. On the iron gate a small metal plate bore only the plain engraved words, Entropy Ranch.

Jersey stood on the metal slats of the cattle guard under the gate and punched the intercom button mounted in one of the posts. "Excuse me? My name is Edmond Jersey. I … received a note."

A filtered drawling voice drifted up from the speaker, "Yes, Mr. Jersey. Please come on up to the house." The lock on the gate clicked open electronically. "You can leave your car where it's at—we're not expecting nobody else."

Uneasy, Jersey pushed open the gate and entered. His dress slacks were starting to get dusty. He strode up toward the house and paused, but forced himself not to turn back, as the gate swung shut behind him. He wiped sweat from his forehead.

When he reached the farmhouse, Jersey noticed a thin black woman reclining on a porch swing in the shade of the cottonwood trees. She stood up, smiling, as he approached. She wore a crisp white lab coat over worn blue jeans. She had soft, wide eyes, high cheekbones, and a hard smile. Her hair was cropped close to her head.

"Welcome, Mr. Jersey. I'm pleased to meet you after all this time. I am Lilith Semper." As she extended her hand, he noticed that she wore no rings, that her nails were clipped close to the fingertip and scrubbed clean. Her voice was cool, educated.

"You sent me an invitation and I came," he said, sounding more impatient than he wanted to. He calmed himself; he'd already had the mother of all dizzy spells today, and did not wish to experience another. "Now what's this all about?"

Lilith Semper smiled invitingly. "Step inside. We've already saved your life twice today, but we'd like to check out a few things, if you don't mind."

Before he could mutter a baffled question, she opened the front door of the farmhouse.

Inside the house's facade stood glass double-doors, behind which sprawled great banks of computers, clean white walls, and giant viewscreens the size of picture windows. Cold, dry air came out at him, heavily air-conditioned to shield computer units from the humid heat. Jersey counted five other technicians within sight, moving, checking instruments.

Lilith Semper startled him by placing a hand on his elbow. "Come on inside—have a look around. This is Entropy Ranch."

He followed her across the threshold between the two doors. He stepped on a square of sticky gray material that grabbed the soles of his shoes.

"For the dust," she explained. Then, from a bin in the foyer, Lilith pulled out plastic booties—instinctively, he scanned for the Grovemont label—and slid one set over her own shoes. She reached into a locker and handed him a stiff lab coat that smelled of bleach.

Jersey shrugged into the lab coat and worked the plastic coverings over his shoes. He forced himself not to say anything. She waited for him, then opened the second set of doors.

On one wall, the large viewscreen simulated a detailed sequence of an airplane collision. Most of the technicians stood by a monitor that showed three children trapped in the blazing interior of a burning house. A screen on the far wall, partially hidden behind a bank of control panels, displayed the scenario of some kind of bus accident. Near the door, a police scanner crackled and occasionally spat out a string of words. A notepad and a dot-matrix printer sat beside the scanner on the same table.

Jersey swallowed, feeling a thickness in his throat. A dull ache began to pry at his temples again. Movie special effects? No, that wasn't it. Actual film? Or detailed accident simulations ... what kind of morbid interests did these people have?

Lilith Semper gripped his upper arm. "I know what you're going to ask, Mr. Jersey. But wait a second—let it all sink in."

He continued to stare. One of the technicians, a freckle-faced and sunburnt young man, smiled at Jersey knowingly, then turned back to the freeze-frame image of the burning house. Jersey could see the gruesome detail, the graphic portrayal of the children dying in the fire. The sunburnt technician spoke to his companions, who seemed to be pondering deeply.

"It's time travel, Mr. Jersey," Lilith leaned over and said into his ear.

Startled by her voice, it took him a moment to realize what she had said. "What?"

"We can go back to change the past, or the future, depending on how you want to look at it. As I said, we've already saved your life twice today."

She took his arm and steered him toward the back of the room. The buzzing sounds of the air-exchangers began to make Jersey dizzy. "I'm sorry we have to show you like this—it'll be unpleasant, sure enough. But if I can convince you at the outset, we'll save us a lot of doubts later on."

She took him to the large screen showing the bus accident. As he looked at the image of the yellow shuttle bus, Jersey felt a chill creep inside him. It looked too familiar. He could recognize the front of the Hilton; he thought he even recognized the shadowy bus driver behind the windshield. But the mangled pedestrian under the bus tires—

"Rerun timeloop 0804 A," Lilith said to the attending technician, then turned to Jersey. "We can stop this at any time, if it disturbs you too much."

A new scene appeared, then began to move: the bus arrived, people stood in front of the Hilton. Jersey watched in horror as he came into view, looking around, distracted. Then the missionary woman walked up to him … he tried to escape across the street, and stepped in front of the bus.

Jersey did not even think to cover his eyes. "That's our original attempt. We tried to stop it from happening, but we weren't aggressive enough at first. We have to change as little as possible each time, you see."

A new tape played. Jersey appeared on the screen again, the missionary woman came, they bantered, he snickered and tried to dash across the street—and, again, the bus struck him. But Lilith froze the image on the screen before the picture could actually show his death.

"Have faith, Mr. Jersey," she said with a beatific smile, "We'll tell you everything, of course."

Jersey felt beads of sweat standing on his forehead, dampening his hair. The inside of his skull began to throb. He took several deep breaths, forcing the nausea away. Not another dizzy spell.

She patted him on the shoulder, failing to comfort him. "It'll be fine now. We just go back in time and do a little tweaking, here and there, to prevent such tragedies from happening."

"But … why?" Stupid question! Nothing else came to mind.

Lilith Semper looked at him with a confident smile. "Why, it's our Christian duty."

She seemed ready to defend her assertion, but Jersey refused to take his eyes from the image on the screen—the expression on his reflected face, the oncoming bus, the deadly impact hanging only a second away.

"But how can you change what's already happened? Isn't it set in stone? If time is …" he faltered, not sure what he wanted to say.

Lilith stiffened, and her voice carried a sudden sharp edge. "We are Baptists here, Mr. Jersey, not Calvinists. If you want to talk about Predestination, you'll have to find a Presbyterian." She scowled, but before Jersey could understand how he had insulted her, Lilith's expression softened again. "If you feel up to it, let me show you something, like a demonstration."

Jersey fought down his unsteadiness as she led him to the screen displaying the burning house. He could see toys littered about, a pair of bunk beds and an extra twin bed on the opposite side. One set of sheets had begun to smolder. The boy's form underneath sprawled half out on the floor, but he lay motionless. One girl retched on her knees, choking and screaming; her hair caught fire. The girl in the upper bunk lay mercifully still, apparently strangled by the thick smoke. The paint on a small blue rocking chair in the corner bubbled away from the wood.

Jersey glanced at Lilith. Her eyes glistened with tears, but her voice came out strong and angry. "Meet Tammy, Cindy, and their brother Brett. The door is locked. You see, Tammy, Cindy, and Brett forgot to come home before six this evening. They were playing down by the creek, catching crawdads and water bugs. They lost track of time, that's all. But they … they came home late, and all muddy, and their daddy got angry. Ten swats for each one of them, and then to their room with no supper." She drew a deep breath, and blew it out slowly. "He locked them in while he went on off to play softball.

"We don't know how the fire started yet. The children are going to be killed—they already have been killed—but how can we just leave them? What kind of world can let that happen?" Lilith stared at him as if demanding an answer.

"Now, by changing a few parameters, we might be able to save them. We can influence precursor events so that this tragedy does not happen.

"Ethically, we have to interfere as little as possible to achieve our results. We don't want to damage the future. We have developed our own rules, set ourselves a time limit of ten 'subjective' hours to fix a disaster. You see, if we go back only an hour or two, it shouldn't set up significant ripples in future events. But the longer we wait, the greater a chance for a backlash. You must have heard plenty of stories about time-travel paradoxes."

She fell silent for a moment, almost brooding. "That means if we can't find a way to save these children soon, they're gonna die like this, in flames."

Jersey stared at the screen, mulling over Lilith's words. "What do you mean, subjective hours? And how can you sit here and manipulate events—once you change something, then it never really did occur, so how can you know about it. I mean ... this is confusing."

"Believe me, Mr. Jersey, all of us here have studied paradoxes until our heads spin. We're safe because we're in this place, Entropy Ranch. Within the boundaries of our fence is a sheltered area, like an island in the timestream. All timelines come here, ripple around, and move on. We can reach in, stir the waters where we like, and watch what happens."

She shrugged. "We've got operatives on the outside, like the lady who distracted you this morning. These operatives change little things, interact in tiny ways, and we observe from here. Sometimes we have to do it over and over again until we achieve what we want.

"For instance, maybe we'll have someone give the daddy a rose on his way home from work, get him in a better mood when he sees his kids getting home late and muddy. Maybe then he won't lock the door, and they'll be able to get out of there. That's the type of thing I'm talking about."

"But why did you pick me? What have I ever done for you?"

Lilith shrugged, and somehow that infuriated him. "Entropy Ranch is just starting out—we need test cases, success stories. Right now we can only respond to local accidents, whatever we pick up on the Dallas-Fort Worth police radio.

"We heard on the scanner that you were killed in an accident this morning. We thought we could fix it. We sent one of our operatives to the scene and, after three attempts, finally managed to distract you long enough so you didn't step in front of that bus. You were very persistent about being killed, Mr. Jersey."

Her eyes took on a passion. Jersey could feel her perspiration as she gripped his hand. "Think of it—we can eliminate awful fires like this, prevent plane crashes, terrorist attacks, stop all those stupid accidents that ..." she faltered, then pushed on, "that needlessly claim so many lives. We can do something about it, even after it's happened.

"But we need to know the effects of what we do. We need to study you, Mr. Jersey, because after we had changed time to save your life, you suddenly collapsed on the bus. What did we do to you—have you uncovered some very peculiar side effect? We have to know before we go on. That's why we broke our secrecy and called you here."

Lilith led him away from the image of the burning house. "The techs need to get on back to work. Come over here —I want you to meet someone." She motioned to one of the other workers.

The man was thin enough that the lab coat sagged around him like a discarded skin, but he moved with an effeminate grace. His silvery gray hair had been swirled and molded with generous amounts of hair oil. A braided bolo tie hung around his neck, secured by a garish lump of turquoise.

"This here is Dr. Barens," she introduced them, "And Mr. Edmond Jersey."

Automatically, Jersey extended his hand. Barens shook it and then took his cue, moving over to the third screen, which still showed the image of Jersey on the verge of death. "We want to check you out, Jersey. Maybe we set up some backlash when we sidestepped you from your appointed meeting with death."

Barens called up a file from the terminal. The image on the screen dissolved and returned to show Jersey climbing the steps of the shuttlebus. The missionary woman chased after him. Suddenly, the other Jersey's expression turned gray and waxen. He stumbled against the railing, sinking to the bus steps. The missionary woman hurried up, looking professional now, feeling his pulse, checking under his eyelids.

"We've never seen anything like your attack before," Barens continued. "It looks serious, and we want to check it out, to see if our tweaking caused some unexpected physical response."

Jersey chuckled a little to himself. "You're both jumping to conclusions. That was just one of my dizzy spells—I've been having them for a month. I doubt they have anything to do with your, er, activities. Not unless you've been 'rescuing' me since April."

Lilith Semper's face wore an almost comically shocked expression. Barens himself cringed, as if stunned. The noise of the air exchangers grew to a loud buzzing as Jersey felt the other techs in the room fall quiet. Some of them watched him openly; others glanced out of the corners of their eyes.

"We never did consider that, Lilith," Barens mumbled. She

pursed her lips and finally turned to Jersey but continued to speak to the doctor. "Then we got to find out what's wrong with him anyway. It's our Christian duty to help, remember?

"Mr. Jersey, won't you please go with Dr. Barens and give him complete details of your symptoms? He may want to do some tests after all."

Barens reacted uncertainly, but Lilith glared at him. The doctor motioned Jersey out another set of double doors into a small sitting room. Barens began to interrogate him in detail about the history and background of his dizzy spells. About halfway through the discussion, the doctor grew concerned enough to start taking notes.

Jersey fidgeted on the sofa as Barens sat in silence. The doctor got to his feet, concentrating on his notes and his thoughts. "Wait here," he said and began to walk back toward the main control room.

"Bullshit!" Jersey said, "I want to know what's going on."

"All right, come on then."

Lilith Semper watched them, hopeful. She raised her eyes, waiting for the doctor to speak. At the other viewscreen, the technicians working on the burning house scenario chattered to themselves about a possible solution. "Well?" she asked.

"His symptoms are pretty clear, but I can't tell how serious it is without different equipment." He continued, as if intentionally ignoring Jersey. "You know, I'm supposed to put in a thousand qualifiers that say 'maybe' and 'possibly' and 'some symptoms suggest'—it's standard bedside manner. But the patient never listens to them anyway, so why bother? I think it's either an aneurysm or a brain tumor. But I'd need a CAT scan to verify it. We're not set up for that kind of sophisticated stuff here—this isn't a medical research lab, you know."

Lilith looked stricken and turned an ashamed expression at Jersey, but he felt too sickened himself to answer. Finally he muttered, "I've got to get out of here."

"He's right," Barens agreed, "If this has been going on for a month, then he should get himself into a hospital soon."

Lilith looked around in anguish for support from the other technicians, but they rapidly turned their heads away. "But we can't let him go. Not now!"

Jersey, Dr. Barens, and Lilith Semper joined the technicians in the large dining room. Stripped of their lab coats, the people took on a more relaxed air. Lilith helped some of the techs bring in empty bowls, baskets of bread, and two large pots containing green or red chili. Dr. Barens brought him a can of cold beer, and Jersey savored it.

"This is a dry county we're in, but somebody runs in to Dallas once a month to pick up a couple cases of Pearl." Barens sighed. "We can't be expected to sacrifice ol' demon alcohol for science or for God, you know."

Three of the places remained empty as they all sat down. "Somebody had another idea to save the children," Lilith said. "Not much time left, so they couldn't take a meal break."

She opened up the windows, and the sound of grasshoppers came from outside. Everyone sat quiet for a moment. Jersey reached for the basket of bread. Then Lilith started intoning a prayer, which grew to several minutes in length.

Jersey had little appetite. Aneurysm. Brain tumor. Possibly malignant—fatal. Now he felt angry and helpless, upset at the people of Entropy Ranch. He should be back in a Dallas hospital, undergoing real tests, seeing what the best medical techniques could do to save him. Instead, they wanted to keep him here for a couple of days—We don't have the facilities for more than a blood test and some other high-school chemistry experiments—where he would only grow worse, hour after hour.

When Lilith Semper finished her rambling prayer, and the others had echoed "Amen," the technicians began to serve themselves, ladling out chili and breaking off chunks of bread.

"The green is hot, the red is milder," Dr. Barens said in his thin voice. Jersey took a small bowl of the red chili, sniffing it suspiciously.

"Since I already know too much for you to ever let me get out alive," Jersey said, "why don't you tell me how you managed to put this little research facility out here without anybody knowing about it."

"Oh, Mr. Jersey," Lilith said, "don't you be so melodramatic."

"Am I?"

She took a spoonful of chili and followed it with a bite of cornbread. "Entropy Ranch, this entire giant project, is funded by one of the better-known TV evangelists. Don't look so surprised. We're taking that money and turning it to the benefit of all of us, as God wants us to do. Our scientists were able to do work with a more open mind than all them party-line physicists, and they found a different way to look at relativity. You see, our people start out with the assumption that miracles can happen, and they look for an explanation. Most other researchers break their backs proving that things are impossible, not possible. Our engineers came up with a way to map the time streams, and once you get to seeing something, it's a relatively simple step to manipulate it.

"So, rather than just learning from our mistakes, we can now go back and fix them in the first place. Just like we saved you this morning. Love one another, strive for peace, do unto others, and turn the other cheek. Those are all admirable goals, aren't they?"

"No other reason, huh? No profit? No glory?"

"No publicity whatsoever. Now that we have the technology, how can we not use it to help other people?"

Jersey ate his chili, keeping a sour expression on his face. "Well, I thank you for saving me—but if you don't mind, I'd best be saving myself. Get to a hospital, you know?"

"We're trying, Jersey," Dr. Barens interrupted, "But we need a little time to work out some technical difficulties."

"What's to stop me from just leaving? Are you going to force me to stay? Whatever happened to Christian charity and doing all that stuff unto others?"

Lilith sighed and met his eyes with a sympathetic expression. Barens pushed himself away from the table and went into the kitchen to get Jersey another beer.

"It's easy to get into the Ranch," she explained, "because all time streams converge here. But we're reaching out, manipulating dozens of different futures that all intersect right here and then branch off in their own directions, swirling around the fence line. At the moment, our most crucial problem is to save the children in the burning house, and we may have to try something desperate, something unorthodox." Her dark eyes went distant for a moment, then she stared back at him.

"But bear in mind that we are working for your best interests.

Give us time to put everything straight. We can set you back down at a point in time that everybody'll see as 'this afternoon.' Nobody will even notice you've been gone."

Jersey still felt indignant. "You're going to erase my memory or something?"

Lilith lowered her eyes. "We would like to hypnotize you for our own protection, but that needs your complete cooperation. If you choose not to cooperate, well—we are Christians, you know, and we do prefer to think the best of people."

He ate the last of his chili and concentrated wholeheartedly on finishing the beer.

"We'd like you to stay in our guest house tonight."

Jersey lay back on the unfamiliar bed, listening to it creak as he moved. He could see the oak bedposts in the moonlight that came through the window. A sluggish breeze stirred the curtain, but Jersey felt sweaty and uncomfortable. Though they had provided him with a pair of light cotton pajamas, he preferred to sleep in his own underwear.

How long did they really want to keep him there? He closed his eyes, turned his thoughts inward—he could sense the alien presence of something growing inside his head, like a parasite. Even if they put him back a day into the past, the tumor would still have grown a day's worth in his 'subjective' time or the aneurysm would have worsened. If he could only get to a hospital.

Outside, crickets thrummed, but otherwise the ranch seemed quiet, asleep. He got up and crept to the door, certain he would find it locked—but the door swung open, revealing the small sitting room in the guest house. No guards either. These people were absurd in their trust. Feeling exposed, he slipped back into the bedroom and pulled on his slacks, holding the car keys and coin purse in his pocket to keep them from jingling.

How could he possibly benefit by waiting? His life lay on the line, after all, not theirs. It seemed an ironic denial of their own Christian charity. They couldn't do anything for him here—they said as much. Holding him over for an extra day or two was just a stalling routine. Pointless. Maybe an extra day would make the difference for him in a real hospital, if things were as serious as Dr. Barens suggested.

He buttoned his shirt and took a deep breath. What would they do if they caught him trying to escape? Not that it mattered—he had to try. He pushed open the screen door, careful not to let it slam, and stood on the porch. Just to his right, the tall white farmhouse blotted out the stars, surrounded by the black masses of giant cottonwood trees. He saw lights on inside, a thin figure silhouetted in the window; it looked like Lilith Semper, watching. But, standing in the bright room, she would not be able to see him.

He paused, listening and waiting. He expected some kind of security, but he'd seen no evidence of dogs, not even the typical ranch-hand German shepherd wandering the grounds. None of the doors were locked. We are Christians, you know, and we prefer to think the best of people. He wondered if they'd be interested in buying some nice swampland in Florida....

Jersey began to walk down the drive, walking on the grass to avoid crunching the gravel. His heart beat heavily, and he drew air in short, quick breaths. He moved faster, but forced control on himself, making sure he didn't run in panic.

Down at the bottom of the hill, he neared the wrought-iron gate, but he stopped, suspicious. If anything, the gate might be alarmed or tied to a motion sensor. If he was going to have to climb over the wrought-iron, he might just as well scramble through the barbed wire instead.

Jersey saw the outline of his rental car on the opposite side of the gate, and that reassured him. If they had truly meant to keep him trapped, they would have moved the car first thing. This was laughably easy—did they want him to leave?

He waded through the weedy alfalfa until he came to the barbed-wire fence. Jersey had made up his mind that he wouldn't tell anyone—explaining Entropy Ranch would be too awkward, and he did owe Lilith Semper that much, for saving his life the first time. Turn the other cheek, and all that.

With a last glance at the spectral silhouette of the ranch house, he pried the strands of barbed wire apart and, careful not to snag his slacks, he climbed through—

—and landed in the middle of the burning bedroom. Flames licked at the side of a child's rocking chair. Clotted smoke in the air blurred the outlines of a pair of bunk beds and an extra twin bed. Stunned disorientation made him lose his balance as intense heat blasted him, singeing the hair on his arms and head and scouring the insides of his nostrils. He whirled, staggered back, but the barbed wire fence, the ranch house, all had vanished, leaving only an impenetrable bedroom wall.

How could he have fallen into a different timeline? His eyes filled with water and then, it seemed, with steam. He dropped to his knees. When he drew in a deep breath to scream, the hot air scorched his lungs

If he died, would the people at Entropy Ranch know where to look? Would they come back to rescue him again? Then sick despair slammed into him with double force. Their ten-hour time limit to save the children had expired—Lilith Semper wouldn't look at all.

Or had they somehow set this up for him? Was this the "something desperate, something unorthodox" plan Lilith Semper had concocted? Because they had saved him once today, did that give them the right to throw him into this?

Jersey lurched to his feet, pawing his hands in front of him. The fire roared, blistering in the air. He could smell the awful reek of incinerating wood, plastic, paint. The door would be locked; he knew it was locked.

And then, in deeper horror, he saw the three children. The boy Brett sprawled half out of his bed, stricken down while trying to escape. One girl lay motionless in the upper bunk; the other girl was coughing on the floor.

He would not refuse to help them, just to spite Lilith Semper if she was watching. Edmond Jersey could Do Unto Others as well as anyone else. His anger made him want to curse Lilith, but it wasn't worth wasting precious seconds. Recklessly, he yanked at the girl on the upper bunk as he dragged the other girl to her feet. He jerked the comforters off the beds, then slapped the boy several times, rousing him from his unconsciousness.

"Come on! Come on!" He tossed the thick comforter around himself and the motionless girl. He blanketed the other two children and hustled them along with him.

Jersey's brown hair seemed to be flaking off in silky ash, and his face burned, raw. Jersey did not hesitate as he savagely kicked at the door with his heel.

The door shuddered in its frame, and he stepped back to kick again. He felt something crack in his leg, but wood splintered around the doorknob. He struck out one last time, and the wood around the lock bolt shattered to pieces. The door swung open to another sequence of the inferno.

The hallway looked alien, filled with a jungle of flames. Never having been in the house before, Jersey hadn't the slightest idea where he was—he couldn't even tell if they were upstairs or downstairs. They could never get out that way.

He didn't blink, but lowered his head and pulled the comforter around him as a shield. "Out! We have to get out!" Jersey held tightly to Brett and the girl Tammy as Cindy choked and cried. She sobbed and almost fell to her knees again, but he jabbed her in the ribs and shouted harshly. "Dammit! Cry later!"

He pulled them back into the room. Opening the door had been a mistake. Stupid, Jersey! On the opposite wall of the bedroom, a small window stood partially covered by the frame of the bunk bed. That would have to do. He hoped they weren't on the second floor.

He had to let go of the children. Cindy managed to stay on her feet, but the other two children slid to their knees, choking. Jersey burned his hands as he picked up the small rocking chair, but he smashed it through the window. A cross draft roared through the room, sucking heat along with it.

Jersey heard noises outside—axes splintering wood, shattering glass. He pushed Brett toward the window blindly. The boy crawled over the frame, cutting himself on the glass but seeming not to notice. Jersey turned to drag Tammy to the window without watching Brett disappear.

He had to wrestle the girl up to the sill. She squirmed, just moving and not cooperating. On the floor behind him, Cindy continued to cry. He could hear her even over the roar of the fire.

Tammy fell to the ground. Jersey saw a glimpse of Brett managing to crawl away across the lawn.

Then he saw moving figures, like monsters from outer space. Echoes of stray thoughts ricocheted through his head. 'Is my life flashing before me?' After he had broken open the door, the heat in the room had grown ten times worse. The comforter on his back burst into flames. He could not breathe at all anymore. He needed oxygen, but he felt his lungs burn. He couldn't see anything right.

But he still needed to get Cindy out the window. Jersey could barely move—every step pushed the hot wind against his face. His feet seemed like someone else's appendages. The girl was hot to the touch, but his fingers were beyond feeling. She seemed incredibly light, like a rag doll he tossed out the window.

He leaned through the window himself. He tried to shout for help, but his vocal cords seemed to have been turned to ash. The cold air outside felt like heaven, allowing him to breathe. But the window was too narrow. His shoulders wedged against the bunk bed frame and the side of the window. Glass cut into his arm as he pushed, but he could not fit through the window.

All right, he would just die here then. Keep Lilith Semper happy. Breathing the air and looking outside. That was a better way to go than a brain tumor anyway. He didn't want to die, but he couldn't make any more effort. He surrendered entirely to the fire and slumped forward.

Someone grabbed his arms, his shoulders, pulled him through. He screamed as the glass cut into his biceps, then in a last anguished moment, he fell into the outside early-evening air.

For a moment, Jersey blinked stinging tears out of his eyes, then barely discerned the shapes of fire trucks, people moving about, water being sprayed onto the flame-filled shell of the house. The three children lay collapsed on the ground, but they were being taken care of. They would be all right. Jersey knew he had saved them, and that filled him with an overwhelming sense of wonder.

He preferred his way to the subtle manipulation of Entropy Ranch. Jersey's breath hitched in his burning throat as he whispered, "While you were biting your nails, I was saving them!"

He collapsed and began to sob, but he could feel only the monotonous symphony of pain all over his body. But that was good. The pain meant he would survive, the pain meant that he was not burned as badly as he imagined.

"… delirious," a voice said. Jersey's ears still rumbled from the roaring sound of fire.

"He's in shock, I think. But he'll be okay—those burns will heal."

"Better get him off to a hospital."

Jersey tried to sit up, but other hands grabbed his arms, lifting him. It hurt him deeply, but that didn't seem to matter anymore. He heard one of the girls, Tammy, begin to cry.

"Yes," he sighed, looking up and trying to see faces. Everything remained a blur, but they were going where he wanted to be. He had done his good deed. He had earned it. Everything would be all right now.

"Take me to a hospital … a hospital."

It's well-known that I am an avid hiker and mountain climber. Upon first moving to Colorado, my brother-in-law Tim got me a guidebook with the routes to climb all 54 peaks in the state higher than 14,000 ft—and the two of us spent the next five years climbing every single one, checking them off the list.

Then we tackled the entire Colorado Trail together, 486 miles. I've got a shelf full of other hiking books with the trails marked off as I completed them.

Tim and I produced several beautiful calendars with our hiking photographs and short vignettes of our adventures; Tim has published two books of anecdotes and lessons learned from the trail, Tales from the Trails *and* Trail Mix.

Many of my colleagues, friends, editors, and publishers couldn't understand my passion for the outdoors. I tried to explain it many times, but my armchair colleagues simply didn't get it. Instead, I took a different approach—I wrote a science fiction story about two friends trying to complete the greatest hikes in the galaxy. Maybe that *will do the trick....*

LANDSCAPES

By the time our clunky shuttle finished two weeks in roundabout transit to the "designated wilderness" planet of Bifrost, Craig and I were more than ready to stretch our legs on the trails of a new alien world. I just hoped we weren't too out of shape for vigorous trekking.

The uniformed ranger who piloted us wasn't altogether happy with his chauffeur duties, but his gruff answers to our many questions could not diminish my exuberance. We were two hard-working guys, looking forward to having the peace and solitude of an entire world to ourselves, and determined to take the long, risky hike to see one of the greatest sights in the Galaxy. With humanity spreading across practically every habitable world, it was nearly impossible to get away from it all. Yet time and again we managed it.

Craig had filled out the sheaf of required forms, and I had paid all of the fees. We were not just tourists of the "pull over, look, then drive on" variety. We were *authorized* to be here on Bifrost. We had the best modern backpacking equipment, semisentient adventure clothing, and camp supplies—not to mention embarrassingly detailed maps. These expeditions had become an annual ritual for us.

Scenery. Solitude. Adventure. This was going to be heaven.

To minimize the impact of visitors on the environment, our ship touched down in a meadow, the single authorized landing zone for official vehicles. When the shuttle's hatch opened, Craig and I stuffed the appropriate allergen filters into our noses, then took deep breaths of the clean alien air. Ready to go.

"I have been counting down the nanoseconds until today," Craig said. "Oh, I was looking forward to this." He had looked tired and a little withdrawn during the long trip, but now he seemed to come alive again. Though he spends most of his life inside an artificially lit starship cabin, Hawaiian genes from somewhere back in Craig's bloodline endowed him with honey-tan skin, deep-brown eyes, and blue-black hair. I, on the other hand, am freckled and pale as protoplasm; despite undergoing melanin treatments and applying sunfilms, I'd probably burn beet red before the end of the trek.

The ranger unloaded our packs from the shuttle's cargo bin. Craig and I hoisted the heavy loads onto our shoulders, carefully adjusted the straps and clamps for balance, and double-checked each other's equipment as if we were orbital construction workers suiting up for a spacewalk.

For us, no first-person-tourist simulations would do: no 3-D images of scenery, no implanted memories of the perfect vacation. This was the real thing. We were going to be entirely and blissfully alone in the wilderness of Bifrost. Making a memory.

"You've got seven days," the ranger said. "Make sure you're back in time, or I'm gone."

Craig turned his wide face to the sky. "If you don't see us in a week, maybe we don't want to go back!"

"Uh-huh." The ranger expressed an encyclopedia of skepticism in those two syllables.

"How often do you really lose people out here?" I asked him.

"About one in twelve miss the scheduled pickup and are never found."

"Maybe they decided to turn Robinson Crusoe," Craig suggested.

"Probably got eaten." The ranger shrugged. "With budget cuts, the Planetary Wilderness Bureau can't afford to go looking for everybody. It's all in the waiver you signed."

"We can handle ourselves," I said. "We do a wilderness trip every year. Even if we get lost, we know how to find our way back."

The ranger stared at us with a grim frown, convinced this would be the last time anyone would ever see us alive. I see that look on my wife's face every time I leave on one of my outdoorsy expeditions with Craig. She never believes me when I promise to be careful, though I have survived every adventure relatively unscathed. So far.

Craig grabbed his walking stick and tossed the other one to me. "Come on, Steve, we'd better start relaxing as fast as we can. Only seven days to cure a year's worth of headaches."

We activated the staffs, which would help us navigate and could also act as cattle-prod defenses if we were harassed by wild animals —though we'd face severe fines and time on a penal planet if we dared to *hurt* any endangered alien species.

"Right," I said. "Asgaard awaits."

Bifrost vegetation had more blues and oranges than a typical chlorophyll-based ecosystem. We passed between scaly ferns and ethereal lichentrees that looked like upside-down waterfalls, and got a view of an ugly swatch of clear-cut ground where loggers had managed to chop down everything before strict preservation regulations had been passed. Now, gray-white stumps thrust up from the soil like razor stubble on a giant's face.

Neither Craig nor I are foaming-at-the-mouth environmentalists, but when you're utterly alone on a wilderness planet, it changes your perspective, clears your head. The scars left by human greed or carelessness tend to look like a big steaming pile of dog shit right in the middle of a playground—*our* playground for the next week.

"I'm glad I never had to haul freight for lumber jockeys or strip miners." Craig scowled, taking the environmental damage as a personal affront. "In a beautiful place like this, what the hell were they thinking?"

"I didn't think the company gave you any choice about the cargoes you carry," I said.

"Screw the company—they've done it to me enough times. Gotta take a stand once in a while." Frowning, he stumped off, as if turning his back on the problems of his real life. "I came here to get away from all that."

Craig is a long-distance cargo hauler who flies a company-owned transport ship around five systems, picking up percentages along the way. He has always dreamed of buying his ship from the company and becoming an independent hauler—and he's gotten close—though recent months had brought a series of setbacks. I didn't know the details, but I would probably hear plenty during the long trek.

At some point each year Craig and I need to get away, escape our jobs and civilized home lives, no matter how much it costs or how far away we have to go. Forget spas and empathic massages, nightlife and interactive entertainment experiences. Sometimes a guy just wants to get sweaty, be miserable, sleep in an uncomfortable tent, eat bad-tasting food, get lost, and then find the way back again, ready to face another year of reality.

Before long the faint path descended toward the distinctive rushing-wind sound of a wide creek. We picked our way over boulders toward the cascade. Wiping perspiration off his brow, Craig climbed up onto a squarish talus slab and shook his head. "This is a *trail?*"

"It's a *route.*" I flipped the filter over my right eye and turned it on so I could see the infrared cairns, little beacons invisible to the naked eye—and presumably to the Bifrost wildlife as well— that marked the trail without defacing the nearly pristine wilderness.

A ribbon of foamy lavender water etched its way through pock-marked stone. Some sort of indigenous algae gave the stream the peculiar tint that in itself served as a reminder not to drink the water without treating it first. In a narrow spot over the creek, three wobbly looking lichentree logs had been knocked over to form a corduroy bridge.

I gingerly started across, looking down into the angry cascade. Although none of the guidebooks had mentioned the presence of aquatic carnivores on Bifrost, the very idea made me scuttle quickly to the other side. Craig paused, bent over, and ceremoniously spat a glob of phlegm into the water. Although he's four years older than me, being out in the wilderness always seems to transform him into a little kid.

Once we were over the bridge, I let my eyes move back and forth, tracing the discouraging zigzag pattern of steep switchbacks up the other side of the canyon wall. When I groaned in dismay,

Craig reminded me, "We do this for fun, remember? Asgaard awaits."

"Yeah, yeah, Asgaard awaits. It's sure better than sitting in my environmentally controlled cubicle."

I had long suspected that Craig envied my stable job with its regular salary, though he assured me he'd rather be footloose, traveling from system to system, than stuck at a desk. For most of the year I work sealed in a cubicle chamber surrounded by screens and interfaces, exploring all manner of networks, following faint data trails. I'm a specialist in tracking certain violations in the business world, a hunter hired by clients to scan the labyrinth of entertainment loops, advertising, and news stories for unauthorized use of someone else's intellectual property. In most cases the perpetrators are too naïve or stupid to be a real threat. Still, just because they're idiots doesn't mean they can't cause disasters. I'm paid to avert disaster. It's a subtle job, and I'm good at it.

Even so, I spend much of my time dreaming of Getting Away From It All, while looking at the images in my *Fifty Most Spectacular Sites* guidebook. Craig does the same on his long-distance hauls. And now that we were on Bifrost, we intended to make the most of our limited time here, and make a year's worth of memories along the way.

Soon after we began the climb, with my thighs hauling every gram of mass against Bifrost's gravity, I found myself regretting all of the supplies I had put into my pack. I reconsidered each item from a new angle: Why should I require a first-aid kit, if I was careful enough? Would I actually miss my sanitation amenities if I left them behind on the trail? And did I really need to eat *every* day? Besides, the ecosystem and indigenous species here were compatible with our biochemistry, so we could just live off the land, despite the potential fines. How would the rangers ever know?

Unfortunately for my weary legs, my ingrained commitment to averting disasters brought me to my senses, and we plodded onward and upward. After two switchbacks, we rested ten minutes, then staggered up two more. By early afternoon we climbed over the canyon rim and were greeted by the glorious sight of a thin, cool stream running across the mesa top. We bounded toward it and stopped on the bank to unlace boots, strip off self-cleaning socks, and dunk our feet into the frigid water.

Craig let out a long "Ahhhh!", put his hands behind him, and stared up into the sky where vulture-sized butterflies drifted about on the breezes. There's nothing like the sheer delight of a simple pleasure when you're tired and dirty. "This is the sort of experience wives just don't understand," he said.

"Some wives do," I said.

"None of mine ever have," Craig said, and a shadow crossed his face. I thought he was about to say something more, but he yelped and yanked his feet out of the water. Several small scallop-mouthed bivalves clung to his bare toes and ankles, nipping at the flesh.

In the stream I saw a swarm of these small nibblers approaching my own exposed flesh and pulled my feet out of the water just in time. Inspecting his toes, Craig found only a pinch mark, no broken skin.

"We're making a memory," I reminded him—a phrase that had become a private joke between us when we ran into something unexpected.

He chuckled to himself as he pulled his socks back onto his moist feet and relaced his boots. I understood what he was thinking: After waiting so long and working so hard to get to Bifrost, we weren't about to let anything ruin our trip. "Rest stop's over."

On backpacking trips, I prefer to put on an extra kilometer or two the first day, when my energy is greatest. Craig has the opposite philosophy, not wanting to burn himself out too soon, so he likes to break off early. Therefore, we compromised and called a halt exactly where we had decided to stop during the months of planning for the trip.

In a pleasant clearing surrounded by huge blue ferns, we unshouldered our burdens, activated the self-erecting tent systems, strung up phosphors for light, and turned on the discourager beacons to drive away any nocturnal predators. Since regulations prohibit real campfires, we settled for a high-resolution hologram of crackling flames and rough logs. I'd considered bringing a can of aerosol woodsmoke, but discarded it when paring down the weight of my pack.

Craig selected a self-heating gloppy concoction of noodles and sauce while I, in a show of macho fortitude, intentionally chose a Spampak. He looked at me with a frown. "You're crazy. I'd rather eat indigenous invertebrates."

"On the trail is the only place this stuff tastes good." I proceeded to eat my meal with much lip-smacking.

We sat outside in the growing darkness under the camp lights and talked. When you're hiking all day, you don't have much extra breath for conversation, so you can let your thoughts wander, clear your head, work out personal problems and questions or, better yet, just think about *nothing*. That's a luxury most people in the frenetic civilized world with families and careers and daily schedule grids don't have.

"I wish my life could be like this all the time," Craig said with a sigh.

"You'd miss the amenities of civilization. Eventually."

He gave an eloquent shrug. "But there are plenty of things I wouldn't miss at all." He leaned closer to the campfire image. "What a year! I don't know how I'm ever going to dig out from under the crap, Steve. Maybe it's impossible."

I waited. Craig didn't need me to ask questions. He'd tell me what he wanted to tell me.

"First, I lost a huge account. A shipment of extremely delicate— and extremely valuable—skreel embryos hatched prematurely while my ship was under heavy acceleration, killing every one of them. In the wake of that disaster, my transspace insurance carrier dropped me."

"Without insurance, how will you—"

"Then, before I could get even probationary coverage, I misaligned my ship in a spacedock on Klamath Station—and *that* caused damage totaling just about my entire net worth."

"Are you going to have to declare bankruptcy?"

From the dark forest came the sound of crashing trees, a loud roar, and a frightened-sounding trumpet as two large animals collided with each other. Craig listened for a minute, then with utter faith in our discourager field, continued, "The company's already planning to sever my contract, and if I declare bankruptcy, I'll lose my ship and any chance at a livelihood. At that point, my options narrow down to submitting myself for scientific research or volunteering for hard labor on a terraform colony."

"I hear terraformers get paid well. At least that's a possibility."

"And where could I spend the credits on a raw world?"

I groaned in commiseration. No wonder he needed to get away. "Trust me, someday when it's all over, this will seem funny."

"I don't think so, Steve. It's hard to imagine."

I might have tried to cheer him up, but then the large indigenous animals—any guidebook would have called them "monsters"—lumbered into view. One, an elephant-sized panther, ripped into a house-sized spiny ungulate that looked like a cross between a porcupine and a woolly mammoth. The ungulate tried to duck into a defensive posture, but the panther-thing slipped under its guard.

They snorted and snarled. Spittle and blood flew. Lichentrees crashed into splinters. The porcupine creature raked a spine down the predator's flank, but the beast didn't seem to notice. The ungulate fled crashing away from our campsite. Without so much as a look at us, the panther sprang after it.

Resigned, Craig said, "Well, that gives me a whole new perspective on my trivial human problems."

"Amen," I said. "I'm turning in."

All the next day the trail led along a sinuous arid ridge dotted with surrealistic hoodoos, hardened clay that stuck out from the softer sandstone like a petrified alien army waiting to advance. I used my clicker to snap large files of images, though Craig just stared in peaceful satisfaction, drinking in the details, taking pictures with his mind. "I store the images in my brain," he'd once told me, "since I'm the only one who really cares about them anyway." I had to agree. There's nothing more boring than looking at pictures of someone else's vacation, no matter what planet it's on.

Late in the afternoon, the wind picked up and the sky congealed with ugly gray clouds, and I became uncomfortably aware of how exposed we were on this ridge. Rain and hail struck with the force of Thor's hammer, stinging my bare arms. I dropped my pack and ducked under one of the hoodoos for shelter. Overhead, sheets of static lightning and blue balls of Saint Elmo's Fire whipped about.

I scrambled to get out my electrostatic rain shield, but my hands were already wet, and I fumbled it. An earsplitting clap of thunder was followed by a rumbling boom, and I dropped the shield projector. Naturally, it struck a rock, and the device sparked and fizzled out. "Great."

Craig crouched under the inadequate shelter with me, his head covered by his own electrostatic umbrella, a twinkling net that deflected the raindrops and the gravel-sized hail. He shifted it over so I could huddle under the meager protection that had never been designed to cover more than one person. "Here, I'll tough it out."

"You're getting drenched and bruised!" I said.

"I'm making a memory." Craig smiled, shrugging the droplets away. "Isn't that part of the charm of this back-to-nature stuff?"

"It's supposed to be a pleasant sort of misery," I said. "The kind that makes you appreciate your everyday life a bit more."

"Bifrost is going to need to toss some pretty big loads of 'pleasant misery' at me."

Watching the majestic storm and waiting for the hail to end, we each ate several handfuls of hyper-granola and chased it with some energized water. Then we passed the time chatting.

Craig was having problems with his current soon-to-be-ex-wife Grace, who had filed divorce forms while he was on a long-distance run, making it impossible for him to finish the rebuttal phase in time unless he dropped his cargo and raced back home—which she knew, as did I, that Craig would never do.

"Grace figured out a new tactic for increasing alimony. She claims that since I'm flitting around between star systems all the time, the time-dilation effect, though small, is still significant. Therefore she has effectively put more time into this marriage than I have. She's trying to get 1.3 times the standard alimony calculation."

"Never heard that one before." It was just another nail in the coffin of his disastrous year.

As the storm rumbled and swirled around us, Craig continued to tell me about how all of his previous divorces had gone wrong. I'd lost track, unable to remember which of the women were legally bound wives and which were just long-term live-ins. He never learned to be more wary of the women he hooked up with.

But we were here on Bifrost, with only a few days to forget about the nonsense of our normal life. I tried to get Craig thinking about good times, positive things.

We both got a chuckle reminiscing about the previous year's

trip, shooting the Hundred Mile Rapids on Beta Kowalski. No one could survive the legendary whitewater stretch in a traditional kayak or raft, so Craig and I rented armored ballistic projectiles. We both found them uncomfortably similar to coffins with picture windows built into every side. Unable to control our own paths, we simply laid back for the ride, in occasional radio contact, though the thundering rapids drowned out most transmissions as we went over cascades, plunged down giant drop-offs, then shot along the current to the next set of even worse rapids. It had been an adrenaline rush for five hours straight, and we were both so weak and shaky by the time we reached the pickup point that the expedition managers had carted us off for a routine medical check. The recovery facilities and the numerous saloons at the bottom of the cascades proved that we weren't alone in being stunned by the trip.

Afterward, Craig and I each had a different look in our eyes. "Most people don't do that, you know," I said.

He nodded. "Most people aren't crazy."

"Most people are boring."

When we showed my wife the pictures, she was predictably horrified and made me promise I would never try such an outrageous stunt again. It wasn't hard to agree, since I didn't need to shoot the Hundred Mile Rapids a second time. I had already checked that one off the list, and there were other things to see and do. I had them all in my guidebook, *The Fifty Most Spectacular Sites in Galactic Sector A*. Everybody needs goals.

The next morning we descended steeply into a swamp, with rivulets of water snaking around dubious-looking tufts of drier ground. I found it ironic that our discourager fields were effective at keeping large predatory animals away, yet somehow they did nothing to block swarms of annoying skeeters. The small biting insects couldn't possibly have a natural appetite for Terran-based blood, but that didn't stop them from biting us.

The swamp foliage was so dense and the muddy ground so uncertain that we had to keep IR filters over our eyes just to spot the trail beacons, many of which were covered with moss or slimy fungus. I had to unroll the mapfilm and uplink to the surveillance satellites and zoom in on the detailed topography.

Splashing across the marsh, Craig misjudged a stepping stone and sank in up to his knee. He pulled out his foot, dripping with greenish-black muck so viscous as it crawled off his boot that it seemed alive. Maybe it was.

Halfway through a thicket, I saw some other hiker's carelessly discarded food foils, and my face pinched with annoyance. "Can you believe someone would go to all the trouble of coming to Bifrost, then be stupid enough to throw litter on the ground?" I worked my way off the marked trail to clean up after the slob. When I pulled at a polymer strap from a hiking pack, it came out of the muck connected to the gnawed remains of a human femur. Now it dawned on me that this wasn't merely careless litter.

"Yeah. I think we've found that one-out-of-twelve the ranger was talking about," Craig said, reading my sober expression. "He wasn't very successful at the Robinson Crusoe bit."

I know it sounds warped, but the only thing I could think of was, "I hope the poor guy got munched on the way *back* from his hike, so that at least he got to see the Asgaard Bridge." Sometimes my priorities sound screwy even to me.

I let the bone drop back into the swamp. "I'd better leave a radio flare so the rangers can come and gather the remains." I took one of the pulsers from my belt, activated it on non-emergency locator mode, and tossed it into the water. If I remembered right, the terms of our backcountry permits required the hiker or his surviving family members to pay all the costs of such a retrieval operation. Maintaining a wilderness planet is serious business....

A large fern sprang back and slapped me in the face after Craig pushed into the drier forest beyond the wet marsh. I wiped slime off my cheeks. We were both tired, but we had to do at least another kilometer. Otherwise, we wouldn't reach our destination tomorrow, and the whole schedule would fall apart.

We found an adequate campsite just after dusk. Too tired to talk much, we ate our meals. That night we went to sleep early after looking at our guidebooks again and drooling over the glorious pictures of the Asgaard Bridge—certainly one of the fifty most spectacular sights in Sector A, if not in the whole Galaxy. I couldn't wait to see it with my own eyes.

As luck would have it, thick fog had settled into the lowlands. The trail took us into a narrow gorge, where we couldn't see anything but a gauzy mist that hung like a suffocating pillow. We moved quickly: After days of hiking, our goal was near. We were about to join the very short list of privileged people who had actually been to the Asgaard Bridge. Mere pictures would never be the same as personally experiencing this wonder first-hand.

We began our long ascent, and once in a while we broke above the low-lying mists and saw outcroppings like islands in a gray-white sea. We climbed toward our destination—the grail. As if by some malicious joke, the clouds thickened even further, making it impossible to see more than a hundred meters in front of us, then fifty, and then twenty. In clear weather, the trail would have been plain, but we had to use the IR cairns just to find our way through the mist.

"Can't see a thing," Craig muttered. "This is *not* the memory I wanted to make."

"We're not there yet."

We kept hoping against hope that the fog would lift by the time we reached the Asgaard Bridge. It was mid-morning, and the sun ought to burn away the fog and leave us with clear skies and a beautiful view. It *had* to.

We reached the top of a mesa, then headed toward the edge of the gorge. Both the map and the IR indicators told us that we had reached our ultimate goal. And we could see nothing. Absolutely nothing. Days of hiking, months of preparations, countless permits, enormous expenses—all to get here.

To see thick fog.

The claustrophobic air intensified sounds, and we could hear the roar of the lavender river charging through the rocks and cascading into the distant gorge. I squinted, demanding optimism from myself, but I couldn't discern even a silhouette.

"The perfect ending to a perfect year." Craig shook his head. "It defies belief."

"You say that every time something like this happens." Resigned, I opened my pack, removing a snack and some juice. "Might as well have lunch."

Troubled and sulking, he tossed pebbles into the unseen chasm, while I opened the map and the guidebook, looked at the image of the Asgaard Bridge again, and tried to calculate just how long we could wait there. This weather couldn't last forever, but it could last longer than we had. We both remembered the ranger's admonition that he wouldn't wait for us—and I couldn't stop thinking of the skeleton in the swamp.

"Three hours is all I'm comfortable with. I sure don't want to miss the pickup shuttle. I've got a performance review and a raise justification when I get back to work."

"Yeah. And I've got my alimony hearing." Craig hurled another rock over the edge. "Sure wouldn't want to miss that."

I started figuring out how fast I could make my way back at top speed, how many extra kilometers I could put on my feet each day, but I doubted Craig could keep up.

On the other hand, I really wanted to see the Asgaard Bridge.

After three hours of growing frustration, the gray mist grew whiter and brighter, thinning. I finished packing up, reluctant to leave but watching my chronometer. We had never turned back before. Never. But our time was up.

Feeling as if a neutron star were weighing me down, I hefted my pack. "That's it." Many other choice words were running through my mind.

Craig didn't move to pick up his pack, just sat staring into the opaque fog. "You go ahead."

"You'll never catch up." My pace was always faster than his.

"I don't have to." He finally turned to me. I'd never seen such a bleak yet simultaneously peaceful expression on his face. "I'm not going. I'm staying here."

What could I say to that? "You're crazy! Come on."

"I mean it. What do I have to go back for? I'd rather go native here. I've got my equipment, supplies, guidebooks." The way he rattled off his justifications, I could tell Craig had been thinking about this for a long time—maybe even before the ranger had dropped us off. "The life forms are compatible, so I can hunt and forage. I can build myself a cabin. I'll be Robinson Crusoe, living off the land. Peace. Solitude. Adventure. *You* of all people should understand that, Steve."

"I understand it as a *game*, a break, a vacation. Not everyday life." Craig's expression wavered. I was articulating his own doubts. "Sure, we like doing this primitive thing every year, mainly because it makes our regular lives tolerable by comparison. The only reason we have fun getting miserable is because we know we're going back to reality when it's over. It gives us an appreciation for the simple pleasures."

"I don't have any simple pleasures left," he said. "I've got nothing. No job, no money, no ship, no wife. Tell the ranger that a monster ate me, or that I fell off a cliff. Make up a good story."

I could only stare at him. "You'll regret it in a week, Craig. A month at most. And nobody'll be there to throw you a lifeline."

"No other options that I can see. And I sure don't want to sign up for a bioresearch project. I like camping, roughing it, surviving by my own hands—" He stopped in mid-sentence and jumped to his feet, grinning. "You better take a look, Buddy! Get ready to hear a chorus of angels."

And he was right. The mist parted, and golden sunbeams stabbed down enough to impress even the most jaded photographer. Suddenly, there was the Asgaard Bridge, an impossibly delicate and poignant sliver of rock stretched across a gorge as deep and as sharp as if a cosmic scalpel had sliced the flesh of the sandstone all the way down to the bone. Directly beneath the arch flowed a foaming cascade of pink quicksilver, a perfect strand of water, pouring from between walls of natural diamondplate crystal. Showers of rainbows filled the air all around us. It was more stunning than anything I had ever seen, more breathtaking than any image in any guidebook. High spires of quartz-laced rock rose like crystalline spears on either side of the gorge, dazzling in the light.

Putting aside the crisis for a moment, Craig and I raised hands, and gave each other a high-five. This was exactly what we'd come out here for. "By far the best one on the whole list!" He said that every time.

I pounced. "And if you stay here, who am I going to see the rest of them with?" I pulled the guidebook from my pack. *The Fifty Most Spectacular Sights in Galactic Sector A.* "We've only done seventeen, Craig—that leaves thirty-three more to go!"

He wavered, looking at the Asgaard Bridge, then back at the open book. Just to prod him, as the final part of the ritual, I found the Bifrost page and marked a big fat X on the checklist box. Another one down.

"I really wanted to see the singing cliffs of Golhem," he admitted. "And the refractory eclipses of Tarawna."

"Don't forget the fungus reefs and phosphor labyrinths on Kendrick Five-A. I was thinking of a way we could combine two separate checklist locations into a single vacation for next year. We *can* bag all fifty, Craig. But not if you're stuck here."

He looked as if his engines and life-support systems had all just shut down. I knew him well enough to read a flicker of doubt in his expression. Even he hadn't been so sure about his decision. "But what else can I do? This seemed like a decent way—make my own home, settle a plot of land.… I could pull it off. I know I could."

I had an idea. "If you're going to do that, then why not sign up for one of the terraform colonies instead? Same idea, but you'll get a huge financial incentive and gain title to half a continent. Pick yourself a hardworking colonist wife and form a dynasty."

He scratched his rumpled and sweaty hair. "Terraformers? I always heard that was miserable, no amenities, living with minimal resources … *no* amenities …" His words slowed.

"And exactly how is that different from turning Robinson Crusoe here?"

He remained silent. Then, like the mists evaporating to give us a view of the Asgaard Bridge, an uncertain smile broke through on his face. "The difference is, if I become a land baron, *I* can foot the bill for our next expedition."

Though I was anxious to start back, I handed Craig the guidebook and let him spend a few minutes mulling over the images. *The Fifty Most Spectacular Sights in Galactic Sector A*. I set the hook: "You know, there are books like that for Sectors B and C, too."

Craig shouldered his pack and looked at the Asgaard Bridge one last time before returning the guidebook. Shaken and still uncertain, he took the lead with a new spring in his step. "We'll have plenty to do for years to come, Steve—if you and I make the time to go to these planets."

"We will. As long as we get back to the shuttle in time."

What if a population was so rigidly controlled that for every baby born, one other person had to die? It's the sort of horrific Hobson's Choice that science fiction explores so well. I found that idea so intriguing that I wrote it down and taped it above my desk so I wouldn't forget it.

I kept pondering what kind of scenario would lead to a rigid rule like that. I considered and rejected several possibilities because they all seemed too hokey or contrived. Then I struck the right one, and the story unfolded.

Finally, in between novel deadlines, I went out on a beautiful mountain hike with my digital recorder. I knew this was the only spare time I would have, so I needed to finish the story in a single day, a single hike. Ray Bradbury wrote all his short stories in a day and so did many prolific and well-respected pulp fiction authors. I could do the same.

A DELICATE BALANCE

The test results came back positive. Birenda felt her life change in a cold instant, as if one of the colony airlock doors had burst open and sucked her out into the planet's poisonous atmosphere.

In another time and place, she would have felt great joy to learn that she was pregnant, but this was not old Earth; it wasn't even how the Antorra colony was *supposed to be* before the disasters happened.

Inside their private family quarters, her father, Walton Fleer, received the results with better grace than Birenda did. "We knew this would happen sooner or later." The weight of administrative responsibility and the rigors of harsh colony life had aged him greatly, and everyone knew—statistically speaking—he wouldn't live to be an old man. "A new life comes, an old life must go. It's the way of the colony, the only way we can maintain the delicate balance."

A new life comes, an old life must go. How Birenda hated those words.

"And my name is next on the list." Walton gave a little shrug, pretending it didn't matter to him. "Only some of us survive, or *none* of us survive."

She clung to her father as if clipping a lifeline to his belt. "I never meant to be the one." Her voice hitched. "I'm sorry." But she could apologize, and pray, the whole day cycle, and that wouldn't change the fact.

Walton sounded so stoic, as if he were giving a speech to the members of the colony. "This way, at least I'll know I have a new grandchild coming."

"A grandchild you'll never see," Birenda said, then clenched her jaw so tightly she thought her teeth might crack.

Pregnancy tests were rarely needed on the desperate colony, since everyone knew the consequences of population growth and took careful precautions. As the current head of the small colony, Walton Fleer had managed to purloin one of the kits from a locked med-center cabinet after Birenda whispered her fears to him. It was just the two of them, counting on each other. After she used the test strip, the older man waited dutifully beside her, kneading his fists together as they waited an agonizing five minutes for the chemicals to work their damning magic. *Pregnant.*

Walton did not rail against her for being stupid and careless; Birenda had done enough of that herself. Birth-control measures were available to all colonists, everyone knew how to use them, and everyone understood that "accidents" were not acceptable. Each new life was a miracle, a blessing not to be spurned, but for a colony existing on the razor edge of survival, pregnancies must be meticulously *planned.* When the others in the colony did find out, they would hate her for such irresponsibility, particularly those couples who had already petitioned the colony council to be next in line for having a child.

Her father tried to sound soothing. "You won't show for a few months, so we don't have to do anything yet. Nobody else needs to know. We can figure out what to do."

Birenda bit her lower lip and nodded, cursing herself for her weakness. "That'll buy us a little time."

She reached out to embrace her father. In a few months, she could always hope that a deadly accident might happen to someone else, and then there would be no need for drastic action to maintain the delicate population balance. Maybe she could pray for that.

The Antorra Colony had started out so well, when measured by hopes and dreams. The original ship carrying two hundred first-wave colonists all bound together by common beliefs had been dispatched from Earth to one of a handful of planets that long-range probes had identified as suitable for Terran life. Although the ten-year voyage had seemed difficult enough, their vanguard ship was much faster than the huge main colony vessel that plodded along behind them. The initial vessel would arrive fifty years before the main group of colonists did.

As true pioneers on an untamed world, the first-wave colonists carried all the basic equipment, survival modules, prefab shelters, seed stock and embryos they would need to establish a settlement and prepare the world for human habitation. The pioneers were expected to have a thriving colony ready-made by the time the rest of the settlers came. That was the plan.

Birenda had been born en route and was four years old when the vanguard ship reached Antorra. She'd been much too young to understand the miscalculation that doomed them, but she remembered the shockwaves of terror, dismay, and hopelessness as soon as they had arrived.

The long-range scientific probes were wrong, miscalibrated somehow; vital measurements had been scrambled by cosmic rays during the transmission, or perhaps the analytical instruments were poorly engineered. Antorra was not fit for human life after all. Although other parameters were within Terran norms, the chlorine concentration in the air was far too high. Not even the hardiest Earth algae could gain a foothold and begin converting the atmosphere.

The pioneers had traveled in space for a decade, with no turning back, only to reach a place where they could not survive.

Captain Tyrson marshaled all the colony equipment and pulled his people together. The habitation domes were self-contained, and the colonists could huddle down and eke out an existence. Antorra would never be the bright new home the faithful pioneers had hoped for, but if they could last for half a century, then the main colony vessel would arrive with all the expansive domes, materials, and scientific experts required to create a rough, but viable colony.

First-wave engineers erected power arrays outside to gather energy from sunlight that filtered through the caustic greenish clouds, but the chlorine corroded the arrays, and they failed one by one. However, with certain austerity measures imposed, an emergency nuclear generator provided enough energy to meet their immediate requirements. For a while, it looked as if the colony just might survive.

Then the corrosive atmosphere ate through the seals in the greenhouse dome, killing seven workers and, worst of all, obliterating much of their seed stock, the only food they could hope for on Antorra. A death sentence.

All of the data had already been transmitted to the main colony vessel that was plodding its way across the interstellar gulf. Among the hundreds of scientists and terraforming specialists aboard the huge vessel, somebody would find a solution in the decades available before they arrived—but that didn't help the initial colonists survive in the meantime....

The captain had sealed himself in his main quarters with the full inventory of all their tools, their food stock, their energy supplies, as well as a breakdown of their bare-minimum needs. He did the math, double-checked his results, and could not refute the cold equations.

Now, as Birenda brooded alone in her chamber for hours during the sleep period, she reviewed the analysis and grim rationale that Captain Tyrson had left behind in his video farewell. The recordings were required study for every one of the children who had been born and taught on the Antorra colony.

Captain Tyrson called a special meeting of hand-picked individuals from among the colonists—himself and eighteen others. It was an eclectic mix of specialties, and no one could guess why they had been chosen. The tense and curious group gathered in the loading-dock module that contained the machinery, environment suits, and equipment needed for exploring the hostile planet.

Monitor cameras captured the captain's last speech. Birenda had watched it over and over, and it still brought tears to her eyes each time.

As he faced the eighteen men and women he had selected, Captain Tyrson said, "This colony's resources can support—at most —174 people. No matter how we tighten our belts, no matter how we conserve, there isn't enough to sustain more people than that. According to computer models, only 174 can survive until the main colony vessel arrives. The choice is hard: only some of us will survive ... or *none* of us will survive."

Then he had opened the airlock and dumped the nineteen "extraneous personnel" into the deadly atmosphere, himself included. No one lasted out there longer than two minutes.

In a calm and detailed video message left in his quarters, Tyrson explained exactly why he had chosen those particular nineteen— because their skill sets, their health, their age made them the most dispensable. Birenda's mother was among them.

In the twelve years since Captain Tyrson's brutal decision, 174 had become a sacred number, rigidly controlled. Although the actual minimum number for survival could not be precise, due to individual weights, metabolic rates, or behavior patterns, the criterion had to be absolute so that it could be followed without question. It was the only way they could follow the grim necessity.

When leaving Earth with high hopes, the initial colonists had all expected to marry and have large families, to spread humanity across a verdant new planet. Now that was impossible.

Rigid birth-control measures were imposed and strictly enforced, but the colonists could not outlaw all births, because the Antorra colony needed a new generation, a turnover of personnel to stay alive for the next half century until rescue arrived—there had to be children, had to be replacements. Each time a colonist died in an accident, one carefully selected couple was granted dispensation to have a child.

In Year 3, when a female chemical engineer developed abdominal cancer from radiation exposure, the colony doctor suggested she might recover with thorough treatment, but the treatment would render her sterile. By unanimous vote—Birenda was seven at the time—the Council decided to euthanize the woman, and she had accepted her fate for the good of the colony. *Some of us survive, or none of us survive.* After her death, one of the healthy young couples received approval to have a child.

Once the first such decision had been made, the rest became so much easier.

In the following nine years, the Council developed several lists— waiting lists for couples who wanted to have children, and ranking lists of all Antorra settlers prioritized by age and value to the colony. Birenda's father had been an astute colony leader for the past two years, but he was now the oldest member, and his name was next on the mortality list.

It was a delicate balance—174. No more, no less.

And Birenda had gotten pregnant.

"How could this happen?" Deputy Bill Orrick pretended to be horrified. "Do we need to impose mandatory sterilization on all fertile young women except for those approved to breed?"

Her father tried to sound calm and reasonable. "This is our colony's first accidental pregnancy in a decade. Haven't we already taken enough extreme measures?"

Birenda could see the strange smile as the deputy considered the consequences and came to the obvious conclusion. Before she could answer him in front of the Council members, Orrick shot a glare at her father. "You know what this means, Administrator Fleer. I'm sorry, but the list cannot be changed. It's agreed upon by every member of the colony."

"I know what it means," said Walton Fleer. "I always knew this day was coming, and I'm content to know that I will get a new grandchild out of it."

She and her father had kept the secret for as long as they could: Birenda hid her morning sickness and wore looser clothes so the swell of her abdomen didn't show, but it was only a temporary fix. Everything about Antorra Colony was only a temporary fix.

She had considered finding a way to abort the baby, researching techniques or drugs in the colony databases. She had told her father this was the only solution, but he was deeply upset. "I will not stay alive on those terms, at the price of an innocent child. We may have set aside many of our beliefs in order to survive here, but I will not ignore that one."

Each day, during the dreadful waiting, she had watched engineering teams work outside in the hazardous environment trying to build a new habitation dome out of scrap materials. It was hazardous duty, and accidents happened—frequently. A fatal mishap, or even a sufficiently grave injury that warranted euthanasia, would even the numbers, keep the 174, and her father wouldn't have to die so that she could have her baby. Then he could live for a little while longer, be a grandfather, hold his baby grandchild. With the colony's reality, Birenda knew it couldn't last, but everyone on Antorra clung to each day, grasped every moment.

But, week after week, all the workers remained safe. No one developed a terminal disease. No one accidentally died. And the time came when Birenda and her father could no longer hide the pregnancy.

"But she wasn't next on the list to have a child!" said Lucia Boma before the Council. "My husband and I petitioned two years ago. We were supposed to be next."

With tears streaming down her face, Birenda had been forced to confess the full story, raising herself up for censure—not for immoral behavior, but because she had upset the delicate balance of the colony.

She and Ando Rivera were about the same age, and it was assumed that they would be matched as a couple, since the colony offered so few possible candidates. Every settler had his or her set of duties; she and Ando were often assigned to go outside to set up racks of genetically modified algae webs, testing strain after strain to see if anything could survive in Antorra's environment.

One day, while returning from their duties, Birenda and Ando had been in the changing room, removing their suits, stripping down to clean jumpsuits as they had done hundreds of times before. They both were sixteen, saturated with hormones, half naked, alone together—and it had just happened. They hadn't paused to consider preventive measures.

Ando had avoided her for many days afterward, and she hadn't even been able to tell him when she first knew about the pregnancy....

"She will keep the baby," her father said to the Council, as if daring anyone to countermand him. "There will be no talk of forcing her to get rid of it, just because this wasn't in our plans. I know what it means, and I have several months to prepare myself before my daughter gives birth."

Deputy Orrick looked pleased and self-important; he'd been waiting for his turn as the next administrator, as soon as Walton Fleer was gone. Birenda despised the man. Her father was a long-term thinker who planned for the future of the colony, aware that he would be long gone when the main colony ship arrived in thirty-eight years to save them all; Orrick, on the other hand, considered only his own brief flash of prominence once he became the colony administrator. (He shouldn't be looking too far forward, Birenda thought, since his name was also on the list, and only a handful of names from the top.)

After glancing at his fellow Council members, the deputy folded his hands and gave a solemn nod. "One life begins, and another ends. Some will survive, or none will survive."

Birenda's stomach knotted, and she forced herself not to say anything. When the solution came to her, it seemed so clear and so obvious, she caught her breath.

She would have to kill Orrick.

For the next several months, Birenda concocted and discarded numerous possibilities, all the while hoping that her thoughts of death did not taint the life within her. She felt overwhelmed with love for the unborn baby inside her, a powerful nurturing instinct. She wanted to protect it, provide a home for it.

Dr. Hajid provided basic prenatal care but performed only cursory tests, clearly resenting her for her indiscretion, which had sent repercussions through the fragile equilibrium.

Even before leaving Earth, the bulk of the colonists on the main ship had considered the tough, conservative pioneers to be a little backward; they refused to check the sex of a baby or perform anything but the most rudimentary of prenatal screenings. The colony doctor was even more aloof than necessary with Birenda, though, as if he didn't care whether the baby was healthy or not. She realized that some in the colony secretly hoped for her to miscarry, or perhaps die in childbirth, so they could get their chance.

Nevertheless, Birenda knew that the baby was progressing well. She studied all the information available in the colony library about pregnancy and childbirth—and she found plenty, because Antorra should have been a place teeming with children after only the first few years.

As she thought of the future, Birenda was sure that her child would still be alive, perhaps even the colony administrator, when the main ship arrived. Thirty-eight years ... that wasn't so much to ask for her son or daughter. What seemed less likely, though, was that her father would survive long enough for the baby to remember its grandfather. The vagaries of the list would shift and change, and sooner or later Walton Fleer would be the one.

But perhaps not now.

When she reached her eighth month, Birenda felt a growing sense of urgency. As soon as the baby was born, her father would be taken away. She was young, and since this was her first pregnancy, she knew she could easily go into premature labor. She had to put one of her plans into practice, before it was too late. She had to get rid of Deputy Orrick, so the numbers remained balanced.

Birenda reviewed Captain Tyrson's last message again and again, drawing strength from his brave words. All her life she had been taught the realities of the colony. Every person inside the sheltered domes knew the math and the reasons for it. The colony had to survive. Some of them, or none of them. *All* was never an option.

It wasn't hard to think of a way to kill Deputy Orrick; she simply had to choose which method would be easiest. Since life on Antorra was already so hazardous, a slight tweaking of life-support parameters would do the trick. Perhaps she could loosen a seal in his environment suit the next time he was scheduled to do outside work. Or she could arrange for a leak in his private quarters, allowing poisonous chlorine air to seep in while he was sleeping.

Planning a fatal mishap for the obnoxious deputy did not strike her with any undue terror. She'd seen people euthanized all her life as their names rose to the top of the list, and accidents claimed many more. Only the number 174 remained a constant....

Day after day, Birenda sat for long hours with her father, resting her hands on the curve of her stomach, but she kept her dark thoughts to herself. Back in their quiet quarters, Walton Fleer was preoccupied, his mood bittersweet. He savored every remaining moment he had with his daughter. She didn't dare tell him what she planned, because then he would feel obligated either to stop her or report her to the Council. Deep inside, she didn't want him to know.

Walton talked wistfully of her mother, his wife, and the times they had spent together during the long journey from Earth, the plans they had made for their future, and how they had hoped Birenda would be only the first of many children. Birenda remembered the woman, but not well. Her most vivid image of her mother was from Captain Tyrson's security tape. She had studied her mother's face, then watched as the woman and eighteen others were sucked out the airlock, sacrificed so the rest of the colonists could survive.

Birenda wished she had known her better.

"We'll only have a few more weeks together, child," her father said, then let out a sigh. "It'll be enough."

To kill Orrick, Birenda decided to use one of the new mutated strains of algae that, according to preliminary tests, exuded an extremely toxic substance. It was a trivial thing for her to slip it into the deputy's daily food ration. In a way, she thought, his death and autopsy would provide valuable medical data for the colony's benefit.

Sitting next to her father, she was distracted, thinking of her plans. Walton Fleer just stared at her, drinking in every detail of her face. "I love you, Birenda," he said.

Because she had already planned it through, and also because she felt the ticking time-bomb inside her womb, Birenda acted quickly. She did not feel guilty, made no effort to speak with Deputy Orrick one last time. She was simply moving his name to the top of the list, maintaining the colony balance. 174. Her father would stay alive, and the baby would have another loving, nurturing presence for as long as it might last.

She supposed she would have to marry Ando Rivera. After her confession during the bitter Council meeting, the young man had acted strangely around Birenda, as if he didn't want to see her, as if he blamed *her* for getting pregnant. But that would change after the baby was born—for the good of the colony. Maybe someday their son or daughter would look up to Ando with the same warmth and appreciation as Birenda looked up to Walton Fleer. She smiled at the thought.

When her father came back to their quarters, his sickened expression told her that she had succeeded. "It seems I have been given a reprieve," he said. "Deputy Orrick just died."

"That's terrible." Birenda needed all of her strength to keep from jumping up with joy. "How did it happen?" The words sounded false even to her ears.

"Extreme allergic reaction to one of the algae strains in his food. They'll be running other tests, but he's dead … we're in balance. 174." He sank into the hard chair, shaking. "I was ready. I had my mind made up. But I can't pretend that I wouldn't like to see my grandchild."

Birenda clamped her mouth shut before she could reveal what she had done. He must never know.

Then the first hard contractions hit.

In the medical center, Dr. Hajid tended her, fully professional now, though he still didn't approve. With the baby coming, a new life for the colony, he was the doctor and he took his responsibilities seriously. His face was pinched, his dark eyes intent, but he voiced no criticism. He didn't really know what he was doing, with little opportunity to gain obstetrics expertise, considering the few births allowed, but he was the best the colony had.

Her father was there in the delivery room—she saw his face watching over her, and she felt comforted. Birenda knew that everything was all right. The delicate balance was kept at 174, thanks to Deputy Orrick's unfortunate end.

Even when she heard Dr. Hajid say something about complications, as if from a distance even farther away than the main colony ship, Birenda wasn't concerned. She was hazy through it all. Perhaps Hajid gave her too many painkillers. The doctor's face looked grave as he said he needed to do a Caesarean, and her father granted permission.

Birenda lay back under the anesthetic, drifting, comforted. As the gray fuzz tightened to a pinprick around her eyes, she had a last glimpse of her father looking worried, but giving her a smile of reassurance….

When she awoke, she had a hard time focusing on Dr. Hajid's face in front of her. She felt disoriented, tried to concentrate. He was speaking in words as sharp and hard as his medical instruments. "The delivery was successful."

Her eyes tried to fall closed again, but she forced them open. *Of course it was successful*, she thought. But she didn't notice her father there, and wondered if he was holding the baby.

She wanted to see him, croaked his name, but the doctor wasn't finished. "There has been one surprise—fortunate or unfortunate, depending on how you look at it."

"Where is my father?" she asked.

"I am sorry to say that he is gone." Hajid didn't look sorry at all.

Then the doctor and his assistant came close to her at the bedside. He was holding a blanket-wrapped bundle, as was his assistant.

Two babies. Birenda didn't understand.

"Administrator Fleer surrendered himself right away, while you were still unconscious. He felt it would be better that way." The doctor gave her a shallow smile. "But he did want to congratulate you on the birth of your twins."

In my first quarter of courses to get my recent MFA (a bureaucratic requirement so that I could be "qualified" to teach writing at the graduate level at my university, even though I've had over 140 books published), I took a focused class on flash fiction. I've always written stories according to the length they needed to be, and never focused on extreme brevity, but this was an interesting exercise.

At first, I started out with extremely short, clever bits, like …

"Last Will and Testament"

The immortal man wrote his "last" will and testament, again, knowing full well it would never be his last.

Or …

"Paradox"

The time traveler contemplated whether he should go back in time to talk himself out of inventing the time machine, but he couldn't seem to come to a decision.

Those are cute, but an actual story has characters and emotions, a plot progression and a point—can you do that in a thousand words or less? I began this collection with the very short "Memorial," my first published work (which was flash fiction, though I didn't realize it at the time). This is a new piece written for the flash fiction course, a story that gets to the heart of why every science fiction fan loves Mars. It's in our DNA.

GHOSTS OF MARS

At the end of a long, slow journey across space, the expedition finally arrived at Mars. The great copper disk hung below the mothership, ominous, enticing.

The lander detached from the mothership, leaving only Pasternak behind to mind the store; he had drawn the short straw and would not accompany the others to the surface. Strapped in the lander's pilot seat, Commander Tomkins felt a pang in his heart for the man left behind. Had the Russian dreamed about Mars all his life, as Tomkins had? Had he, too, been inspired by the stories he had read, adventures that fired the imagination … and now, finally, the reality?

Tomkins rode with Suvi and Chen as they began the slow-motion gravitational ballet down to the surface. The atmosphere whispered against the outer hull as the lander swung around Mars.

Tomkins opened the comm channel. "Descent nominal as we head around to the far side." His voice was dry and professional, but in his heart he was speaking to the entire human race, everyone who had dreamed of the Red Planet. "Ionization front building." He could already hear the static crackling.

Pasternak responded from above, "All is on schedule, yes? We expect twelve minutes of radio silence."

"We'll talk to you on the other side," Suvi added. She and Chen had barely cracked a smile during the long trip from Earth. The best in their fields, respected scientific colleagues, but they had never softened into friends. This was a job for them, not a *dream*. Tomkins was the wide-eyed one, filled with wonder by the very idea of the voyage. He thought of all the books, all those visionary writers who had traveled here first with their own tales ...

The lander dropped into sudden, blissful silence, cruising over the rusty red landscape, looking down at an olive-green sky, air a thousand times fainter than a baby's smallest breath.

When they did land, Tomkins, as commander, would be the first to emerge, the first human to leave footprints on the red sands. Once again, he pondered what he would say upon achieving one of the grandest dreams of humanity. How could anyone improve on "One small step for man, one giant leap for mankind"? What was he going to say?

The reddish mountains and canyons below tugged at his heart as the lander flew over the deep gash of Valles Marineris, the conical mound of Olympus Mons: magical names, the stuff of legends.

As the lander continued to burn through the atmosphere surrounded by an impenetrable shield of ionized air, Tomkins heard static on the comm. And then the faintest breathy whispers:

You made it.

It wasn't a real voice, but something ghostly and inspired by his own imagination. He perked up, curious, and somehow he knew who was speaking.

Look for the canals, said the long-gone voice of Percival Lowell. *The Martian race on a dying world, their civilization struggling to survive, pumping water from the ice caps, erecting domed cities. That is what I imagined. How I envy you the sight! It must be marvelous.*

Another voice came through the static. *Beware of their tripods and their heat ray,* said H.G. Wells. *The Martians have long regarded the Earth with envious eyes. Even now they may be building their invasion cylinders to rain down upon us in a war of the worlds. They do not know you come in peace.*

Tomkins listened, unable to believe what he heard. Preoccupied at their own consoles, Suvi and Chen didn't seem to notice. These were voices from his own inspiration, his own past. These were the original dreamers who had created the quest for Mars in the human spirit.

Barsoom is a beautiful world with a wondrous civilization, said Edgar

Rice Burroughs. *I wish I could be there to see the great oxygen factories, the four-armed green Martian warriors led by Tars Tarkas. And the lovely, incomparable Dejah Thoris! In my stories, I sent John Carter there many times, but I myself would go out at night and stare at the red star, wishing with all my heart to be transported there. But it never worked for me.*

The last voice seemed most earnest of all. *My heart is about to burst,* said Ray Bradbury. *Take care that you don't contaminate the pristine civilizations there. The Martians are majestic, but maybe incomprehensible. They will love you and lure you, but you are there. Really there! At long last. The human race truly made it. Your lander wasn't just built by scientists and engineers. The road was paved with the dreams of writers like us.*

Our adventures weren't just whimsical stories, said Burroughs. *They were an inspiration.*

I watched through my great telescope in Flagstaff, Arizona, Lowell said. *In my journals I painted a picture clarified by hope rather than through the lenses of the long refractor.*

Humans will always speculate, Wells said. *They will always explore and discover. We have traveled in our hearts and minds, but you are actually there. We wish we could be with you.*

"You are!" Tomkins said aloud, startling Suvi and Chen, who turned to give him a curious look. He lowered his voice, and repeated, "You *are* with us. And you got here long before we did." He felt tears in his eyes.

The lander broke out of radio silence, and the other two crewmembers quickly transmitted updates, worked the controls to adjust the craft, but Tomkins took a moment just to stare out the window at the raw, pristine landscape. He smiled and nodded. "We won't let you down," he whispered. He finally thought of the line he would speak. "*We leave the first footprints in the red sands of Mars, but other dreamers left their mark here long before we arrived.*"

With a gentle spray of dust, the lander touched down with a sound like a sigh of long anticipation, and victory.

Wait, we're not leaving Mars yet. What would science fiction be without the mysterious Red Planet? You'll see throughout these collections how my fascination for Mars has influenced my career. It was, in fact, Mars that made me decide to become a science fiction writer in the first place, when I became enthralled with the classic film The War of the Worlds *as a kid.*

The core inspiration for this story, though, comes not from Mars, but from obsolete computer software. I worked in a large government research lab in the 1980s and 1990s, when personal computers were just beginning to gain a foothold in office work. I was one of the first to have a Mac Plus on my desk, and I loved it.

It was also the first time I encountered the phenomenon of obsolete software. As upgrades were made and new versions became available, we would toss out the old versions and install the new, better versions. But it struck me that there was nothing intrinsically wrong with the old version of the software—which still worked the same as it always had, perfectly adequate to do the work. Yet, it was obsolete, discarded.

What if a certain group of people were modified to perform a specialized task, and they did that job well ... but still became obsolete as the task was completed or a better "version" of them came along? How would those people react to being discarded?

This scenario was so rich that even this novelette wasn't enough room to explore all the things I wanted to do. "Human, Martian—One, Two, Three" is the springboard for my novel Climbing Olympus.

HUMAN, MARTIAN—ONE, TWO, THREE

I ce, the color of spilled platinum on ochre dust, extended from the breached pipeline. Water had spewed into the thin atmosphere and frozen in lumpy stalactites dangling from the pipe. Before long the solid lake would erase itself again, volatilizing into the Martian sky.

As she brought the crawler vehicle toward the pumping station, Rachel Dycek tried to assess the area of spilled ice. "Thousands of liters," she said to herself, "many thousands. A disaster."

She turned a sharp eye from the clinging scabs of ice on metal to the broken pipe itself. The thin-walled pipe was more than just breached; someone had torn it apart with a crowbar.

That almost piqued her interest. Almost. But Rachel didn't let it happen. Her successor would have to deal with this debacle. Let him show off his talents. He deserved the trouble. She no longer considered herself in charge of the Mars colony.

As she drove up, three *dva* emerged from the insulated Quonset hut beside the pumping station. The *dva*—from the Russian word for "two"—were second-stage augmented humans, surgically altered and enhanced to survive the rigors of the Martian environment. Rachel watched them approach; she recognized none of them, but she had done little hands-on work herself with the second stage. Only the first.

She parked the crawler, checked her suit's O$_2$ regenerator system, then cycled through the airlock.

"Commissioner Dycek!" the leading *dva* greeted her. He was a squat man covered with thick silver and black body hair, wearing loose overalls, no environment suit. Rachel looked at him clinically; she had spent a great deal of her time in UN hearings justifying every surgical change she had made to the *dva* and their more extremely modified predecessors the *adin*.

The man's nose and ears lay flat against his head to protect against heat loss, and his nostrils were wide sinks on his face. The skin had a milky, unreal coloration from the long-chain polymers grafted into his hide. His chest ballooned to contain grossly expanded lungs.

The other two *dva*, both females also wearing padded overalls, clung beside him like superstitious children. They let the man do the talking.

"We did not expect someone of such importance to investigate our mishap," the *dva* man said. His accent was thick and exotic; from the southern Republics, Azerbaijan or Kazakhstan most likely. He shuffled his feet in the rusty sand, kicking loose fragments of rock. "You see, it is much worse than we reported in our initial transmission."

Rachel stepped forward, turning her head inside the environment suit. "What do you mean, is worse? How much water was lost?"

"No, the loss is what you see here." The *dva* man gestured to the metallic sheet of ice. Wisps of steam rose from its surface. The salmon-colored sky had an olive tinge from the algal colonies that had proliferated in the atmosphere for nearly a century. Rachel saw no sign of the seasonal dust storm she knew to be on its way.

"Come with me," the man said, "we will show you what else."

As the *dva* man turned with the two women beside him, Rachel finally placed him and his ethnic group. Kazakh, from one of the abandoned villages around the dried-up Aral Sea. The Aral Sea had been one of Earth's largest fresh-water bodies until the early twentieth century, when it had been obliterated by Joseph Stalin. Trying to rework the desert landscape to fit his whim, Stalin had expended all that water to irrigate rice fields in the desert—rice, of all things!—until the Aral shoreline had retreated kilometers and kilometers inland, leaving boats high on dry land, leaving fishing villages starving and disease-ridden. The area had never recovered, and when the call went out for *dva* volunteers, many families from the Aral region had leaped at the chance to come to Mars, to make a new start. Even here on a new planet, though, they clung to their ethnic groupings.

Rachel followed the *dva* man. Her suit crinkled, unwieldy from its high internal pressure. The three *dva* led her to their hut and then behind it. Part of the back wall had been knocked down and then shored up. Bright scars showed where someone had battered his way in from the outside.

Under a coating of reddish dust and tendrils of frost, two iron-hard corpses lay on the ground. Rachel bent down to look at the wide, frozen eyes, the splotched, bloodstained fur, the ragged slashed throats.

With a grim smile, Rachel could think only of how the new commissioner, Jesús Keefer, was going to have a terrible blot on his first month as her successor. So far Keefer and the UN had kept everything cordial, a comfortable transition period between two commissioners who held nothing but outward respect for each other. But Rachel had been cut out of all responsibility, with nothing to do but twiddle her thumbs in the pressurized habitation domes until the supply ship came to take her back to Earth. After she had gone, Keefer would probably find some way to connect this event with something Rachel had done during her administration. He had to keep his own record clean, after all.

"We left this other one by himself." The *dva* man took her to the far side of the Quonset hut. "We did not want him tainting the soil beside our comrades."

The third body lay sprawled, arms akimbo, head cocked against a boulder as if the *dva* survivors had tossed his body there in disgust. Inside her helmet, Rachel Dycek let out a gasp.

"*Adin*," the *dva* man said, stating the obvious. First-phase augmented human.

"I thought they were all dead by now," Rachel said.

"Not all," the *dva* man answered, gesturing with his stubby hand at the exaggerated adaptations of the *adin*. "One other escaped."

The *dva* looked human—distorted to the point of the caricatures found in Western newspapers, but human nevertheless. But the *adin*, placed on Mars in an earlier stage of the terraforming process, had endured more extreme transformational surgery. The eyes were deep-set under a continuous frill that hooded the eyes to shelter them from cold and blowing dust; the nostrils were covered with an extra membrane to retain exhaled moisture. A second set of lungs made bulbous protrusions in the *adin*'s back, half hidden by this one's skewed position in the dust. The *adin*'s body lay naked in the freezing air.

"He came out of the darkness," the *dva* man said. The two women nodded beside him. "His comrade smashed the pipeline, and we were distracted by the screaming sound of the water. This *adin* came through the back wall of our dwelling and attacked us. He slashed the throats of our two comrades while they were still trying to wake up. We managed to club him to death."

Rachel noticed what she should have seen right away. Frozen blood trailed dark lines from the *adin*'s ears; his eyes had shattered. "Down here on the plain the air pressure must have been killing him. The *adin* were adapted for conditions much worse than this."

She heard faint sounds from the chemical O_2 regenerator system in her suit. It hissed and burbled as it made her air. She marveled at the irony of the atmosphere being too thick, the temperature too warm for the first group of Mars-adapted humans.

Rachel turned back to the lake of ice and the broken pipeline that stretched from the water-rich volcanic rocks of the Tharsis highlands. "Can you repair this yourselves?" she asked. She did not want to report back to the UN base if she didn't need to.

The *dva* man nodded as if it were a matter of pride. "We are self-sufficient here. But we hope there will be replacements for … for our lost comrades. We have much work to do."

Rachel made a noncommittal response. No more *dva* would be created, and both of them knew it. Though conditions on Mars remained worse than a bad day in Antarctica, tough unmodified humans would soon be making an earnest attempt at colonization, more than just the token UN base Rachel Dycek had overseen. Politics had changed, and the days of augmented humans—and their creator—were over.

"You will need to make your repairs with haste," Rachel said. "A Class-Four dust storm is on its way from the north and should arrive late today."

The *dva* women looked at her with sharp, deep-set eyes. The man nodded again and took a step backward. "Thank you, Commissioner. We already know about the storm. We can smell it in the air."

The response took her aback. Of course the *dva* would know such things just by living closer to the Martian environment.

Rachel herself had been concerned only with how the storm would obliterate her own tracks, allowing her to disappear forever....

The breached water pipeline had been a mere pretext for her to take one of the crawlers from the inflatable base. Everyone else had duties, and no one had complained when she volunteered to make the long trip. Now the *dva* would perform their repair tasks, and Commissioner Keefer would think Rachel had taken care of everything. She would be long gone before anybody suspected something might be wrong.

After cycling back through the crawler's airlock, she drove off toward the volcanic highlands and the mighty rise of Olympus Mons, leaving the *dva* behind with their spilled ice and their dead. She had no intention of ever returning to them, or to her base.

Even on the highest slopes, the Martian air tasted spoiled to Boris Tiban. His first inclination would have been to mutter a curse and spit at the ground, but he had learned decades ago never to waste valuable moisture in pointless gestures. All the *adin* had learned that in their first days on Mars.

Boris reached the opening of the cave and turned to survey the endless slope that stretched down to the horizon. The climb from the plains to the highlands had not even left him out of breath. With only a third of the gravity that his body had been born to, Mars made him feel like a superman. He belonged here at high altitudes, where he could still breathe.

Two of the other *adin* came out to greet him as he stood in the cave entrance. They appeared unkempt, inhuman—as they had been designed to look. When they saw him alone, they hesitated. Stroganov asked, "Where is Nicholas?"

"Dead. The *dva* killed him." But the cause of death had been more than the *dva*. He and Nicholas had descended too rapidly, and the atmospheric pressure had maddened him with pain. Nicholas had begun to hemorrhage before the *dva* struck their first blow.

"Oh, Boris!" Bebez said. Her words sounded too human coming from the tight, insulated lips, the flattened face.

Boris leaned against his pointed metal staff, torn from the center of a transmitting dish, and closed his eyes. *Boris Tiban.* That was what they had called him in the camps in Siberia, decades ago on Earth before his surgical transformation into *adin*. Prior to that he had worked in the Baku oil fields near the Caspian Sea; his superiors had showed no mercy when a fire in his area caused a major explosion that destroyed a week's production of petroleum. Sentenced to Siberia, Boris Tiban had grown strong in the hellish winter wasteland, the harsh labor. And then they had snatched him away again, put him through rigorous selection procedures, made him sign forms written in English, a language he could not read, and then worked their black cyborg magic on him.

"Is Boris all right? Why doesn't he come inside?"

Boris had never heard Cora Marisov's voice in the rich atmosphere of Earth, but he imagined it had been deep and musical, not the shrill tones caused by the thin air. Cora herself must have been beautiful. She refused to leave the shadows now, especially now.

He stepped into the cave. "We destroyed one of the water pumping stations. It will do no good. Nicholas died."

Inside, the caves were comfortable, the air breathable. The dim light hid the traces of green lichen crawling over the rocks. Boris remembered how excited he had been, all the *adin* had been, when their terraforming efforts began to show results: the lichens, the algae, the changing hue of the sky. They had worked together in selfless exertion, tearing themselves apart to terraform the planet, to make it a better place for *themselves*.

The *adin* had been the first true Martians, feeling the soil with their bare feet, breathing the razor-thin air directly into their enhanced lungs. They had set out to conquer a world, and they had succeeded—too well. Now none of them could breathe the dense air below.

Cora came out, swaying as she walked. She went to him, and he embraced her. "I am glad you came back. I was worried."

Boris could not feel the details of her body against him. The long-chain polymers lacing his skin insulated against heat loss but also deadened the nerve endings. He felt like a man in a rubber monster suit from a ridiculous twentieth century film about Martians. But like those costumed actors, Boris Tiban was human inside. Human!

With the death of Nicholas, only five of the *adin* remained of the initial 100. He, and Cora, and three others.

And Cora frightened him most of all.

Through the trapezoidal windowports of the crawler, Rachel Dycek could look out at the Martian sky and see bright stars even during the daytime. Twice a day the burning dot of Phobos swam from horizon to horizon, running through its phases—full, to quarter, to crescent, to new—though they were visible only in telescopes. The other moon, Deimos, seemed nailed to the sky, hanging in nearly the same place day after day, as it slowly lost pace with the planet's rotation.

The uphill slope of Olympus Mons was shallow, taking forever to rise up from the Tharsis Plain until it pushed itself clear of the lower atmosphere. The crawler vehicle made steady progress, kilometer after kilometer.

The monotonous landscape sprawled out on all sides. Rachel felt small and insignificant, unable to believe the arrogance with which she had tried to change all this. She had been successful against a world; because of her work, adapted humans could live in the open air of Mars—but now her successors were tossing her aside as casually as if she had been the most miserable failure. That phase of the project was over, they said.

The terraforming of Mars had begun with atmospheric seeding of algae many decades before the first permanent human presence on the planet. The algae latched onto the reddish dust continually whipped into the air, gobbled the abundant carbon dioxide, photosynthesized the weak sunshine, and laid the groundwork of terrestrial ecology.

Encke Basin, in the Southern Highlands, showed the great recent scar where the united space program had diverted a near-Earth comet into Mars. The comet brought with it a huge load of water, and the heat of impact measurably (though only temporarily) raised the planet's temperature. Encke Sea had volatilized entirely within seven years, further raising the atmospheric pressure.

But the terraforming had been an enormous and unending drain on Earth's coffers, siphoning off funds and resources that—some said—might better be spent at home. Fifty years had passed, and still no humans smiled under the olive sky or romped through the rust-colored sands as the propaganda posters had promised. Popular interest in the project had dropped to its lowest point. The beginning of a worldwide recession nearly spelled the end of a resurrected fourth planet.

No wonder the Sovereign Republics looked on Rachel Dycek as a national hero. With her secret work, she had succeeded in creating a new type of human that could survive in the harsh environment. Double lungs, altered metabolism, insulated skin like a living protective suit.

In a surprise move, suddenly there were people living on Mars—and they were Russians, Siberians, Ukrainians! The news shocked the world and catapulted Mars back into the headlines again.

Rachel Dycek and her team came out of hiding with their rogue experiments and raised their hands to accolades. A hundred human test subjects began eking out a living on the surface of Mars, breathing the air, setting up terraforming industries, ingesting the algae and lichens and recovered water. They transmitted progress reports that the whole world watched. They were called the *adin*, the first.

After months of interrogation by outraged—or perhaps envious, Rachel thought—investigative commissions from the world scientific community, she and her team had developed a second generation of Mars-adapted humans, the *dva*, who needed less drastic changes to survive on a world growing less hostile year by year.

All the enhanced males were given vasectomies before they were shipped to Mars; since they were not genetically altered, any children conceived by *adin* would have been normal human babies who would die instantly upon taking their first freezing, oxygen-starved breaths.

And finally, just five years ago, a "natural" human presence had been established on the surface, living in thin-walled inflatable colonies set up in canyons protected from the harsh weather. Rachel had been given the title of commissioner of the first Mars base as a reward for her accomplishments. She had watched as her *dva* workers paved the way on the highlands, remaking the world for humans to live on unhindered.

The *dva* project no longer needed her supervision, though; and most of the *adin* had abandoned their work and died out before Rachel ever set foot on the planet. Adapted humans were a short-term phase in the terraforming scheme.

Jesús Keefer, the UN Mars Project advisor, had come to replace her. Rachel's work on Mars was finished, and she had been ordered to go home. Keefer would not want her around, and Rachel's superiors had left her no choice. They would return her to Earth a well-respected scientist and administrator. She would fill her days with celebrity banquets, lecture tours, memoirs, interviews. Charities would want her to endorse causes; corporations would want her to endorse products. Her face would appear on posters. Children would write letters to her.

It would be pathetic. Everything would remind her of how she had been retired. Obsolete. Tossed aside now that she had completed her task. But Mars was her home, her child.

The crawler toiled up the lava slope of Olympus Mons. Black lumps of ejecta thrust out like monoliths from the dust, scoured and polished into contorted shapes by the furious wind. On the sunward side of some of the rocks she could see gray-green smears of lichen, a tendril of frost. It made her heart ache.

Even in the one-third gravity her body felt old and weak. Returning to Earth—and the extra weight it would make her carry—would be hell for her.

Instead she had made up her mind to go to the highest point in the solar system, fourteen miles above the volcanic plain. *Make sure you finish up at the top,* she had always said. Olympus Mons stood proudly above most of the atmosphere, two and a half times the height of Mount Everest on Earth.

On the edge of the eighty-kilometer-wide caldera, Rachel Dycek would stand in her laboring environmental suit and look across her new world.

Already she could see the bruised color of the northern sky as the murky wall of dust stampeded toward the southern hemisphere.

The crawler itself might survive—the vehicles had been designed to be tough—but the sandstorm would obliterate all traces of *her*.

Cora Marisov remained in the shadows of the lava tubes where the *adin* lived, partly out of shyness, partly out of the revulsion she felt toward her changing body.

Fifteen years ago her eyes had been modified for the wan Martian sunlight. They had been dark eyes, beautiful, like polished ebony disks, slanted with the trace of Mongol features retained by many Siberians. Her Martian eyes, though, were set deep within sheltering cheekbones and brow ridges, covered with a thick mesh of lashes. She remembered her grandmother braiding her hair and singing to her, marveling at what a beautiful girl she was. Her grandmother would no doubt run away shrieking now, making the three-fingered sign of the Orthodox cross.

Cora made her way up the sloping passageway to where sunlight warmed the rocks. The wind picked up as she stepped outside. The cramps in her abdomen struck again, making her wince, but she forced herself to keep moving. She used her fingers to collect strands of algae that had clung to the flapping skimmer-screens that captured airborne tendrils. The *adin* would cook the algae down, leach out the dusts, and bake it into dense, edible wafers.

After greeting her upon returning from his raid, Boris Tiban sat brooding in silence below, basking near the volcanic vent. She thought of him as a rogue, one of the legendary Siberian bandits, or perhaps one of the exiled revolutionaries. It had taken her a long time to grow accustomed to the abomination of his body, the lumpy alien appearance, the functional adaptations tacked onto his form.

She recalled her emotions the first time they had made love, more than the usual turmoil she felt when lying with a man for the first time. This was no longer a man, but a freak, with whom she grappled in a charade of love.

He had taken her under the dim sun, inside a sheltering ring of lava rock that reminded her of a primitive temple. She lay back in the cold, red dust but could not feel the sharp rocks against her padded back. When Boris held her and caressed her and lay his body on top of her, she could enjoy little of his touch. Too much of her skin's sensitivity had been surgically blocked.

Thin wind had whistled around the rocks, but she could hear Boris's breathing, faster and faster, as he pushed into her. Her external skin may have been deadened, but she squirmed and made a small noise deep in her throat; the nerves inside had not been changed at all. They moved and grabbed at each other, making an indentation in the dust that looked afterwards as if a great struggle had occurred there.

They had nothing to worry about. The Earther doctors had made sure they were all sterile before dumping them on this planet. Sex was one of the few pleasures they could still enjoy. Cora and Boris had made love often. *What did they have to lose?* she thought bitterly.

A hundred of the *adin* had set out to establish new lives on Mars. Eight had died within the first week when their adaptations did not function as expected; more than half succumbed within the first year, unable to adapt to the harsh new environment.

As good workers, they had transmitted regular reports back to Earth, at first every day, then every week, then intermittently. With a forty-minute round-trip transmission lag, they could transmit their report and be gone again from the station before the Earth monitors could respond. Boris had liked using the delayed messages to taunt and frustrate. The Earthers couldn't do a damned thing about it.

After three years, cocky with invulnerability, Boris had spoken to the remaining *adin*. The Earthers had abandoned them on Mars, he said, to sink or swim depending on their own resourcefulness. Earth wanted to watch a soap opera, the quaint outcasts' struggle for survival. Finally, Boris transmitted an arrogant refusal to do terraforming work anymore, and then destroyed the station. He had taken the metal spire from the tip of the dish and kept it as his royal staff.

By that time, only thirty *adin* remained. They moved to higher altitudes where the climate was more comfortable, the air thinner and easier to breathe.

Within a Martian year, the first *dva* arrived. They had been planned to replace the *adin* all along....

Now, her arms laden with wind-borne algae strands, Cora turned and listened to an approaching mechanical noise, tinny in the thin air. She looked down the slope and saw the human crawler in the distance, raising an orangish-red cloud behind it.

Cora stumbled back down into the cave, but already the other *adin* had heard it. Boris leaped to his feet from where he had been brooding; his body glistened with diamonds of frozen vapor. He held the pointed staff in his hand and peered out the window opening. The other three *adin* hurried to him.

No one paid attention to her. She couldn't be much help to them right now anyway.

Cora slumped down against the rough rock wall, breathing heavily and sorting out the algae strands. She felt tears spring to the corners of her eyes as she patted her swollen belly—the last great practical joke of all.

The crawler helped Rachel choose the best course. She opted to follow a gaping chasm that spilled down the slope of Olympus Mons, possibly extending to the base of the towering cliff that lifted the volcano from the Tharsis bulge. The chasm was one of the only landmarks she found on the vast uphill plain. It suggested days long past when liquid water had spilled downhill from melting ice. Or perhaps the enormous shield volcano had simply split its seams. She knew little about geology; it was not her area of expertise. If she had been a geologist on Mars, her specialty would never have become obsolete.

Gauges showed the outside air pressure dropping as she ascended. The wind speed picked up, bringing gusts that carried enough muscle to rattle the crawler. She had been climbing for half a day. The distant sun had passed overhead and dropped to the northwestern horizon. Behind her reeled two parallel treads, marking the path of the crawler. They would be erased when the storm hit, certainly before anyone thought to come looking for her.

With a momentary twinge of guilt, Rachel hoped the *dva* at the pumping station would be all right, but she knew they had been trained—and made—to survive the weather conditions of this new transitional Mars.

Ahead Rachel saw areas that looked like ancient volcanic steam vents, lava tubes, and towering jagged teeth of black rock rotten with cavities formed by blowing dust. It looked like an extraterrestrial Stonehenge guarding a gateway to a wonderland under Mars. Long sunset shadows stretched like dark oil spilling down the slope.

And then figures stepped away from the rocks, emerging from the lava tubes. Human figures—no, not quite human. In the fading light she recognized them.

Adin.

She saw three at first, and then a fourth stepped out. This one carried a long metal staff. Her heart leaped with amazement, awe, and a little fear. Rachel's first impulse was to turn the crawler around and flee back downslope to report the presence of this encampment of rogue "Martians." What would they do to her if they caught her?

But instead she stopped and parked the vehicle, locking its treads. So what might they do, and what did it matter? She sealed the protective plates over the windowports, then stood up. The recompressed air in her suit tasted cold and metallic.

Rachel had nothing to lose, and she wanted to know how the *adin* had fared, what they had done, why they had broken off contact with Earth. At least she would know that much before she died, and it would bring closure to her work. She had to find out for herself, even if no one else would know. She was probably the only one who cared anyway.

She cycled through the door of the crawler and turned back to key the locking combination. Rachel stepped forward to meet the *adin* survivors as they bounded toward her.

The Earther inside the suit looked fragile, like eggshells strung together with spiderwebs. She would never survive ten seconds unprotected outside.

Assisted by Stroganov, Boris took the captive woman's arm and lifted her off the ground. Her reflective suit, bloated from internal pressure, felt slick and unnatural in his grip. He noticed that the suit design had changed somewhat since he had last dealt with Earthers, when they had first deposited the *adin* on the Martian surface.

He and Stroganov carried their captive easily in the low gravity; oddly, she did not struggle. Boris set the woman down in the dimness of the lava tube and scrutinized her small body. Apparently nonplussed, she straightened herself and looked around the grotto. Through the faceplate of her helmet, Boris saw dark eyes and an angular face, salt-and-pepper hair. He discerned no expression of helplessness and fear. He found it disconcerting.

"I recognize you," the Earther woman said. Her words filtered through the speaker patch below the faceplate in crisp textbook Russian straight from Moscow schooling. "You are Boris Petrovich Tiban."

Pleased that she knew him but also angry at where she must have seen him, Boris said, "You must have been entertained by our struggle for survival on this world, while you sat warm and cozy on yours? How often do they replay my last transmission to Earth, just before I dismantled the dish?" He rang his staff on the porous lava floor for emphasis.

"No, Boris Tiban, I remember you from my selection procedures." She paused. "Let me see, Siberian labor camp, correct? You had been a worker at the Baku oil fields in Azerbaijan. Your record showed that you got into many brawls, you came to work drunk more often than not. During one shift you had an accident that started a fire in one of the refinery complexes. The resulting explosion killed two people and ruined a week's oil production."

The other three *adin* stepped away, looking at her in amazement. Bebez grabbed onto Elia's arm. Boris felt a cold shiver crawl up his spine that had nothing to do with the temperature of Mars. Flickers of memory brought him fuzzy glimpses of this woman, dressed in a white uniform, bustling down cold tile halls. "How do you know all this?"

The woman's response was a short laugh. She seemed genuinely amused. "I selected the final *adin* candidates myself. I performed some of the surgery. I *made* you, Boris Tiban. You have survived here because of the augmentations I added to your body. You should be grateful to me with every breath you take of Martian air." She turned around, flexing her arm. The suit made crinkling noises.

"I do not remember these others as well," she continued. "There were so many candidates in the first phase."

Boris felt the fury boil within him. It all came back to him now. "Doctor ... Dycek—is that your name, or have I remembered it wrong?" She was provoking him, taunting him—perhaps she did not know him as well as she thought. Stroganov gawked at her, then at him; yes, he remembered her, too, the smell of chemicals, the slice of pain, the promises of freedom, the exile on this planet.

Boris brought the metal staff up. "Maybe I should just smash open your helmet."

"Do what you will. I never intended to return anyway."

Boris stared into her dark eyes distorted by the transparent polymer. He could not say anything. She had made him helpless.

"Tell me why you are so angry," she continued. "We set you free of your labor camp. You signed all the papers. We gave you a world to tame and all the freedom to do it. Better to rule in hell than to serve in heaven, is that not correct?"

All the clever words tumbled in his throat, clambering over each other to come out. Where was the tough, charismatic leader who had conquered Mars? He had made his speeches over and over to the surviving *adin*; but now he had the proper target in front of him. He clenched his hand so tightly that he actually felt the nails against his thick, numb palm.

The anger finally burst out, and Boris shouted in a way that overrode all his training for shallow breaths and conservation of exhaled moisture. "You created us for Mars—and then you took Mars away!"

He gestured out beyond the cave walls. In his mind he held a picture of the growing lichen, the tracings of frost on the lava rock, the thickening air. Dr. Dycek looked at him through the faceplate. He saw a weary patience in her eyes, which made him even angrier. She did not understand.

"Why is she here?" Elia asked him. "Find out why she is here."

Boris looked down at Dr. Dycek. "Yes, why?"

"I am being replaced. I have no more work on Mars, and I am to be shuttled back to Earth."

Boris tightened his grip on her thin metallic suit. "So now you know what it feels to be obsolete yourself. We watch our world slipping away with each new *dva* establishment, with each water-recovery station, with every normal human setting foot on our planet! The time has come to send them a message they cannot ignore."

Dr. Dycek put her gloved hands on her hips. "I came up here to be swept away in the dust storm. They will never find my body. If you kill me it makes no difference."

"We could dump your body just outside of the flimsy inflatable base. They would find you then."

"Then someone would have to hunt you down," Dr. Dycek said. "Why bloody your hands? No need to add murder to your conscience."

Boris laughed at that. He felt easier now, more in control. "Murder? It is murder only when a human kills another human. *Mars* will be killing you, Dr. Dycek. Not me." He hefted the metal staff over his head, ready to swing it down upon the curved faceplate. She tilted her head up. "It is the way with all creatures: those who cannot adapt to their environment must die. So here, breathe the clear, cold air of Mars. It will be a grand gesture for the *adin!*"

"Oh Boris, stop!" It was Cora's voice, sounding annoyed. She made her way out of the shadows from the back of the cave. "I once admired your ways, but now I am tired of how you must make a grand gesture of everything. Tearing up our transmitter, sabotaging the *dva* pumping station, even blowing up the Baku oil refinery."

"That was all justified!" Boris snapped. But he watched Dr. Dycek's attention flick away from him as soon as Cora stepped into the light. Cora panted, then winced at internal pain.

"She's pregnant!" Dr. Dycek said. "How? That's impossible!"

For a moment, Boris thought her comment so ludicrous that he stifled a chuckle. How? Does a doctor not know how a woman gets pregnant?

"Even the best Russian sterilization procedures must not be one hundred percent effective," Cora answered.

Dr. Dycek's entire attitude altered. "Your baby will die if it is born up here! It will have none of your adaptations. Just a normal, human child."

"We know that!" Boris shouted.

"This changes everything. An *adin* having a child! The first human born on Mars!" Her voice rose with command as if they were her slaves—just as she had sounded in the *adin* training and therapy sessions back on Earth. "We will have to take you in the crawler vehicle back down," she said to Cora. "I can pressurize the cabin slowly so you will acclimate and tolerate the atmosphere below for a short time."

Boris felt his control of the other *adin* slipping like red dust through his fingertips. Stroganov and Bebez nodded, looking at the suited figure and ignoring him. Cora stepped forward, so intent with new hope and excitement that she did not try to hide her swollen appearance. "You can save my baby?"

"Perhaps. If we get you back to the base."

"This is good news, Boris!" Elia said. "We thought the baby would die for certain."

Boris released his hold on Dr. Dycek's arm and turned to face his four companions in the cave. "Yes, save the child! And then what? Then everything will be perfect? Then all our problems will be solved? No! Then the Earthers will know where we are. They will come here and watch us die off, one by one. They will make a documentary program about us, the failed experiment. Maybe it will be on worldwide *National Geographic*?"

He moved toward the cave opening to the deepening dusk outside. It was difficult for him to stomp in anger in the low gravity. "You are all fools! I can have more intelligent conversations with the rocks."

Boris Tiban stalked out into the air to stare at the brightening stars, at Phobos rising again in the east and the pinprick of Deimos suspended partway up the sky. He felt like the king of all Mars, a king who had just been overthrown.

Not even Boris's tantrum could disturb Rachel's concentration as she stared at the rounded abdomen of the *adin* woman. The survival of these augmented humans impressed her, but the simple miracle of this pregnancy that should never have happened amazed her much more. A pregnancy, the type of thing men and women had been doing for millions of years—but never before on this planet.

She and her medical team had seen no need to sterilize the female *adin*, a much more difficult operation than a vasectomy.

Though Rachel had heard of men siring children years after they had had vasectomies, she and her team considered that possibility to be an acceptable risk. Russian medicine had somewhat low standards for "acceptable risks." Rachel could hardly believe it herself.

But the tight skin stretched over Cora's belly spoke otherwise. The thick *adin* fur wisped up and curled over, showing white patches where toughened skin had been stretched to its limits. Rachel reached out with a gloved hand to touch the bulge, but she could feel little through the protective material.

Cora seemed more preoccupied with excusing Boris's temper. "He is not always like this. He is strong and has kept us alive by our own wits for ten years now, but everything is running through his fingers. He lost our companion Nicholas two nights ago in a raid." She drew a deep breath. Her words carried a rich Siberian accent that evoked thoughts of wild lands and simple people. "These grand gestures of his always backfire."

Suddenly Cora's mouth clamped shut and she let out a hiss. She squeezed her eyelids together. The skin on her abdomen tightened until it had a waxy texture and was as hard as the rind of a melon. Her hands groped for something to grab onto, finally seizing a lump of lava. She squeezed the sharp edges until blood oozed from shallow cuts in her palms, freezing into a sparkling smear on the rock.

Rachel knelt beside Cora while the other *adin* came closer, showing their concern. Rachel had never had children of her own; she had been too preoccupied with her work, too driven, too dedicated. She had never regretted it, though—had she not done something far more important by preparing the first human to set foot on Mars?

Cora gasped out her next words after the spasm passed. "It's all right. For now. That has been happening for days. I can bear the pain, but I can concentrate on little else."

"You must not have the child here," Rachel repeated. She didn't know if the baby would be getting enough oxygen through the mother's bloodstream even now, but it certainly could not survive in the open air. "How frequent are the contractions?"

"I have no idea," Cora snapped in a voice filled more with pain and weariness than anger. "I don't exactly have a chronometer! Boris left all that behind when we came to the highlands."

"They are about every fifteen minutes," said one of the *adin*, Bebez. "You must get her away from here. Give her whatever help you can offer. The baby will surely die up here."

Rachel would have to give up her own pointless gesture of defiance, standing on the volcano top while the dust storm swept her away. But it seemed a ridiculous thing to do now, like something Boris Tiban would attempt. A grand gesture that would impress no one. Instead, she would accomplish something to hold up in front of Jesús Keefer's face.

Cora's infant would focus Earth's attention once again on the *adin* and the *dva*, and on Rachel's own efforts. She might even get a reprieve, be allowed to stay on Mars to study the remaining altered humans and how they adapted to their changing planet. But she felt she was doing this for something else as well. Better to save a life than to take her own.

"Let us go and save your child, Cora. My crawler is not far."

Cora stood up and Rachel touched her shoulder. The other three *adin* nodded their agreement but made no move to help as the two women went to the door opening into the Martian dusk.

Outside, Boris Tiban was nowhere to be seen. The sky's green had turned a muddy ochre. The upthrust rocks were stark against the smooth slope of Olympus Mons.

The crawler was gone.

Leaving Cora to stand against a rock, Rachel ran over to where she had stopped the vehicle. The low gravity made her feel light on her feet. The wind ran groping fingers over her suit.

She found the crawler's tracks, already beginning to blur in the wind, then she came to a sloughed-off portion of the chasm wall where a large object had been toppled over the edge. Pry marks in the lava soil showed how Boris had used his metal staff.

As dread surged inside her, Rachel went to the brink of the gorge. More lava rock lay strewn a hundred meters below. In the gathering shadows of night, she could make out the squared-off form of her vehicle, out of reach far below.

In darkness, they used tough cables and harsh white spotlights to reach the bottom of the chasm. The *adin* had taken the equipment from the remaining cache of supplies they had brought with them when they had abandoned the Martian lowlands. Low gravity made the climb easier.

Cora allowed Stroganov and Dr. Dycek to help her over the roughest patches. She had to stop four times during the descent while cramps seized her body, demanding all her attention.

Over the past two days the cramps had clenched her stomach muscles, squeezing and pushing, then gradually loosening again. At first they had been intermittent, several an hour and then giving her a few hours' rest before they started again. But the pain grew worse, more regular, more intense, as her muscles lowered the baby, helped position it, started to open Cora up inside. Cora knew the baby could come within hours, or she could have to endure this for several more days.

She watched Stroganov jerk the thin cable as his spotlight shone down on the crawler vehicle surrounded by broken scree. He had never told anyone his first name, but clung to his family identity; he traced his lineage back to the first nobles sent by Peter the Great to conquer the wilds of Siberia.

The crawler had plowed a clean path down the cliff as it fell, and its low center of mass had brought it to a rest upright, though canted against a mound of rubble. As Stroganov played the light over the scratched and dust-smeared hull, Cora looked for the disastrous damage she expected to see.

"It appears to be intact," Dr. Dycek said. She squeezed Cora's shoulder and jumped the last few meters to the bottom of the chasm, landing with deeply bent knees. Her voice sounded thin and far away as she shouted through her faceplate. "This vehicle is tough, built to withstand Mars—as you were."

Dr. Dycek held out her hands for Elia to toss down one of the spotlights. From above, Cora tried to pay attention to the operation. Using the spotlight beam, Dr. Dycek climbed around the vehicle, inspecting the metal plates protecting the trapezoidal windowports. She rapped on one with her gloved fist, then held her fist high in satisfaction.

On her own initiative, Cora began the last part of the descent. Stroganov and Elia helped her until they all stood on the jumbled floor of the chasm. Loose boulders the size of houses lay strewn about. Cora looked up to the top of the cliff wall, a black razor-edge that blocked all view of the stars. Bebez had remained in the caves, and Cora saw no figure looking down at them.

They had called into the darkness for Boris to come and help them, but he had remained silent and hidden.

Dr. Dycek trudged up to them. "The door-lock mechanism is still functioning. The antenna is smashed, though, so we will not be able to let anyone on the base know we are coming." She paused. "From the dents around the antenna base, it looks to me as if Boris knocked it off himself."

The other *adin* said nothing. Cora nodded to herself. Yes, that was the way Boris would do it. He was so predictable.

Then her knees buckled as a new labor spasm squeezed her like a fist and sucked away thoughts of the outside world. Stroganov caught her and held her upright.

Dr. Dycek grabbed one of Cora's arms and began to stumble-walk her toward the crawler. "Come on. We have at least a day's journey before we get back to the base. Even at that, I cannot be certain this chasm will lead us anywhere but a blind end. But there is no other way. The crawler is down here, and we have no choice of roads. You have no time to waste."

Dr. Dycek hauled her into the tilted opening of the crawler's small airlock. Stroganov and Elia helped, each of the *adin* men squeezing Cora's numb skin in a silent gesture of farewell.

"The storm is coming," Stroganov said, sniffing the air.

"I know," Dr. Dycek answered. She made no other comment about it, but faced Cora instead. "We will get you inside and begin the slow pressurization of the interior. We have to make the atmosphere thick enough so the baby can breathe, in case it is born along the way."

Cora dreaded the thought of air as thick as soup and heavy as bricks on her chest, making an ordeal out of every breath— especially during the most exhausting hours of her life.

She doubted the baby would wait until they reached the Earthers' inflatable base.

The airlock door closed behind them, leaving them in claustrophobic darkness. Already Cora longed for one last breath of the cold air on top of Olympus Mons.

As the southern hemisphere of the planet Mars entered its winter season, the falling temperature caused great portions of the atmosphere to freeze out. Water vapor and carbon dioxide piled up in layers to form a polar icecap. The resulting drop in air pressure sucked wind from the northern hemisphere down across the equator. Gathering force, the wind rushed to fill the invisible hole at the bottom of the world, picking up dust particles in a fist as tall as the sky.

The storm hit them three hours after they had left the *adin* encampment. Rachel could barely see as the roiling murk pounded and shook the crawler from side to side. The brilliant high beams of the vehicle's lights revealed only an opaque haze; the low beams illuminated no more than a shallow puddle of ground directly in front of her. Rachel squinted through the whirlwind, hoping to swerve in time to avoid the largest rocks or another gaping chasm. The walls of the crevasse sheltered them from the worst gusts, but vicious crosscurrents forced her to wrestle with the controls.

Rachel had no idea where the narrow canyon would take her, but she had to follow it. She wound her way along the crevasse floor, hoping it would spill out onto the Tharsis plain or climb back up to the flat surface of Olympus Mons. She did not know where the nearest settlement would be, or if she would have a better chance heading straight for the main base facilities.

As they continued, Rachel increased the air pressure in the crawler, gradually acclimating Cora to the change. The muffled sounds of the scouring gale came through only as distant whispers. Her suit worked double-time to absorb her perspiration. She no longer felt like someone who wanted to surrender.

A wry smile came to Rachel's face; she had never imagined she would be facing the dust storm in such a manner. Her planned suicide had seemed poignant and dramatic at the time, like a great hero going to meet doom—but now she realized that most people would have shaken their heads sadly and pitied her instead. They would have found her pathetic. They would have reevaluated all of her successes, used her final madness to brush aside the accomplishments and then forgotten about her.

She kept her mind focused on moving ahead, on the need to

return to the main base, where she could show Jesús Keefer how important she still was to the Mars project. Keefer had always been impatient with the slow work of the *adin* and the *dva*, wanting instead to have humans scrape out a direct existence on Mars from the start.

But Rachel and her team had made it possible for the first humans to walk free on another world. No matter how the future changed, no one could alter that. Her work had resulted in the birth of the first Martian, a landmark event never before rivaled in human history.

Behind her on one of the passenger benches, Cora Marisov spoke little, gasping as another labor spasm hit. Rachel used the vehicle's chronometer to time them. They occurred about every four and a half minutes. Cora seemed oblivious to the storm outside.

"I think ..." Cora said, gasping words that Rachel heard muffled through her helmet, "you had better find a place to stop the crawler. Park it. Shelter. I need you now."

Rachel slowed the vehicle and risked a glance backward.

Cora lay on the floor, her back propped against the curved metal wall and her legs spread as far apart as she could manage around the mound of her belly. Between her legs a gush of liquid spilled out, steaming and freezing in the icy air.

Her water has broken! Rachel lurched the crawler over to the canyon wall under what she could dimly see as an overhang. Now what would she do? Rachel was a doctor, no problem. No problem! But she had studied environmental adaptation, worked with cyborg enhancements. The closest she had come to witnessing birth was in staring at cells dividing under a microscope. It had been a long time since her basic training, and she had used none of it in practical situations.

She looked down the treads of the crawler and turned back to Cora. The pregnant *adin* woman looked up at her; Rachel hoped the faceplate hid her uncertainty.

"I may be able to help you now," Cora said, "but when the final part of labor comes, I will not be able to hold your hand through this."

The thought of Cora helping *her* in the emergency made Rachel stifle a raw-edged giggle, but Cora continued. "I helped my grandmother deliver two babies when I was small. Midwives still do much of that work in Siberia."

Rachel fought away her scattered emotions and stared into Cora's dark, slanted eyes. "All right, should I check to see how far you are dilated?"

"Yes. Reach … inside me. Then we will know how much time I have."

Rachel looked down at her clumsy gloved hand. She checked the external air pressure monitor; though the suit seemed more flexible now that the differential was not so great, she still could not survive unprotected in the crawler cabin. "I dare not remove my suit yet. There is not enough air for me. And the glove is too big as it is. I would hurt you."

Cora's eyes shut in a wince and her body shook. Rachel watched her body straining, the augmented muscles stretched to a point where they seemed to hum from the tension. Cora's fingers scrabbled on the smooth metal floor, looking for something to grasp. After a minute or two, the spasm passed.

Cora took five deep breaths, then brought her attention back to the problem. "We need to learn how long it will be. If I am not fully dilated, we might have enough time to reach your base. If I am, then the baby could come in as little as an hour."

Rachel drove the panic away and tried to dredge up alternatives from the thin air. "There are small cutting tools in the repair box, and some metal tape." She looked down at her suit. "I could cut off my glove, seal the sleeve around my arm with the tape. Then I could feel inside you."

Cora looked at her, saying nothing, as Rachel continued. "My hand would get numb in this cold, but I can raise the internal temperature here as much as you can stand."

"If you damage the suit, you will never be able to go outside until we reach your base." Cora closed her eyes in anticipation of another labor pain. "Perhaps you should keep driving. Hope we will find help within another hour or so."

Instead, Rachel made up her mind and went to the crawler's tool locker. In this storm, and with the distance yet to travel, they would never get to a safe haven in an hour. She had spent most of a day maneuvering the crawler up the smooth slope of Olympus Mons, making good time and seeing exactly where she was going. She had now been driving barely four hours, over rough terrain, unable to see for the past hour. They would never make it. Better to prepare here.

First, she wrapped the tape around her forearm as tightly as she could, making a crude tourniquet. Then she pulled up the slick fabric around her wrist and removed one of the small cutting tools from the locker. The tough suit material could resist most severe abrasions, but not intentional sawing. Keeping the metal tape at hand, she pulled in a deep lungful of air and sliced across the fabric.

Her ears popped as air gushed out. She could feel the wind and the cold pushing against her skin. The tourniquet could not make a perfect seal. She cut the gash longer, enough that she could pull her fingers out of the glove and thrust her hand through the ragged opening. With her protected hand, she wrapped more metal tape around her wrist where the suit material met the skin. She taped back the flopping, empty glove, then sealed the seam over and over.

Panting, Rachel tried to catch her breath as the suit re-inflated. The chemical oxygen regenerator on her back hissed and burbled, adding to the ringing in her ears. Her head pounded, but her thoughts cleared moment by moment.

Cora squirmed on the floor in her own ordeal. Rachel knelt in front of her. "Cora? Cora, I am ready." She touched the *adin* woman's bristly coating of fur, the waxy texture of her polymerized skin. Rachel's hand felt crisp from the cold, then sensitivity faded as it grew numb. "Tell me what I should expect to feel inside you."

Cora blinked and nodded.

The placental water on the crawler floor had sheeted over with a film of ice, clinging in gummy knots to Cora's inner thighs. Rachel slowly felt the folds of skin between Cora's legs, dipped her fingers into them, then slid her hand inside.

At first the temperature felt too hot, like melted butter, in startling contrast to the frigid air. She forced herself not to withdraw. Her skin burned.

"Feel the opening deep inside. It is surrounded by a ridge," Cora said, biting off each word as she said it. "Tell me how wide it is."

"A little wider than my hand and thumb."

Cora bit her lip.

Rachel withdrew and grabbed the other woman's arm. The

biting cold of the air felt like acid on her wet hand. "Is that good or bad? I can't remember my training."

"Bad. No, good. That means this should be over much sooner. A few hours, perhaps."

The sound of the storm outside suddenly turned into a monster's roar, a grinding, crunching sound that pounded through the walls of the crawler. The rock outcropping above them came crashing down, tossing boulders and blankets of dirt.

Rachel fell on her side, clawing at the air; Cora rolled over and curled into a ball to protect her abdomen. Rocks pummeled the top of the crawler, bouncing and thudding. Reddish smears clogged the view from the main front windowports, blowing away in patches as gusts of wind tore it free of the smooth glass.

Rachel got to her knees. She felt herself shaking. The palm of her bare hand seemed to burn into the frigid metal of the floor. "Are you all right?" she asked Cora. The *adin* woman nodded.

The sounds of the avalanche faded into the roar of the storm, but then another, softer thump sounded on top of the crawler. Cora froze, and her eyes widened.

Rachel got up to go to the crawler's control panel. Luckily none of the falling rocks had smashed through the front windowports.

Then a face and shoulders appeared from above, hands reaching down from the roof of the crawler, brushing the dust aside. The face pressed against the glass, peering inside and grinning.

An *adin*. Boris Tiban.

In shock, Rachel caught herself from crying out. She smacked her hands down on the controls for the protective plates, which slammed over the windowports. The last thing she saw was Boris Tiban leaping aside in surprise, vanishing into the tangled murk of the storm. Then the metal clanged into place, leaving the crawler in dimness. The central illumination automatically stepped up, bathing the interior in a blue-white glow.

Cora stared wide-eyed at the sealed windowport. "Boris!" she muttered. She seemed to have forgotten about her labor. "He caused the avalanche. He must have been working at it ever since we stopped."

"Out in the storm?" Rachel could hardly believe what she had seen herself. "How could he survive without shelter?"

Cora shook her head; Rachel saw a smile on her lips. "He likes to do that, pit himself against the elements. He is proud of how he can cope with anything Mars throws at him. Tamer of Worlds—that is what he wants to be called. He does not like to see you domesticating this planet. Then he will be obsolete."

"I know what that feels like," Rachel muttered, then stopped. "But if Boris tries to kill me, he will also destroy you, and his baby. Does he not realize he will murder his own child?"

Cora hung her head, then shuddered with another spasm. Rachel adjusted the air compressors to increase the pressure inside the crawler more rapidly. When Cora recovered, she looked Rachel in the eye and kept her voice flat.

"He needs the baby to die. He has always planned on it."

Rachel opened and closed her mouth without words; she knew that behind the faceplate she must look like a dying fish in a bowl. "I don't understand."

Cora let her slanted eyes fall shut beneath the thick lash membranes. "His grandest gesture of all. He has been anticipating it for months. We have always known the baby would die at birth. I should never have gotten pregnant. That loss would be a direct fault of the Earthers. He has found a way to blame all of our troubles on you. He is good at that.

"When the baby dies, he will have all the reason he needs to strike back. It will be a catalyst, an excuse. Everything must be perfectly justified. Those are the rules by which he plays." She sighed. "No one ever thought someone like you would come."

Rachel struggled with the sick logic. "What will he do?"

"He plans to go to your inflatable base and destroy it. With his metal staff, he can tear holes right through the sides of the walls. He can run from one section to the next as fast as his legs will take him, striking and moving. He can do it. The alarms will send everyone into confusion. He can burst every module even after they seal themselves. The people inside will be trapped and he can pick them off, one room at a time. The Earthers might repair some of the walls, but Boris can just strike again. He can wait longer than any of them."

"But what about you? He's trying to kill you now, too!"

"That is incidental. He loves me in his own way, but he sees the cause as more important. Just like a great revolutionary."

Rachel felt anger welling up inside of her. "Well then, I must make sure he has no reason to attack the base. Your baby will live." She patted Cora's bulging stomach with her bare hand and turned to look at the heavy metal plates covering the windowports. "We are safe here, for now."

Surrounded by the muffled whirlwind of the storm, Cora Marisov gave birth to a daughter. The crawler walls creaked and groaned as the wind tried to push in, but the shelter remained secure.

As soon as Cora's final labor began, Rachel had no choice but to begin pressurizing the crawler interior as rapidly as the pumps could bring in more air. Many of the intake vents had been clogged with dust from the storm and the avalanche, but the gauges showed the air pressure increasing.

Cora cried out with the effort of her labor, but also gasped, complaining about how difficult breathing had become. "Like a metal band around my chest! My head!"

"There is nothing for it. The baby must breathe when it comes." *No matter what it does to Cora,* Rachel thought. "You are strong. I made you that way."

"I ... know!"

When Rachel had pulled the slick baby free, it steamed in the air, glistening with red wetness. "A girl!" she said.

Cora's mouth remained open, gasping to fill her lungs. The baby, too, worked the tiny dark hole of her mouth in a silent agonized cry of new life, but she could not find enough air.

Rachel moved quickly now. As she had planned, she shucked her suit and popped open the faceplate, letting the blessed warm air gush out. The shock stunned her, but she forced herself to keep moving, to plow through the black specks in front of her vision. A bright pain flashed behind her forehead. Moments later, a warm, thick trickle of blood came from her nostrils.

She grasped the loose end of the metal tape sealing her wrist to the suit. The grip slipped twice before her numb fingers clutched it and tore it off. She let out a howl of pain, releasing half the air left in her lungs. She felt as if she had just flayed the skin off her arm.

She had to hurry. Grogginess started to claim her, but she stumbled through the motions.

Shivering already, she stepped out of the empty suit, letting the metallic fabric fall in a rough puddle on the floor. She wore only a light jumpsuit underneath, clammy with sweat that froze in icy needles against her skin.

Rachel clamped shut the empty faceplate and grabbed up the baby. The infant skin, smeared with red from the birth, took on a bluish tinge as she tried to breathe. The umbilical cord, tied in a crude knot, still oozed some blood.

Cora found the strength to reach over and touch the infant one last time before Rachel slid the girl inside the loose folds of the suit and sealed her whispered cries into silence. She began pressurizing it immediately. The folds began to straighten themselves as air pumped inside.

Heaving huge breaths but still starving for oxygen, Rachel grasped the limp sleeve where she had cut off the glove and knotted it. Suit-warmed air blew from the edge, squirting onto her skin. Rachel clutched the roll of metallic tape and wrapped it around and around the end of the sleeve. The hissing noise stopped, replaced by the ringing in her ears. She crawled over to where regenerated air streamed into the chamber, but that helped only a little.

Cora, though, grew worse. "Can't inhale," she said. "Like stones on my chest. Breathing soup." She was too weak to cope with the increasing difficulty.

Rachel felt all her words go away as she looked at the exhausted new mother, at the mess of blood and amniotic fluid and afterbirth tissue on the crawler floor. This had not been clean and quick like the make-believe births shown in entertainment disks. It looked like some slaughter had occurred here. But not slaughter—new life.

Somehow, Cora got to her knees, wavered as she tried—and failed—to draw a deep breath, then crawled toward the airlock. "You must let me out. Dying. Need to breathe."

Rachel, dizzy from her own lack of air, tried to fight against confusion. "Not in the storm! Not right after the baby. You are too weak." But she knew Cora was right. If the *adin* woman had any chance for surviving, it had to be outside, not in here.

Cora reached the door and rested her head against it, panting. "Strong enough," she said, repeating Rachel's words. "You made us that way."

Rachel watched her open the inner door and haul herself into the airlock. The noise of the storm outside doubled. Cora looked at the sagging environment suit on the floor, focused on the squirming lump that showed the girl's movements, then raised her deep-set eyes to meet Rachel's. She looked intensely human and inhuman at the same time.

"I will tell Boris his daughter is alive. Safe." With great effort, she filled her lungs one more time. "He must face that. Adapt to new conditions—his own words." She raised her hand in a gesture of farewell, then sealed the door.

Somehow, her words about Boris Tiban did not reassure Rachel.

The noise of the storm muffled again, grew louder as Cora opened the outer door, then finally resettled into relative quiet. Rachel found herself alone with the newborn baby.

She had to push the crawler into overdrive to break free of the avalanche rubble. The vehicle groaned and lurched as it heaved over boulders, bucking from side to side. Rachel wished she had strapped herself in. Unsupported on the floor, the baby in the environment suit slid over to one corner and came to rest against a passenger bench. She could not hear the infant's cries over the sound of the storm and the straining engine.

"Come on!" Rachel muttered to herself, pounding the plastic control panel. The effort sent a wash of dizziness over her. Her jaws chattered in the cold. The back of the crawler rose up at an angle over the worst of the obstacles, then she found herself free of the rock slide.

She slid the protective plates aside so she could see her course, though the storm made that nearly impossible. Using less caution now, she increased the crawler's speed, trusting the vehicle to crush medium-sized rocks under its treads so she would not need to pick a path around them.

The chasm walls lowered and the floor widened within half an hour. She felt the urgency slackening as confidence grew; she would be out on the flat slope of Olympus Mons in a few moments, and she could use the guidance gear to choose the most direct course back home. She eased the crawler to greater speed.

She turned around to glance at the baby, to make sure it had not been injured.

Then Boris Tiban sprang out in front of the vehicle again and bounded onto its sloping hood. The dust swirled around him, but he seemed to draw energy from the storm. He hefted his metal staff over his head like a harpoon. The expression on his face made him look like a savage beast from the wilds of Mars.

Instinctively, Rachel ducked back. She did not think quickly enough to slam the protective plates over the windowports.

Boris brought the pointed rod down with a crunch in the center of the trapezoidal glass plate. A white flower of damage burst around the tip, and a high whine of air screamed out as he withdrew the staff. He brought the tip down again even harder, puncturing another, larger hole through the thick glass.

Rachel heard the wind's roar and a distant howl that might have been triumph from the *adin* leader. "Stop!" she shouted, expending precious air. She yanked back on the control levers, bringing the crawler to a sudden halt.

The lurch tossed Boris Tiban from his perch, and he rolled nearly out of sight a few meters away. He staggered to his feet, using the metal staff.

She slapped at the control panel. The brilliant high beams on the crawler stabbed out like an explosion of light. Boris froze, blinded. He wrapped a forearm over his eyes.

Rachel could have accelerated the vehicle then and crushed him under the tread. But she could not do it. She stared at him, listening to the scream of escaping air from the puncture holes. She had created Boris Tiban and exiled him here. He had survived everything Mars could throw at him, and she could not kill him now.

Still unable to see, Boris staggered toward the crawler, raising his staff to strike again.

Cora appeared out of the whirlwind, stumbling and off balance —but perhaps only due to the wind, for she looked stronger than she had when she departed from the crawler. She kept her back to the bright lights.

Boris seemed to sense her presence and turned. He blinked at her in astonishment. Before he could react, Cora snatched the pointed metal staff out of his hand. Delayed by surprise, he did not grab it back immediately. He turned, as if shouting something through the storm at her.

Then Cora shoved the staff through his chest. In the low gravity, her strength was great enough for the thrust to lift him completely off the ground. The spear protruded from his body, puncturing the second set of lungs that rose like a hump on his back. Then she tossed him away from her.

Rachel slapped the palm of her hand against the largest hole in the windowport, picturing herself as the legendary Dutch boy who put his finger in the leaking dike. Instantly she felt the biting cold and the suction tearing at her hand, trying to rip it through the hole. She screamed.

Cora had fallen to the ground outside, but she staggered to her feet and stood in front of the vehicle. She made frantic motions with her arms. Their meaning was clear: Go! Now!

Rachel tore her hand away from the windowport, leaving a chunk of meat behind that dribbled blood and slurped as it was sucked outside. A frosty red smear coated the white cracks in the glass.

Blood dripping from her torn palm, Rachel found the metal tape and pushed several pieces over the punctures in the windowport. The tape dug into the hole, pulled toward the outside. She added a second and then third strip of tape over the punctures, and then began to breathe easier.

Outside, red dust had begun to pile around the body of Boris Tiban. Already Mars hurried to erase all traces of the intruder. Boris had thought himself invincible because he could withstand the rigors of the harsh environment. But Mars had not killed him—a human had, an *adin* human.

Hours later, she continued on a straight downhill course. The slope of the volcano offered a relatively gentle road, scoured clean. The wind continued to hammer at her—such storms rarely let up in less than four days—but it no longer seemed such a difficult thing to withstand.

The layers of metal tape sealed the punctures in the front windowport, but air still hummed out. The compressors kept laboring to fill the crawler with air; the heaters warmed the interior as fast as the Martian cold could suck it away. Rachel hoped she could remain conscious for as long as it might take.

The indicators showed the general direction of travel, though the storm and the iron oxide dust in the air could ruin the accuracy of her onboard compass. Boris had smashed her antenna, so she could not pick up the homing beacons of any nearby settlements, nor could she send out a distress signal.

But if she continued down to the base of Olympus Mons, she might encounter one of the *dva* materials-processing settlements that tapped into leftover volcanic heat, unleashing water from hydrated rock, smelting metals. She had been squinting through the dust for hours—and hoping. She could barely hear the baby crying inside her suit.

Rachel thought her eyes had begun to swim with weariness when she finally saw the yellow lights of a *dva* encampment. The squat, smooth-curved walls made the outbuildings look like hulking giants. Much of the complex would be underground.

Rachel let herself slump back in the driver's chair.

She had made it back with the baby. She had returned to her world, when she had intended to be gone forever. Rachel felt a moment of bittersweet failure, wondering now if she could ever have stood alone and faced the onrushing wall of the storm, to let it carry her away into death.

And what would have been the point? An empty gesture for no one but herself.

There was no use mourning the completion of a job well done. Strong people found new goals to achieve, new challenges to face. Weak people bemoaned the loss of great days. Beside her on the crawler floor, this new baby was trying to be strong, to survive against all odds. Rachel Dycek could be strong, too, stronger than Jesús Keefer or the UN administrative council. *Adapt to the hostile environment, and defeat it,* Boris Tiban would have said. Humanity, in all its forms, would never be obsolete. Rachel would not be obsolete until she surrendered to obsolescence.

Ahead, the dim yellow lights of the *dva* settlement looked as welcoming as a New Year's tree. The cold air of Mars whistled outside the windowport of her vehicle, moaning as it tried to enter through the metal tape. But she would not let it harm her.

She had work to do.

This is my favorite Alternitech story.

When my professional writing career started to take off, I eagerly pursued book contracts, built up my name, sold stories to the major magazines, and clawed myself up one step at a time. Then a hot new author exploded onto the scene with a universally celebrated first novel that won a bunch of awards. Everybody read it, everybody talked about it. He was the greatest new writer.

And we never heard from him again. No second novel (that I know of), no other short story publications. The guy had achieved the pinnacle of success that so many of us longed for—and then he just stopped writing and disappeared. Why would anyone do that? The question obsessed me, and I still don't know the answer.

"Rough Draft" explores that question, and I think it's one of my most powerful stories.

ROUGH DRAFT

(with Rebecca Moesta)

After a decade during which he wrote and published nothing new, the fan letters dwindled to a few a year.

"Dear Mr. Coren, You're the best science fiction writer ever!"

"Dear Mr. Coren, Your book Divergent Lines changed my life. I felt as if you were speaking directly to me, and you helped me work through some major issues."

The entire experience, though great for the ego, had ultimately proved meaningless. Eventually he'd been forced to return the money for the second book advance, because he simply couldn't do it again. After enjoying a pleasant day in the sun, Mitchell Coren had retreated to his small apartment to live a normal life. The gleaming Nebula Award and the silver Hugo—both dusty now— were little more than knickknacks on the mantel of a fireplace that he never used.

Having convinced himself of the wisdom of J.D. Salinger's approach to authorial fame, Mitchell had squelched all thoughts of returning to writing. He immersed himself in a normal life with all its petty concerns.

Today, with an indifference born of long practice, Mitchell opened his bills and junk mail before finally tearing open the padded envelope that obviously contained a book. Another intrusion, no doubt. An annoying reminder of his old life. He still received advance reading copies from editors trying to wheedle a rare cover quote from him, rough draft manuscripts from aspiring authors who begged for comments or critiques, and books presented to him by new authors who had been inspired by his lone published novel.

Inside this envelope, however, he found his own name on the dust jacket of a novel he had never written.

Infernities

Mitchell Coren

Multiple Award-winning Author of *Divergent Lines*

Whirling flakes of confusion compacted into a hard snowball in the pit of his stomach. "What the hell?"

His initial, and obvious, thought was that someone had stolen his name. But that didn't make sense. Though many editorial positions had changed in the decade since he'd published *Divergent Lines*, Mitchell was still well enough known in the insular science fiction community that somebody in the field would have noticed an imposter. Besides, how much could his byline be worth after all this time? It wasn't worth stealing.

Someone had tucked a folded sheet of paper between the book's front cover and the endpaper. He read it warily.

Dear Mr. Coren,

As a longtime fan of yours, I thought you'd appreciate seeing this novel I came across in a parallel universe.

I'm a timeline hunter by profession. Perhaps you've heard of Alternitech? Our company uses a proprietary technology to open gateways into alternate realities. My colleagues and I explore these parallel universes for breakthroughs or useful discrepancies that Alternitech can profitably exploit: medical and scientific advances, historical discoveries, artistic variations. My specialty is the creative arts.

I stumbled upon this book in an alternate timeline while searching for a new Mario Puzo. Since the science fiction market isn't nearly as large or profitable as the mainstream, I couldn't spend much time checking out its background, but a brief search showed that the "alternate" Mitchell Coren published a dozen or so short stories after Divergent Lines, then produced this second novel. I'm hoping Alternitech will want to arrange for its publication, but naturally I felt you should see it first.

With deepest respect,

Jeremy Cardiff

Mitchell stared at the letter with mistrust and growing irritation.

He had heard of this company that searched alternate realities for everything from new Beatles records, to evidence of UFOs or Kennedy assassination conspiracies, to cures for obscure diseases. He could understand the more humanitarian objectives, but why *fiction*? What gave Alternitech the right to infringe on his life like this?

He opened to the dust jacket photo and saw that the picture did resemble him, though this other Mitchell Coren wore a different hairstyle and a cocky, self-assured grin. The bio mentioned that after completing *Infernities* he was "already at work on his next novel."

Oddly unsettled, Mitchell pushed the book away. Its very existence raised too many disturbing questions.

Three increasingly urgent phone calls to his former agent went unreturned. Since Mitchell had neither delivered anything new nor generated much income, his agent wasn't in a great hurry to attend to his so-called emergency. Even in the days when he'd briefly been a hot client, Mitchell had been relatively high-maintenance, needing encouragement and constant contact.

He decided to contact his entertainment attorney instead. After all, Sheldon Freiburg charged by the hour and therefore had an incentive to get right on the matter.

"Mitch Coren! I haven't heard from you since the last ice age." Freiburg's voice was bluff and hearty on the telephone. "What on earth have you been doing? You dropped off the map."

"I've been working a real-world job, Sheldon. You know, regular paycheck, benefits … security?"

"Yeah, I've heard of those. Hopped off the old fame-and-fortune bandwagon, eh?"

"A modicum of fame, not a whole lot of fortune—as you well know."

Freiburg had handled the entertainment contracts for the two movie options on *Divergent Lines*. Mitchell had been young and naïve then, believing the Hollywood hype and enthusiasm. He'd been surrounded by smiling fast-talkers whose eager assertions of certain box-office appeal and guaranteed studio support were built on a foundation as strong as a soap bubble. After the attorney's fees and the agent's commission, the option money had been just enough to pay off his car, which was now ten years old.

"So, Mitchell," Freiburg said now, "people don't call me unless they have a situation—either good or bad—so let's hear it."

"Someone's trying to publish an unauthorized Mitchell Coren novel."

"You've actually done other work?" The lawyer sounded surprised. "Something new? I thought you'd turned hermit on us. Did somebody steal your manuscript?"

"This is trickier than that. It isn't exactly a matter of stealing. This is a novel from a parallel universe, and Alternitech wants to get it published here." He explained the situation in full.

"Oh, that *is* tricky—but not unheard of. Listen, since it's Tuesday, I'll give you a special deal, a quick and inexpensive answer."

"Inexpensive? You've changed in the last ten years, Sheldon."

The lawyer chuckled. "How could I help it? The whole world has changed. But you're not going to like what I have to say."

Mitchell braced himself, clutching the receiver; thankfully, Freiburg could not see his tense expression.

"Precedents have been set in this area. In every dispute about the use of materials from alternate universes, Alternitech has come out the winner. I'm convinced the company spends as much money each year on their team of lawyers as they did developing their parallel universe gateway. You'd be wasting your money to try and block the publication. Compared to the rest of the entertainment industry, authors and books are minnows in an ocean. Even the big fish in the music and film industries haven't won a single case.

"Alternitech's timeline hunters bring back intellectual property that might conceivably belong to a counterpart in this universe. The first big case was when one of their music specialists, a guy named Jeremy Cardiff—"

"That's who sent me the novel."

"Great," Freiburg said, then continued, ignoring the interruption. "In Alternitech v. the Carpenter Estate, Cardiff found several new albums by the Carpenters, in an alternate reality where Karen Carpenter never died of anorexia. The CDs sounded like the same old shit to me, but don't underestimate the huge amount of money generated by piped-in background music. The Carpenter

Estate sued, citing copyright infringement and unlawful exploitation of a creative work.

"Alternitech countered that since Karen Carpenter was dead in this universe, she could not 'create' new works after the date of her death. They also argued, using an old favorite of the pharmaceutical companies, that since Alternitech had made such a substantial investment developing their technology, they deserved to reap the benefits of its commercial exploitation.

"The ruling sided with the Carpenter Estate insofar as establishing a 'fair percentage' of profits that should go to the creator's counterpart in this reality—fifteen percent, I think it was. But since Alternitech's timeline hunters did all the work to obtain the property, kind of like salvage hunters on the high seas, they were granted full control of its use. Similar lawsuits have been raised by individual movie producers, screenwriters, directors, and even actors who resent the release of 'new films' starring them for which they never got paid. Like I said, in every case, they lose."

Mitchell remembered that one of the alternate Mel Gibson films had caused something of a stir, because the parallel-universe-version of the actor had received an Academy Award for a role that this timeline's Gibson had turned down.

Freiburg continued: "When you get right down to it, Mitch, record companies and movie studios don't *want* the individual artists to win. Alternitech provides them with completely finished new work for a fraction of the cost or effort of making it themselves. Much less hassle, too. They just distribute the work through their normal channels and pay a standard percentage of artists' royalties directly to Alternitech. Then, if and only if the court orders it, Alternitech cuts a teeny-weeny check to our own world's parallel artist or company or estate, and everyone is happy. Well, almost everyone."

"So you're saying I shouldn't even try, Sheldon? It's not … not *right!*"

"Mitch, if Paul McCartney can't win, then a mere sci-fi novelist doesn't stand a snowball's chance." He paused as if reconsidering. "On the other hand, Mitch my friend, I just thought of a factor that's ironically in your favor, if you really want to stop publication. There's a very real chance that Alternitech won't even bother with your little book. Look at your royalty statements. You're a science fiction writer ten years out of the public eye. Oh sure, there'd be a limited audience for a 'lost unpublished work' by Mitchell Coren ... but it isn't exactly a Margaret Mitchell sequel to *Gone with the Wind*. If this Cardiff guy is a fan of yours, contact him and tell him how you feel. Who knows, he might do you a favor and pretend he never found it."

Mitchell didn't know whether to feel stung or take heart from the possibility.

Distracted and fretting, he polished the two awards on his mantel—something he hadn't done for the better part of a year. They looked quite impressive, he had to admit, and certainly gave him bragging rights. His occasional visitors asked about them, and he answered with feigned modesty. The awards seemed so irrelevant to his current life.

These days, Mitchell used his skills as a wordsmith in the unglamorous but stable profession of technical writing, producing essential documentation and annual reports for a manufacturing firm. Although it was a challenge to write compelling prose about new cereal box designs or recyclable plastic bottles, he was a master at slanting his text toward investors or consumers or environmental agencies, as needed.

Many of his coworkers—what the science fiction world called "mundanes"—were aspiring writers who never managed to finish or submit stories. Few of them knew about his past, however, since Mitchell rarely mentioned his novel.

As he rubbed a fingerprint off the Nebula's clear Lucite surface, looking at the suspended bits of metal shavings and semi-precious stones that formed a sparkling galaxy, he thought back to those brief, heady days. They were just memories now, but he wouldn't trade them for anything.

Divergent Lines had appeared with a splash like a giant water balloon. An excerpt of the novel had been published in *Analog* as the cover story and won that month's readers' poll. The novel itself had generated rave reviews and was immediately dubbed "a new classic" by critics and his fellow SF authors.

He had been welcomed as a hero at the World Science Fiction

Convention. He'd always read science fiction, but had never attended a con before. The fans surprised him at panels, listening to everything he said. They lined up for his book signings in the autograph hall or followed him and asked embarrassingly earnest questions about details he himself had never considered.

When Mitchell went to the Hugo Awards ceremony, he found himself plunged into a sea of unreality as the emcee announced his name as the winner. Astonished and grinning, he stumbled up to the podium and held up his silver rocket ship with mixed feelings of shock and giddy triumph.

The following spring, thanks to the continued buzz, *Divergent Lines* had been a shoo-in for the final Nebula ballot. New to the entire experience, Mitchell stood like a lost puppy in the lobby and the bar, surrounded by luminaries of the genre. He recognized their names from the covers of well-loved books, famous writers ranging from Grand Masters to prolific hacks, all of them legendary and, for the most part, *personable.*

He'd been in a daze. These Titans of science fiction talked to him as a peer, praised his novel. Mitchell found it unnerving, and he began to wonder how he could ever live up to their expectations. Did he deserve so much praise and success? What if his next work didn't measure up to their expectations? Would he be exposed as a fraud and cast out of this distinguished circle of authors? How would he bear the humiliation?

His publisher paid for his Nebula banquet ticket, and Mitchell was treated as a celebrity at their table. With his stomach tied in knots, he could summon no appetite at all. In an agony of anticipation, he endured the drawn-out meal, the mandatory chitchat, the interminable banquet speaker. By the time the awards finally began, plodding through each category as if in a calculated effort to increase his anxiety, Mitchell had convinced himself that he had no chance of winning. He was a newcomer. He had no track record. He had never played the politics of exchanging recommendations. He had not campaigned for the award. These writers couldn't possibly consider him a friend and certainly didn't owe him any favors.

And yet the name in the presenter's envelope said *Divergent Lines.* The Nebula seemed even more amazing than the Hugo, because this honor came from his *peers,* fellow professionals who supposedly knew good writing when they saw it. As Mitchell stood clutching the award, he imagined that someday, when he stood at the Pearly Gates and looked back on his entire life, this would be the high point....

After that night, though, Mitchell Coren never wrote another word of fiction. He had left the science fiction community behind and let *Divergent Lines* stand as his sole legacy.

Even in his heyday, Mitchell had not spent much time with die-hard science fiction fans. Not because he didn't like them—he appreciated anyone who bought and loved his novel. But he didn't understand their intensity or their passions and usually ended up feeling outclassed when they wanted to talk shop.

He met Jeremy Cardiff at a quiet place called Mrs. Coffee, a small bistro with shaded outside tables where they could have a conversation in a pleasant atmosphere. Mitchell didn't know which of them was more nervous. He could see in the timeline hunter's eyes that Jeremy was a bona fide Fan.

"This is really an honor, Mr. Coren. I've always been an admirer of *Divergent Lines*, and now that I've read *Infernities*, there's no doubt in my mind that you're one of my all-time favorite authors. I felt so surprised and fortunate to have found the book." Jeremy, a youngish man with a thin face, long hair, and a neatly-trimmed brown beard, looked like a waif hoping for a pat on the head. His blue eyes were wide, his smile tentative.

Mitchell took a drink of coffee, then cleared his throat. "Well, Mr. Cardiff, that's what I'm here to talk to you about."

"Please, call me Jeremy." Then the younger man's face fell as he interpreted Mitchell's reluctant tone.

Mitchell chose his words as carefully as he would have in preparing a viewgraph presentation for the board of the manufacturing company. He wasn't sure his reasons would make sense to anyone but himself. Though he knew he didn't exactly have a legal case, he might be able to play the celebrity card. Perhaps by asking a special favor from his number one fan, he could get what he needed. "I think you're perceptive enough to understand why I don't want the novel published here. It's not *my* book. Somebody else wrote it."

"No, Mr. Coren. You wrote it. Another version of you, maybe, but it was still your talent, your creativity. When I was in college I read and reread *Divergent Lines* until my copy fell apart, and I've been waiting ten years for a new novel by the same author. When I found *Infernities*, I sent you the physical book I brought back through the portal, but I made a photocopy. I'm already on my second time through it. It's brilliant—full of intricate layers and nuances."

Mitchell desperately wanted to ask which book he thought was better. Dedicated readers like Jeremy were generally his toughest customers and his harshest critics and, because Mitchell didn't think a new novel could ever live up to their expectations, he had decided not to try.

"That man may have the same name and the same genetics as I do, but he grew up in a parallel universe with a different set of circumstances. He's not me. He obviously reached a different decision about his career. But I didn't write *Infernities*, and if you published it here in our universe, people would see it as my own work, no matter how many disclaimers you put on it."

"But it's good, sir. Have you read it?"

"No, I don't dare. It would seem almost … plagiaristic."

As if clinging to hope, Jeremy said, "So … are you writing something of your own? Maybe a book that's similar to *Infernities*?"

"No. I'm not writing anything."

The young man looked at his coffee as if it were poison. He didn't seem angry at Mitchell's attitude, just deeply disappointed. "Then I don't understand. What made you stop writing? I mean, you got the royal treatment. People were lined up waiting for your next book. You had a contract to fulfill, didn't you?"

"Yes. And I … decided to return the advance."

"But why? It just doesn't make sense."

"Why? I'd already won the highest accolades in my field." Mitchell spoke softly, but his voice grew more intense. "Whether through brilliance or sheer dumb luck I muddled my way to the pinnacle of success my first time out of the starting gate. *Divergent Lines* was hailed as the best book of the year, won all the awards, got spectacular reviews in every periodical from *Publishers Weekly* and

Kirkus to *Locus* and *Chronicle*. *Library Journal* called it an instant classic."

Mitchell sighed. "Don't you see? The weight of it all gets oppressive. Where could I possibly go from there? There's no place but down." An edge of bitterness sharpened his tone. "It's a very long way down. No matter how good it was, my second book—*Infernities* or whatever I might've called it—would never be good enough. The fans and the critics certainly aren't kind unless your sophomore effort is unbelievably spectacular.

"As it stands right now, I'll go down in history as the author of a great novel. But if I published twenty other books, regardless of how well-written they might be, I can tell you some of the review quotes already: 'A solid novel, but not as inspired as *Divergent Lines*.' Or 'A fine effort, though it doesn't live up to the promise of its predecessor.' Or, worse yet, 'A disappointing follow-on to the author's first novel.'"

Jeremy frowned at what Mitchell was saying. "I think you're too hard on your fans, sir. We would have followed you. Even after ten years, most of us still want to read whatever you have to say."

"Maybe I don't have anything else to say," Mitchell said. "I can name author after author who falls into that category. Being successful is a Catch-22. If your first novel is a smash hit, an award winner and a critical success, it might mean your career has momentum and you're launched. On the other hand, it could mean your writing will never be good enough again. What should I have done—expanded *Divergent Lines* and written a couple of unnecessary sequels, so I could call it a trilogy? I could have licensed my universe, farmed it out to other authors, but that just didn't seem right to me. Either way, I would have been crucified by the fans and the critics."

"Just by the snobs," Jeremy said, "not by the *fans*. But you disappeared from fandom altogether. When's the last time you went to a science fiction convention?"

"The WorldCon where I got my Hugo was the first and last. I stopped reading *Locus* and *Chronicle* and *Ansible* after one of them ran an editorial about one-hit wonders that led off with 'What ever happened to Mitchell Coren?'" He looked at his coffee. "I didn't stand a chance of keeping up the momentum in my career. Fans and critics are too unpredictable. So I controlled the only part of the equation that I *could* control: I stopped writing fiction. My life is stable now that I've accepted the wisdom of anonymity. But if Alternitech publishes this apocryphal second novel that I didn't really write, then I'll be at the mercy of the public's expectations again. Please, don't do it."

Disappointment and resignation filled Jeremy's eyes as he unzipped his backpack and reached inside to withdraw a thick stack of photocopied pages. "Look, this is my only copy. What happens to it is not really supposed to be my decision. Alternitech owns proprietary rights to whatever I bring back through parallel universes. Still, no matter how much *I* loved this novel, I have to admit that this doesn't have the equivalent value to Alternitech of, say, an unknown collection of Sherlock Holmes stories by Arthur Conan Doyle or the Dean Koontz/Stephen King collaboration I uncovered once. I think people deserve to read it. I was going to have you autograph this for me." Jeremy slid the stack of papers across the table. "But now I guess you'd better keep it, so you'll know there aren't any other copies in existence. You decide what to do. It's your call, Mr. Coren. It's your book."

"I—" Mitchell started to speak, but found his voice choked with emotion. He took a long drink of his now-tepid coffee and started again. "Well ... don't you want to keep it? You said you were reading it."

Jeremy shook his head. "If you know I have a copy, you'd always worry that someday I'd be tempted to post it on the Internet. It's better if you keep it."

The papers felt warm in Mitchell's hands. His vision blurred, and he took a moment to compose himself. "I ... didn't expect this."

"I'm a musician myself, Mr. Coren. I write and record songs, but I haven't had much success so far. It was a minor consolation when I found that I did have a hit record in an alternate universe, but nothing here yet. I was the one who brought back the new music for that whole Karen Carpenter debacle, and I don't feel very good about it. As a musician, I thought Carpenter or her estate should have had some control over her own creative work, no matter which incarnation made the album. The same goes for you, sir. If you're uncomfortable about having *Infernities* published, then ..." He shrugged.

"I can't tell you how much this means to me."

"I think I understand." Jeremy slurped his decaf cappuccino. "Besides, I'm your fan. I can't think of anything cooler than to know I am the only person in this entire universe who's read your new novel."

Dozens of the loose photocopy sheets wadded up under the fireplace grate made for good kindling. Mitchell rolled the remaining loose pages of twenty-pound bond into plump literary logs, rubber-banded them, and set them on the log holder above the crumpled pages. Then he fanned out the hardcover book and flattened it across the white paper logs. He stood back to observe the diminutive funeral pyre with a sense of uneasiness.

He should have felt relieved.

This potential source of humiliation or disruption would soon be dealt with. The book would no longer be in his life, could no longer irritate or goad him by its very existence. No fans would have a chance to either criticize or clamor for more. The chapter would be closed.

Yes, Mitchell was definitely relieved.

After he lit the match, he hesitated for a long, indecisive moment before finally touching the flame to the edge of one of the loose sheets. There. A burnt offering to a cruel muse.

As the fire caught, guilt gnawed at the ragged edges of his mind. There was something intrinsically criminal about burning a book, especially the only copies of a book. While this event would not go down in history with the sacking of the Library of Alexandria, it was still a loss to at least some tiny backwater of the literary sea—espccially to the hopeful fans who had waited so long for any work by Mitchell Coren.

The flames grew higher, devouring the loose pages and curling the glossy dust jacket of *Infernities*. An interesting play on words, he thought. Infinity, Alternative, and Eternity all rolled together. Now he could add "Inferno" to make it a quadruple entendre. He wondered how it related to the story.

Didn't he owe it to himself at least to read his own work, to see what he could have done with his talent? *Infernities* was tangible proof that in some other reality his author-self had overcome the pressure and the expectations. But how? Didn't that mean that he, too, could do it?

No. He'd made the right decision. He thought with some satisfaction of the author photo blackening and blistering, cremating his cocksure successful doppelgänger. The man had dared to risk his reputation, his spotless literary legacy, to write this second novel and offer it to an unpredictable reading public. He had dared. Had risked …

With a groan of annoyance and frustration Mitchell snatched the hardcover from the fire, dropped it to the floor, and stamped on it to put out the flames at the edges. He bent and picked up the singed novel that had disrupted his calm life.

As he picked up the blackened book, Mitchell's lips flickered in a smile. Though he still had no intention of publishing the novel, he would hold onto the book as a goad. Just to keep him honest. To remind himself of what could be.

He had his own ideas for new stories and novels, of course. Every writer did. The ideas had never stopped coming, and he had jotted down notes during lunch hours at his tech-writing job. Some of the outlines were damn good, but he had been too afraid of failure to write the books, believing it better to let readers live with his mysterious seclusion than to risk them shaking their heads in disappointment.

Yet his alternate self had somehow shaken off the fear of failure. Therefore, it could be done. And that sincere, appreciative look he had seen in Jeremy Cardiff's eyes told Mitchell he still had an audience, no matter how small....

Some authors were motivated to write strictly for the critics, for the kudos and awards. Others wanted the money and name recognition of sales, with big print runs and splashy publicity. Some wrote only for themselves, giving the finger to anyone else's expectations. But why had *he* become a writer?

Now there was a group to whom he owed something: his fans—the readers who understood what he was trying to do and who saw him as a human being with a talent that should not simply be thrown away. *Those* fans would enjoy whatever he wrote.

Certainly, a few of them went to the crazy fringe, seeing him as a guru with unparalleled insight into their particular problems. But most were just regular people. If he struck the right note, his pool of fans would be large; if he chose a path that was too esoteric, the numbers might dwindle. In either case, the readers still deserved his respect.

Mitchell looked at the charred copy of *Infernities* he held. He realized now that burning the novel was selfish. There were thousands (or maybe only dozens) of people like Jeremy Cardiff, who would have enjoyed this book if he allowed it to be published.

Setting the burned hardcover down, he opened the bottom file drawer of his desk where he kept the folder of notes and ideas that were just too good to throw away. If he was going to bury this cuckoo's egg of a book, then he was obligated to give the readers something in exchange.

Mitchell skimmed his outlines. He had forgotten how clever or thought-provoking many of them were. Had he intended to be an Emily Dickinson, locking his notes away in a box for someone else to find after he died? Not long ago, he had been tempted to burn these, too.

Now he would write some of them.

As he flipped through his notes, the ideas reached a critical mass, and Mitchell saw how he could combine concepts and characters. What might have been simple short story ideas now became enough material for a multi-layered novel. It wouldn't be just like *Divergent Lines*, but so what? It would still be good, still be worth writing.

He spread the papers out on his desk. He had an old, outdated laptop computer and plenty of time during his lunch hours. Some of the greatest works of literature had been completed a few pages at a time during lunch breaks....

Mitchell glanced at the fireplace, where the fire had now died to a pile of orange embers. The photocopied novel was now nothing but ash.

On the mantel above, his Hugo and Nebula awards reflected the dull glow. He turned away from them and focused on his desk. *Divergent Lines* had been an unnecessary ball-and-chain to his creativity, along with all the other excuses he had made up over the past ten years. That was enough procrastination.

He looked at the charred but still readable hardcover of *Infernities*. First, before he started on any new book or short story, he had to write a letter.

"Dear Mr. Cardiff, let me make you a bargain." He proposed that if he had not produced any new novels or short stories in the next five years, then Jeremy had his blessing to publish *Infernities*, if only to reward the fans who had waited so long. He packaged the letter with the scorched book and mailed it to his "number one fan." Simply knowing the novel existed would be all the inspiration he really needed.

On the way back from the mailbox, he smiled to himself, convinced it would never be necessary for the other Mitchell Coren's book to be published here. He would take that risk for himself.

IF YOU LIKED ...

If you liked *Science Fiction Stories: Volume 1*, you might also enjoy other WordFire Press titles by Kevin J. Anderson.

Our list of other WordFire Press authors and titles is always growing. To find out more and shop our selection of titles, visit us at:
wordfirepress.com